SEARCH SWEET COUNTRY

SEARCH SWEET COUNTRY

B. Kojo Laing

BⱵB
BEECH TREE BOOKS
WILLIAM MORROW
New York

There is a glossary of Ghanaian words and
author's neologisms on pages 302–308.

Library of Congress Cataloging-in-Publication Data

Laing, B. Kojo.
  Search sweet country.

1. Ghana—History—1957–   —Fiction.   I. Title.
PR9379.9.L35S44   1987   823   86-32030
ISBN 0-688-06905-3

Printed in the United States of America

First U.S. Edition

1 2 3 4 5 6 7 8 9 10

BOOK DESIGN BY KATHRYN PARISE

The word "book" is said to derive from *boka,* or beech.
The beech tree has been the patron tree of writers since ancient times and
represents the flowering of literature and knowledge.

For
Judi Panyin
and
Judi Kakraba

SEARCH SWEET COUNTRY

Chapter 1

In the bush just beyond Accra, the bush that handfuls of wild guinea fowl raised with their cries, sat Beni Baidoo. One hand held blackberries picked from thorny branches, the other hand held a jot whose smoke passed through the taste of the berry first. When this cigarette smoke got too much, he would rush to the sea and steal some of the freshness of the breeze. The language of the sea spoke in shells that he could understand: as the waves rolled uselessly over the sand, so his years rolled over him speaking of waste, of events that only showed through his wrinkles, and through the lives of others. He watched others as he did not watch his own life . . .

Beni Baidoo was Accra, was the bird standing alive by the pot that should receive it, and hoping that, after being defeathered, it would triumphantly fly out before it was fried. But when he was lonely—which was not very often—his skin crawled all over him, unmaking and remaking wrinkles, tightening his eyes, and making his heart shrink smaller into his faded shirt; this heart could shrink so much that he feared it would secretly crawl out through the back of his chest . . . leaving its pumping and beating to his laughter. His laughter was part of his shirt. He was a sprightly old man who had retired twice: he had been a second-division clerk with an outrageous jaunt in his walk; and then he had become a letter writer in Post Office Square, the trouble there being his habit of adding his own facts to the complaints of illiterate customers: often a story about a stolen piece of land ended up with a stolen wife added . . . so he had to retire again. Thus, shrewd and shriveled, he went around Accra with his one obsession: to found a village. And if some of his friends were making serious and half-serious searches in their lives, he felt it his duty to balance this with his own type of search. The search of a fool touches other lives . . . Beni Baidoo usually had as much laughter with his food as possible, and finding himself in 1975, had broken up the year into different grades of laughter, sharing the teeth and noise among his friends Kofi Loww, Kojo Okay Pol, ½-Allotey, Professor Sackey, Dr. Boadi and others. He brought to friendship a fine quality: nuisance value; and then flowed with his one obsession in and out of the lives he met . . .

The two beards crowded in one corner of Accra did not agree . . . under the shoeshine tree whose breeze polished both souls, in Mamprobi. The mango tree grew, laying its fruit lazily on the unfinished wall. The fruit ripened but the city did not. The father's beard shifted and pulled at different angles, taking in the sun and folding its rays under the hair. This hair saluted from a chin too small for it. The son's beard was soft and vast with Vaseline, the hair parting ways at the middle, in confusion, and finally lying against its own big chin exhausted. Both beards were, in the brotherhood of hair, heavy with commas; and showed that full stops above the necks of father and son were rare, that permanence was scarce. Erzuah the father's beard had more fluff, more earth, more answers, more Saturday-night powder, more tradition, and more smoke than the other. And this other was Kofi Loww the son's, which defined the face less clearly, the hair hanging on in the pose of an afterthought . . . but this same beard being so still, could gather the whole city; and as it gathered, the hair spoke to the five feet of space between his chin and foot, filling the talking with cassava, aimless wandering, long stares at worlds that would not stay still, papaw and tart, and the up-down absence of Adwoa Adde, for Adwoa held a room in his heart. Erzuah's beard had a web of wisdom, but the resident spider was missing; so that his sense of absence, which was far less than his son's, would immediately be filled with goodness qualified, and with drinking . . . whether the spider was found or not. It was the learning to stretch his skin to fit the being of the moment that gave him gray hair at the back of his head . . . especially when the extra skin was needed for anger or for laughter. He believed his pipe to be richer than his mouth, and that a true hunter's pipe shone and made value long before the mouth did: the hole of the mouth was second to the hole of the

10

pipe. The son's face was blacker, and had hopes in it brightening the small slanted eyes, which the deep obstinacy there whitened. In a meal, there was a path of okro leading from one mouth to the other, so that okro-mouth Erzuah talked the world into shreds, while Kofi Loww's life slipped from another region of the face, with a curious dignity. After all, it was not doubted in areas of Accra that Kofi could walk yards backward, without anyone telling the difference between his back and his front: the surplus slant of his beard did this, the jut of his bashi did that . . . the man with the traveling horizon at the nape of his neck. The dust, the ginger and rumors piled up against the walls, and shook them. Now, Erzuah's eyes were so quick, so arrowed that they traveled in anger around the jutting bridge of his wide nose. This nose, smelling the world with suspicion, edged down with contempt at the ridiculously small mouth, a mouth that in days past was usually crowded with akpeteshie and abuse. The son took the spiritual weight of his father, two kilos; and when this spirit entered his beard—through three out of every ten hairs, he thought—he stooped with the thrust of the weight. Over by the scantlings in the higher grounds, Kofi Loww could see the vulcanizer eating his waakyi, sitting on the tires that rounded his life. As the years wore on, Erzuah had become alarmed to see that he had been measuring important events in his life by the heat of each drunken tot, and by the linking spice of his pipe . . . so that one day he had not been able to tell the difference between gin and smoke. But he could still face the sea and blow fuse with Ghana aromatic schnapps.

In those days, Erzuah's wife Maame was a proud tower of fat, and when this fat was heated with his taunts, it fried and burned his dignity . . . then spread between his legs. Years of emotional walls, across which no mangoes lay, had taught her how to ignore him when he asked for anything. She talked to little Kofi alone when she had anything to pass on to Erzuah. This one-way she-mouth almost halved Erzuah's face with the anger it grew there. He accused her of trying to make him manless, of putting stones in his rice and beans. He rushed to her in his rage—in this compound yellowing—his pipe dangling in his mouth, and he shouted as she cooked, "You, your kitchen is full of hate! I can't keep your food down in my stomach, it could be my grave on the fire now! All these years you think I haven't seen you shake your buttocks at Yaw Brago . . . he's rich, though there's nothing between his legs.

11

It's money, not manhood, that he has between his legs! Bright coins, that's all. At least for me I've fathered someone! You will bear him only pounds and pennies . . . and as for your face, hmmm, I've only tolerated it all these years, it's not fit for daylight, and it's just like your mother's . . ." He then moved his dry, smirking body, dancing around her, puffing his smoke just above her duku. Kofi Loww was a little child, and he sat in the terrified corner of the world, the compound of which he was trying to push away with a desperate frown. His widened eyes saw his parents as two beasts from an Ananse story. He hated it when his mother insulted his father back, and included him, small as he was, in the insults. What had he Kofi done? His few words of despair sent to the middle of the quarrel were only like kerosene for their fire. Little Kofi lifted up one foot, as if to lessen the surface of terror on the earth. Maame changed her position, and then slowly rose, presenting a different target for the bursts of fresh abuse. At such moments, she was torn between the guilt she felt at listening with interest to the sly persuasions of Yaw Brago, and the need to fight back and make the point that Erzuah's guilt should be far greater than hers. She began to walk slowly. The snails and onions she was cooking with fell at her feet. Her arms had started to shake, as if exorcising the space around them. As the walls moved closer to the three of them, the passing car's horn increased the turmoil. With her eyes searching the compound sky—the onion sky she looked at so often—she began to sing a song of supplication to God, showing her anger now only in the shaking of her big arms. Her brown cloth brightened with injustice, and her song was her twin. Then as she went on singing, her hand reached to her waist and loosened this cloth. As it fell onto the old concrete, she turned around with speed, pulled her underwear down, and completely bared her buttocks. She continued to sing, her eyes up high. Her beads defined her outrage, were the roundabouts of the utter confusion in the eyes of Erzuah. He could not move; Kofi wanted to borrow his father's feet, but he could not move to do so either . . . four feet stuck in the depths of the world. Maame then started to walk backward toward Erzuah, slowly, contempt on her face, and screaming with terrifying weight, "Yes, look! look well! You haven't seen it for years! I will stand here like this till Yaw Brago and everyone else come to the house! If you don't want me, others do! I can have more trousers than you can ever count. And this son of yours always takes your side. Fools together! I will claim back every expense I've made on the two of you. Yaw Brago wants to give me a cloth so what, so what, I'll take it . . . I'll take it at night lying down. So God help me!" She resumed her singing, and stood still, throwing her head from side to side.

The hearts of father and son became one, turned and turned in their one desperate chest. In Erzuah's head Maame had become fire, had become a witch with her powers turned in evil toward his destruction. He rushed across the compound with his batakari flying, and covered the tear-stained face of his son. "Kofi, don't look, don't look. She's mad, she's mad in the buttocks!" Maame still followed Erzuah backward, in her abomination. The compound was the Bedford—just passed—in reverse gear, with all the roars now quiet. Erzuah's own daze cooled him down, it reached his depths, forcing out of him a calm that both broke and raised the last barriers in his head: he suddenly had a feeling of righteousness. For an action beyond his own excesses had been thrown at him, and this released him from any feeling of responsibility. He welcomed her outrage, and yet wanted to kill her for it. His pipe, that weapon of war, held his jaws in determination. He drew at it with both hands, and no smoke, no comfort came. As his hands shook with one useless match after another, he pushed aside his ambivalence, took hold of his son's hand and was walking out of the compound. Kofi pulled his hand away from his father's and looked in terror at his mother. "Cover yourself, Maame, cover yourself," he said to her with prayers shining in his eyes. She stood, stiffening herself with the mercy of her son's tears. But she ignored him, she looked through him as the light changed the color of her skin, casting a deep purple of controlled shame around her. Erzuah's shame had already vanished with the absence of his son's withdrawn hand. He had gone out to the streets in a mad glee, shouting, "Come and see this woman! Come and see! She has found a new way of bringing up her child . . . She's bringing up her child with her buttocks! Come and see, come and buy! As for this, it is cheeeaapp! Cheap! Come and see something you have never seen before! Come!" The compound filled up in seconds with curious, gaping people of all ages, hooting, laughing, chattering in uproar, with little Kofi desperately trying to cover his mother. Erzuah joined them in their cries of "shame, shame, shame!" There was a voice: "Her buttocks are copper colored paa!" Then two women came, they pushed

Maame, with finality, into the nearest room, covering her and shouting at her, and asking her how deep she wanted to go to shame her womanhood, just for a man . . . Maame replied, shaking, "Deep as the sea, the man is a devil!" "Then," one of the women said sadly, "you have made all women naked in Accra today. Did you not, did you not see the face of the men?" Maame merely gathered her shaking and held it in her unstill arms. She looked down deep. The women left her as quickly as they had come, and drove away the crowd in the compound.

Not a word was said to Erzuah, whose eyes they avoided like a great sickness. He had risen from his exhausted stool, his hand-kerchief full of the powder of other people's passing sympathy: "What a wife to live with," they had said. Kofi could neither comfort nor even look at his mother. The walls moved far away, and the dying muttering outside them was more than a judgment; it was an intrusion into the shattered heart. The probing breeze had nothing for the father, nothing for the mother; the bird it had blown over sang by the gnarled tree near Kofi. Erzuah rose again, his heart under the fuel of a new resolve, this in turn being fueled by shame . . . as if all the years of waste had been redefined then. He was leaving the house: he gathered his clothes, his gun, his photographs, his cloths, his railway testimonials, his pipe, and his son . . . who stood there rigid and unleaving. When Kofi finally moved broken to his mother, all she said was, "Go, go, go to your father! I can't look after a mistake, my whole life with him has been a mistake . . ." Kofi did not wait. He threw his broken heart at her, and left, running to his father at the gate, shouting, "Papa Erzuah, if I must stay with you, I will. I will help you to move everything." Father and son left in their doubt, and Erzuah's hat could fit both of them since the pain was so wide. They did not see Maame stare after them with an intensity that felt nothing and for a long time lived nothing. She built up a bank of silence that she later withdrew from, sharing her indignation—and guilt—among her sisters until it was all finished, all forgotten.

The sun broke into his face and bisected it. Kofi Loww, now thirty and living on the wandering side of doubt, walked along the High Street of Accra. His head was slightly lower than it should be, so that much of the world, even when laden with a breeze of fresh

14

kyenam, raced immediately above him. Everything seemed to happen at a distance, yet could come back later with a sly poignancy.
His father, whom he had changed over the years, was now trying
hard to change him: Erzuah deeply wanted Kofi Loww to realize,
through his wanderings, that it was necessary to continue with
university, since he, Loww, had persevered with his diploma course.
It was a matter of degree, Loww would think with irony; and
standing under a sudden orange tree he thought his doubts would
come to fruit. So his whole being, except for his okra, moved faster,
as if the postponement of this decision was a dam raising his seeing
level and letting it flow. His neck was tilted to one side away from
the thrust of Accra. Each corner, each new vista opening out behind
a building, a crowd, or cars was an intrusion and a release at the
same time: interruptions ceased to be such, and became successive
presences on their own. The neem trees held and brushed Accra,
yet the corner breezes only moved the heat from one person to
another, and to no other person than Beni Baidoo deep in thought
and sitting on his donkey.

Beni Baidoo wanted to found a village, away from his own Mfantse
area . . . where he knew he was poorly regarded. He drove this
desire as usual into other people's garages, and Kofi Loww was the
space that Baidoo saw now. "Hey young man! Is your father driving
you to dream again! I know everybody in Accra except dignity!
See my donkey, I bought it with my retiring benefits. I ride it with
one buttock so that it will eat less and last longer. All I need now
is a little help from my goooooooood friends to start my village. I
can get land, I have my donkey, and all I need is a few human
beings, some furniture, several superhuman girls, a family god, an
okyeame, a village fool and a village thief . . . to steal from the
rich to give to me gently. You should be more like Dr. Boadi: he
gives me beer to keep me quiet, but I have to talk to earn the beer
first. Young man, how much can you contribute to this great new
village?" Baidoo said at great speed. Kofi Loww looked at his watch
to see whether there was any luck in meeting Baidoo. He found
none, he found only ten o'clock, and said nothing. "That's right!
Quiet as usual! I fear your silence as I fear your father's noise . . .
as for me I know everybody, and the rumor I have to pass on to
you is that they want to arrest you, so stop walking about, and

start making money for your little boy. I've told you, and I love sugar bread! Get me some, so that I explain to you how you managed to turn your father from a boozer into a half-drunk domesticated philosopher . . ." Loww scowled, but put a cedi note behind the donkey's ear, and walked on past the chattering Baidoo. "I am the explainer, this unimported explainer thanks you, Kofi . . . from the bottom of my heart and from my wife's bottom too . . ."

Passing Ussher Fort by Sraha Market where the Pentecostal church clapped its walls, Loww saw how clearly everything—from fresh water and churches to governments and castles—could fit so easily in reflection in the gutters. This city could not satisfy the hunger of gutters, for there was nothing yet which had not been reflected in them. The Bukom building gaped through its small windows at the ancient coconut tree . . . which danced with the odd rhythm of his own heartbeats. The old fisherman mending his net had hair the same color as the passing clouds; and this same color was thrown down in different shades onto so many buildings, buildings sharing among themselves the poverty and richness of different decades, different centuries. One hundred feet from Kofi Loww to the shore, the tides threw up good and evil as plentiful as Keta schoolboys: he found no answer there, not even with the one shell that defined the entire dirt of the Jamestown sea. Each piece of doubt had the status of a grain of sand. Bebreee. And the sun rose from the prison yard after thirty minutes of custody. Everyone took the sunshine, the earth, and the streets freeee! The sun was the brightest sister! The sun was a baker: heads, laws, fish, backs, beauty, chiefs, and history all browned under it; and the deepest assessment of the two-sided coin of life, the life of fufu, the life of pito, ended up with the same brown. And it was exactly this brown that Kofi Loww saw in the faces that laughed, frowned, mocked, and loved. Fatima bumped into him so that his thoughts fell down with her groundnuts. Fatima lived in a hut smelling of groundnut skins. She screamed: "Owula, you don't look where you're going? You are lucky that these nuts are still in their shells! And look at the dream on your face!" Fatima had been trying to work out the number of groundnuts she could eat without her mother finding out, so she threw a grimace every few seconds at Loww as they picked them up. Loww stared above her so that, without looking, he was picking up as many stones and bits of alokoto, as nuts. When she saw this she shouted, "Please go, please go. I'll do this myself. Whaaaat! For all

I know you have put half my nuts in your beard. My mother will kill me if I don't hurry up and go and boil the rest!" The bicycle repairer was pumping somebody's patience into the shape of a tire, for it could burst. When Fatima finished with her nuts, she carried some words quickly over to her friend who was selling oranges; as soon as the words were put down, they both burst into laughter at the disappearing Loww. But that tough aplankey with the smoke in his eyes thought they were laughing at him. So he spat out, as his old trotro passed. Fatima and her friend cursed him, chattering and laughing.

As Kofi Loww went around a corner near the post office, he saw his father standing before him with folded arms. "Ah, I knew I would hear your footsteps here! Let's move on quickly: it's dangerous to stand in one place with two beards!" Erzuah said with a laugh. "And what I need you for requires the support of the back sitting down: it is serious, it is heavy." Old Erzuah had the gift of giving each of his features a different mood or meaning, as he spoke: his eyes darted impatiently around his son's face so that his words looked unreasonably breathless; his nose waited calmly for any answer that he could immediately refute; and his mouth reflected the irony he felt in finding his own son with that strange disposition that was both so serious and so aimless. Their strides shared Accra as they walked along in silence; they covered the city in hair of different grades. Then suddenly Kofi Loww could not see Erzuah at all. He stood near Glamour Stores vaguely, looking for his father, even for signs of his absence. He thought he could faintly smell the old tobacco smoke, but he saw nothing. He was going to resume his slow walking when Erzuah bounced back beside him, almost knocking him over. "But what are you . . ." Loww began. "No no no, don't talk. I prefer your silence in this case. You see, I had to secretly go for a quick gin. After all I need a little fortification, old as I am," the old man interrupted, "I've told you that what I'm going to tell you needs support! And as you know, these days I do this drinking small-small. And if anything controls my mouth at all, it's my pipe." "But who is with Ahomka now?" Kofi Loww asked of his son, whom his father looked after, and looked after so well. "I will tell you soon, soon. It's a pity that you feel you must climb so many mountains to reach such a small anthill of life. After all what do you want to know yourself better for? What is there to know? I think you have read too many books. How many young

17

Africans like yourself have you seen chasing their own shadow? None! They are all busy getting what should be due them!" "I will get what I want when I know what I want," Loww said with surprising force. "We've said all this before, and we're even saying it in the middle of the street now." Then he lapsed back into his customary silence. "If only you could make your silence roar!" Erzuah shouted. "Apart from your diploma, the only sensible thing you've done is to have a child. Of course I agree that you can't marry Ahomka's mother. For her, her noise is as dangerous as your silence! Hahaha. Don't mind your old father, I'm talking now from the heat in my throat. But I think that Adwoa will be good for you. Only be careful you don't lose her!" Loww smiled with the front of his mouth, heightening the hair there, raising the convictions there. Children in the streets of Mamprobi would point to Kofi Loww as the man who walked with the sky in his eyes. Tall trees dusted the sky, and so would he. "Why don't you tell me what you want to tell me now, Papaa?" Loww asked his father with the mildest hint of impatience. Kofi Loww's legs were bow and long, had an almost sideways shift that met the world as if it had all been walked before. And his soul was the same . . . walking, and putting its strength right where others had left their weaknesses long ago. And his eyes: it was said they contained so much that was unclear that there had to be more than one human being wearing them . . . true some dissatisfied ancestor used the same eyes in this double world of seeing. Erzuah ignored his son's question, and added another warning: "If you keep on living the same way, someone can easily take over your spirit!"

The silence was filled with other people's words, other people's cars. Kofi Loww walked his father rather quickly to the Community Center where they sat down at different heights. "It looks as if my words have to climb up a bit to reach you . . . but let me finish this tatale first," Erzuah said absentmindedly, handing Loww some of the brilliantly fresh tatale. They ate different thoughts. "Now both my back and my belly have support! Look, young man, I'm going to tell you something strange. But you are made for strange things, so it shouldn't surprise you. I was sitting playing with Ahomka, answering his questions and fooling his fooling—he likes no one to beat him at his own tricks, Hmmm!—when this white man came to the door and asked for you. I said to myself: good, at long last my son is moving toward the riches of Europe; his friends are whitening! If you want direction, move away from Accra and go to the villages, if that doesn't work then leave these wonderful shores, leave these mighty forests, these endless savannas. Go to the white lands where it was believed that people went to the toilet but once a year! Hmmm. As I was saying before the akpeteshie spoke, this white man said he knew you through one Ebo, and that he had come with a visitor, a woman, an old woman, who wanted to see you. I then realized that it was your own friend Ebo. He went back to his car and produced, yes produced this woman: and this woman was Maame, your mother!"

There was suddenly a great confusion in Loww's eyes. He rose and stared at the sun, his chest beat a different drum. Then he added with an evenness that he did not feel, "After all these years what does she want? Is she the one looking after Ahomka?" Erzuah paused to light his pipe, but when he coughed, the foreboding did not leave his throat. "I haven't even asked her her mission yet, so don't panic. I am still thinking you have more appetite for the unexpected than I have. But true, Kofi, true, she looks like an old witch; she's become so thin too! Was Yaw Brago not able to look after her? Her eyes don't look like yours anymore," Erzuah said all in one breath. He looked as if he were trying to avoid his son's eyes, and Loww felt an anger that he could not explain. He stared at Erzuah, as if the old man should receive this anger: "But why should you leave Ahomka with her? You know, you know that it's really me that you have left behind with her. How could you leave me behind like that? Do you think she will leave me behind this time too? Papa, she has come to take me away through Ahomka; she knows I'm Ahomka . . . the only difference is a few years and different bodies. She wants the years back. Her regret is the same! She wants to use her bitterness! Let's go before it's too late, Papa Erzuah, let's go!" Kofi Loww had been shouting while he spoke. The sweat could have been misplaced tears. Erzuah looked at him curiously, and said, "I don't understand all this you are saying. Surely you are not Ahomka . . . what are you saying?" Loww replied, racing off, "So all these years you haven't realized that she can sometimes think and speak through me? Let's go to the house." Breathless, Erzuah was saying, "But the white man was there, the white man was there!" The panic he warned against in his son had now gone into his own chest; in the taxi, his body was traveling far faster than this Datsun. Distance had lengthened, his body was stretched, his eyes looked in one direction. Loww finally said, not making much difference to the silence in the taxi, "Once Dr. Pinn knows she's Ahomka's grandmother, he won't stop her from going out to the street, from taking him away." Erzuah just shook his head vigorously. As if to say that when you shook your head, you shook the world away too. After all, the truth could be in the shock absorbers, which shook even more.

The house looked desperately quiet when they finally reached Mamprobi. Erzuah was out first, like lightning. As they both entered the two rooms they heard an angry shout outside: the taxi driver was shouting for his money, which they had forgotten to pay. "Owula, sorry!" Loww said hastily as he threw the money into the car without looking at the driver. Then there was a quiet knock at the door. Father and son both rushed to it. But there was nowhere to put the rush: it was only Dr. Pinn standing there holding his chin. There was an ordinary calm in his eyes—blue for nothing, blue for nothing, Loww felt himself think irrationally, as his son's absence filled his mind—which was an affront to the agitation filling the two men. Loww spoke first, without greeting: "Dr. Pinn, where has the old woman taken my son? Where did they go?" "Good afternoon," Dr. Pinn began, determined to keep to the civilities, in spite of being taken aback by the heat of the questions. Erzuah's mouth was shut but his eyes asked just as many questions. "The old lady said she was going around the corner to buy her grandson some sweets . . . but Mr. Loww, is she not your mother? Is there something I don't know?" Dr. Pinn continued, "And you know, I have never seen you like this . . . not even when you stayed with Ebo at my house for a few days. Anyway I myself had something to tell you: the rumor is that the security people are after you. But more of that later . . ." Dr. Pinn's face had taken on that earnestness that forcibly stopped itself from drifting into an ironic frown. He was being rushed. He added as an afterthought, "Of course if your father had left me any instructions . . ." "Yes, it's my fault! Wherever they are it's my fault. I should have known that old witch of old! She has stolen the child as a final revenge. And what is this about the security people?" Kofi Loww pushed his father down into a chair without thinking, and said, "Rest." The room smelled of crushed red ants, and old Erzuah's eyes looked just like an anthill would look with the sun just moving off it. "Take it easy both of you. A little boy with his grandmother is nothing to get hysterical about . . . I'll go and return later with Ebo if you don't come to my house first. We'll all look for them if they haven't come back by then. But of course you know her house?" "That is part of the problem, you see. We have had no contact with her for years," Erzuah replied, his eyes still reddening, "apart from the evil messages she sometimes sends demanding money which she never gets; not from me."

Kofi Loww thanked Dr. Pinn and saw him off. As soon as he returned to the room there was another knock at the door. "Agooo!" It was Maame's voice. The two men sprang up. "Dada, look at my chewing gum! I've made it from the alasa that grandmother bought me. She likes me, paaa. Look, isn't she nice? Papa Erzuah said she is a witch, but I don't think so. Ha! Watch me blow a bubble. Have you seen a bubble blown from alasa chewing gum?" said Ahomka all in one breath, holding his grandmother's hand. "Yes," Kofi Loww said to his son, "I mean No, I haven't seen this trick before, but let me see it later." Then he pulled Ahomka away from his grandmother. Maame laughed without mirth, then looked at her son with a full directness, as if she were looking back twenty years. Then something rushed into her eyes: tears; and rushed back out again. She looked with fear and longing. Then just as quickly she calmed herself down. "No chair for me?" She asked Erzuah with a new combination of sarcasm and timidity. "There is no chair strong enough to contain you here, Maame. But let me give you this one . . . no one sits on it except the angels or the devils." Erzuah's features had become so sharp, so intensely outlined that they looked as if they would take off from his face. He had a terrible feeling of vindication and anger, a vindication that stretched back more than two decades, and had now ended up in the open with the visit of this woman. She thanked him for the chair and sat looking down. Kofi Loww, getting up, looked at his father and shrugged off a feeling of involvement.

"Don't go!" Erzuah said a little too loudly. "Help me to ask her what her mission is. As for water she won't want any. And maybe the water in this house is poisoned. If, on the other hand, she has come here to collect some dead hearts . . . hahahaha!" Erzuah's laughter dropped on the chair with him as he sat down opposite Maame. She looked at him with a sudden assertiveness, then withdrew again, saying nothing. "Mother, what's your mission?" Kofi Loww asked almost inaudibly, himself surprised at the

21

growing indifference in his heart; and he did not yet know whether this feeling was real or merely protective. Maame hesitated, her eyes full of a barely concealed pain. "I don't come with anything bad. I just wanted to see my grandson. I know my own son hates me. As for his father he's sorry I'm alive . . ." Loww gave her a piercing look, and asked her, "Yaw Brago is dead isn't he? He's dead!" She looked down even more deeply, shaking her head. Her faded cloth wanted no sympathy, and she did not get any. The silence would explode if any one of the three of them cared enough. "He's not alive," Maame said finally. "Oh, not alive, eh? As for today I'm learning! It's not that a person is dead, it's just that he's not alive! Ewurade! So have you come here to see your grandson or to display your tears for your dead lover? And who told you you have a grandson? He's been in this world for the last eight years, and you are now coming to . . . to see him for what? Ei! If I could see Ahomka's mother now—God forgive me—I would try to push the little boy back into the womb, so that you would have the joy of seeing your own grandson being born again! God help me! What is your real mission, Maame? Is it not money? Your Yaw is no longer around to push the gold at you! And don't fool me with your faded cloth . . . you have put it on deliberately. Now you must have property! What do you want money for?" Erzuah finally stopped speaking, and took out his pipe. He had decided to store his talking in it. "I know what you have really come here for, Maame. You want us to go with you to the house that you have at last inherited from Yaw Brago. You want us to live with you," Loww said with a strange low voice. "You see, she has no shame!" Erzuah said, biting her with words.

Maame turned her face to the ceiling and produced silent tears from points in past time that were both clear and hidden to all of them. She spoke through her tears: "The past was as much your father's fault as mine," she said appealing to Kofi Loww. Loww got up and went out of the room. Erzuah looked at her with a complete lack of pity, and said, "We have our different lives now. Don't come and disturb us! All these years that you were living in wealth, we were struggling. You disgraced us. I know my faults, but what you did almost broke Kofi and me." Then he stored his words again. Kofi Loww came back in and met the silence. Maame's eyes were dry, dryer than sand, and she had a change of mouth: "Ei, Kofi, have you no love left for an old woman like me? Won't

22

you visit me, with my little grandson?" she asked, her face brittle with self-protection. "But Maame, where are your other children? I mean your children with Yaw Brago . . ." "We had none," she said curtly. "Ah, did I not tell you? Did I not tell you!" Erzuah broke in, his face shining with the second layer of vindication. But there was a sadness in the shine. "I loved your mother once," he began, looking at Kofi Loww, "out of all the women that loved the words in my mouth, and the hair on my chin, I chose her. I admit my drinking, but did that give her the right to shake her buttocks at someone else? She didn't even think about her only child. You Kofi, you . . ."

Loww looked away. He felt a sudden weight on his chest. He said to his mother, "Maame, go in peace. One day Ahomka and myself, we'll come and see where you are . . . I don't think Papa Erzuah will stop us . . ." Then Ahomka rushed in with his most adult look, inspected all the faces, saw the sadness, saw the defiance, saw the growing pity, and said, "You big people! you are so serious! Should I start preparing the evening meal, since you are all so busy? And have you all decided whether grandmother is a good woman or a bad woman? Tell me! Papa Erzuah never hides anything from me. I'm his friend. And now that I have been listening to you, I would like to give her alasa back. But she would cry. So I think we should forgive her . . . I mean not now. We should hoot at her now, then forgive her later when we visit her. Papa Erzuah, my old friend, do you agree? You big, big people. Okay, I'm going to begin the cooking. I love snails, so tonight it will be snails!" Loww took his son out before he could say more. "I wish I could give the little rascal my beard, and he needs a slap on the wrist," Erzuah said to himself as he saw Maame off. He did not look at her, he did not speak to her. She disappeared into the silence, into the distance.

"Maame-oooo, Maaaame! It's me Baidoo. If you don't want Erzuah now, why don't you try me? We can lie down together, and whisper our skins to each other!" Beni Baidoo shouted in a high-pitched voice to Maame, who just stood and stared. When she realized who it was, she went on, quickening her steps, trying as hard as possible to wave Baidoo out of her life. "Maame, don't go, my bed is made. I've never forgotten the story about the way you bared yourself to Erzuah. They say your back flesh is the same color as my face, and beautiful! Ei! Didn't I warn you about old Erzuah years ago? Be careful and don't go looking for revenge, leave them alone. Your lives together are now past-ooooo. Your thinness equals my bones, we can knock ourselves together, like old drums better with age! You are now old and left alone. I can comfort you-ooooo. At least one of my buttocks is fresh, I don't use it for this donkey . . . half a buttock is long life to man and animal . . . Oh, don't go, I wish I could see half your heart . . . the other half is crushed between Erzuah and Yaw Brago. Maaaameeeee-O, don't dream of revenge!"

Maame climbed into a crowded taxi, and shook Baidoo's words out of her duku. And as Baidoo floundered after the slowly crawling taxi, Maame did something without thinking: she threw half a loaf of bread out of the window hard at Baidoo. It hit his head, and then bounced up the sky, so that when he eventually caught it, his teeth had a sharper grip of it than his hands.

Chapter 2

All over Accra Baidoo the Beni was thought a dazzling fool that came to rest often like a damp squib on other people's hospitality. As he repassed Kofi Loww passing the Bank of Ghana building, their shadows joined, forming the image of one huge beggar: Loww begged the universe, and Baidoo begged Accra. The latter seemed to be stalking the former. "Kofi, it's me, and don't let all your teeth speak at once . . . I have collected twenty more cedis toward the founding of my village, fifteen from Dr. Boadi and five from Kojo Pol. I'm progressing beyond my letter-writing days, there is no longer any alphabet in my blood . . . I looked at a biology book and it seems to be cedi plasma I'm collecting! But I have a problem: my donkey won't come out of my room; it doesn't get on very well with my old rascal of a dog: they quarreled, and now it's in a huff with all its four legs. Ewurade! Incidentally your father has told me not to step in your house again. He says my donkey eased itself in your compound. Now, I surely can't control such a stubborn animal's bowels! And I could tell by the furious way he smoked his pipe that he was trying to burn Maame out of his life. Kofi, the only way to make your old man happy is to stay out of politics, thinking, and wandering . . . and then to marry. My room is full of elephant grass, stale bread and the permanent smell of failure. But don't vex, I'll invite you to the official opening of my brandnew village. But really, Kofi, I came to you to ask you for something, not too big, not too small . . ." Loww's silence would travel a path in his own beard if the words hadn't left his mouth first: "I have nothing more to give toward your village, Baidoo . . ."

25

"Nonono, I don't want money . . ." Baidoo interrupted, then lowered his voice, "I hear your father has a powerful family god . . . could I borrow it for a few weeks just to start my village properly . . ." Loww laughed and Baidoo laughed to lengthen it. "He has nothing of the kind, Papa Erzuah's only god is in the Methodist Church . . ." Loww said looking straight at Beni Baidoo, who was determined to keep his laugh above the look. "Confide in me, young man, I can keep secrets. There's one more space left in my head for one more secret. Tell me, O, for a moment I thought your beard was on fire, but it was only the sun catching and coloring it. I could be your uncle you know, and I'm one of the few masters of donkeys in Accra . . . as soon as you take your eyes off me, then you know I deserve respect. And it has been said that my voice is like that of an ambitious frog croaking high and coming out drunk from Star Hotel . . ." Baidoo tried to share the smirk on his face but Loww took none of it. "Ask my father if you don't believe me," Loww said with an absentminded frown, and then walked off with determined steps, for his mother's visit had cut angles from his wandering. Baidoo's knees knocked. "But what about my donkey, can't you solve its legs for me? When you were small, you were my little pet; now look at what you are doing to me! Okay, if you can't give me a god, then pass me a jot . . ." Baidoo shouted to the disappearing Loww. Gods and jots, now. "You know I don't smoke," Loww replied taking his voice into the corner and out of earshot.

The Beni stood with hands on his outer pelvis bones—no hips were visible—and stared into the absence before him. The stairs of the bank guarded nothing, and they were tired throwing feet up and down in daylight, and had to rest in the evening, crawling up and down each other with slow luxurious movement . . . fast day, slow night. Beni Baidoo's words were still stuck like rubber round the ears of Kofi Loww, who had to go a few more yards before they snapped out of his head . . . to be replaced by his decision to visit Ebo the Food, and thus to see how mad or how wise wisdom itself had become. The number of streets that tripped and got in each other's way was amazing, so that the best way to Kanda was through confusion, or through kelewele, cars and what he thought was uninventive architecture.

The dusk was both a cheat and a truth, for it framed the beauty of a people faithfully, yet stylized it as if this beauty should only have belonged to places more rural than this city. Each time Loww took a step, he lifted a whole country. It looked as if each space given to each person to walk in was a source of art: the movement of people was nothing less than a series of abandoned dances controlled marvelously in the most ordinary, in the most triumphant ways. Kofi Loww saw this highly expectant space waiting for, and getting, the slightest touch of bodies that were in turn touched back by this same space. Thus the universe was danced in all the walking of Ghana. A sudden call to Kofi Loww broke his small world: "Ei, wofa!" a strange female voice called him, "Won't you come and buy some of my kaklo? For you, you look as if no woman would want you at aaaaall, unless she wanted to marry you first! How about me? The more of my kaklo you buy, the better chance you will have of getting me to love you!" Then she ran away, holding her breasts and spreading her laughter as if it were corn for chickens. She shouted back, "Let my younger sister serve you this time. I'll keep myself for you next week, eh?" Kofi Loww bought what he had to buy, and shouted to her in spite of himself, "Now what sort of running is this? You run as if running had never been invented before. You run as if your legs are holding cassava sticks . . . what sort of beauty is that?" One man's smile, low, one woman's laugh, high again. The horizon fell, and the streets were higher, Kanda was coming . . . soon. Loww walked on with his part-crouch part-march, carrying himself like a rectangle of darkness around all the lights of talking: they talked kerosene, they talked electricity. And little children shouted to him through Adabraka, "Only your beard, only your walk. Which one will you keep, and which one will you throw to us, Oooooh!" On the streets the sellers made a way of life, they almost guarded his thinking.

And as he finally sat at Avenida Hotel, chasing the terrace flies from his beer with controlled impatience, he saw an old man in a white robe coming to his table. "Kofiiiiii!" Mustapha shouted with no regard for other ears, "I'm bringing my retirement to you-oooo! They say make a go for retirement, so I de go. Sister Adwoa, she greet you, ibi the one she sent me for here. She say I go find you here. She give me money to buy you kyinkyinga two, fresh ones paa. Ibi here, the meat, commot am with your beer. As you know, for me I no drink, koraa. Sister Adwoa say make you come to house, she has small palaver with you. But Kofi, you koraa you have fine woman like this, and you treat am basabasa . . . i no be

27

good!" Loww gave Mustapha a withdrawn look, and thanked him only with his eyes. Mustapha spoke so fast that the words shot out before they could be heard, and his gown flowed with quick ironic movements. He was often sent by Adwoa Adde to Loww, and he knew old Erzuah well, but he did not like the way sadness was pressed into Kofi Loww's trousers so often, like a starch that still showed white. "Hey, Kofi, wake, wake! listen to me! the ministries i die paa long time, awu: I go for retirement siz months now, and I no fit get my social security. Now I no have cedi fit buy kola self . . ." Mustapha said, digging deep into his pockets, for nothing. Loww gave him two cedis without a word. "Ah," Mustapha continued, "Allah bless you! For me I no sabe spend kube, I no sabe spend money; money self, i finish too-too quick, so one day I go spend all my pikin! Masa . . ." Mustapha at last lowered his voice, "Masa, something de trouble me paaaa . . . you see, my t'in, my popylonkwe, i no fit rise again, i no fit commot my wife. When she shake her big-big buttocks, i no make stiff koraa! I beg you, help me! Take me for big doctor." Loww looked to see whether Mustapha was serious or not, and when he saw that he was, he rose and patted the old man, and told him, "Soon I take you for Owula Allotey. He go make am fine for you." Mustapha then thanked him and said, "I tell Sister Adwoa that you go come soon." As he took his leave of Loww, he walked on briskly, shouting to himself, "We go rise, Yes-yes! the t'in go rise, Yes-yes! Allah is good!" Mustapha left the smell of chewed tobacco behind. Kofi Loww could almost hear the deep freezers mourn in Kanda, so he rose and made his way there.

Finally the moon was a truth that he did not arrive at Kanda with: it lay fat in the sky like sinking sugar in the morning koko, it was eaten behind the gray clouds . . . he no longer had to drag it behind him. And there was Ebo the Food—he ate and drank other people's goodness—standing near the Pinns' gate, cool, running the Pinns' two dogs in different directions, with his limp in between. One of his eyes was mad: "Kofi, be quiet, the dogs are praying! This is a solemn moment for booklong people. The dogs and you are the only ones that can take my limp naturally." Ebo stood solemn by the motionless dogs. Kofi Loww looked interested but unimpressed; his eyes were vaguer than the cream color of the bungalow. Then he said out of passing indignation, "I haven't spoken yet, and you say be quiet . . ." "And that's the best time not to speak, when you are quiet!" the Food hissed in his impossibly loud whisper. "I thought Ghanaian hospitality was never postponed. Doesn't it just flow without end?" Loww said, as his mind turned again to his mother, and then back to the incident at the Kotaka airport. "I suppose sometimes it's the security people that bring us the hospitality." Then Loww was quiet, he stared away from Ebo the Food. "Ah, you see, I am not so stupid! I have recognized a few adinkra patterns in the movement of the dogs! You think because I can't speak this mad English language properly I am not wise?" Ebo shouted. He looked at Loww properly for the first time. Then he sent his controlled limp to welcome him, while he himself stood guarding his own bright smile.

For Ebo, one half of the world was always lower than the other, so that his limp became almost a moral force: when he misbehaved, he defined the world as of the lower half; and when he was good, he could hardly reach the higher half of his limp, his real world of value. Then Ebo said, parting the strands of silence, "You need boiled groundnuts, you are getting thin; I am crowding some into my mouth now. Have some." Different groundnuts moved in different mouths. The Food's chewing was more or less wild. "Why don't we make some money out of these security people that are chasing you?" Ebo asked, with the gleam of charcoal in his sane eye. "I came to talk about my mother first," Loww said irritably, feeling quite unready for any of his friend's schemes. "Is it not money that makes mothers? Did your own mother not really come for money, after all these years? Money is something in my head; look, come and shake it, you will hear the coins and the notes, Let's finish with money first!" "Can we not go into your room? I want to give Dr. Pinn a message . . ." Loww said, with a frown. "Why not! custom is custom! I'll offer you water when we reach the quarters. Have you noticed how all boys' quarters stare so enviously and with such anger at the masters' main buildings? It's good I like the Pinns, otherwise their house would crumble with all the staring!" the Food said, as he moved through the gate with the dogs. "And besides, Dr. Pinn is not in. And you are lucky that the dogs know you. Madame is the boss of this house, but she's also out."

Kofi Loww's frustration moved from one eye to the other, and then back again. The water in Ebo's room was Club beer, and the custom was a fast handshake by the window against which a young, dry flamboyant tree outlined its groping: its flower was suspended high in the middle of February, and it had spent months under the words of the Food. And as they talked, the harmattan cooled their talking. Loww gathered his words about him and locked them up high. Ebo talked through his beer: "But you, I always ask you, you never reply: where do you get all this seriousness from? Are you not in Ghana? You young men with the wise looks are the most dangerous! For me it's the women I study more. One thing: the yawns of these alombos have become longer. Why? It is because they want lunch and drink before they lie down. They have lengthened everything! Ei, this is Ghanawoman 1975: every yawn costs money, every money costs a yawn if it's too small! Eventually when she lies down, she is already self-sufficient in money and attention, and doesn't want that logologo cargo between a man's legs. That's why the young men are serious! Dr. Pinn thinks, laughing, that they should have me in the sociology department. But me, I'm illiterate, I stopped school at standard seven and even then my standard did not go past six. But I've been talking and listening to the people ever since . . . he was even going to arrange for me— I mean Dr. Pinn—to meet one Professor Sackey . . . but Pinn is himself too generous, and so he sometimes assesses human man through his Fante wife. As for animal man, he leaves him alone. Imagine one man having four eyes all controlled by his wife! As for Madame, I fear her oooooh, she tries to boogie my drinking altogether. Now, what about your mother? Leave the old witch alone! I don't trust fat women who become thin, and then try to open up the past. Never let your money or your son go to her. Fine, we've now finished with your mother, I lie? Let's move on to the security people. Tell them you have all the information about the way the government tried to bring horses into the country secretly. Tell them that if they don't . . ." Loww was staring at the Food with an intensity that made him stop talking. "What is it?" Ebo asked. "I saw dust go into your mouth as you talked. And leave me alone," Loww said to his friend, vaguely.

Then they both heard the horn of the Pinns' little Fiat. The curve of the wheels was the curve on the Food's mouth as he rushed to brush his teeth, saying, "I promised madame that I would not drink today. You see, the more promises I make, the longer I can stay here . . ." Two dogs and two men went out to greet the Pinns. EsiMay Pinn had a traveled smile, and she looked with suspicion at Ebo's mouth as she got out of the car and said, "Ebo! So you've been brushing your teeth . . . at this time? What are you trying to hide? Oh, I see your friend is here again. I'll check up on your tricks later . . . Good evening, Kofi Loww. I'm sure you got your little son all right . . . Andy was telling me." "Yes, thanks. I came to tell you all," Loww replied. Andy Pinn went in with a comic pained look at Loww, saying "This hunger! Imagine a married man like me feeling so hungry. You would think I were a little neglected, wouldn't you!" EsiMay gave him a look somewhat stronger than tenderness as the two children Yooku and John rushed in. The building swelled with their entry. Kofi Loww stayed out in the garden, watching the special shimmer that the harmattan often gave to lights.

He was thinking that the Pinns' family history could easily have lain on the lawn: it looked just as neat from the outside. Their children brought brown into their lives; after them, all colors changed, Loww could see. From the inside came the bursts and rhythms of talk and laughter. Ebo the Food's voice rose. Pinn, an economic consultant, was a careful man born in the heather whose wife broadened his roads, thus letting in characters like Ebo. He also renewed, every now and again, the need to reach out beyond the confines of his own world, so that he could tolerate the Food and his like better. This need fired his sense of irony whenever it came: he found it ironic that Ebo had such a passion to help Kofi Loww, rather than as usual be helped. He laughed through himself at the neatness that he thought his life was turning into. It became, even, ironic that he enjoyed this irony: he would look severely at the usually beaming face of the Food, take in the solidity there, and then enjoy—with a peculiar sense of Presbyterian woundedness—his sense of caution being overwhelmed. Pinn thus loved to owe little moral debts to those he was already helping . . . Ebo refused payment for keeping a relaxed eye on the house . . . for these debts balanced things, and restored, at the appropriate times, the elements of caution that he still needed. On the Food's part he just enjoyed living under someone else's sense of responsibility. He just gave sun under the shade, under the roof of Pinn. And their talk inside fed the history that Loww, outside, felt and only felt, that he knew some of Pinn's decision to marry EsiMay was found a great risk by the latter's family, which wondered what its energic daughter was doing picking up such a loose, pale pebble from such a deserted beach, the beach of life . . . and then marrying it. As such views changed over

31

the years, so did Andy Pinn, considering that the only real risk he took was falling in love at all: he refused to listen to his heart for weeks, even in the frost and smog of Glasgow, steadying himself with the confusion he felt at her indifference toward him. In desperation, he had tried a bit of tenderness usually beyond him. He was so clumsy in this that she laughed it away. And then, magically, a strong earnestness filled the space left: he suddenly looked, to her, like a planner and a provider. As soon as she finally agreed, he became, almost imperceptibly, exactly as she wanted him to be: full of purpose, and somehow a little older than his thirty-four years. Since EsiMay loved to laugh, other qualities that he showed or tried to show, sustained the relationship: she was satisfied with laughing at his pretensions, and he in turn was pushed into better shape by the same laughter. So that by the time they both felt more secure materially, some adventure had gone out of their living; but a store of laughter and love remained, binding them to their children. Now, what it meant was that Ebo helped EsiMay push Pinn's smile an aggregate of a few yards a year . . . which gladdened her for it was sometimes tiring to push her husband's smile along alone.

The Food finally came out of the history of laughing, and prodded the startled Loww, "Hey Kofi, let's go and drink. Madam EsiMay says I can entertain you small, and do without tomorrow. She worries about my health too much. After all, isn't it only a limp I have?" And sometimes his limp did more walking than he himself did. There was a silence as they both looked out of Ebo's window sideways into the street. The food was feeling vulnerable, wondering where his life was going, for he was only slightly younger than Kofi Loww. The bicycle that went around the corner could have gone around a whole emotional world. The brown articulator with evening minerals passed, and all size passed with it. "Hey my friend, you're not my friend, my friend. You make me think too much. I don't want to waste time thinking. I want to waste time making money!" The Food was restless, and dancing a suggestive dance . . .

There was a soft knock at the door. When Loww opened it, a short, frowning girl with cold eyes rushed into the room, and held the Food's shirt, shouting, "Give me my money! You think you'll fool who. Give me my money now! Or you get trouble!" "Ewuraba, good evening. Sit down and join us," the Food said with the utmost calm, ignoring the hand on his shirt, "or you want to spoil your beauty with this burst of anger. How did you manage to come through the gate with the dogs there? Not even one bark followed you. But you can hear them gathering barks now! Oh, Kofi, look at her beauty!" Kofi Loww looked with his boldest disinterest, so that his eyes did not need any words from his mouth. He drank his beer with a peculiar look at the girl. "So you Ebo you didn't hear me? You don't know I'm a human being? I'll show you, paa! I will shout until the white man hears me . . . ." Baby Yaa said with her small yoyi eyes beaming their blackness out of her round, fawn face. It was a face that corn had once grown near, noisily, when she was in the village planting seeds reluctantly, and when her mother had taken seed every year. The city had shortened her already short smile, so that she now spoke at double the speed that she used to last year. There was no longer any village left on her teeth.

Ebo was still being a studied, if rather desperate, gentleman. His shoulders broadened in necessary confidence, but he only looked a bigger target to Baby Yaa, to whom he appeared ridiculous in his calm. Then she started to pull his shirt hard, so that the stretch looked like a pig squealing in a witch's hands. But the Food went on talking in an offhand way with Loww, who had still not uttered a word. The blue room changed color, and there was silence. Ebo broke it: "You see I told you that women like my limp! Baby Yaa loves me. She even loves my shirt. My dear Yaa, hold my shirt harder! Hold it harder! I know that if we were alone, it wouldn't be my shirt you would be holding so hard, eh! Hahaha!" The laughter reminded Loww of masqueraders when he was a child: they were so colorful, and leaped over roofs with their stilts; but they sometimes fell, just like the Food's laughter, now inches from the ground, finishing. "Give her her money. How can we stand here watching her concert without doing anything? Ebo, how much is it?" Kofi Loww asked. The anger had now come a little forward into Ebo's eyes, his shoulders narrowed as if ready to spring. He said, "I've been eating kelewele from her tray. I've paid her some, and I'm left with some." Then with a mad smile he lurched at her throat, kicking her legs, and shaking her violently. There was a loud scream from Baby Yaa: "He's killing me-oooooh, he's killing me! mewuooo!" Kofi Loww held the Food's arms, and separated them quickly with a twist of the wrist, and then held him back.

There was a knock on the door. All three of them understood

straightaway what was to be done: they sat down with an amazing and sudden calm, holding two glasses and one bottle. Then the Food started to chat about rising prices. Mrs. EsiMay Pinn looked in with a question on her face, asking, "Was there a noise from here, Ebo? I thought I heard a scream or a loud laugh or something . . ." "We heard it too, madam, and I've just looked out the window to see what it was. I saw nothing. Kanda is getting more and more drunks these days, Hmmm, Yaa am I not right?" The Food said all this with a smile. But Baby Yaa drank beer sullenly to stop herself from talking. "Ah, as for your friend Kofi, he doesn't talk much. A wife would soon cure that, eh!" EsiMay said, and slammed the door with her laugh still stuck in it.

As soon as she left Baby Yaa rose and held Ebo's shirt again. Kofi Loww pressed her hand, twisted it slightly and disengaged it, saying "Awura, stop this nonsense. How much does he owe you?" "Thirty cedis," she said, looking at her hand rubbing it. "Thirty cedis. And I may have to add something for all this pain I'm getting. I'll be dead before I leave here." "She's a liar!" Ebo roared. "It's only twenty cedis. Don't force me to beat you again! You, Yaa-for-nothing!" "You try it and see!" Baby Yaa shouted back. "Your friend here is a gentleman, he will not let you kill me!" Then she rose and pressed herself gently against Loww. He moved back and looked at her with thirty cedis in his hand, which the Food tried to snatch. "She's a liar! Don't give her a free ten cedis." Kofi Loww moved the money out of the way, put it quickly in Baby Yaa's small bag, and led her out, telling her, "Next time don't do such a dangerous thing like holding shirts. Is this how you always collect your money?" Ebo followed with anger in his limp, and then suddenly stopped and went back into his room. As soon as Baby Yaa was outside the gate, Loww went back to the room . . . to redeem his money in turn from Ebo. The Food was not there. And the window was wide open. He looked around pulled, then suddenly shot out of the room and the gate into the street, realizing what had happened.

He ran to the right toward the GNTC at the corner. Then he saw Ebo, Baby Yaa and a police constable standing together. "Officer!" the Food was saying, "she's my wife. I wasn't beating her. I was giving her money to buy kerosene. Aha, here's Kofi, my brother. He will verify what I'm saying . . ." Loww said: "True. Don't mind them officer, they love each other so much, but still

34

they're always fighting!" "After all," said the doubtful constable, "this is a nyamanyama marriage! You fight in the street like this! Breach of peace, first class!" "Yes, my dear husband, give the officer ten cedis for his trouble. After all you are holding my ten cedis there . . ." The Food gave the money after a slight hesitation and stormed off, dragging Loww behind him. "He's a very good husband, you see. Only, officer . . . something between his legs has to be serviced!" Then she laughed and laughed, running off, and shouting back at the constable still standing there alone vaguely scrutinizing the ten cedis. "I will never have such a fool for a husband! Now that you have ten cedis—awoof money!—I can talk: he's not my husband, and he's a fool! Haha." Kofi Loww and Ebo quickened their steps, hearing only half of what Baby Yaa was saying to the policeman.

"You have to learn some patience," was all Loww said when they returned to the room. "Patience with a thief-woman holding my shirt? Impossible! Kofi, here's half your money . . . as for the ten cedis I won't pay. I told you she was lying and then laughing too on top." "Ebo, you people are all actors, you are all GBC one-to-thousand," Loww said looking beyond the room. "Don't thousand me!" the Food shouted laughing. "You especially. I can hundred you: you are the man of a hundred moods, all quiet . . . even when they are chasing you! But you are my friend, and I like you. I will eat banku with you when you come again. Are you going?" As they reached the gate, Pinn called from his front door, "So you are going away without saying goodbye, Mr. Loww . . ." The glint of irony in his eye did not reach his mouth this time. Kofi Loww went to him, with a directness bordering on the abrupt, shook his hand and moved back. Pinn continued, "Are those people still after you? . . ." "Oh, I don't know whether it's as definite as that," Loww said, with a start, wondering whether the spreading of this information would finally make it a more serious reality. "I only wanted you to know that if you need any support at all, my wife and myself would gladly . . ." Ebo interrupted, "Oh, you do enough for me already, especially madam EsiMay; and if you help me, then you help my friend. Your help is enough. I will pass some on to Kofi here and anyway nothing bothers him." Pinn smiled through the interruption, adding, "Of course I mean moral support." Then he winked at Loww, without the Food seeing this. Loww smiled back at the wink, then waved and left.

Back in the streets Accra had one eye shut: at nine o'clock, the taxis were driving toward sleep; and with the open eye, with the one bright headlight, they moved to the cines, the wake-keepings, the spiritual churches, the still-talking compounds, the society meetings, the discos, the night classes, the late journeys, the night kenkeys, the kelewele, and the evening profits. Kofi Loww was hardly even a point in space: it seemed that every human being, everything else, was so decided, had such purpose, that he was automatically and constantly engulfed by the more active space of every such thing, every such person. He had his hopes in points of time, hoping that each minute would eventually draw together enough space to either rush along in perdition or explode . . . and he would be there at that instant when a purpose could be taken or left out of the debris; when a sense of self, perhaps vanishing, would finally give him, too, a little space for himself. In the old days, he thought—sometimes sadly, sometimes with a smile—that he would have been an old elder that others came to, especially the young, to pour out their hearts to, and then would leave feeling that they had talked to a safe man, a man who was neither traditionally nor emotionally dangerous. The propellers of his soul sliced nothing in revenge, and he certainly did not want to move into any imported philosophy of action or absence, neither Marxism in palm wine nor existentialism in pito . . . if there were any absence at all, it was merely the absence of one thing or one thought as opposed to the other; of one way of life as opposed to another way; of the collision of decisions or attitudes, one of which would not vanish but would move into a different relationship, a different collision. He wondered, as he suddenly smelled the rich shitoh, whether this was the basis of his reluctance to go and take in other people's ideas at university, again. He wondered whether a quiet persistence to find what he could do with both old and new was a sin or a taboo. He ate shitoh, kenkey and doubt: but what was old, what was new, after all? Hundreds of years of experience before and after strangers came to this land should have created a brilliant freedom in him. The world was open, no matter how many cultures you shut it in, including your own. As he neared Kaneshie, the sellers preparing to go to sleep contoured him: they marked him out as someone not buying, someone not rising to a quick gossip on his way to bed. There was no money in his beard. In the distance as he crossed the huge, new market . . . that vast, concrete monument to sell-

36

ing: . . . he saw one star shine on one kiosk with the records in it returning sound up there for the light coming down. Exchange in light and sound. Late akpeteshie in a late mouth shone through a man's cheeks. Loww suddenly stopped walking, stopped by a sudden and overwhelming need for Adwoa Adde. Ebo had once told him that a man of hesitations was a wasteful thing to behold. He had been pointing to Loww's relationship with Adwoa and wondering what all the thinking on Loww's part was for. They all knocked with this certainty at the closed door of his heart; but it was Adwoa herself that never pressed too hard, she waited as if she were not waiting at all.

And true to form, with blurred eyes that blurred the whole corner stood the stooping form of Beni Baidoo, omnipresent, eating kenkey with two hands, worrying the pepper on his plate, and smiling through the stubs on his chin. All he said to Loww was, "I vote for sister Adwoa, for when she settles you down, then you'll be able to help me more more one hundred times!"

Chapter 3

Baidoo was involved with driblets of divination; he was the explainer whose buffoonery ranged over the city . . . fools got reputations fast in Accra. He divined that Adwoa Adde was going to have spiritual children soon, and he was obliquely one of the children. He therefore tried hard to let his cigarette smoke ascend the sky as vertically as possible. But when he wanted to pray, his knees refused to reach the ground even though they were bent toward it. He saw Adwoa everywhere, even when his vision was blocked by goats, Mercedes Benzes, semiprostitutes, harmattan or plantain cake . . .

Adwoa Adde's underbelly was the city, her heart was higher than Loww's, whom she suddenly saw at the old Polo grounds, without calling him; her mouth traveled to him in silence. She had thought her type of feeling for him grew stronger with stealth and suffering. Sometimes she was his oxygen as she followed him without his knowing. New truths were coming to her, and she at first laughed at them, laughed at what her own head was telling her: she felt that the daylight, being female, was lighter in weight than the darkness which was speaking to her in a new way: it was trying to give her the power to push day toward night by a few minutes, whenever she felt her heart in danger. Her aftersmile spread into the doubt in her eyes when her head told her that she would soon be able to carry the daylight on her back. In order to give more meaning to what was happening to her she created two obsessions in her life: her love and her God; and then God also dragged into her head the lives of other people. She said to herself, "Some gods are making me their trotro." Her food sizzled with religion, with caring. Sometimes she saw herself only as knees . . . angled toward the skies, as she listened to traditional religious songs. Her eyes brightened like butterflies, and were as restless. When she felt her mind leaving her body, then her necklace shone and orbited around Accra. It was only when she was able to wear the daylight completely that she knew she had been pulled into magic and witchery. She mastered the sunlight, but she could make only half her darkness a force for good; her intentions were the faint dot under the question mark of the city. She started to sell fruit that, when it was all mixed, was the color of her tongue; and she saw colors and shapes in patterns changing with the intensities of her central concerns: fresh tomatoes and mangoes made one bunch with horizons, almost creating new adinkra designs; pyramids and figures-of-eight stood before her; intermediate patterns moving from buying hands to fruit to baskets and bags, put strong lines around her world for miles and miles; that leaf unwrapped could be an opening soul. When she was bargaining, her mouth became rounder than ever before, making a beauty that further tightened her fine lean body. Oh Adwoa! It was as if the new simpleness and tension of things led to the shattering nights . . . this was her test.

Near the Accra Community Center, the sand of which would rise to meet the sea and remain dry, Adwoa saw a man with a dog following Kofi Loww; Beni Baidoo followed the dog. The man was Kojo Pol, was tall, thin and nervous, and he shared his eyes with the dog: both man and dog had expressions of tremendous annoyance and embarrassment, and they shared one wrapper of groundnuts, which the dog kept glancing suspiciously at . . . feeling that Okay Pol was having more than it was. The snout of the dog huffed and puffed against the African concrete, and some streets of Accra were shaped exactly like its tail. But it was the cigarette stuck behind the dog's ear that Baidoo was chasing. Baidoo wanted the canine jot, and so the dog appeared beautiful to him, with the possibility of a smoke freeeeeee. Okay Pol had no idea who put the jot there, but the dog would not have it taken off; it snarled the finest hands away. Eventually Beni started to talk to the dog in a series of barks and supplications.

"Beni Baidoo, I am busy on a national assignment! Leave this stupid dog alone!" Okay Pol shouted with his frown spreading into his hair. "Young man!" shouted Baidoo back. "Teach your police dogs to be kind! All I want to do is to smoke a jot that an animal can't possibly smoke with its ear! I know the language of barking, but this dog is stubborn with all the Ga bones it can't eat! Kojo the Pol, I demand on the authority of my wizened age, that you allow me the pleasure of an African smoke . . . you know smoke like a woman moves more slowly in the tropics . . . I say allow!" Some boys appeared through the dust of Baidoo's noise, and tossed obscenities at Pol . . . national duty obscenities that filled the sweat in his fez. Without any warning, Okay Pol gathered the ungatherable dog with its street tail questioning the city, and threw it at the boys . . . and just before the dog fell, Beni Baidoo expertly freed the cigarette, laughing high and low before lighting the jot that brightened Accra.

The boys clapped Kofi Loww awake, but he saw nothing that went on around him. Adwoa edged out of sight, out of the dust settling on Pol's shoes, her eyes opening and lowering by sun and shade.

The edge of the fufu pounder rounded the sky. Adwoa Adde had reached her two rented rooms at Odorkor, feeling ridiculous that love had sent her so much after an aimless man whose interest in her seemed such as to fill only one eye; and sometimes she felt so small that she could fit into his toothache . . . the pain in his life. She finished her fufu and abenkwan, dried her mouth of music and prayers. And then saw Beni Baidoo stiff at attention at her window. What was he doing there? "Sister! these days I speak stylishly through the glass of other people's windows. Can I half-come in? Half-wits should not fully enter wise houses! And true, Sister, I vote for the fine weddings of spiritual women and vague male thinkers: add Adwoa to Loww! and the rain will fall, even in the harmattan. You will have your quiet Kofi! Sister, I now have one leg hanging out of your window, but forgive me and listen to my two problems: I am desperate about founding a village; and secondly, my donkey is on strike. No one is giving me real help over this village. Why? At my age shouldn't I command more respect than I do? I usually help the clouds by my smoking, too! But Sister, what's happening to you? You are changing . . . your eyes are shining, and your room looks upside down . . . Sister, I'm going, I'm afraid of spirits. I fear fear itself; but don't forget to solve my problems for me when you are free again. I'm gooooooiiiing! Sister, I told you you would have porters . . ." Baidoo ran.

40

Adwoa felt a strange weight on her breasts. She had a sudden urge for height and her room seemed upside down and deadly quiet, in spite of the argument about lotto between two other tenants in the corner house. Her mind had been broken into two by a line of black powder vaguely seen, and she felt the presence of a black pot reflecting, deeply and with sound, her kerosene light. Then she saw in a flash in the corner a young woman whose limbs had been taken out of her and arranged in a line in front of her, all at the same level; her pelvis had been turned backward and pushed against one eye; the other eye, which gushed with tears, was between two fingers pressing it in terror; the sound of wailing came not from her mouth, which was lying on the floor, but from her ear obviously borrowed from an ancestor as a gift not to be returned; her other hand was moving around the room in fiery cartwheels; the ceiling lowered, pushing the woman's bottom down onto a sudden miniature silk cotton tree which had a storm of its own in its six inches of space; when Adwoa Adde tried to scream there was no sound; her own neck danced; then the woman quickly formed herself whole again, kneeling down in mock reverence and making grave begging movements with her bleeding hands, and shouting in a voice unnaturally high. "It is the prayers that will kill you, ooooooh, Adwoa, it's the prayers . . . come to us, we will eat and drink, can't you see that you can borrow a body any time you want! Heeeeyyyyy! Tie your hair to mine, we are together, you are mine!"

As the woman floated toward her with laughter in her hot eyes, Adwoa Adde dropped her ring, and flew . . . from some force by her breasts through the open staring window. The window closed by itself after she had gained height, still praying, and feeling a strange brown underbelly of love as she flew over Accra. She flew around the Central Post Office clock twice, moving it to dong with a wave of her fingers. She felt herself going through the looking phase, seeing the city within her own movement of time, disorganizing all sleeping clocks, seeing the night and the day at the same time; Accra was cut up into varying intensities of light and dark, of good and bad, in such a way that she could only describe and feel for what she saw . . . she could not distinguish what was good and what was bad, for she was forced into relationship with everything, and her pulse was the movements of thousands in sleep. She could suddenly see her friend Sally Soon flying from London, they waved across the skies . . . And Adwoa took her own breeze, she wore the wind. And her spiritual children floated below her . . .

But Kwaku Duah the fitter was chattering into a gasket under the flying eyes of Adwoa; he had contributed nothing to his Asona clan meetings, and had no feeling at all for the owner of that Peugeot 404 car. He didn't care for the streets either, which he used merely to walk, and drive, and spit on . . . but the streets were alive, were the holders of human crying when all city hearts slept. As soon as a path became a road and a street, it was spiritual movement for the earth, the street was the earth's long grown-up child; but Kwaku Duah stood as if he owned it, spreading oil and broken metal on it. When he arrived from Offinso fifteen years ago as an apprentice, he helped lift heavy engines and was teased and bullied. He took it all in his stride, finding it quite easy to learn all that he had to learn from his Togolese master and two cruel chief apprentices. Kwaku Duah was strong, but he did not see Adwoa Adde lift and embrace High Street, raising it with the banks, the churches, the stores and the houses. Love could lift high, and the eyes of the streets were closed, especially the sleeping watchmen with their arrows lost in their bows . . .

Manager Agyemang looked with scorn at the territory of his desk; he had been pushing goods and paper for years, and was now watching the sly lizard catch a grasshopper at his window. The tongue of the lizard was the tongue of the manager, momentarily . . . only, he caught different things; he ate life's different insects; the night lay on his eyes as he went home with his hypertension. Three fish slept on his plate by the kenkey, each one representing the graded silences of his wife; the gravy wore neat onions, shouted through its pepper; when he ate, his jaws were lonely, so he rushed out to a Lodge meeting, trailing her silence behind him and wishing she were dead. He knew he himself would die almost forgotten at his condemned desk. Condemned? It had built him a house, this desk, it knew half his secrets, and traveled with him everywhere in spirit, but the heaviest thing it felt it had to carry was his name . . .

Akosua with the blue cloth and the faded cheeks powdered double had quarreled with her green-green mother by the huge odum trees that steadied her village; she felt tough because her mother had cried, and she walked an agitated confident quarreler's walk. Her wisdom, deep as her tiny bag, had led her out of Obogu

42

into Accra against her mother's wish; and she had spread among the winding slopes of Obogu the question that if all the parents in all the towns and villages had given up bringing up their children in the colo way, why should she sit down and let her mother force her into the fields? She had danced with victory among the silent golden eyes of old cocoa farms holding the heavy shades in their leaves; but Akosua's fists were the same size as the small jaws of Adwoa Adde, jaws that her prayers forced to receive in silence the fighting of other people's fists. Now in the city even Akosua's walk was different for the whole family had now moved to Accra . . .

Aboagye Hispeed smelled of Sunday akpeteshie but he would not admit it. That day he refused everything: he refused to admit he had a mouth with which he could drink; he denied he had a wife, adding that it was not because she was ugly; he insisted that his children were chickens pecking around the bush of his disgrace; then he finally admitted, crying, that the spirit from which he came was pulling him with the longest fingers in the world, back to the spirit world, and that was why he drank, for protection through just that secret brand of akpeteshie that certain spirits, like his, did not like. When his skin finally collapsed, leaving his wasted bones knocking out of rhythm, he screamed around Maamobi far into the ears of the Nima people that he would buy his own coffin, that all those waiting impatiently for his death would not have the chance to insult his bones, that he would bury himself in the first automatic one-man funeral ever seen in Accra . . .

One of Abena's eyes was constantly quarreling with the other, for they could not agree on the angle at which the world should be looked at; so the crossing routes of her eyes made Adwoa roll in flight, made confusion among the stars; Abena's rubber frown was taken from her rubber bag which had no money; she was a telephonist but the only person she wanted to phone was God; she would draw a telephone in the dust and try to call God thus, but God's phone was always engaged; "G—O—D ooo! God!" she would shout without answer; so she took to baking: Abena had been told to collect some flour, but she had to open her legs to get it, and she shared her tears with the rain as that bad man with no smile koraa lay on top of her; but when she collected her flour and made her bread, she baked her shame into the first hundred loaves; after that it did not matter for she covered her heart with the same thick dough and became a stylish young mammy powdering and lightening herself through all the best spots in Accra until she found Kusi . . .

Kofi Kobi-ooo, Kofi, you had to walk with your pioto showing, for your wife with the amazingly broad back was leaving you for the rascal with the long legs, for when he walked he took away all her contradictions, and you just made them grow! She hated your mouth, she hated your head, she hated your voice, and she finally hated your thing; Kofi-oooo Kofi, remember the plan you had to trap them, these wicked lovers? You followed your wife and her lover from bar to bar, secretly, until you yourself became so drunk in the concealed corners that when you finally decided to attack, you attacked the wrong couple; and when you managed to bribe your way out of the police station and went home you were too weak to do anything to the real culprits doing the logologo in your own bed, and they insulted you on top without even stopping what they were doing . . .

Jato with the wrong chin and the kokakola eyes bubbling with brown mischief, had bullied his younger brother for years, until they both grew up on yoo ke gari, with little variations boiled nut by boiled nut; then Kwao the younger goat grabbed education by the horns, bleated until he made money, then got his revenge by releasing the smallest droppings of money to Jato the poor; Jato would polish his jealousy every day and present it hidden as humility; but Kwao gave him exactly what he had always given him from the time he made his money; so Jato tried lies: he filled the Homowo with rumors about how his brother made his money: the money was juju money, was the reward for destroying spirits, the money was robbery, the money was politics; people laughed, Kwao laughed then completely stopped giving Jato money to chase women with . . .

As for Amina she lived under the shadow of her father's cola so that her light-brown eyes, something like the underside of a deer, shone when she was alone in the market with hundreds of strangers; but she was looking for only one stranger: Adwoa Adde, whom she dreamed about while still in the North; Amina could see miles of pain, waste and hope, and her hope was the lamp that led her in wild search for Adwoa Adde whom she did not know in body; her father had finally let her go to the South, thinking there was a devil taking her over, and hoping her uncle would cure her; in Accra Amina's eyes were up, and she knew she would find her spiritual mother . . .

Beni Baidoo moved in and out of the spiritual children, gathering tears and laughter in a cup. He said to the flying Adwoa, "Sister, don't mind them, they want to burden you with their lives. At least I have an excuse: I am old and need support, my life is behind me yet thrusting toward the ancestors . . . I will probably die under a packet of exploding jots, just when I'm about to win a million cedis on the lotto! with my dog and donkey dancing with joy. Don't mind Kwaku Dua the fitter: he does not live in a fitting manner; don't mind Manager Agyeman: he manages to make a mess of his life; Aboagye Hispeed is a smelly wizard; Akosua and Abena are merely semisupertobolo alombos! And Kofi Kobi merely foots his legs all over Accra after women; and Jato is a stupid boogieboy mad in one ball! Sister forgive meeeeeee! I've told you part of my story already, but I think they want too much meaning from you. I only want my *village*, where I will be served by young-young women who have a complete disregard for wrinkles . . . Sister, while others move toward meaning I move toward my village . . ."

Adwoa Adde looked at all the hands moving around in the dark in this city. She saw the thousands making love, the thousands crying, the thousands laughing. Coconuts held the hardness of Accra. The delayed twilight was a train that did not move from its station now; and below the clouds Adwoa saw Kojo Okay Pol too gauche to search, yet searching enough to get his gauche answer: and this answer was to ride on a contrived innocence, on a calculated trip that got him bigger goals than he deserved yet kept his means clumsy enough for a continual need to reassess himself. Okay Pol was asleep in Kaneshie but his bed was awake. And back at Legon, by Adwoa's last high flight, Professor Kwesi Sackey talked in his sleep, but managed to contradict his wife Sofi even in his dream, when she wondered what he was saying. ½-Allotey was in danger at Kuse, for he wanted to go too fast in traditional change, for the elders . . . only his shoulders and his stare saved him from their devastations. As for Dr. Boadi, she only saw his belly heavy and political, sustained by Guinness and the gentleness of his wife Yaaba. To the left, in the east, where the shopgirls slept, cockroaches chewed the Bank of Ghana. Fate was a cola nut: when you spat it out you put another bit back in. Incense reached out with brilliant hands and touched anything modern in a man's head, then pulled the head back in time . . . the earth was the boss; dwarfs, herbs, beads, meat, soap, lavender and juju held the football matches in their grip, brushed the heads of lotto stakers, pushed the hands of draught and oware players, bunched the secret societies, and slept the lovers; the late man or the man late moved indistinct in the truck station with a whole village in his head; he was comfortable in this sad type of sankofa for after he repaired his master's car, he traveled two hundred years back to go and eat his kenkey and kyenam with an extraordinarily comfortable body. Adwoa saw the dead as more adventurous, as more prepared to experiment . . .

Then in the hospital with the wailing buildings she saw Kojo the Joke—the son of a strict standard seven scholar newly dead with his square head—picking the pockets of the sick, without disturbing the two mosquitoes on his shoulder; this showed he was a real expert. After picking six pockets he wanted to try one more. He chose Auntie Lala who looked tough enough to have money; her florida water spread even into her night shadow, and her big legs were unmovingly geographic. It was a fight with her small husband that had sent her to hospital with a bitten finger. The same teeth he used to sing and praise God were what he used to bite her. She would explain with a dignity that would hide the real event, how disgraceful it was for a man to fight with a woman, and bite her to save himself from a proper beating. Her words would fall around the closed ears of the doctor. She saw Kojo the Joke almost straight-away, watched him for a few minutes counting his takings, and then raised the alarm as soon as he came near her. The sick jumped, dragging the Joke outside, hitting him without mercy, with sudden blocks, with metal sticks with healthy fists; legs were pistons; the Joke's screams were serious. He shouted "My mother!" They laughed. He was dragged half-alive to the mortuary whose arms were so unshut. In utter silence a man took a length of old iron rod and stuck it slowly and with purpose up the anus of Kojo the Joke. His spasms were watched almost without interest, his blood was spat at. "Throw him in among the dead," was the shout. Mortuary attendants stood by as the Joke entered, his head dragged and dying with a ten-cedi note stuck with a vengeance in his mouth, and the rod trailing behind like the last tail.

Sally Soon was crying, but she had too much London in her

mouth. And she took notes through her tears. The desperate sounds had moved wildly the course of Adwoa Adde's flight; her heart shrank with pain; but she still avoided the sea, for the sea's juju was always fresh. At the urine-soaked corner of a spare-parts shop in Osu she saw the wondering spirit of Kofi Loww; her heart let in more blood immediately; she turned with a grimace, hovering, directing her breasts in circles; her sudden beauty crowded the sky, as she looked with pity at the love that caused so much restlessness both to himself and to her. His spirit was as confused as he was, yet he would not offer any small sacrifice; she landed and hugged the unknowing spirit, she moved up and down with the weight of her own caring; his spirit understood her and that was what kept her positive about him, but his strange ways were almost taking this understanding away. Adwoa Adde was exhausted. She laid down her bit of daylight as the dawn moved sideways into the city. She was no longer upside down, and she could not fly.

Her eyes closed, crossed and closed; and over at the beach, the receding fury of waves was only southern lions roaring wet in thousands; perception was an X, was a squint of eye, was the suffering of others; trees changed and rechanged roots, filling the underground, the rats, the termites, foundations, and graves with movement; the State House had superstitious foundations, and was a witch, and was usually borrowed by Osu cemetery for numinous meetings . . . and the poor stadium: it was taken for spiritual roaring with thousands of stolen mouths. And this city carried too many centuries on its back at the same time. Adwoa could not believe it as she saw the sky lightening with the descent of hundreds of witches, most of them speaking silently of blood and bone, as snakes slithered into bodies again, and as pots, rings, beads, padlocks, knives, disembodied hearts and black powder lay charmed.

Adwoa Adde found herself back on her bed, almost awake. Sally Soon could be taking her notes in the clouds. The bed did not face the usual wall, her powder had been slightly spilled, there were paths of it; the light seemed to come through her windows reluctantly; the sound of absence was loud. When she frowned the sky frowned; her window did not frame her sense of perception, she felt free and she thought free. Her prayers decorated her knees. God came down with the sun and pushed her yawn aside, God was ready for koko. Fresh morning water washed the love from lovers; Adwoa's heart moved miles and back, in peace. But when the dawn left, she rushed to market and disappeared inside her own haggling, and she sold biscuits even to bishops, desperately . . . so that all Sally Soon had to do was to fly by, trailing behind her: stone walls, midges, daffodils, a few accents and wild bursts of snow.

Chapter 4

Kojo Okay Pol was the optimist, was the monkey that believed he could climb down his own tail in any emergency. In the rush to trail Kofi Loww he had changed from a slightly quiet man into a slightly talkative one. His slanting eyebrows were two little steps of doubt leading up to a bewildered frown. His height suddenly ended up crowded at his hunched shoulders, with his head and neck almost irrelevant, until he smiled teeth shut yet with such light that his whole upper body glowed. This happened even when there was a fly on his shoulder. Under a thick brofo-nut tree he stood deep in thought; then he moved in fits and starts, much like a preset hiccup. He approached the corner carrying a breeze which had pushed too many faces aside before now reaching his own; and his jaws thus carried the weight of wind, their shape showing this: gently hollowed, almost crouching under the high cheekbones, so that words left his mouth as if over a bridge. The space between his hopes and his life stretched further than Navrongo. But his faint-green fez, worn in a short period of sudden inspiration, added the touch of ridicule that both freed and imprisoned him. When he was sure of himself he took advantage of other people's underestimation of him, and when he was confused the entire universe—a look, a remark, a situation, tomatoes, cars, the moon—crushed him. Sometimes, caught between the jet and the village, he whistled; he insisted that culture was just what you did, so he was free to do anything, especially with a Northern father and an Akan mother. To confuse things still further, he usually felt he was bigger than any situation he found himself in, but the fact that he could not often control

49

these situations gave him an acute sense of injustice. He therefore tried to choose a sense of innocence, which was temperamentally true, to go with his sense of ridicule. And this led him to create unnecessary complexities around people.

He thought, for instance, that Kofi Loww was desperately trying to think up schemes of betrayal and escape; he also thought the latter was always laughing at him, laughter at the Rex, laughter in Ghana House, even laughter in the Accra plains . . . corners were especially dangerous for gusts of it. Okay Pol was given to looking for clues and signs of persecution from Loww. The dog: twice Pol looked at the underpart of a dog and saw Loww's fingerprints there, he assumed, from long hands unwashed after a meal of crabs and snails in abenkwan with fufu, thick; eventually his own shitoh finger marks fooled him, and he released the dog; but it was a stubborn animal, the very one that caused a scene and demanded its share of sympathy and groundnuts. The tree: Pol was convinced, on a hunch provided by an ancestral presence and a bottle of Guinness mixed with palm wine, that Loww was on top of that particular neem tree looking for incriminating signs of disgrace; Pol climbed up and down the tree several times, leaving his fez at the foot and collecting it at each climb; he knew his foolishness spread among the leaves, greening them. And what a burst of sound and shame when the crows came and retook the tree! The cinema hall: as Pol searched for Loww during the film, each seat became an enemy and each enemy gave a curse when he stepped on a toe; Pol left himself here, and collected himself later in strange seats there; the whole hall at last rose against him just at the moment when what Pol was doing was exactly what was happening in the film; they thought he was a wizard, knocked his fez off, and drove him out. Outside by the fried fish under the moon he stood, chewing his desperation into the gum in his mouth. He dusted the principles in his sunglasses, and said to himself: "Enough! Dr. Boadi must find another African donkey to chase his shadows; for after all couldn't something better be done, even with a secondary education?" But when he went back to Dr. Boadi, he was talked into renewing the security contract for another month.

August weather could redirect a life or release it, and usually did neither to Pol, with its breeze of the left hand, though even Pol's brains were cool then, and he did not cough above the weather. If there were any heat at all then it belonged to the hearts that shared

50

passion. The grass lay down and became brown only in stretches under the city trees showing the full glow of their hard-won green. The harvests had come and were coming, queueing like anything else behind the engine of the seasons. Pol could not, even in this trading country, buy the sky, but it was cheap for small joys when hard rain, hard sun and hard dust slept. Under the rainbow, being God's gentle kente worn quickly and put down, the palm tree waved spirits on. Pol suddenly decided not to join the police force after all . . . so the uniforms marched away from his head; for no reason he felt like giving his country a hug, and he knew the woman to do this with: Araba Fynn, whose indifference and stylish languor was a challenge to his new mouth, his new confidence. There was a physical speed of general movement about Pol which came fitfully. When his hurried jaws took a simple ampesi, two rays of the sun sent left light and right light to either side of him. His teeth were decorated with sunlight, and were chewing in thought as he remembered the first time he saw Kofi Loww insignificant at the Kotoka International airport. He thought Loww looked as if he desperately wanted fufu, soft; and everything else soft. He also thought Loww walked as if he were climbing hills all the time, as if some sly ancestor had rented his body, and was swaggering with it without regard for the borrowed nature of the body being used.

And so that Okay Pol came to the fading airport, where the front door of the country was really the back door. The concrete was being eaten by the roar of jets; the glass sometimes mirrored beautiful people, sometimes the decay of a whole country; the steps leading up to the departure lounge jumped on each other with the same rush as the people; the chandeliers hung in baroque dust, like well-dressed thieves at a festival; and the staff, trained or untrained as symbols of Ghana 1975, were exactly that: they sat there frozen like traditional masks though they did not have the meaning, they did not have the color. Pol instinctively disliked the place, but he was there on duty: he had to make sure that the horses, deceptively padded in six high boxes, would be delivered safely to Dr. Boadi and his Commissioner; no publicity no palaver. Boadi's political ambitions depended much on this operation. To him Pol looked naïve and clever enough to do this for he thought that any future favors for Pol could easily be met without much debt or inconvenience. Thus, with the weight of responsibility, Pol's fez tilted left in the opposite direction from his head; his soft hair caught the air in bunches, and shaped it from the back. Boadi had hinted that he and his masters wanted two of the horses, of a different breed from the rest, to start a private race club for themselves, "with betting and things. For after all who in Ghana knows the difference between a racehorse and farmhorse like the Clydesdale?" Boadi added. Pol ignored this, pretending he had not heard the last point. He treated his task as morally neutral, but when he thought of Dr. Boadi too often the doubt would start circulating in his head, like a canoe on the Volta without a bank. But Dr. Boadi was persuasive, was an expert in ironing out moral creases. He was well dressed, with a whaaaat jacket bordering on silver, even for ordinary occasions; his belly was formed almost with a cosmic curve, and it seemed to lead him like a guide pushing back the world and making way for the small important buttocks following. Beer brewed in his brain. His Chevrolet, a fine aging American tart, brought the ghetto to Ghana, and was usually crowded with friends and relatives, all of whom could smell the stews ahead. His ambitions were the umbrella for all and sundry. And his broad smile, which Pol often looked reluctantly into, contained biting schemes as big as caves. Pol stared in amusement when Boadi suggested that the contrast between the two of them could give off sparks of profit . . .

The trouble at Kotoka first started in Pol's head when the parking lot crows scattered their black-and-white cries over the wings of stationary airplanes. This broadened the range of noise and put Pol on edge, so that you could see his narrow back tightening. Then the group of porters, much like doctorate kayakaya, complained of the weight of the boxes, complained that the ventilated boxes were breathing more air than they were . . . "How can this adaka fit punish man like this?" was the cry. Their overalls were buttoned together with the obstinacy of mutual suffering. Their movements took on that slow rebellion that moved their work forward barely inch by inch . . . then they dropped one box from the gangway onto the tarmac. That was a quiet box, its noise light and brittle against the deep "swine" that escaped from that fat porter whose left shin the box heavily grazed through the haste of his early-fleeing co-workers. They passed among themselves, after the recovery of their lethargy, feelings of indignation, pain and embarrassment. Atanga got the trumpet in his mouth ready: "You think this be good matter? Man's belly no chop, then you make am commot this heavy t'in. For me I no de fit take am, my hand, i' cut." His

52

upper lip would first quiver, then burst into a series of ironic laughs, with the words shooting out from the hungry side of his mouth, just as the kola scattered. He had suddenly remembered that his wife, whom he had not yet properly married, had stopped cooking and selling waakyi because she felt she was supporting his laziness; so whenever he spoke he seemed to push everything to a crisis, as if he had very little to lose anymore.

"This box," he continued, "ibi heavy pass airplane self. For me i no sabe this nyamanyama t'in at aaall. Him who pack this adaka bambala in UK no get sense koraa. You fit give me kenkey for my belly, then I too fit lift whole airplane self. Rrrubish! Rrrru-bishsh! again my frien', I lie?" Atanga threw this question like groundnut paper at Kofi Loww half-sleeping up at the balcony. He threw the paper back: "Make I come down for help?" Loww mumbled through a mouthful of corn. "Ah, my brother, nexx time, but so the world be . . ." Atanga said over his shoulder as he joined his fellow workers, who were examining the shin of Yaovi more from an excuse to have a break from lifting than from any sympathy. The workers slowly became curious about the nature of cargo they were lifting and decided to let drop a second box, deliberately, to see whether it would open and show its secrets. There was new concentration, as their blue overalls pocketed the same color of sky; and there were suddenly new muscles, and Atan-ga's tongue was locked, was untrumpeting; their grunts took over the airplanes.

Pol, watching with a curious frown, decided immediately to go to lift the rest of the boxes with the workers. He was impressed with their new energy, but there was still something odd. He showed his card as he walked quickly onto the tarmac toward the plane, wondering, in passing, what Atanga had said to the stranger on the balcony; and he took mental note of this. The manner of the porters let Pol know straightaway that he was not welcome at all. Their eyes formed a barrier over which he jumped with his long legs. Then they moved more quickly. "Tsooboi! Yei!" came the war cry as a final effort was made with resounding success, with a resound-ing crash . . . kpa! As it broke open, the big box pushed its sounds out in echo, driving out other sounds, mixing suddenly the bright-ness of sun with the brightness of the eyes watching. Out came the brown horse with a snarl, covering the view to Accra with its mane; it had worn the terrible confines of the box, and it now wore the airport. It had now become a presence: the short angles of its kicking and galloping both broke up and focused the confusion; speed and surprise, taking the glare of the eyes back from the sun, turned the horse into an Ananse monster, a visitation or a huge dog, as if the last match in the middle of all the villages in Ghana had not quite gone out, as if revelation were still possible. Gasps and OOOooohs varied the air, tilted Pol's fez in consternation. He worried in rhythm to the hooves. Over by his red eyes the world grew beyond his control. The radar took his fear round and round on useless rides, and the small handful of people suddenly looked like thousands. When he rushed, his shadow rushed and then stood still without him. The rumor was that this was a plane of ghosts, ampa; was that this was an invasion force, with the horses sent ahead while the white riders took the wrong plane, ampa; was that the gods were coming.

Pol walked furiously among the instant stories, ending up at the office of the duty security officer who was smoking with both hands, and doing his banker to banker stakes. Kwaku Tia lowered his cigarette with one hand; the urgency on Okay Pol's face seemed to have made his smoke lighter to carry. Four airport eyes grew and rounded with hate . . . then with questions: Kwaku Tia knew what was in the boxes but was annoyed that the task of delivering them was not entirely entrusted to him, but rather to a complete amateur like Pol; Pol knew he thought this, but felt only contempt for a security officer who appeared so incompetent. So each asked in his mind what the other was doing intruding on the other's bush. And this question led to doubt about Dr. Boadi's own wisdom in selecting the two of them together. Kwaku Tia had a mobile forehead with which he headed the world away in emergencies, with looks of intense concentration. Pol pushed the silence away: "C'mon, have you no work to do? The horses . . . the boxes are breaking! See to your men . . . I will speak to the small crowd on the balcony, I will warn them about the government's need for secrecy, for after all as Dr. Boadi says, if Ghanaians help the government, the government will help Ghanaians . . . Eh?" Pol was gone in a flash with these last words almost sticking in his throat, with doubts about Dr. Boadi still trailing his head. As soon as Pol left, Kwaku Tia let his mouth fill easily with contempt: was this how things were now run? He was going back to his lotto when he remembered the blame he too would get if the horses did not canter to safety and secrecy.

He grew bold with yawning, then suddenly leaped up, his short legs almost levitating, and ran toward the action . . . ending up with a scream, both feet stuck in a pile of dung, his rolling eyes staring at the shanks of a momentarily stationary horse.

"In the name of the law," he shouted, "in the name of the law, what language do these animals speak? are they Twi-speaking horses?" There was a roar from the crowd, and this started the horse moving wildly again. Kwaku Tia saluted in desperation, for something to do; but the laughter brought his hand down with force. His belly sagged to the sound of cheers. The horse bristled, stood at attention, forcing Tia to do the same by the sheer force of its stillness. Pol stared in disbelief at man and horse standing motionless at attention, their shadows joined into a different animal, much like the map of Ghana with huge jaws eating it. Two more horses broke loose, with one snorting and galloping sideways and drawing more cheers from the crowd. History said: galloping usually gathered roars. Pol saw, with panic, tens of footprints on fresh heaps of dung on the runway; the airport seemed soft and offensive, the airport seemed stepped upon, and the small crowd representing all shades of Accra shared much more laughter than its mouths could hold. The tarmac took off with the force of African laughter, and every laugh was a cry in the head of Okay Pol. "Ma frien'," someone shouted from above, "horse toilet dey for your hat, I swear!" Pol froze in the beloved capital, removing his fez and cleaning it so that Accra itself was cleaner. A feeling of persecution in his large Oh-eyes had destroyed the light there and pulled the eyelids down lower than sensible. Kwaku Tia used one half of his jaw to suffer for his confusion, and the other half to enjoy the plight Pol was in; and his sense of decision crashed between the two halves.

Pol now was a one-man wail, rushing suddenly and with decision into the stares of the crowd. He tried to scatter the look of ridicule in each eye by appearing masterful even with his thin legs. He shouted, "I must warn all of you that what you are seeing here is not true . . . the eyes have been known to deceive . . . you must be interrogated to confirm this . . . the government needs your support in this hour of galloping, I mean this hour of crisis . . . these are agricultural horses, to push on Operation Feed Yourself, and they will pull the plow . . . you are in the name of the law asked to remain here until further notice . . . you may continue to look but don't pass water—I mean don't pass judgment." Pol was gasping, but felt confident, adding, "Look at the hooves, don't waste your eyes looking for horse skin much higher than that." His smile was not passed back, his smile just burst in his own face. Kofi Loww's eyes held heat, were angry and round like kpakpo shitohs. He had been watching and listening with foreboding. Though he considered himself a quiet if rather odd man, struggling for his stomach and for his soul with touches of obstinacy at the temperament, with a slow but sometimes raging temper, he insisted that he would not be told *when* to leave an airport in his own country. The neemberry in his mouth picked yesterday in a moment of absent thinking, balanced the sense of fight in his heart, gave his feet the right space between. On the rare occasions that he felt like fighting, he also had feelings of peace and expectation; in his head the buildings, the markets, the streets, became alive, became almost passionate with existence.

Some could see the confrontation coming, but were laughing, thinking that Pol and the security men were not really serious . . . but Loww saw the agitation in Pol's face, a face that was heavy with a naïveté that could not be put down; and he had to answer this agitation, this challenge, for he could not be kayakaya to his own silence, and finally to his own conscience. The back of his head moved the anger to the front, as he said almost casually, "No one has the right to stop me or anyone else from leaving here . . . You, my friend, you don't really look as if you belong to the politicians . . . and what's all this dreaming on the tarmac you were doing? When will some of you stop invading our dignity? You would think there were enough mad concerts in town . . ." Kofi Loww remembered his uncle, Wofa Kobina, who always spoke so deliberately that his words could lie down singly and rest. He had learned something of this. The sun pushed two small clouds aside, gauging its dying light onto the scene. After the roar of approval, there was a silence which no one's mother could fill. If that man chewing so fast laughed through his corn, it was a bitter laugh pushing the corn to one side of his mouth. Kojo Okay Pol beckoned sssss to Kwaku Tia, with the latter wearing a face that showed the fear of things getting out of control now, yet ready to follow any decision that would both solve them and absolve him from responsibility for any effects. Kofi Loww's body stiffened, on the alert, as the two men advanced toward him. Someone suddenly shouted. "We're going we're going, we're going only if we want!"

The crowd joined him: "We're going-oooooooo! only if we want!" With the contemptuous angle it was at, Loww's beard gathered this roar, in silence, and threw it in Pol's direction. Pol and Tia suddenly stopped, and put their heads together, whispering. "Hey! the government doesn't whisper," someone else shouted. "Say it loud! let's all hear some."

Pol and Tia had seen what looked like a ghost coming around corners so fast, and pushing shoulders aside. "Something is coming to save us or damn us," whispered Pol, half hopefully half ironically. Osofo Ocran had arrived with his quick, squat steps: "Stop stop stop all you gentlemen, three times stop. Remember the trinity, in the name of the Lord, not the law. Hey, don't forget your forefathers. This morning I have polished the knees of Jesus Christ with all my prayers for all of you. I have seen everything, I have seen these two young men getting ready to fight. Why why why? . . . remember the trinity, again and again and again. You all belong to one country, a country blessed with . . ." "Curses!" someone shouted from the back. Osofo ignored this and went on, " . . . blessed with peace, in the sky and in the earth. I am Osofo Ocran. I look up to my bishop looking down at the flock. Bless these horses, bless these broken boxes. Is it not good to eat banku on these broken boxes, for it may be a sign from God that we must not break, we must put and stay together. OOOOOH, your smiles are beautiful and God-given! I belong to the church of the Smiling Saint, SS church. I have collected everything and given it to God, even your laughter. But look at all the people around with stooped shoulders; and maybe the country is stooping too! I only ate one kenkey and half a fish this morning, but it's enough, I have been blessed, my belly is a little temple of food, African food. And may the horses bring good tidings, even if some of us think it's a foolish idea. Be careful with each other. Alleluya! If you waken the devils in you, you will surely fight, and you will surely see hell. Up goodness, down sin! Amen. Please stop grumbling; you have to listen to me, for on Thursdays I am not permitted to smile, except alone in prayer. The church suffers with the people, so the smile is locked up once a week, and only God sees it. You know, my own grandmother cried at this spot before this airport was built; she said that flying was a bad omen for this country, she said that sinners should not ascend the sky! So I'm sure that her tears have not yet been dried by the Lord . . . she cried for her tribe but I cry for the whole country! And don't be surprised if her ghost still worries around this airport putting the cobwebs back up when they are dusted once a year. I come here at regular intervals to look for her . . ." When Osofo saw that he had only half-won the crowd, he suddenly turned around, faced Pol and Tia, and shouted with the deepest gravity, raising his shoulders nearer the medium height of his neck, "I command you in the name of the Almighty to let these people go! This is their country, this is their air, they own all this glass in trust for God. Let them go!" Then Osofo went in among the crowd pushing, forcing people to kneel; some did not, but others did. Kofi Loww had rushed into a corner in bewilderment, not knowing what to do with something he felt he had started. "All right, pray if you like, pray. If the press come and see this scene here, nobody can blame me," shouted Kwaku Tia, looking knowingly at Pol, and Pol passed on this same look to the sky. The two of them stood rooted, lost in the gloom that both bound and separated them.

There was another sharp crack, and out came the most handsome horse, black and beautiful, tossing its own style around its mane as the sun burnished it. Okay Pol was shattered, biting his lip and cracking his fingers . . . all he had to do now was to put his hands at the back of his head to let his mother and father die. "A ship would have been better," Tia suddenly said, with what Pol felt was boring finality. "I know Dr. Boadi likes hot air too much . . . he should have chosen water this time; after all his beer is made of water and boats can sail on it." Pol's eyes had reached the lowest point of their own depths, and had taken on that vacant look that was both a resignation and a defense; and any air of new confidence that he had remained with the quick movements of his legs, which looked like scissors cutting all the mad gray of the tarmac, in no particular direction. Kwaku Tia was so short that when he smoked one jot after another, in this atmosphere of confusion, he was almost hidden by his own smoke; so that when Pol wanted to talk to him he had to jump behind the smoke or blow it away. Out of resentment for what he saw as Tia's basic disinterest, Pol blew the smoke into the former's eyes, reddening them instantly. And when Kwaku Tia tried to cough philosophically, he could not: insults came scattering out of his mouth toward Pol who had suddenly moved away and found himself face to face with Kofi Loww . . . Loww was asleep with that same expression of bearded and bewildered contempt that Pol now wanted to punch out of the crowded balcony.

58

But he could not: Osofo was holding his shoulders with such strength that he could not move; and Pol was thus pulled with this strength and a perpetual holy smile on Osofo's face, down onto the tarmac. "Prepare your knees and kneel down among the airplanes, on this particular spot, and pray for the success of your life," Osofo shouted at Pol, looking the latter straight in the eye. Pol found himself beginning to resist, indignation rising right up to his raised eyebrows. But Osofo's great arms held Pol down for one minute, and forced a prayer of hope into his head, a prayer of optimism and . . . gentleness. There was a shout: "Just as well there are no foreigners with us here . . . this is an international airport, and it is a disgrace that something like this should be happening here."

The silence, the continuing confusion, and then the renewed noise pleased Kwaku Tia: he had completely forgotten that he had such an important task, and he was quietly singing and dancing to the high life of a stray transistor radio when Pol, at last freeing himself from Osofo, pushed the dance out of him saying almost with a snarl, "What's this dancing? In the name of your cocoyam uncle, why don't you do something befitting your status for a change! This cheche-kule kofi-salanga will get you nowhere! Boadi will squash you flat, hat or no hat!" Kwaku Tia slowly moved further back adjusting his brown hat so that he could send his glare between Pol's eyes. "And you too, young ruffian! When you talk I can, excuse me to say, see all the rubbish you ate with your morning gari . . . now tell me, didn't the beans have stones? Eheeeeeh! I've caught you! No sense ever comes out of a poor breakfast . . . ahh." When Tia laughed his feet almost left the ground, as if to catch more laughter, and he did, shouting at the diminishing crowd, "Wanted for immediate national duty anybody with huge buttocks to sit on the last two boxes. These horses are not like my wife your wife or your boss . . . they are reasonable, they listen to cola. So when you sit on the box, the horse, brown black or white, will listen to the weight of the said buttocks, will know its pressure; after all, these have been African horses for the last three hours . . . they have forgotten the UK snow! Any volunteeeeeers?"

Kwaku Tia, who stood behind a dung of three stories with fashionable shoes printing the sides, felt more in control than his eyes showed; and he had almost forgotten that most unreasonable refusal of his wife's to give him money to collect soap to resell.

59

She knew he was going to drink with it, and she also knew he resented the truth that she knew. He demanded, without words, that she know less about his intrigues; and so whenever she wanted something from him, she became almost portentous with innocence. She paraded her sudden mutually agreed, but unspoken, ignorance of him. They laughed a laugh that crossed at the shallow edge of the throat, yearning for the easier directions of the crossroads there. That morning he had left the house muttering darkly of the injustice in her refusal. You could see the funeral in his mouth. After a heavy fufu breakfast, to which he had contributed nothing, his complaints were both an attack and a defense of his financial failures . . . which had led him into Dr. Boadi's schemes in the first place. Now he stood in his own words, waiting for the ridicule to die down before the meaning itself seeped through. He had borrowed the reasonableness of his wife's face as he caught sight of himself in somebody's mocking eyes; and he was alarmed to see his head looking so much like a papaw about to ripen, and about to be picked, with its seeds staring wildly in all directions. Then the reason went to his head, it was so sudden: "And there will be a reward for the said buttocks!" It was odd, even to him, the way his years in the police force remained in his teeth with the few legal words he spoke; and a quiet sense of theatrical trust, learned again from the force, defined his plea to the crowd: some thought there must be some real sort of reward waiting to be shared out by the eyes of Tia, which were so sad, and so unable to stare straight.

"Yesssss! Yeahhhhhh, yeah! Get up all clans and let us take turns at sitting on the boxes, so that we get something. After all the best way to get something is to sit; this is the country of sitting! Some are born, wear uniforms, seize power, *sit* on government stools, and then die immortal and in disgrace! Forward in reward men of all tribes . . ." The voice died down, and someone else in the crowd picked it up: "True, true! we want democracy in this: revolution, action! Yoo ke revolution, gari-action! This is the buttock-renting service, bottom allowance! Allow, allow, I talk true! Which man wants to lose which tooth by disagreeing with me? We shall work out the charge, by the pressure of each buttock. Beautiful women get bonus! I lie?" The roar brought on another voice: "Okay okay, look at my motoway. I'm grown, I'm gray and I'm a man of vital parts. I want to be paid in check. For me I chop only checks! Some of you think a few years at secondary school plus plenty of ambition

60

entitle you to throw abuse around like this! Well, for me I had half a year at university, ten years ago, so I can speak my five-foot-six-inches of nonsense! Does any woman here love me? I am very very available soooonest . . ." Another mouth rushed in when that one rushed out: "Oh, we're doing all this for Ghana, Ghana is the name Ghana, we wish to proclaim . . . this country is good-ooooo; it gives us sun, kente, ampesi and palm wine, fresh, all fresh! After all we're all good crows after awoof money! Only your kalabule!" The crowd continued to drive the soul of its own laughter: "I have been doing this agreed sitting for thirty minutes now . . . and this is the first time I have ridden a horse in a box. We want our money now now now! Sika ye na! Showboy be broke, and he sleeps at the bus stop tonggg. See these fat and no-fat peeeeeople doing all this sitting! Accra be shut, Ghana de sleep! Money na han' . . ." "Yes, ampa. No delay no trouble . . . contrey don't delay; don't let my tongue talk so, it will lose shape, paaaa." Then some started to dance to the rhythm of money . . . "Money be beauty, Yessss!"

Kwaku Tia was pushed out of the police force because they said he was too soft and that he had stood on tiptoe when being measured for the statutory height. He was now filled with the terror of losing this job too. He stood there feeling his biceps, gauging the flow of his own sweat. The horses were now quiet and under control, with Pol exhausted and leaning against a pillar in a corner, feeling triumphant that he had at least achieved something in spite of Tia's lazy contempt; but he could not find Kofi Loww anywhere. The look of alarm on Tia's face widened the space between his short legs; and the legs moved about in worried abandon, gathering dung freely. The little tufts of hair across his motoway dammed the sweat at awkward angles and intervals: his forehead was patterned with deflected sweat, making his whole head look like ancient waterworks. In times of crisis he always retained the memory of his wife, flooding his head with images of her acts of kindness and comfort which were impossible to touch now. His face was angular; his nose had risen in a flare and looked down the moist wastes of his mouth. The teeth came down together on the lip in a sad, sharp hold. When a man was hot, paa, they piled on the heat, he thought. Look at the steam from his spirit, and all the hissing that came from thoughts pressing and pushing in opposite directions. And when he talked, his eyes spoke a different language from his mouth, and his skin was raised and sensitive to everything, except his own scratching.

When he suddenly realized that he could put the blame of failure of secrecy on Kojo Okay Pol, he brightened in the eyes, raised a triumphant frown, and disappeared to do his lotto. Okay Pol now climbing down his own tail at last had saved the day by shouting, after prior arrangement, "Beer is served, all you kind people that don't see what you see, you can have free beer . . . Keep that a secret too . . . and those sitting on the boxes and controlling the horses will have something extra. Long live Ghana!" There was a roar and a rush to the bar, where the preaching of Osofo had a flow that did not match the flow of Club beer. And the spreading of any stories and rumors would now, surely in Pol's head, only come from Kofi Loww the disappearing one . . . but Loww was thinking about more permanent things . . .

And there under the surprised gaze of Poly lay old Beni Baidoo drunk and asleep, having arrived just in time to enjoy the beer, and shouting out just before his drunken collapse, "I will bring my village to the airport. After all, anything that takes place here is faster than anywhere else because here everything flies . . . my village is a tiny old man's quest for love, luvvvvv! and for this love, I will search governments, private people, hills, churches, and best of all private parts if necessary . . . luuuuvvvvv . . ."

Chapter 5

When Osofo's baked-block church cast a shadow in the mornings, he chose the coolest bits in which to pray, joining it with his own shadows of the soul. He had sold five Bibles at the airport, and had now returned to base to throw the world out of his head. For each buyer had been less religious than the last. Slowly the morning opened the door of his spirit, and the presences of God came around him, dancing above his thoughts and prayers; and near his knees the herbs of the fetish priest appeared without warning, and joined Jesus Christ in giving his life meaning. For years Osofo had kept this marriage of Christ and herbs to himself, and when he finally told Bishop Budu, leader of the church, the direction in which his spirit was going, the bishop was quiet for days . . . his usual wisdom said nothing, though behind the small sparkle in his eyes there was a touch of challenge and sadness. Osofo's life had started to move away from the comfort and ritual of his church, scattering dust on those who, like Bishop Budu, perceived this and were filled with foreboding. Osofo had made his bishop defensive about his silks, his perfume and his rings, though what kept Osofo still close to him was his basic goodness and simplicity. The bishop's cool and calm opened all paths to and from the SS church, so that though Osofo would joke with an ironic smile that bishop Budu would retire into his wardrobe, he knew that it was his bishop that kept this growing church together. Budu would say with a smile: "Under this fine cassock, my brother, lies the passion of worship." At such moments you could almost see the commotion of the marketplace in the face of the bishop; then the calm reasonableness would appear again, driving slowly into his face through his left eye.

Budu gave trances to others, but did not keep any for himself: except when God made him cry at His will, he usually kept his heart clean, in the spirit of a polyethylene bag. So that morning when his shadow crossed Osofo's and did not reshape it, he kept his usual calm, passing the praying Osofo with a blessing. He was hurrying to spread his deep Alleluya into the trees and the people of the morning. When Bishop Budu was happy he had a childlike air about him, brought out smiles from faces that had over the years become grimaces in the dusts of the soul; his hurrying feet hurried joy there, and when some threw flowers at him in this ascending goodwill in this morning ritual, he stopped abruptly, and with an avuncular frown, said, "Throw your love at God, not at an easy sinner like myself." He would thus banter with his congregation, carrying their worries to God on a broad bright back just as they carried his blessings. When Osofo entered this morning scene with his brooding, there would be a short sharp silence. Then Bishop Budu would say with a laugh, "My brothers and sisters, don't you know that the wilderness is sometimes useful on the forehead? Don't worry, Osofo is just bringing us love on the lines of his forehead. Look! God is on his face!" Some of the laughter would be free, some would be bitter at the intrusion of a spirit coming with the wrong fire at the wrong moment. Osofo, though deeply sad at this growing resentment, used it to fuel his inner desire for pace and change.

The membership of the church began ten years ago in the mid-sixties, when they said Ghanaians were taking a new direction into the same old road; a different brood of wild guinea fowl was nibbling at the same unready cassava; the tall guinea grass, the flat thicket grass, the soft ferns, the reeds, the PWD grass and the hard crab grass were all pressed down, this time with boots of fine bush shine, reflecting stream beside stream. When the grasses rose up again they were a little less resilient . . . as if the weight of the footwear that marched through history, through grassland, forest and brush, was the same whether the boots were shoes or whether the shoes were boots. The church held its first six members in the valley between Madina and Ashalley Botchwey with gentle hands. The brilliant lilies that suddenly made earrings on the listening land pushed into their colors a warning: every blade of grass that was destroyed stunted the beauty of the lilies, and the beauty was in the great trees, was in the mid trees too, was in the berries, nuts and seeds crushed by the huge beak of the akyinkyina, was in the hills that broke the long line of sky, was in the yoyi tree, and was even in the snakes and insects. At the beginning the church was so poor that as the bishop said, it almost had to wait for two lizards to cross tails before it had a Cross. And it seemed that as these lizards aimed their wise nods into the mud, so grew the patience and wisdom of Brother Budu, as he was then. The prayers were the roof, and formed beams of different intensity, slates of unequal strength.

Ama Serwa was beautiful, her food bowl always full of prayer and trance, her mouth almost as strong as Budu's for calling God; and she was one of six founding members. Osofo had squeezed in as the sixth founder, abandoning his own dreams of founding a church, for he admired Brother Budu's extra spiritual weight. Ama would pray and sell: she brought in more women and more money than anyone else. They would joke without this truth being changed in any way that she built the church on the foundations of her groundnuts. Budu admired and avoided her, for he knew that the moment they would be alone for too long, he would see crumble all the excuses and defenses he had built up between himself and his passion for her. It was Old Man Mensah who first noticed this hidden passion. Since he had already seen Ama's love for brother Budu, he tried as quietly as possible to bring them together. Often after late prayers Brother Budu would find Ama agonizingly close, by the luminous flowers, in the open spaces where the marks of restless knees, just risen from the sands of God, still showed. Her shoulders narrowed his eyes and widened his love; the shadows of trees brushed them by the staring lanterns. As he stood almost rigid looking straight ahead, she moved about picking up stray leaves, gathering her outer cloth closer about her. The talking of members in the distance went over the rising slopes, so that in the end the two of them were left sharing the weight of the sudden silence. His hand moved unthinkingly onto her shoulder, and at last he looked at her. But for him the danger and the tension were past: he could speak to her of other things, other than those on their minds. She was still so drawn to him that, with his hand on her shoulder, only an intense prayer for God to control her heart saved her from the risk of holding his hand as tightly as her hopes held her own life. Then for her too, this period of possession passed. They escaped into talk of increasing church membership, they huddled in peripheries, leaving the center cooling and almost irrelevant. Then just as they were parting for the night, he said, "We will wait until we build the church . . ." She looked at him with eyes open like the widest skies. She said "Yes" almost too quickly, and then ran off with a thrown-back good-night, her speed still like a little girl's, and her back so soft.

Ten years further on they still shared this love spoken so rarely, but she was exhausted with waiting, and with work. So she became bolder in love and quieter in religion, paying him visits in the night. He was alarmed, and prayed more often than usual under the incense, scattering supplications into the corn. Old Man Mensah had taken Bishop Budu into a corner and, with a penetrating look, had said, "Bishop, we now have hundreds of members; you have built a church, now build a father's life, build a mother." There was a look of shock on Budu's face, which he quickly changed into his usual genial smile, and replied, "Yes, Brother Mensah, Nyame-bekyere, God will provide and show the way." Then he patted the old man on the back and hurried on. Mensah shouted after him, "Babies are dancing here, God is answering, the drums beat in our swish walls . . . it's only the heart that is slow, Bishop, it's only the heart that is slow. What hard hard standards do you think you are setting? Even in the established churches . . ." Bishop Budu had run out of earshot, and waved in exasperation as he stepped onto a fallen orange and leaped away in controlled alarm.

It was said unfairly that Osofo deliberately brought his own crises up against the crises of others, to show how superior his heat was. The more he came across these little misrepresentations of his soul, the more stubborn he became, though in this case he had been completely unaware of the personal crisis of Bishop Budu and Ama Serwa. Whether he would have acted differently if he knew was another matter. Osofo hounded and pounded the consciousness of his bishop: he insisted that certain practices of fetish priests had to be introduced into the church; he thought the church should know healing trees and sacred trees, powders and herbs. Sometimes Budu reacted to these pressures of the new with wild charges of heresy. But when he calmed down, he watched his own pot cooling as Osofo filled it with food for thought. And after the calm, he obliterated the one road that made the crossroads a crisis: he remembered his own one-way break from the Anglican church, and,

66

resignedly with his eyes raised, allowed Osofo to raise some doctrinal speed, to renew the path beating that he himself began so intently but with so much less obsession than Osofo had. To be happy with God, the bishop thought, was what the church was all about. But Osofo was thrashing about the divine feet, trying to force new clothes, cloths to be precise, onto God's shoulders. The bishop allowed the happy peace of God to inform his own almost lethargic gentleness, and it was this sense of basic happiness with God's ways that drew together—in a pull of the head—excessive patience with the world, as well as an optimism of such breadth that little decisions did not matter, and dragged on with a flow that could shatter or elevate lesser lives. Beside him, Osofo seemed a wild man, both more practical and more probing. Bishop Budu said to him, "Osofo, you can't cast a spell on the head; one thing you have to do is to find a way to men's hearts first. You want the head at once!" Then he would laugh his deep slow laugh, while Osofo stared in the opposite direction, trying to take the wild look of disappointment and anguish out of his own eyes; but his eyes did not reach the peace of the patterned blue in the sky.

The world always moved back before his frown. The bishop continued to speak from the perfume in his handkerchief: "You worry too much, Osofo; one day some heavenly hands will take you into a corner, and talk to you, paa. Now I have almost stopped reading; I read until my head was crowded, no room at all, not even for a foot of the heart. But whatever I read now comes out as big blocks of certainty, as if as soon as my head receives it, it is sent to my soul which shapes it and throws it down large and simple. I have no head. For you, you are trying to have too much . . . but forgive me, it is the Lord that fills your head. Osofo you are the engine of this church! Only don't go too fast for the passengers . . . hahaha!" Osofo hesitated then said quietly, "I want God's glory now now now, I want God in a batakari . . . you can't really understand half of my hurry . . . when you form something new, you keep pushing it, we don't want other churches to overtake us in their Africanness . . ." That look of intense earnestness had, for a change, no touch at the edges of irony or impatience. Osofo brought his hands tightly together in silent prayer, as if Budu was not there at all. The latter, being seven years older than the youngish man suffering in silence before him, looked hard and with pity at his brother-in-Christ, and said, "Young man, I think you really could be suffering . . . Don't let this pushing you talk of itself push you into pride; after all the church council has agreed to some of your changes . . . Don't let your great arms come together in worry again. God has given you strong arms . . . Work in the grounds when you feel overwhelmed with His wisdom . . . These days I don't see you among the orange trees at all, they are not doing well without your care."

Osofo stood stiff and vacant, thanked the bishop, in whose friendly stare he had felt the beginnings of his own trance, and went to his house, itself ready to spring its peace into him as he went into it in the west of the compound. As Osofo sat down his head had already broken itself up into sparks of questions, bits of balancing pain: where was this church going? In many ways would it not be easier to be a rebel in the established churches, away from feelings of loyalty in such a small community? And when you questioned an idea or a practice there were always real people behind them, so ready to test their humanity against your prodding. And after all where was this new passion coming from? Why the race to change? Each question, each level of pain both reinforced and undercut the other. Into his cooler of water he looked; angels spoke through the neck of the cool water; the world was a dance without the proper music; the sun was one plus one but had been marked three and wrong that morning by demons eating green-green; Jesus Christ had left the polished cross, where food was kept, and was swinging in hunger toward him; after all the hill was a dying breast; into the hymn he composed, in Twi, ran the panting voices of unknown languages; look at the cassock, look, it was spread on the tower of the church like a scarecrow; God's blessings came down in harsh words of incantation; Osofo the standard-seven scholar had destroyed the rigid symbols of philosophers; couldn't the bishop, consecrated especially at Osofo's wild, almost mad insistence, share some of his peace, couldn't Osofo have some of this gentleness? Share, Osofo, share your own solitude, bring to Madina the sound of God coming down; into the ritual of herbs danced the angels; Osofo blessed his walls, blessed his books, his stool with the kente cushion, Osofo blessed his table as it gave him food he could not eat. And in his dreams clapping had become a form of art begun and continued by the young churches, and he was almost clapped awake; but he went deeper: the drums and the walls bounced off each other, made a symbol of the new in their echoes. His head moved among the religions, in delirium, separating some religions from their cultural houses, and his soul said through his dream that he must bring into these walls the pouring of libation and the puberty rite. The flies in the dream could not find any fruit to land on . . . the way the forefathers mourned their dead had to be the foundation of dust to dust . . . the crows talked into the bishop's sermon yesterday and shined it black and white with their wild chorus: This world was mad! This world was mad! they cried, and you saw it more when you were a crow! One beak moved with that hop of crow confidence, wakening Osofo with the sharp cries aimed at his head through the roofing sheets. He came out with a headache to find the daylight waiting with so much light. He took his drained body to the goats, among whom he knelt, trying to find his balance again. He threw plantain skin at them, shouting, "Eat God's meal, eat, eat." He scattered them with the force of his prayers, moving around the back of the compound on his knees; the Word did not go into the heads of goats. The branches pointed at Osofo who was desperately trying to shake off the aftereffects of the trance and the dream. He knew some of the congregation would be saying, "Osofo is having one of his fits again. The bishop should go and hold him." But there was nothing he could do about other people's contempt, and it did not particularly worry him. He had a fast walk for moving through other people's opinions, and he walked it, arriving late for prayers.

So Osofo and Bishop Budu balanced each other, one—at different times and in different moods—the solid earth to the other's flying wings, the roots, in terms of temperament, to the tops of the trees. When next they met for an evangelizing walk through Madina, Budu's slightly hooded eyes made a special effort to be earnest with Osofo: something in his extraordinarily open manner that morning suggested a need to make an unspecified apology, and also to show a protective concern toward his brother . . . and not because of Osofo's "fit" on Tuesday. Apart from his gentle platonic love, the bishop had another secret, if he himself would call it that: he discovered halfway through the life of the church that he sometimes had special powers in his stare when it was concentrated with special intensity and with both eyes, at a particular angle; a power to transmit a trance, almost instantly, whenever he thought that the person he was looking at needed his help to solve some deep problems. This was less prolonged and much more ruthless than the usual trances that he helped induce during services. He sometimes felt like a dangerous man, and would kneel in utter humility before the smile of the nameless Saint, and before God, begging for release from this gift . . . or curse. He had looked at Osofo in just that way; and this had made the latter delirious. And above all, with a feeling of contrite shame, he suspected that even at the beginning of the life of the SS church, he had this power . . . and that this power was used almost unknowingly on Ama Serwaa. Even with his years of self-searching he never dwelt too long on this thought; it was a door at which his self-knowledge usually stopped abruptly. With a feeling of horror, he wondered, with the deep and dramatic gestures that the Ghanaian sometimes reserved for moments of stress and shock, whether the source of his humility to God and man was the need to banish his guilt. He whispered the questions and answers over this to himself only, hoping—with a laugh—that God would be too busy with other hearts to look inside his own. With the tension of this mood he believed that everyone, especially Osofo, must see through him. But all these slow and tortuous thoughts came out fresh as earnestness, and genuinely too. He loved, and had mastered, the joy of letting simplicity in action take over, with a gentle pull, the complexities of his inner anguish. Old Man Mensah would not understand that it was not "standards" that kept him back from Ama, but the guilt that he had tricked her with his eyes; which meant that even at the apex, or at the furthermost point of symbolic traditional thought, of what he hoped were pure motives, was a baneful, compromised way of dealing with the world. So, that openness of spirit that he thought he had reached could be false. The thoughts were like ants at his feet, and he hoped and prayed that no one in Madina saw his frantic dancing, dancing away from these stings. Nor saw that he did not know how long the simple actions could contain the anguish. In his weak moments he dismissed these thoughts without any grappling, saying to himself, "What is a joyful, badly educated Ghanaian doing with these broken thoughts in his sunny head!" Then he smiled and put his hand on Osofo's shoulder as they went up the valley.

As they walked, Osofo's quick steps stretched, without increasing the speed of the bishop's slow and fatherly steps . . . the slowness of which his bullneck emphasized. Budu was animated, completely oblivious to the small crowd, mainly children, that was following them: " . . . and you see, my brother, some of these new young churches are so fast, so full of business and travel, so political that their spiritual food will be finished, even between the journey from the hand to the mouth, eh? Haha! What is the difference between them and the established churches? None at all! They are even more secular! We too have our little thoughts, our little hopes, even our little education . . . but with you around, Osofo, we will never be happy with the fast cars, the smart suits and the athletically preaching Americans! Osofo, I think we want to keep the spirit fresh and simple, for the Madina streets, and for those ordinary men and women who want to touch the world through the fewest pretenses . . . yet the most meaningful ritual. Perhaps your soul is that bit more naked than mine . . . I can see you so often exasperated with me. Under my cheap silks—you thought they were expensive! well, only one is, and it was a gift!—my eyes weep for this country. Sometimes I wonder . . . there are even more important things than official cultural or political direction: the ordinary people go on with their ordinary Ghanaian eating, living and dying; do they really feel that their soul has been imported? Not at all! You young men may think I'm too slow! But it's not direction we need, it is not the slogans of revolution and self-reliance that Acheampong speaks of that we need. We need hard work, humility in the right doses and consistency. Eh, my Brother!" The bishop laughed and seemed to be a little breathless, finally noticing the children and old women, and showering them with blessings.

Osofo had listened with a curious agitation, buttoning and un-buttoning his cassock several times. Then he said in his peculiar high voice, "Brother, I used to believe that to go to God through a little vanity may be better than not to go at all . . . like watching women dance up to communion in the old churches, all powdered, perfumed and pressed; there was an air of the festival, a test of the smartness of the body, about communion . . . you see it's beauty before the Lord that will kill Ghanaians. That's what I think now! You see, Brother Bishop, this is where I now disagree with you: we Ghanaians are far too comfortable in our bodies . . . look at the way we move, look at the way the women walk! as if every single one of them is a queen. Fine, fine, but queens should be inventive and hardworking before their subjects. And we have no Yaa As-antewaas now! Have you ever seen a country where everyone is a chief deep down in his or her heart, so that effort and a little thought are only a means to money or power or, excuse-me-to-say, sex? Brother, we must push, *push* hard, sweep aside everything; especially in the church! Change, change!" Osofo had stopped, and was wiping the sweat from his face. He had seen a look of alarm come to, and leave, the bishop's face. He asked, "Brother, what's wrong?" Budu made a joke out of his spiritual crisis, saying, "Osofo, I sometimes get dizzy listening to you young men, at the speed you go! At least we both agree on hard work; so two different mouths can after all speak one confused language! But don't forget, we must have ritual and continuity before we can attract new members . . . and I see a little contradiction in your passion—you book-long people may call it paradox! For someone who wants so much change, why do you want to introduce so much more tradition? Why not try to invent a new Ghanaian culture fresh from the mud oven? You want to make the new out of the old old things and ways!"

The bishop was startled to find the children laughing with him, though they did not understand what was being said, even though some of it was said in Twi. The children seemed a little afraid of the abrupt wild ways of Osofo, and had decided that anything that he was not doing, must be good and must be joined in . . . and the bishop looked so kind that he may even throw them a few pesewas. Budu, in truth, loved the children, loved their dust, their bare feet, their mischief and their ready smiles . . . but Osofo wanted to start his radical changes right from the babies on their mothers' backs . . . to him children were there to be better fed than they were, to be cured, and above all to be molded and trained! Then Osofo was suddenly pointing a finger at his bishop, and shouting and swaying left and right, "What do you mean paradox, Brother Bishop? If I didn't love and respect you I would almost say that you are one of the most comfortable Ghanaians! You you you! And as for the tradition, I only want a little authenticity! You can put this paradox with all the other tricks of Ananse . . . well, senior brother, I'm sorry, I'm sorry, I'm sorry, I . . ." "Of course you can!" said the bishop with a smile. "This is how we have been making our new membership these days! God is fire as well as water! And you are wonderful!" They both laughed and went, drawing more children with their laughter, their very slow strolling.

As they reached the northern tip of the New Road, with the children gone, each head jumped into its own silence; and the edges of the old conversation did not touch at all. The last sound was the coins Budu gave to the children. As Osofo looked back at the untarred road, he saw that the imprint of Bishop Budu's right foot was heavier than his left . . . when he was tired he had a slight limp . . . as if quietly as the day wore on his heart wore down. Osofo looked at him with concern. There was a strange blue light as the dusk, almost animal in its stealth, pushed at the doors of sheer, square houses with no part of the ribs in any old architecture, except in the idea of the compound. Only the people made the life bright in them, and each door that opened its teeth needed dental attention . . . to repair either its structure or its beauty. There was a plan in the bishop's face, for the face took on the darkening light with a disturbed glow. Across his simple black hat lay a stray leaf rising and falling with his slow gait, and changing color as it did so, as if it were trying to explain something important in the head below. The two men stopped, almost expecting something from each other; and the bishop's eyes spoke before his mouth: "I have to think about retiring before long . . ." Osofo stood, his own eyes swaying with the leaves of a saluting coconut tree. He heard nothing, though he felt uneasy with the echo of gravity in Budu's voice . . . which finally repeated itself, like the strategy of early mosquitoes coming back to bite again and again: "I will retire very soon; I can see myself that the church does not have the direction it had. I'm waiting for you to learn to forgive, to broaden out . . ." he laughed his laugh, "before we release you onto the flock alone!" Osofo had heard now and turned full circle, an unnatural calm on his face. He scratched his chin, spreading the shock there. He said, with suppressed fire in eyes, "I have for some time suspected that you want to leave, or—if you'll forgive me—run away with the weight of your own humanity . . . or perhaps enter the world again through the love of a woman. But you can't do it, you can't do it!" As they looked at each other, with the bishop's face fuller with expectation, each set of eyes pulled intensely at any possible secret knowledge the other may have contained. Osofo shook his head at last, shouting, "God has not really spoken to you that you should leave now. If you leave, the whole flock will also leave . . . they will be lost. I will be a madman that cannot keep them, even for one day. And as you can see, Brother, I'm not broadening out; I'm rather narrowing down with a strength and a pull that I cannot explain; my river of God will capsize all the canoes calmly rowing now . . . all the canoes that you shelter from the storm. You are a father, you are an odum. Even I am under the shelter of your leaves. Neither the church council nor anyone else will agree with what you've just said." Osofo laughed, took his bishop's hand with a shrug of his heavy shoulders saying, "How can you talk of going when there's God's work to do!" Bishop Budu, looking far into the distance, said to himself more than to Osofo: "No, not for a woman, I suppose not . . . at least not yet, Osofo, not yet."

Chapter 6

Professor Sackey sat down with a glare in the east corner of his house, and watched himself grow into middle age in the west corner. His strong jaw and permanently angled elbows, angled for war angled for pride, pushed the world aside into broad classes, each of which had its level of pain and frustration. One long level was the utter stupidity of most people before him; another was the impertinence of being ultimately under the control of fate. His wife was soft and vulnerable, caught between all the levels at the same time; so that when she talked, the theories in his head roared in disapproval. His love for his few friends, pushing impatiently, at the back of his love for his family, had much pepper in it. And the hate for his enemies, which sprang continually onto the stage of his constant play for peace, busied his eyes and shaped them. By his window, that same fistful of cloud punching through the empty sky gathered his heart with the force of bitterness: after years of companionship, no companion could give him the true peace he wanted. Sackey, Professor of Sociology, could not manage the society of his house. His two children Kwame and Katie had learned from him the skill of hoarding in their eyes devastating looks of arrogance and irony, doubly strong when turned on their father; so that Sackey had long divorced childhood from innocence, and could hardly carry the weight of his own heart when he saw, so often, his own reflection thrown at him from the power of these four young eyes. And they protected their mother from him with the same fire he protected himself: sly fire would enter all the little emotional interstices, in a run from father to children and back to father. Like: "But Papa," his son Kwame would say, "Mother just does not feel like talking this morning; after such a poor breakfast her mouth is too weak to talk . . . Papa, we beg you, leave her alone," Sackey would shake with rage, but he did not believe in beating his children. He valued independence more than respect . . . and a feeling of guilt at the back of his head controlled his reaction to their words and saw them merely as an advance party for the battlefield of his wife's silences.

As he rose from the window of his South Legon house, he caught a glimpse of himself, motoway polished, big eyes unnaturally bright, and skin the color of coffee. His look of controlled wildness roared into his gidigidi reputation, and made a mockery of his dream of being a quiet farmer somewhere hoeing the land . . . with the land saying nothing. Land with no mouth, he thought, Sackey wanted you! And it was land that led Professor Sackey to Owula ½-Allotey, the oddest farmer in the plains nearest Accra. It was this semisecret wish of her husband's . . . to till the land . . . that gave the extra dimension of patience to Sofi Sackey's character: she hoped he would change for the better, once they had left Legon. She even became the earth for him: she would lie down and receive the flood of his dammed-up anger as often as she could . . . not always . . . in the same way that a farm already watered would receive more rain; and she hoped the harvest would not die, for there was a limit, a limit to the size of her draining . . . "It's my brains!" Sackey would say to her in a rare moment of confession, "I have been doing nothing but reading writing and talking all my life; and my father did the same; we don't have the rural peace of my grandfather. My brains won't let me rest, because I suspect I wasn't built for this artificial life."

Sofi Sackey was trying to tell him that it was precisely because of his brains that it was unnecessary to throw books at students, hold the shirts of people, and generally blast through the world. She would, to his irritation, remind him of some of their problems on past sabbaticals abroad: he would insist to a confused waitress that it was not bacon and eggs he had ordered for breakfast, and that she should be smarter, for after all most of her people insisted they were God's gift to the world . . . and he would laugh ironically at this. And when the poor waitress would be dashing back to make another order, he would call her back and devour the "wrong" order without a word to her. Or the uproarious nature of his lectures here . . . "But how do you expect me to handle asses that will, like their forebears, ruin collectively and cumulatively all this country's wealth?" From the side, his whole face took on the shape of a fist. "But how do you know they are all alike?" Mrs. Sackey answered him, knowing instinctively that he would immediately be criticizing in his head the quality of her points and arguments. "OOOOH, Sofi, don't sail your canoe into deep water . . . From institutions to personalities, I see all their actions so interrelated, and so lethal, that I can't bear it. You see, you can take institutions apart, criticize them till there is nothing left . . . but it is the great big egos behind them that make things unbearable: the entire country is performing badly enough, but when you see a fool rise up to defend himself with pompous words more foolish than himself, then you know there's no hope! How would you like to suffer the frustration every day of dealing with people that don't deserve respect?"

At the mention of "frustration" Mrs. Sackey closed her eyes without his noticing; she did not want to bring her own heart into this discussion, but the effort of seeing her own ironies in him, of trying to resolve some of her own inconsistencies by seizing this opportunity, was almost too much for her. She merely kept nodding and saying to herself in Mfantse, "It's a problem, but it will be all right." He ignored her and went on, "Besides they are forcing me to look at problems that I'm not basically interested in: I get up, I have my kyenam and kenkey, but I'm not particularly interested in how a country works politically in day-to-day terms. And then I get indigestion while I eat, thinking of questions like, what philosophies should we have, what sort of spirit do we bring to technology, or how much of ourselves are we prepared to cast off, if we should at all, before we leap into all aspects of this century? And all our disciplines are busy collecting material, in a sort of empty-headed positivist sort of way . . . then after all the data, some pirate rushes into Ghana, makes patterns with the raw material available, and then leaves the structures and theories around for our bright and unoriginal professors to tussle with. Sofi, this is crazy! I have no time for the great traditionalists or these modern carpenters of the head either, making chairs to preset designs!"

Sackey was shaking, holding his hands together as if he were pulling something out of the floor. Sofi Sackey looked hard at him, determined not to go and calm him down, withholding her sympathy with difficulty, but withholding it all the same, knowing that

77

he would probably drive her love away with a sarcastic remark. She stood still, and stared at him, her eye unfocused and unfinished in its stare, suddenly wanting him to make a gesture of friendship. He in turn looked at her with his sarcastic frown, shouting, "Isn't there something burning on the fire?" When she heard "burning" she suddenly looked at her heart, without thinking, before rushing into the kitchen to see the garden egg stew. Sackey rushed after her, shouting, "Let it burn! Just when I'm talking of some of the fundamental things of life, you choose to let food burn! You complain I don't talk to you about important things . . ." Before he could finish Sofi had lifted the burning food, had run to the table and placed it, brown and defiant, at the place where Sackey usually sat. She was crying and shouting, "Kwesi, be reasonable, I'm somebody's daughter, just as you are somebody's son. I come from a respectable home. If you feel you have married the wrong woman after all these years, there's nothing to stop you from telling my people about this . . ."

But Sackey did not hear most of this. He did not even realize that she had in any way attacked him. He had already stormed out of the sitting room, and was pacing up and down, muttering to his book and eating boiled groundnuts at the same time. His neat mouth had lost shape with snarling. The lines on his face took the lanes of worry into his fair skin, where the youthful glow still lurked like a thief. There seemed to be an edge to everything he said, and beyond this edge was a precipice which, of its own volition, was deepening over the years. His energy was the basis for most of his friendships, the speed of his mouth drew people to him, but eventually he built walls around himself with his gesticulating hands: those who wanted to persevere with him had to climb high over these walls, with patience. He was a mason of the mouth. He carried himself by himself as he was fond of saying; some knew him as "Professor Carry Yourself." To him, the world was light, and yet his moods were so heavy. When he eventually went to table, he found everything ready; he looked quizzical as he remembered the food burning. Sofi Sackey had chosen the path of peace, had calmed down while she recooked the meal; but she avoided her husband's eyes as he sat down with a sigh. He looked at her averted red eyes and wondered why she had been crying. "Sofi," he began almost absentmindedly, "don't flaunt your weakness. Let's be sorry for whatever happened . . . what exactly did happen? Fortitude is

78

good . . . the water in your eyes has come too late for the rainy season, eh!" He laughed, and noticed how she stiffened herself when he perfunctorily put his hand on her shoulder.

When he was leaving "for an appointment" she had already sewn her mouth, she had armed her muteness. And was at last becoming expert in withdrawing just when she could provide some sort of inner walking stick for this stumbling man. So they took leave of each other's silence, with each heart . . . Sackey's out of annoyance . . . wishing for some desperate release from the responsibility of being a watchman over the other. Under the mango tree the red ants took Mrs. Sackey's thoughts up, down, and across; at the top of the tree, two small green mangoes pressed against each other, in mockery. When a car slowly passed the corner curve of the house, its round horn gave her an instant tune: leave him first, madam, before he leaves you . . . leave him, leave him . . . the tune went round and round her vulnerable neck, until she was wearing the saddest necklace of tunes in Accra. And it was only the comfort from her children just then come in, which made her head straight again.

The afternoon followed Professor Sackey like a dog out of the house, with its heat: there was not a paw he could send back there . . . where nothing cool could be returned to him, even as he huddled in sweat. When he reached his office, he found that Dr. Pinn had come early and had let cigarette smoke fill the room, to Sackey's disgust. "This smoke is evil. Could I ask you not to light the one you're about to light . . ." Sackey said and then left his office to Pinn, standing by the steps for fresh air, and writing while waiting for Pinn's smoke to clear. Pinn thought Sackey odd and disconcertingly without ceremony, but he did not leave the office himself to join the professor, thinking that the latter could at least have excused himself before leaving the smoke. Pinn had sudden feelings of mild anger, and for him this was usually followed by images of oak trees in idyllic fields of brilliant weather, where as soon as you found happiness you lost it again. He pressed the redness into his hands and waited. He remembered Sackey's mouth as a machine or a furnace, though he did not feel involved enough with him to carry this impression further to a judgment about the whole of Sackey's character.

When the latter finally came in, he behaved as if Pinn were not there; he glanced through some papers, and was about to go out

again when Pinn offered a cough as proof of his existence. "Oh,"
laughed Sackey, "I couldn't see you through the smoke! Sorry . . .
if this word is appropriate at all in this circumstance." Pinn nodded
with the vaguest of smiles, looking at the fine joromi patterns on
Sackey's shirt, and asked, "Is it true you have something important
to discuss with me? That was the message I got when I came up
to Legon for my usual part-time lectures two days ago . . ." "Oh,
it's amazing we've met so little, though I hear you do consultancy
work for UNDP down in the wilds of Accra," Sackey interrupted,
waving a seat at last to Pinn, but getting up with a wild laugh when
Pinn saw no chair in the office. Pinn said with his deadpan manner,
"Would that not be the neatest Freudian slip this side of Legon!"
When Sackey came back in with a chair, he had left his laugh behind
and was wearing an irritated look, very much like a broad tie too
tight for his neck; his eyes shone like the easily removed skin of
newly boiled tomatoes held away from the pot. "Yes, yes," mumbled Sackey in answer to nothing said, staring straight at Pinn as
if there were something grave to be found in the latter's blond hair.
And below the near-long hair were eyes that knew patience but did
not quite use often enough the sprung expectation that now played
at their pale edges. The boyish face, looking permanently undecided, held up two red cocked ears like fans for charcoal fires. The
eyes asked Sackey: won't you stop your games and let's get down
to business . . . There was a pause. "Now, I must stop my games
and get down to business . . . is that what you are thinking? . . ."
Sackey shouted, a stray ray of the sun lying on his temple, and
overemphasizing the distance between his eyes, thus giving his face
an X-rayed look, with the bones of his irritation showing. Then a
sudden cloud by the window shortened the sparring between the
two chairs, deepening the movements of four crossed legs while
the careful botanic trees outside held the space that could receive
rain soon. And this silence outside seeped inside snapping up every
little noise, then held Sackey's voice a note lower: "Well, I personally think that you shouldn't—not emotionally, anyway—take what
I'm about to say too seriously, but it may be in your interest as a
stranger . . ." "I've been here ten years, and my wife is Ghanaian"
Pinn put in, his voice rising an additional note and contrasting with
Sackey's. "Oh, then we have a stranger who knows the inside of
the pot!" Sackey added.

They both laughed, looking at themselves for a few seconds,

with Sackey wondering just how deep this man's sense of calm went; and then he continued, "Fine, fine! As I was saying, the story is that you are harboring one Kofi Loww . . . or some ridiculous name like that . . . and he is wanted for some very mild questioning over statements he made—allegedly of a disturbing nature—at the airport. Forgive the legal buffoonery, but it seems to me that in this great country, where even the clouds are sunny!, serious things often start in this clumsy half-engineered way, then gather a sort of crazy momentum of their own, creating little tragedies in their wake of ease, togetherness and laughter, and . . ." There was a second pause, behind which Pinn hid his frown. Sackey continued, adjusting his eyes: "Well, seriously, these things have a way of pulling others, of a well-meaning nature, under, and then holding the innocent down, drowning them right under the big waves of the cruel sea. If what they are saying is true, would it not be better for you if your guest found another place?" Sackey's voice had a touch of impatience, wondering what he was doing passing on this information at all. His spirit bulged like a bag of charcoal with the dust still unsettled.

Busy suppressing something in himself, Pinn pushed forward successive faces of anger and amusement, an ironic fold pressing his mouth smaller and smaller, and throwing out sparks of himself that Sackey had not yet seen: "Kofi Loww, a friend of a friend of mine, is a harmless even slightly depressed young man; you could say he sits in dream between his past and his present . . . the future hasn't risen for him yet! Anyway as a matter of principle he has gone back to his two rooms, somewhere in . . . somewhere by the sea. His friend Ebo who stays with me can give you more detail, but I doubt whether he would. I understand all that Kofi Loww did was refuse to be intimidated. If this is true then I admire the young man for this, and wish he had stayed longer at my house." Dr. Pinn felt oddly heated, as if he were in the dock, yet somehow keeping his weapons of defense in check, almost against his own will. Then he could do so no longer: "Can I make a comment? The very little I know of you Professor, makes me surprised that you've taken an interest in such a small matter, whose implications border so much on the sordid. I'm sure there must be many more gentlemen of the highest caliber sniffing round it!" Professor Sackey rose quickly, his bold eyes taking in light, and roared, "Hey hold your horses or whatever! Don't bring your ungratefulness to me here. I have told you free of charge for your own good! I'm a human being first, a sociologist second, and a black man last, and if I have any interest at all in this, it may be professional. But as a fellow human being I felt I had to tell you! Boadi, Dr. Boadi told me all this, and asked me to approach you, gently if possible; but gentleness is scarce these days and I've always lacked it myself. Of course Boadi is a twit! A presentable madman! and let loose in academia too. I tolerate him because we have beer in common . . . he has, I suspect, some political ambitions . . . be careful, be careful in an alert, minor sort of way . . . I think you understand me, and I wouldn't want you or your Ghanaian family to be troubled. You see, it's not only my gentleness that's scarce! Besides you have a peculiar air of innocence about you." "Thank you," Pinn replied with exaggerated deference. "Then I think I better grow a beard . . . anything to hide this innocence a bit, to have a little savoir faire, eh!" On a sudden impulse which he immediately regretted, on remembering how he left his house, Sackey invited Pinn home for a little of the palm wine that ½-Allotey promised; if not, then they could cross the continent of the mouth and have tea.

Chapter 7

Dr. Pinn reminded Professor Sackey of an old man's cream crackers. It was the sharp point of this Pinn–induced image, Sackey inexplicably thought, that led to the invitation to the house. As they walked, at Sackey's insistence, to South Legon, they looked odd to passersby: Sackey's long strides led him far ahead of Pinn, who ambled behind like a wise duck, half-listening to the torrent of words coming back to him from Sackey with the breeze; and at one point as Sackey disappeared around the tree-lined corner, his words came racing back, hollow with distance and ludicrous with disembodiment: "Look, I thought you Scots were walkers; if you can't keep up, then go for your little Fiat! By the way it occurred to me the other day . . ." There was a wave of leaves rustling, over which the words continued to sail: " . . .that your Fiat is so small that when you and your family are all in it there must be more of you outside the car than in it!" The two levels of laughter, short and tall, passed up and down between them, lengthening Pinn's stride and shortening Sackey's . . . so that when they arrived at the house they had almost met again. Sackey stood and stared at the house, as if he had now come to his senses. The bungalow looked inert, much like a piece of brodo with the yeast of his wife's indifference rising slowly inside it. Pinn was staring curiously at his host, wondering what was wrong. The hibiscus was red with doubt. Over the August grass with the green all going brown, lay the daily history of all Sackey's frustrations. He suddenly felt that his life was all his fault . . . Then there was Sofi Sackey bright with a smile of welcome at the door, long before they could even knock at it.

"Oh Professor Sackey, so you have been hiding such a gracious pretty wife from us all these months!" Pinn ventured after introductions, not knowing that he was carrying more meaning than he meant with his little chatter. "But you don't know that down by the polo club the best horses are kept well fed in the finest stables?" Sackey replied with a shrug of the shoulders. "I'm glad I'm a horse!" Mrs. Sackey laughed, giving the two men the same look, though hoping fervently that her husband would see the sarcasm she intended for him. She continued, "And I knew you would come with a visitor today, so the palm wine is nicely chilled, and sweet; and I've baked some nice plain biscuits for you." She glowed with genuine pleasure, but Sackey saw revenge at the tips of the glow. "So Allotey came?" he asked. "Yes, he was around a few minutes ago; but you know him, he doesn't stay in one place," Sofi Sackey said, keeping her smile firmly on. When they sat she also sat, after getting the children to serve them. Sackey had thrown her a few heavy, wary looks, but she ignored these, knowing that Pinn would be her ally, especially if there was nothing particularly confidential for the two men to talk about. Pinn loved the palm wine and biscuits and, feeling relaxed and at home, asked for more and talked: "I only hope that Dr. Boadi does not start throwing around the persona non grata weapon, because I'll fight him; or better still my wife will fight him!" "Oh no no no, don't panic. It won't reach that stage," Sackey smiled expansively, suddenly feeling flowingly happy with Sofi. "She's tried, she's tried," he said to himself. The fresh new palm wine made a fresh new world, so that his face took on a fuller, less pointed look, his skin came back and settled on his bones. "Well, it's just that one often unnecessarily takes one's life in one's hands . . ." Pinn said gravely, shifting his position on the chair and getting a distant look in his eyes so full of gray first and so full of blue last.

He continued, "I went through a strange case last week. I was bringing two pet snakes from Bolgatanga, where they were given as presents from an old priest friend to my children. At the barrier at Anyinam one indignant narrow-nosed copper-colored cop, if I may say so, demanded the 'purpose of the snakes' saying he had heard of 'diabolical acts perpetrated by foreigners' involving the secret insertion of gold and 'diamon' in reptiles and parrots (and in the most private parts at that!) aided and abetted by their Ghanaian lackeys, and that he Corporal Addo of twenty years standing . . ."

Sackey interjected: "Yes, an upright man literally, certainly not sitting, certainly not sitting!" And Pinn continued with a smile in the direction of Mrs. Sackey, " . . . was not going to stand at ease for this deception, nor lie down either for his dear country to be awoofed, as he said . . . and that this would be like babooning for two deceitful lovers. As Corporal Addo spoke, Private Akakpo fidgeted in the background, casting alternating looks of disdain and alarm at his superior officer. Suddenly the corporal rushed off to the quarters behind the police station, shouting 'Wait' to me. With irritation and curiosity, I asked the private what his bossy boss was going to do. 'He go for commot dictionary, he go check his English . . .' was the reply. When Corporal Addo came back there was a look of triumph on his face. He beamed like a lamp in a swish building, approaching us with slow deliberate steps. He turned around quickly, with momentary embarrassment, staring at a small book and trying to hide it at the same time. Then he turned around again, with his confidence restored, and shouted, 'I also accuse you of trying to travel . . . incognito; and if that is your wife sitting beside you, she may be traveling incognita . . . do you, as a white man, know the difference between incognito and incognita?' 'Well,' I began, with a pause of anger I could hardly now control. 'You see, you see, the alleged imperialist smuggler does not know his own language!' Corporal Addo boomed, his face no longer able to contain the triumph in it, so that his whole body shared it as it shook, 'I think, common corporal that I am, I think that you may not even be a white man after all! I demand that you be bathed! This is a military-cum-police regime and I have the right to order you to be washed very hard with sapo—you know sapo?—and alata samina, the strongest soap!' Then without warning, Private Akakpo heavily tapped his boss on the shoulder—too heavily for the latter's liking—and shouted, 'You fit forget something, sah!' Corporal Addo shrank from him, stood with his calabash belly still, and released his stored contempt, through the redness of his eyes, at Akakpo, saying 'And you too what?' 'Eheeeh,' said Akakpo, his chortling coming from a fount of righteousness, 'You forget say: and anyt'in you wear will be taken down against you in hevidress!' Private Akakpo said this very slowly and with pride, his mouth shaped the words with a sculptor's care. Addo stood up to his own full height, staring at Akakpo with a silence that told the latter that if he were to apply to him, Addo, to be a human being, his application would be wholeheartedly rejected. 'Ahhhh, and you too what, and what again? You get the thing all wrong, I teach you-aaaaa, still you no fit learn . . . you no fit sabe police work koraaaa! You want come spoil my book-book show. Okay, take my book and read am . . . you see you no fit read at aaaaal. Now, order here, order, let the forest be cleared of all noise, all basabasa. Private Akakpo, you will seize the snakes and you will cut them up! After that then the white G-E-N-T-L-E-M-A-N will tell us the difference between intoxication and inebriation; for after all he's failed the first test.' Akakpo made a concealed reassuring face to me, as if to say that all would end soon.

"He thus caught me in a sort of perverse but amiable loyalty, in a little pact that he, I suspect, would one day use against Corporal Addo. Private Akakpo approached the box of snakes, looked in gingerly, making the sign of the cross, and then screamed, 'I swear sah, these snakes fit talk! I hear am say that if we touch them we go die-oo and they say that you—yes they say your name—must hold one, and then you make libation now now now. After that the snake, e' crow like cock, I swear!' Then I saw my chance at last: 'Officer, there may be a rare species of talking snake which is said to be attracted to corporals . . . well, at least the last person it bit while it spoke was a corporal. No, I am not trying to frighten you.' There was a laugh and a pause from Addo as I opened the box and took out with my hand one of the harmless grass snakes, and walked toward him. 'Hey, hey, halt in the name of the Anyinam law! I have not washed you yet. Wait! Wait for your wash, for conclusive proof of your whiteness! For this whiteman, he craze! Akakpo, arrest him, for attempting to intimidate a strong defense-less policeman like me.' Akakpo snarled back, 'Chief, let him take his matter go. For me I no fit arrest man and snake.' Then impul-sively Akakpo went into the box gingerly held out the other snake. Addo watched in horror, and then raced into the station. 'Retreat, Akakpo, retreat, the enemy de come, pasaaaaa!' Akakpo's smile filled the street as he quickly put the snake down. He had finally managed to overpower his cantankerous corporal; and as I drove off, he waved his thanks."

"What a great relief!" Mrs. Sackey shouted, almost involuntar-ily, her mouth broad with this temporary freedom from her hus-band. "But what about your wife in the car?" "Oh she was asleep!" Pinn said with a laugh. Then he suddenly rose, with a puzzled look on his face, and said emphatically, "I feel the presence of my wife . . . Yes, is that not her voice down the drive?" Pinn went to the window. The Sackeys looked with surprise at him, wondering whether the palm wine, unsour as it was, was too strong for him. "I insist that it is my wife. Look down your drive!" Sofi Sackey got to the window first, and saw nothing, saying as Sackey got up reluctantly from his sleepy chair, "Excuse me Dr. Pinn for making this remark, but I can tell by the look in your eyes that you still love your wife . . ." Pinn looked at Sofi Sackey with a bisected intensity: the preoccupation with his wife's presence crossed, stubbornly, his need to give the true answer to Sofi Sackey's direct and risky observation. Then with difficulty he looked at the expression of growing anger on Professor Sackey's face, and quickly added, sending his eyes back to the drive, "Mrs. Sackey, loving your wife is an occupational hazard . . . but I must admit that those of us with attractive wives, like professor and myself, if I may say so, may have an easier time than others. Look! It must be EsiMay!"

The renewed emphasis moved Sofi Sackey's feet toward the drive, but she left her eyes behind still staring at that increasingly wild face of her husband's. Kwesi Sackey was surprisingly quiet: he felt he had been pushed into an uncomfortable corner, with all the talk about tenderness. He was caught between showing his usual contempt . . . especially in his own house . . . and feeling the weight of a host's responsibility. Also the obvious delight Pinn had taken in his, Sackey's, wife had put him on the defensive. It seemed to Sackey to be a market scene: the wares he had so often passed over with such indifference were being, albeit innocently, admired by someone else. And the look of vindication, bordering on triumph, on Sofi's face tested and pulled at his very small sense of control. For once his safety valve, usually dangerously open, let out a difficult silence, betraying its pressure only by the look in his eyes, and this look fascinated Sofi Sackey, since it was so rare. Above all, Kwesi Sackey had no intention of giving Pinn the pleasure, even if concealed, of witnessing a domestic scene under the flowing circumstances of palm wine. The silence of the drive sent the two men, now alone in the sitting room, to the door where a strange sight met them. Yes, there was Mrs. EsiMay Pinn talking quickly to Mrs. Sackey, and beside them were two policemen who had their backs to the window. Without changing the direction of her eyes, Sofi Sackey made a sign to the two husbands to stay out of sight. Andy Pinn reluctantly moved back, whispering to Kwesi Sackey that he was sure the policemen had come over the Anyinam snakes. Sackey could not longer contain himself, and after muttering about the risk of letting the women take control of such delicate situations, stormed out shouting, "Now, what . . ." Sofi Sackey thought very fast, rushed up to her husband, took hold of his hand and said sweetly, "Oh thank you, Professor, for the visit. I'm sorry my husband was not in. I'm now a little busy with these very understanding policemen. Could you please come back in about an hour, and I don't mean a Ghanaian hour . . ." She led an angry confused Sackey down the drive, whispering to him to be calm please for a change. Sackey swore that the palm wine had weakened his resolve, and wondering what was happening, strode into the trees by the curving street. Pinn had already been pulled into the study by the Sackey children who had understood everything straightaway. Kwame thought it was a great conspiracy.

When the women led the two policemen into the lounge, the latter had regained a little self-confidence through the gentler ways of Mrs. Sackey. Mrs. Pinn's combination of sarcasm and charm had been a little too much for them. The sergeant sent his moustache ahead of him to the chair, in a fine jut of confidence, before he himself sat down with an emphatic sigh. The corporal in turn put his smile gently down on the chair before him, but kept standing himself, waiting to be offered a seat, which he was. A slight pause of expectation moved around the room, and as it settled on the lips of Sofi Sackey, she spoke: "Let me offer you a little water." Her smile stretched between the two men, and reproduced itself in Mrs. Pinn's face. The arena of smiling broadened with the arrival of palm wine. The two women, complete strangers before, looked like sisters anticipating each other's moves, with each move calculated to be ahead of anything the policemen would do. "You see, officers, I told you that we would not find my husband here; now you can't arrest a ghost, can you?" "Ah, madam, I would be prepared to arrest a ghost in the interest of the force," the sergeant said with a laugh. The laugh was passed around, slowly, vibrating from mouth to mouth. "Madam," began the speaking sergeant with cheeks shining like overripe plantain with burning oil on them, "your husband could be deported for the way he behaved . . ." EsiMay Pinn bristled, and Sofi Sackey cut in with a complete sense of ease:

"Oh, officer, I think we palaver the same kind of English . . . you look familiar. You did not by any chance do a course at Legon here did you? I can almost swear I've seen you before." "No, madam," said the corporal, "you haven't seen us yet, you haven't seen us at all . . . not even in chambers!" He laughed at his own joke, under the glare of the sergeant, whose stripes could momentarily roar like a tiger's: he knew a serious discussion could lead to a serious arrest or a serious . . . compromise. But before he could speak, the corporal decided to use the appropriate mood, saying, "Yes, the master of that other house, the one close to arrest, is very close to deportation following something serious released forever in the anus of Ghana." The sergeant's eyes reddened, then took on a puzzled look. He said, "Corporal, you're a foko fool, paa. The word is annals, not anus . . . excuse-me-to-say; but go ahead, we have to be democratic with the lower ranks." The two women remained serious only by the mutual balance of the great pressure not to laugh.

"Sir," began Sofi, "you don't know our troubles at all; I can see you are educated . . . almost both of you . . . You see my sister here? She is suffering, paa, with that white man. Let me tell you a secret: she is the one that brings money into the house. She supports him, and the children. Imagine that! And the biggest thing in the secret is that it has been ordained that she will continue to support him until he dies. So . . ." and she paused for effect, "so if you arrest him and eventually deport him, she will have to find pounds, yes pounds, to send over to support him. If this is not done, the whole family will die. This is the problem, officer." She looked with an expression of utmost pity at the sergeant. And here, pity was a building of three stories, each one with a short and immediate story: one was Sofi Sackey's look of pity, the other was EsiMay Pinn's look of helpless yet righteous indignation, and the last was the two women's shared actions of a very easy yet somehow—to the policemen—real sorrow; they touched hands comfortingly, they snapped their fingers in the Ghanaian way of distress, and they were beginning to almost sway in their slow, stooped rhythms of pain; and then the sudden silence demanded sympathy from the men in uniform. One corporal looked at one sergeant, expecting one sergeant to lead the way either in sympathy or in tough professional talk about the necessity of duty. One corporal had nothing in his broken blue pockets, and wished that one sergeant would choose the former way . . . for after all, kindness usually deserved a reward. One sergeant shrank with deep thought, his cap revolving with indecision.

EsiMay broke the circle of the revolving cap: "Please tell us, officers, do you have wives?" This question struck a sudden chord in the heart of the sergeant. He said, "Madam you should see the hardness of my wife's bottom . . . of the heart. If I, poor man that I am, cannot give her the chop money she wants, she will follow me to the station, going everywhere I go, even—excuse-me-to-say—trying to force her way into the latrine . . ." "Whaaaaat!" interjected the corporal, with not a shred of sympathy in his voice. "Oh, how terrible," shouted EsiMay in genuine horror. "Yes," continued the sergeant, "and what was so annoying was that one day she tried to force her way into the easing room; and the terrible thing was that my inspector was the one there, and not me . . . I had slipped out trying to escape this woman. And you should have heard the roar and abuses the boss let out. And I think he let them out standing upright . . . But I was lucky: he didn't see who it was, and she was so frightened that she never put her foot there again. We are now in the middle of divorcing each other. But whenever we reach the middle, then we fall in love again . . ." The sergeant's face was round and sad with the contours of his own story. "Oh, forgive her," Sofi pleaded, yet wondering how their own case was going to end. "Ei, as for sergeant, he never forgives," the corporal said tellingly. The two women froze. The corporal went on, "For me, it's two-two: I married, divorced, which is one-one; then I married and divorced again, two-two. Now I see women in only two ways: either standing up or lying down! Hahahaha!"

The corporal noticed that this time the laughter was not being shared. EsiMay Pinn coughed into the corner, and when her husband's sneeze came in from the study, she coughed again to hide it. The sergeant suddenly rose, and to everyone's surprise shouted "I will never forgive my wife! But for this case, Corporal, we have not been able to trace the abode of the suspect, have we? And I believe suspect's wife is prepared to contribute voluntary beer and birds from her poultry at the back into the 'save the police small fund': no receipts available, eh? Hahahaha!" And all was settled before the two husbands had the chance to come in and spoil everything.

Chapter 8

As soon as Owula ½-Allotey's hat fell down, the ground wore it; the world had a hat to keep all its cruelty under. And all perspectives shrank to his forehead where the line of old brown felt made circling boundaries. This led to a quarrel with the earth, to a war between the farmer and the great farmed earth; you could not tell which east and which west of the tall trees would harbor abuse released by ½-Allotey, or released by the giant miles of the earth's mystery. So Allotey had, over the years, built up a deep resentment over existence, especially the existence of the earth, first, and then the existence of himself, second. This seminegation of himself gave the earth the advantage: it could be tricky with him when it wanted, sending his shadow the wrong way, burying his optimism and letting it grow in little suffering shoots of tomato whose red was not a red of harvest but of sorrow. Eventually he felt the awe of the tropical earth reducing his own humanity in another way: he decided that the best way to trick the earth back, to run away from failed harvests and wrong seasons, was to beat and form his own roads of living; to reduce his link with festivals, with rites, even with the rhythms of communal living . . . so that if he ended up as the merest leaf above the substance of someone else's fat shoot, then it would be a way of furthering his fight with the mother of mud, the earth. For him there was too much substance, too much continuity in his village; the village was a different image for the same earth, and it rooted him to just that existence that he wanted to stretch. And after the stretch he hoped there would be balance:

91

a new commitment, together with the roots below the green, the roots still deep there holding the stems.

½-Allotey sometimes saw red ants take over his mango trees, and he took this as another attack, and prepared himself for worse things. They would even roll down in their balls of leaves when Allotey used a stick to hit them. At first he used to farm in virgin forests, and he was casual amidst the suspicious awe of the giant trees. The odum was a hard schoolmaster, and his own seriousness could not match it; and though he never trusted the space between the root and the trunk—anything could happen in crossing it—it was the only thing he could hold, in a time of crisis . . . Anything could happen: the other afternoon, before a very large wawa, his shadow ate the fruit from the trees while he looked on in hunger . . . his face looked and worked like a clock as he watched. And he knew that forests were jealous of sound, and were able to create and destroy echoes . . . whether echoes of thought, decision or sound. Often the friendliest thing that the trees could do was this: the leaves talked over his bent back, they chattered with profound nonchalance into his circular soul, in which the many questions chased the few answers round and round. Where was the horizon in a forest? In those sudden moments when small clearances dragged down the sky, it would be dangerous to touch the blue . . . the sky was the question, his hand was the answer . . . and all the grasping produced the same endlessly long sky—height was length in a forest—and the same short hand. The forest had thousands of skirts and beads: ivy and weed were formed in a constant hold, from which grew the shapes made by the eyes hunting for signs, at great speed; and from which a dance was forced with the smallest rare breeze, or from the commotion of the cutlass clearing for cassava, corn or plantain. As he cleared, after the previous short work of chainsaws, ½-Allotey sang—he at last had to do something with the silence—about unfaithful women and the rewards they got. The sound was almost physical, and could hang there like anything else in the trees.

The brown hawks, the egrets and the akyinkyina were already poised for mice and insects as the burning of a cleared square began . . . the hawks were like eerie symbols on the treetops. But when the quick shower came out of season, and the wind moved mournfully around the bulk of ancient barks, Allotey's sheltering was useless: the trees had already taken him over, and the ancestors shared bits of him with that playfulness that often hovered at the edges of horror and destruction. His nose was taken anyway for ancestral breathing, his eyes changed sockets, and one of them could see miles of pain ahead, even through the trees which only blocked joy; meals on the treetops were eaten with his stolen mouth, while his stomach was left agonizingly hungry on his own body. He once named himself "half"—and turned it into figures—in a moment of controlled terror, when he was desperately trying to dig a grave and bury half of himself, that half which was slowly strangling him by its borrowed absence. When, out of a sense of justice as well as revenge he refused, on this dark afternoon, to have his half back, it was suddenly thrown at him in a gust of flesh . . . and the terror was in his bones moving and slowly settling in him. His half had acquired such weight that he sagged heavily to one side for days, and the skin seemed further from the flesh, seemed further from the bones. And then he knew the history of all skeletons, felt their music. And no one believed him as he shouted intermittently on his way home, "This half is heavy, they have burdened it with their evil!"

To the village, he became odder until he finally disappeared altogether from their horizon of sense, dipping sharply, with the crows, down into the subsky of sage, buffoon and madman. To himself, he was merely struggling with his new seriousness, failing to see the contradiction in seeking continuity in himself—even if in a series of broken directions—and avoiding it in the village. When he talked, the contortion of his mouth turned his moustache into a lizard nodding wisely . . . something new he could not avoid, this speed of the mouth. He shocked the elders of Kuse by actually suggesting changes, even in the pouring of libation on the black stools. Kwame Mensah, the elder with the crumpled face, and the narrow, red tongue, gave ½-Allotey what appeared to be a re-incarnated stare; the red tongue was moving fast, but the anger, so deep, made it silent; the cheeks moved back in a growl and stayed back. Allotey raised his moustache in defense, feeling the weight of centuries staring at him. And curiously, returning the stare was easier than fighting the trees. His jaws shot the energy back and forth in a useless chew, until Kwame Mensah looked away in disgust, saying, "So of all the things you can change, with Accra so near, why change what would turn the ancestors into mad wandering screaming ghosts? Change some of your own habits, or go

93

to Accra and change the hearts of those city ants, with their souls in cigarette packets, bars, lotto, football parks and women. Go and change them! We don't need your mad changes! We will go at our own speed, you hear!" The crowd that had gathered was on the verge of dragging Allotey down and beating him. But they remembered his great strength, and none wanted to feel the first few blows before overpowering him. He just turned, almost toying with their anger, and went to his house, shouting that nothing like this would ever drive him away, and that he himself was on the verge of going . . . to come back stronger, and with more demands for changes. All the hate flew over his roof and met the empty sky, and the innuendos in their chattering only reinforced his walls, with the thatch above them rising up in a strong salute of the breeze.

½-Allotey had been planning to move for some time, and he had now got a little farming land among the round shrubby hills between Kwabenya and Pokuase . . . he wanted to run into the land of fewer roots, of semisavanna, where songs suddenly sung out above the hoe did not end up abrupt and stopped by the war of trunks . . . he wanted, also, to make some money in Accra. So he left his forest and his clearing to his elder brother. Though it was not as if he were traveling more than thirty miles away, he was drawn to the small forest to make a last survey of the eye. When he entered there was a python climbing two trees at once; the fern by his right foot bowed as the huge toad jumped over his staring; and the branch that supported the parrot sent by the rainbow, supported his pain . . . and let it drop; he felt his back moving by itself in a dance that made use of no feet; and the horns of chiefs roared the warnings: "Be careful, the land already has you, wherever you move, it will claim you"; as Allotey tried to speak he found one side of his mouth locked, with the bright key blocking the other side so that the words pressed the back of his front teeth and made them hot; and the insects cried early, pushing the trees closer together . . . the earth slowly lowered so that his head was further from the darkening sky; the paths were disappearing, and as he held onto the most familiar one with the heat of his footprints still there, it threw him back; the snake rose in a yawn coming from someone else's mouth, and Allotey heard: "I have given you a yawn instead of a scream, are you not happy? After all, this is what the forest is about: happiness!"; as the ants came in columns from the left, he felt his thoughts were more than they were, and he had a feeling of familiarity rather than fear; but he did not know, as he walked out backward, whether it was the laughter of the dwarf that parted the trees and brought the paths back trimmed, and each one exactly the same shape as the snake . . . and the moon at last led him out with its weak young wick. At the entrance to the forest his brother Kwaku stood with a frown. He asked Allotey, "So you too what are you doing at this time here? I thought you were lost. You have to send more money for me to clear this whole place . . . I don't like it at all. I'll tame it with corn and cassava." ½-Allotey stared strangely at his brother, wondering whether he could give him the true meaning of all he had seen in the trees. His brother was even more stubborn than he was, but only about his needs and wants: Kwaku hated ideas and anticipations, and was happiest criticizing other people's exaggerations, especially his brother's. Kwaku told Allotey: "You should either become a fetish priest, or arrange for your own madness in the streets of Accra." Then, kekekekeke, would come Kwaku's laughter, with the frown still miraculously on his forehead. ½-Allotey could not break the laughter even with this: "Kwaku, I'll be here every month . . . don't go and destroy my farm with your drafts, your chacha and your jots. If you do I'll fight you brother to brother!" Kekekeekekeke . . .

But four trees followed Allotey to the semisavanna, in the dotted hamlets behind Kwabenya. The copses breaking the bending hills hid the giant leaves badly; one tree stood openly and aloofly in the valleys, spreading the memory of the Kuse forest in the way it continued to throw squirrels down hard. And there was a proposition in the hands of the branch, which it took ½-Allotey a few weeks to discover: if you threw a squirrel down hard enough, and you had ancient shoulders, you could bury it at the same time, on impact. And the mist continued to curtain the valleys, early; so that, sometimes, he could not even see the end of his own urine. But that was the time he caught the earth asleep . . . not at night: he studied the stillness with such intensity that he could feel the soil under the brush writhe: and as he released his prayers slowly into the valley, he could feel a solid but precarious distance between himself and the visiting trees. As the days wore on, they related with him in a different way. They used him as an interval of distraction between the constant flow of cosmic oneness . . . even the porters of time must play. It was only the great, lone tree that allowed a measure of farming success: it blocked some of the tricks

95

of lesser trees, but it was impossible to see whether this was to fatten Allotey later for a greater sacrifice or not. So his beans grew, and so his fish in the pond also grew . . . by hard work and by grace.

It was the need for a market for his fish and beans that sent Allotey to Legon. When he realized that some of the lecturers wanted to study him, he stayed away again. Finally it was the need for money that committed him to the campus again . . . it was a close, steady market. He took a sample of his produce and decided to try to sell it to the one who had appeared to Allotey to be slightly mad, but who on the other hand, did not treat him as an oddity . . . an oddity was, to them, a man who tilled the land but was restless with it, though he had no need to do a regular job and did his little thinking not about the land but against it.

"I see you have increased the prices. And there was me thinking you were a man of morals . . ." Professor Sackey said curtly to the man with shorts and a batakari, ½- standing so thickly and nonchalantly before him. ½-Allotey did not say anything at first, but just stared at Sackey with what Sackey considered impudence. "You see, Mr. Professor . . . last time it was a discount I offered; but the cost of walking has gone up! You know, every mile in the country has lengthened. If you don't believe me, consult your gadgets . . . you really are a professor are you not? These old sandals I'm wearing have increased the price of my walking. Even my legs are more expensive than they were the last time we met . . ." Allotey said with only a slight play of irony in his small eyes. "Stop stop stop!" shouted Sackey. "What are you talking about?" "Oh," began ½-Allotey, "you are the professor and you should know what I'm talking about!" Sackey rose with rage in his eyes, but before he could speak ½-Allotey interrupted again, saying, "Let me hold you on the shoulder, Professor. I feel smoke and anger in this office. I smell statistics in your eyes . . . forgive me, is that how you pronounce it? I am a man of small education and much mud. I said sit down, Professor; it's not acceptable traditionally to stand up talking with anger in the eyes. I will give you the best terms of sale on the campus. I like you, and maybe you can educate me . . . small small." "Look!" roared Sackey. "No one comes into my office and tells me what to do! I used to be soft on nonsense, in fact I suffered it for ten years. But all I want from life now is what I call

96

essentiality—look at me explaining myself even in anger . . . when did I last do that?—almost like a state of spiritual grace . . . in which the space between your goals and the means to achieve them is almost gone. I will have no ritual or inessentials . . . whether traditional, doctrinal or anything else. People mistake this for impatience—even my wife, who should know better. Now you enter my office and . . . are you trying to use spiritual force or what?"

Sackey felt that he had been pushed into saying something too abstract and too early, far too early. This man's eyes pulled skins of truth out of him. "I wish I had it, this force, to fight the trees," Allotey said with utter seriousness. Professor Sackey looked at him with a combination of scorn and bewilderment. "Cracking somebody's impatience is a small thing, Professor, especially if, as in your case, this impatience hides a true spirit. Ayekoooo, Professor, I was wondering when I would meet a real searcher in Legon. But I came about fish and beans . . .," Allotey said slightly more loudly than usual. His voice had a sureness that seemed to force Sackey to care more about what he was saying himself than how he was saying it . . . a trap, Sackey thought, that he himself and so many other teachers fell into: the how rather than the what of things. There was a pause. Then Professor Sackey asked, "What do you hope to find in those hills?" "Money!" shouted Allotey immediately, with a laugh, then he said more seriously, "A way of living, a way of thinking; and a way of fortifying myself so that I return and attack my village with change, with a type of revenge." Sackey nodded, looking at ½-Allotey with a frown, and said, "But you know that those with such a conscious search . . . something not related to money . . . are usually laughed at or hated. That's one of the unwritten rules of this society! If there is no money or status in it, then it's useless . . . But what I don't understand is this: you've certainly got more than a measure of education, yet you seem to want to hide it. Also, with your age—is it mid-thirties?—you seem to be top-heavy with questions about the meaning of life, and then the meaning of life *here*. You must be a threat to many people. The soldiers would film you for a self-reliance program, the academics would make a case study of your life, the churches would damn you for pulling God into the savannas, the lodges would accuse you of not being interested in togetherness, and the elders would

97

charge you with trying to destroy their way of life." Sackey's lean body was still, as if he were being pulled inside his own head; serious, his motoway shone more.

"Professor, while I want to talk about beans and fish, you want to dwell on the sad little path I'm trying, only trying, to make. Can you give me money for this please?" Allotey said almost in exasperation, adding with a smile after seeing Sackey's eyes drop in disgust, "You higher beings can feed on words and ideas, but we the ordinary people can only live on things like payment for ordinary fish and beans! But I agree with whatever you say! I like you, though if I want to be serious, I must say that I am trying to run away from the beauty—yes, even in poverty!—and the ease of our living . . ." "But others argue that there has been too much change already . . ." began Sackey. "Be serious, Professor! We sat down and let the change, the history, be thrown at us! And in spite of over five hundred years of association with foreigners, we have been very stubborn: we have kept our basic rhythms, we know our languages and have assimilated so much into them, we laugh the way we used to laugh if you take away the bitterness here and there, we dress and eat what we want which is still basically the same. Professor, I am sure that if you compare the proportion of ourselves that we have kept over the centuries with other peoples' histories, you would really find us so stubborn! Professor, part of my secret, if it is a secret at all, is that I don't accept that we are still slaves of our own history! Do you really think our traditional ways were so weak that they could have been so easily swept aside? They were too strong! And we still want to keep an integrity of the past that so many have shed! I, Allotey, want to make my changes *now*, and on what is *still* lived in the villages and towns. This is what drives me . . ." ". . . mad?" Sackey interjected, blocking the torrent in ½-Allotey's face. The two mouths smiled, with Sackey's adding, "It looks as if you have forgotten about beans and fish!"

Allotey stood still with his broad shoulders stooped, his small eyes most astral with intensity. Then he added slowly, "Professor, don't take me too seriously; all those words I used, I read them, my education is barely beyond the standard seven level, with maybe a few years in a poor secondary school, and then trying for some useless diploma . . . All I want now is my payment. I am hungry. Why did you push me to talk so much?" Allotey's huge hands were curiously delicate, almost vulnerable in their strength as he held them out and took his payment. He became surprisingly quiet, looking like an unopened coconut, yet with a suppressed restlessness that halved his sense of self-containment. Sackey looked at this squat thick man with the piercing eyes, with the air of the village about him. He almost gave out peace and Sackey almost took it, for there was a bewilderment of values about Allotey that Sackey took as a challenge, and which drew him away from what he already considered a half-dead campus. As they shared beer in the silence, ½-Allotey brightened in mood, and rose suddenly with a glint in his eye.

"Professor," he shouted, "I have a problem that even the most shiny silver heads of this place cannot deal with easily. You see, it is about my okro farm . . ." Sackey made a grimace. "No, Professor," continued Allotey regardless, "I need a different type of help now! The first problem I want you to know but not to solve is that I eat too much. I eat as much as I sell. Of course you know the story of the Makola women who eat half their produce, and then have to increase their prices to make up for what was eaten . . . I understand them only too well!" "Oh yes, I just have to look at your size to see why you understand . . ." cut in Sackey, just as abruptly as ½-Allotey, in his turn, drove his words on the wrong side of their talking, saying, "Fine, Professor, fine, but it looks as if your food travels higher than mine . . . and wouldn't it need greater quantity than mine for this? Haha. But as I was saying, I have a second problem. Last year my okro farm at my village was taking over my body. I would not be telling you about this now, but there is in my hills an okro farm exactly like the one I had—we farmers know our contours—and it seems to have planted itself alone! I'm serious. And then it vanishes on certain days, and reappears on others, and brings with it a blue earth. Yes a blue soil. Professor, don't look at me as if I'm mad! It is an automatic blue farm in the hills. I don't know what it plans to do this year, but last year, as I said, it wanted to take me over at Kuse. I watched the okros grow, and the first one that matured—a fine thing with a slight bend to it—was the exact copy of my . . . of my thing! The same thing is happening now above my blue earth. And this was where my wife, now my ex-wife, saw the chance for her revenge: she could not have children, after four years of marriage, and she had been dropping hints around the village that I could not do my duty . . . my mat duty properly. After my quarrel with the elders about change, I did hear some of these hints, but I thought the madness was as usual on their side. Now, after I had innocently told Mayo—there was some innocence then—about the okro, she said nothing. But I saw a look of triumph on her face, her two eyes passed whatever secret there was to each other. Then she vanished from the house for hours. Puzzled, I went out to look for her. I followed a distant commotion . . . which to my confusion was leading to my farm. And there to my amazement was Mayo standing at the head of the crowd of women mainly. She was talking fast, as usual, and had picked an okro—oh my god, I thought, it was *the* okro—which everyone was closely examining. They had not yet seen me. 'You are right, Mayo, he is big for nothing! As soon as you see this okro you can tell that its owner's copy is a useless thing . . . it may excite you as a woman, but there's nothing under it!' 'Yes yes yes,' laughed another, 'so all his boldness that some of us secretly admire is nothing but a power that cannot rise, Oooooooh! Poor Mayo, all these years without action.' 'Hmmmm,' Mayo sighed, trying to get her breath back from the mixture of fast talk and laughter, the shitoh to the other's fish . . . Then I screamed out, 'M-A-Y-O! what disgrace and shame is this? Mayo, what have I done to you that you are betraying me with lies like this!' The sudden silence was like a bowl for their shame. I began to advance toward them, slowly and with death in my eyes. And they began to run. One shouted as she ran, 'It is what you *haven't* done to her that she is worried about!' Somebody laughed on top of the running. Mayo stood completely still, almost limp as I lifted her up and threw her down. Then I suddenly left her alone, for I knew then where to put my anger or where not to put it. I shouted to all of them: 'In three months I will have a child with someone else, someone more beautiful than this hard woman lying on the ground before me. Mayo is a liar! But I won't beat her . . .' Professor, I swear to you that I did exactly as I said, and they fear me, paaa. I tell you!"

"Well, some problems can't be solved, and where's your child and its new mother?" Professor Sackey declared flatly, after a long absentminded pause, then continued without an answer, "But watch the papaws. I want to study them, their relationship with the human jaw, just before they are picked, and just before they are eaten . . ." ½-Allotey looked at Sackey as if the latter were trying to get his own back. "The professor is mocking my true experience," ½-

100

Allotey half-laughed. "Oh no!" shouted Sackey, "I'm trying to tell you something, too, that is true. The seeds of the papaw are the eyes of the country. Have you ever seen Ghana looking at its own eyes? The seeds, like Gold Coast eyes, are bright, round and sharp and empty; and Ghana eyes have more seed than fruit to hold them . . . you see, weak sockets! I'm serious, Mr. Allotey! I am so interested in you, partly because my own research is taking new direction, probably just like your life. Now. when I look into the sliced papaw, I go nearly blind with fright. Looking at my own eyes I couldn't see! How can this country see with the same eyes that it has taken out, right in the brightness of the sun! Ghana eyes are rounder than seeds, rounder than coins, and just as blind! You know why we are so slow, in this country? We are still, every day, trying to come to terms with the supernatural . . . we love the past, pounded right into the middle of our fufu! And this is where they say my nonsense research is taking me . . . aspects of the past and the intellectual . . . Now for your problem: there's only one way to beat the earth . . . control it, control it, and control it again!"

The two men went out, and left their laughter uneasily in a corner. "You are giving me the same old 'modern' medicine!" Allotey complained. "And about my new family: they are safe with relatives. I'll return to them one day soon . . ." "Yes, and I think you should. But you need the modern, nothing scares away the ghosts and the dwarfs more than the deadness of gadgets and processes . . . you either live fragmented and half yourself, half your heart, or you keep slow, and whole, and die!" Sackey said. "Well, Professor," Allotey replied, surprisingly sadly, "it's a choice I don't accept. There must be a middle way somewhere . . . no matter who or what is inhabiting me, I want to find this balance!" As the two men walked away from each other, they both shouted, "Beans next week!" at the same time, and Sackey frowned, thinking that it was ½-Allotey's basic core of stubborn naïveté that stretched the ten years difference in age between them; and the stretch annoyed him even though it had only a question mark over it.

As ½-Allotey made his way through the bush valley, down from Legon tower, he glimpsed a face among the leaves. "Ahhhh!" shouted Baidoo the Ben, I see a ½-GENTLEMAN who is a bush expert, and who wants the valleys to bow down and sing to him! . . ." ½-Allotey stiffened, then reluctantly let his smile take over his face, saying, "My old man, where's your village now? Still in your head?

And be careful you don't drown this poor village with all the drink in your head!" The sun polished Allotey's teeth as he spoke, and he periodically drove flies from his dusty hat. "Don't laugh at me, Allotey, we're both searching for the same thing . . . only my search is a little lazier than yours . . . don't laugh. I see trouble for you ahead. Leave the hills, and go and give food to the black stools normally, in the normal way. When I have created my village, then you can come and be creative there! . . . Now, I want to ask you in the most dignified way possible to let me come and eat with you this evening," Baidoo said, lowering his voice, and scratching a thin leg; the leg dangled as it was scratched. "You can't walk that far, my old man," Allotey said gently. "Here's a note or two earned from my beans. Go to the market and fill your mouth." "So there's still some kindness left in your broad shoulders . . ." Baidoo began, "But tell your friend Professor Sackey not to shout at me so much . . . his words have a wind that can blow an old man like me away; also tell him to look after his wife properly, otherwise she may want to run away . . ."

Then with a sudden wave Baidoo limped off, scrutinizing his money. "My belly thanks you, my belly thanks you, and pray for my village," he shouted after ½-Allotey; but the latter had already taken his shoulders beyond the horizon, with his great strides devouring the bush.

Chapter 9

When Dr. Boadi sailed out of his mother's womb forty-five years ago, much like a Vaseline presence, she almost did not realize that he had come out; nor did she know that he would retain this smoothness and his tortoise shape throughout his life, especially in the belly. His mother, as one of her many rewards, became a memory of fresh stew. Now, he was still led by this same belly—a sly, round pioneer—into the crowded bush of money, status and power . . . all held in the strong current of flowing beer. In his rare moments of introspection, he would wonder why others found life so hard. Even in his failures—which he linked logically with his usual successes, as small pauses—he was smooth. He used to laugh aloud that thinking to oneself was like wearing one's skin inside out; so that facts and more facts, preferably dug out by others, was what he ate. Yet he went as far as to have the insight that he knew something of the secrets of life: his secret was to have the sun on his back, to be bright and easy about difficult things; and then, most important, to have the moon in his stomach for two good reasons: first, to take its shape and secret glow, and second, to digest it while others were looking for it. After that there would be nothing but success, for he would drop his secret light whenever and wherever he wanted . . . and others would have to look with the admiration of sunglasses. He had humility to such an extent that he became proud of it; and for the sake of fairness between the two qualities, he would sometimes rest this humility, and take up pride which was lighter to carry and which had a bigger throat for all the food of his world to rush down. In moments of neutrality to either of these qualities, he would say to a friend, "Look at one thousand people dreaming about me like this, and I am only Dr. Boadi!" And his laughter was a dangerous thing: if it caught you, entered you, shook you, and you did not laugh back, you would burst yourself, one time. One of the fine sights of Accra, considering the number of fine noses pushing into posh corners, was Dr. Boadi wearing his whaaaaat silver jacket, and lecturing with exaggerated gestures to students of Regional Planning.

And the words would stand lethargically on his lips before flying off into the void . . . where almost every student was a pen or pencil that never left its paper. And his words often leaped beyond students, threw excess verbs around the campus, sent adjectives rolling past Tetteh Quarshie Circle, where all circles wept, and were absorbed . . . moved nouns in a daring fast crawl through the deepest gutters, gathered one full sentence in the defining pain of Korle Bu hospital, and then moved with a low political bow into the cool office of the Commissioner for Agriculture . . . who took the words and finally sent for Dr. Boadi's mouth and talked to it of the possibilities of working together. One mouth could be hot, one mouth could be cool in this agreement. This meant that when Boadi lectured his students, he could see miles over their heads into Accra, into his own ambition. And he told his favorite ones among them, with only half a smile: "Gather facts, but make sure that someone else gathers them first; when you come up against a theory, avoid it as far as possible, then treat it as another fact . . . Keep the factual car running; never indulge in the luxury of insight until you have all the facts, and by then your minds will be too full to move, to think; and you should have only first and secondary thoughts: the first thought should be about money, and the second should be about getting the degree that would bring in the money. Am I being cynical? Oh no! 1975, you see, is not the year for youthful idealism, Hahaha!" And the laugh was taken around in a relay race, but a few dropped the baton . . . and it was too late, for Boadi had already won the race.

Dr. Sam Yaw Boadi, or Sam the Ram as his enemies called him . . . which enemies? . . . guided his actions by what he called "qualified kindness": he planned things in such a way that his intrigues hid the fact that some of his friends did not know they were really enemies until he had openly taken advantage of them. He did this not only to achieve a particular goal, but also to have a sense of balance in life: he at times felt his own kindnesses suffocating him, and he had to balance this with jugs of ruthlessness, drunk alternately with drafts of beer. He not only believed in the inevitability of fate, but did so even more strongly when the inevitability belonged to a less fortunate man . . . and fate and money went along hand in hand, with the latter pushing the former along prearranged paths. His wild urge to survive contoured his convex front, so that Monday was money, Tuesday was money, while other days of the week were the colors of different types of cedi. "After all," he said, feeling at the highest level of justification, "the Ghanaian is the most material being on earth. After these thousands of years, he still retains a material connection with his ancestors . . . Eventually, when rockets are out of date, and Ghanaians get around to importing a second-hand one, libation will be poured before launching. I swear that every Ghanaian has a true urge to carry body and spirit around his neck for the whole of all eternity, and through the entire universe!"

As soon as Dr. Boadi got his doctorate, he dropped his research and his reading, just like the pot that one threw away after finishing a hasty stew in it. Soon after, his body grew and his skin and eyes took on that carefully scrubbed, oiled look that certain chiefs and businessmen had acquired to bluff through life with . . . a flowering of ebony that was skin jazz, and that outshone the even brighter colors they wore. Boadi had a wife who did not remind him to clean his teeth often, so that his dazzling smile had a bit of misplaced sunset in it. But since his skin was a fine line of defense against his teeth, he reinforced the former and attacked the yellow further with his little axioms. Today, this one was over the carpet on the floor: power led to money led to power, and there was a vision of the commissioner behind the words, as Ghana food steamed behind the alphabet. For Boadi, for practical purposes, politics and economics were the same ampesi. But his wife was lost somewhere in between, for the years of bending to his will had finally bent her angles away from the 180 degrees of his life. She now seemed to know only half his cloth, half his head, and half his heart . . . the other half of which, on the slimmest of rents, belonged to other women.

But the more they lost of each other, the friendlier they became. Yaaba had first thought that this was a paring away of the unimportant in their relationship, so she kept her innocence, which was after all the guardian of her love for him. And this guardian was busier than any watchman near the heart of any building. But it was the day that Boadi bought her a fine piece of cloth that she sadly realized that if it were not for the money—that had almost become a substitute for his sense of responsibility in their marriage—her innocence, and then her love, could have vanished long ago. She was amazed at the way everything narrowed and thinned down, from the bed to the smile to the touching of eyes. The new friendly reasonableness that filled the space thus left was very welcome for Boadi, for it not only gave him more time, both linear and emotional, but it made it possible for him to say with an easy sense of confidence, "You see, Yaaba, the more time passes the more love we share." She squeezed her round delicate face for a second, then asked "But Yaw, how many of us are sharing it?" His laughter was long enough to cover up an answer, and her seriousness silent enough to make dialogue on another subject, as well as the unspoken reprimand in her frown, almost painless for both of them . . . much like children that walked in the mud of a sudden rain with very little looking down at the dirty feet. Yaaba suddenly asked, "Where is this commissioner taking us?" This was a new question to Baodi, a little closer to what was important to him than other questions recently asked by his wife. "Oh, he's taking us to greater responsibility, to . . ." began Dr. Boadi. "No, I mean where is he really leading us to? Are you sure this new thing will not break us apart altogether?" asked Yaaba again, the doubt pulling her eyes closer together and raising her nose, as if to smell the answer. "Ei, with our new love? Certainly not! Our love is a don't min' your wife chop bar love . . . free, mature, and lasting, yes it's lasted," Boadi replied with his finest smile. "Free, yes!" retorted Yaaba, "and it's lasted, but it's now last . . ." When Boadi laughed, Yaaba found herself, to her own horror, saying to herself that at least she had fought back by leaving a film of yellow on his teeth . . . a woman whose husband was slightly neglected was a strong, secret fighter, a tearer of the veins of nkontommire leaves when no one was looking.

Dr. Boadi sat down, half-watching Osofo Dadzie on the television. He was appalled at the difficulties Kojo Okay Pol went through at the airport, his doubt about Pol's capabilities almost spoiling his beer. He looked at his wife, and was glad of her silence now, glad of the questions locked perhaps unwillingly in her mouth. He rose, patted her head, and sat down laughing. She looked at him inquiringly, her small hip-round, upper-lean body sprung into a question mark that looked at its own single dot below and did not look up again. Boadi had been advised to watch carefully those who were witness to the arrival of the horses, especially that young man Kofi Loww who showed signs of stubbornness. In this house, the commissioner was in the curtains, the commissioner was in the water, even though he had visited Boadi only once; his presence was hope to Boadi, was becoming the stroke that completed the visionary cedi sign: cedi in the eye! cedi in the sky!

The commissioner, who was just about to stroll up against that hard signpost of forty-five years, considered himself, in general terms, a kindly man. And he loved to relax in the relaxing manner of Dr. Boadi: difficult decisions and bad decisions were made with the utmost ease. "You make decisions with the easy stylish wisdom of chiefs and you will be successful," Boadi would say to the commissioner as Yaaba looked down. Commissioner Otoo was a tall soldier whose winning nose jutted out like a salute, and whose head, especially when he was sitting at his huge desk, looked as if it had been gently cut off and handed politely back to him to hold, bewildered, in his hand. He loved looking at reasonable people, and he thought most Ghanaians were reasonable, especially when they accepted his policies. At the beginning of his commissionership, he walked through farms, he became excited with new policies, he fought for his budget, he adjusted his cap on television, he got lost, and called for help, in statistics which neatened his papers. Under the meetings, over the committees, across the late fertilizers, beyond the speeches, into the favors, around the late seasons, and through the politics, he felt that results were not being achieved at all: he therefore, in a moment of bold desperation, started loving the constant challenge of failure. He began to find success in two ways: in a slight lessening of the rate of failure, and in the enthusiastic way he was received, usually in the villages.

And at one such village, he never quite recovered from his inspection of a communal poultry farm under the supervision of the District Agricultural Officer . . . an officer so meek and mild in manner that he was able to get away with the outrageous things he said and did. Fred Frempong was leading a whole convoy of cars to the farm when he stopped his car abruptly; he took fast agricultural steps to the commissioner's car: "Sir," he began, "I must confess before you that sometimes I have problems with distance. Everything I look at moves away into all the yards and miles; and just now, I don't see how we can reach the farm when it keeps moving back as we approach . . . I told Nana and the District Chief Executive that it wouldn't be advisable to visit the poulty farm just yet, but they insisted . . ." Commissioner Otoo stared in disbelief, then looked questioningly at the DC, who in turn shouted: "Frempong, onward! I will take the lead to the farm, and you'll of course lead us around when we get there!" There was a general feeling of annoyance, which quite quickly disappeared when Dr. Boadi cracked, "My friend, don't worry, we all sometimes have trouble with our wives!" But Frempong looked so meek, so respectful, and he provided such a sudden change of mood that Lt. Colonel Otoo took him for a little pet, if a rather mad one. Nana Bankahene straightened his cloth, so that the world may also be straightened; and his gray ring squeezed his finger, as it did whenever he felt there was going to be trouble. The small-timbered forest jumped, exhaust smoke climbed an Odum tree like the most elusive snake; and the feeder road could swallow the entire convoy if it dipped deeply and suddenly enough. At last the farm stood still, and they reached it. There was a wonderful sweetness and stillness in the air, so that you could feel the city dropping off the backs of the visitors. There was something like the laying down of souls . . . into deep farms, silences that absorbed all noise, palm wine with the half-world of the calabash, and then a very broad propriety.

"How many hiccups must I go through this morning, my chest is getting finished!" Nana Krontihene said to himself, not realizing that someone or other had heard, and was laughing. "Your farm is very quiet, Mr. Agriculture," the Commissioner said through his cap. Ears were raised in anticipation . . . and true, only the forest spoke. "Now, sir! Nana will confirm that this is a young farm . . . and we are very free with the geography of our birds . . ." Frempong said, shifting from one foot to the other. "Wait," interrupted Dr. Boadi, "make yourself plain, let the commissioner understand you . . ." The clearing of sky moved as Kojo Pol adjusted his fez; his neck grew with looking. "Well, as I said," Fred Frempong continued, his round face traveling its own innocent contours, "as I said, I've said it." There was a pause, but this time the silence did not quite reach the forest: it was swirling about in people's heads, with just a touch of impatience. The meekness added inches to Frempong's height. His shirt whitened with justice: after all, he had warned them, and they had refused his advice. "All right, all right, how many birds are there in the farm? Perhaps Nana can help us here . . .?" an impatient voice asked. "Oh, about two thousand," the chief said proudly, with that special friendliness that he kept in his room and brought out for dignitaries. "Two thousand!" the visitors repeated, impressed. "Then let's go and see the quietest two thousand birds in the world!" Boadi shouted, laughing. "Please stop!" Frempong suddenly commanded, "We must pour libation to the gods and ancestors that have made this day and this farm possible!" "You do not make the program!" the DC shouted, hurling the words at Frempong. But the latter had already rushed to his car and brought out a half-finished schnapps bottle. Nana reluctantly poured libation, for the second time, calling for yet more blessings. Then they all entered the wooden gate. Heads were angled in a confused silence . . . how many necks were at this moment horizontal in Ghana . . . "But where are the birds?" a voice asked. "I told you that we are very free with the geography of feathers . . . free range, free range. There are hundreds of birds out wandering about in the forest . . . It's healthier, we have discovered, by long and local research to let the birds walk about in the forests. Unfortunately, we couldn't catch them all for the commissioner's visit . . ." Dr. Boadi looked at the commissioner; the commissioner looked at Dr. Boadi. Their looks made a pattern. The DC fumed in between, asking Frempong: "Maybe you have the same problem with distance again?"

The Ministry of Information cameramen had to do something, so they took pictures of the empty coops. Pol smiled his sharp smile; the forest seemed to be advancing on their sense of rationality. "But the commissioner may please inspect the two hens that have just laid two fresh eggs in the corner . . ." Frempong ventured. There was thunder in the eyes of Lt. Colonel Otoo as he moved toward the two birds. "But these are cocks, they are not hens!" someone shouted . . . "so in this village, cocks lay eggs!" Fred Frempong was shifting faster from foot to foot, hoping that he would not come to the end of his feet at the crucial moment. Nana and his krontihene were conferring beyond the egg-laying cocks. Then Nana moved forward boldly, faced the commissioner—who was getting ready to go—and said, "Mr. Commissioner, the hens have been transferred! Don't mind Frempong, he's mad. Even these two eggs are boiled! The hens are not in the forest. We have eaten half and we've transferred half to an even bigger farm . . ." The forest laughed at last.

Back in Accra, just at the moment when the commissioner was bordering on being cynical and discouraged about the whole bank-oshie, then Dr. Boadi would sing the song of reason and ease, reminding him that there were only a few tried alternatives available, and that proportionately speaking, Ghanaians were eating more. Eating more? According to the statistics from the agricultural officers the rate of growth of cocoyam and corn was higher than the population growth over the last six months; and since the projected growth for the next six months for other crops was even higher, there seemed to be cause for celebration. Boadi was already arranging a few quiet parties. But Lt. Colonel Otoo heard these voices from the people almost constantly: "We have been left out of the statistics, we have been pushed behind the arithmetic!" When he told Dr. Boadi about these voices, Boadi looked aghast, saying, "Colonel! There is no room for introspection in politics! You have been able to perform your duties ably. After all when people see you coming, they know you are definitely the Commissioner for Agriculture! They know you even when you are not there physically. And look at the welcome we get in the villages, with the drums and the brass bands, the dancing and the tradition! Relax sir! For after all, you are in revolution! You leave the worrying to me." But Colonel Otoo left only half his worry to Dr. Boadi, and used the other half to grow his first six gray hairs. The ease only returned when Boadi calculated that the ministry's aggregate of failure was lower than the caps of failure in the other ministries . . . besides, in agriculture, the sky was really the limit, and clouds were ultimately the unit of measurement; so that the commissioner's cap rose with the mist of success, he walked with a new dignity much like a chief's, and he started to build a house, a large house. Now, Dr. Boadi could calculate in relative peace: failure, plus effort, plus money, plus Ghana, plus more money = MONEY! For some time his axioms and equations were kept, with high interest rates, in the bank of his mouth.

Would that, when Dr. Boadi smiled, more money fell out more often, Okay Pol thought. Pol had agreed to watch Kofi Loww "until further notice," to find out whether the latter had any evil intentions to sabotage the horse policy. Kojo Pol was now in Dr. Boadi's house, eating banku and green-green, and drinking Guin-

110

ness. As far as he was concerned, the Guinness bottle contained exactly what Dr. Boadi contained: flow. And this mixture of flow and authority had pulled Pol to Boadi. Of course, Pol believed there was some merit in having horses for agriculture—especially with the growing misuse of machines in the country—and that if a few were racehorses, then you would obviously have faster farms . . . But still, his innate suspicion of Boadi made him less gullible as time went on. And when Boadi spoke of Revolution, Pol noticed the fan's own aerial revolution: both fan and idea moved in hopeless circles. In addition Pol was intrigued by the self-contained indifference of Loww, an indifference bordering on insolence, so that in "watching" Loww, he had the chance to be vicarious about his own latent contempt for authority, a latency that he had seen in different forms in the young in every part of the country . . . especially when he trekked in the commissioner's entourage.

Suddenly Professor Sackey stormed into the green walls of Boadi's sitting room, wondering why he had been kept standing at the door so long this cool September evening, on such ridiculously small steps. Pol, who had eventually opened the door for Sackey, still stood, open-mouthed at the open door; then he closed the door and his mouth at the same time. "Ah, Uncle Professor, akwaaba, akwaaaaaaba. There's your seat over there while I go for something cool for you. Sorry for the wait, but the TV was too loud. I was entertaining my other guest over there, Kojo Pol, as you can see . . ." Dr. Boadi said, busily generating his smile. "I thought you were being your usual polite self, letting me shake my dust off before you let me in to experience the grandeur of your house," Sackey put in sarcastically. "And I hear you want to be a chief in addition to all your other duties, eh!" Dr. Boadi stiffened imperceptibly, as if too much of himself was being revealed beyond his control, as if he would have timed things differently. But he soon put the stiffness down, picking up his dazzling smile instead and saying, "Professor, you always go too fast for me . . . haha. To you I am a pack of cards, and you deal me out as you like! And pack of cards that I am, I still offer you beer, Uncle!" "Hey, don't uncle me," Sackey roared, sitting by the green wall with his green shirt. "There are only two years between us! Your beer is so cool . . . political beer I suppose, Supreme Military Council ice!" "Ei, Uncle, or is it semi-Uncle, I am still barely at the Redemption level, barely national, hahaha!" Boadi shouted. Then the sound of a goat broke their talking in two; as if as the words scattered, Boadi took the exclamations and Sackey took the expletives. Kojo Pol refereed with his silence, but there seemed to be a look of alarm on his face, which the light reflected away from the other two men. Pol seemed to establish a better relationship with the large picture of Boadi dominating the ornate sitting room: the picture smiled back when Pol smiled, and he exchanged an odd silence with it. Boadi on film was nicer than Boadi in the flesh even if the skin had the copious oil of overfresh tatale. Sackey suddenly looked menacingly at Pol, and shouted without warning at him, "Look, you young men think nothing has been experienced before in this world. You may not believe it, but I was just as innocent as you at your age! Boadi is a different Ananse . . . look at the richness around us! What are you doing giving your youthful energies to this Ghanaman operator?"

There was a slanting silence which Dr. Boadi filled with a loud calculated burp. He began, "Uncle don't spoil me, Oh! All I'm trying to do is, one, to give this young man some living, and, two, to let him see what the real Ghana is like." "Boadi Boadi Boadi! let me say your name three times in disgust! Since when did you politicians arrive at the conclusion that your world was everyone else's world? This has been your tragic mistake for years . . . and you Boadi, you at all, Mr. at-all, you should have kept to your lectures instead of applying to go away next year. Most people on this campus think politics is the ultimate! The sad thing is that you so-called intellectuals probably do as badly as anyone else at governing. Your form, your speeches, your analyses, if any, may be better; you may be able to move, even if with a limp sometimes, on the international plane. But you are hopeless at real day-to-day governing! And you only have a sense of urgency in relation to specific tasks . . . not even policies! Those of us busy in different worlds have nothing but contempt for the type of politics you have been feeding us with over the decades . . ."

"But it's the lavender, sir," Pol interrupted Sackey, almost apologetically. The two men turned and looked at him as if he did not, or should not, exist. But Pol pressed on regardless, looking at the two of them with an intensity that was entirely defensive: two university mouths were leaving one ordinary mouth out with no ceremony at all. Pol then took on a protective, comic earnestness: "It's the lavender which I smell from both of you that is killing this country. This lavender is so powerful that any action, whether good or bad, takes on a fine smell, a neutrality . . ." "Hey wait! where did you learn about fine neutrality?" Boadi asked Pol with an arrogance that was completely innocent. Pol suddenly took off the intensity, as he would trousers that could cut the air with their crease, and Boadi saw a stubbornness that he had feared did not exist in the young man. "Mr. Kojo Pol," began Sackey, "it seems very disrespectful of you to use lavender against us like that. Certainly, I do not know that lavender exists. You know, I only find it occasionally in my handkerchief, my wife puts all sorts of things in my handkerchief! . . ." Pol continued, looking straight ahead of his own line of vision, "What I really meant to say was that none of you as a group would give us any hope in the quality of your lives. I may have been sitting here quietly, but I see more than you think! Believe it or not, but a little bit of hope drew me to Dr. Boadi . . . at first, but now . . ." "But now, what?" asked Boadi with an ironic frown.

"Look Boadi," said Professor Sackey, "don't force him; this young man could turn out interesting. He is only overasserting himself now, as earnest young men sometimes do. Now, this should bring me to my mission, which you failed to ask . . . Purely out of moral interest, I would advise you to leave the Pinns and that young man once staying with them for a few days alone. That young man has some high-sounding name . . ." "Kofi Loww," broke in Pol. "Yes, I thought the lower part was high-sounding," continued Sackey. "Boadi, they are harmless! They are not interested in that ridiculous horse affair! The more you harass them the easier it will be to force them to take a stand, and then you'll have enemies. And I really must be frank now . . . eh? Oh, I know I'm always frank, you don't have to say it! . . . I think that the direction you've taken toward politics and the way you've taken it is suspicious and unscrupulous. You have actually stooped to letting people be followed. Of course, I'm not surprised, since, normally, when the Legon connection . . . can I call it that, Your Excellency! . . . enters the wide corridors of power—where the harmattan is constant but sweet—they are immediately led from the rear, the backside, if you prefer! And why does this happen? Of course basically it is a question of weakness of character . . . strong drinkers with weak stomachs! . . . You all become defensive about your education: you are either afraid of your advice being thought unrealistic, and mere showmanship, or you don't want to be accused

113

of being out of touch with the people. So that your choice is either to be compensatingly tough, or to close your eyes to the excesses around you. What a choice! Fine, I can understand that these are some of the pitfalls of pluralistic society; but hold it: weren't most of us running about in bare feet like the rest? Did some of us not sell things after school, like everyone else? Did we also not have yoo ke gari like the people? Have we not been common before? The funniest thing is that when you go and see the mess around the throne or the stool, you very rarely think about resigning. Resignation is something you read of and admired in your student days! And you can't resist the march-past, the whiskeys, the trekking, the durbars, the sirens, the women, the salutes, Oh God!" Professor Sackey's fire consumed his lips which had become pink with angry biting, his neck seemed to grow longer, out of his shirt, into the walls, seeking some truth, seeking something far thinner and tauter than his own country.

Dr. Boadi had risen once or twice during Sackey's outburst, but with a great effort he pushed the gates of his smile open. Pol saw his teeth singly, each one sharp with suppressed anger . . . but Boadi's large belly secretly grew and absorbed the tension above it; then the belly bank, the belly pit, rounded with success as the mouth above it decided to answer to Sackey: "Uncle Kwesi! there you go making me dizzy with your speed again! You will spoil this young man with your cynicism! Now look, we are talking about the reality of Ghana politics . . . whoever told you that morality and subtlety are the moving passions! Surely a professor does not need to be told the difference between what is and what ought to be. I am for life, and you are for the ivory tower; which makes you a member of the tall elephant brigade, Hahaha! And I am the grass cutter down low in the earth, with the burrowers and the worms! I am the norm and you are the normative!" Dr. Boadi's hands were usually absolutely still, but now they moved about in agitation as if he were in the middle of a lecture.

Kojo Pol had not seen him like this before, and he felt stronger as he saw Boadi's unshakable confidence shaken somewhat. Professor Sackey rose with a scowl, unbuttoned his shirt as the hairs on his chest stood ready, in their grays and blacks. To Pol this seemed to be a different type of moral chest. "Young man," Sackey shouted, with contempt in his voice, "you are my witness: I accuse Dr. Boadi of exhibiting his lavender—your creation, Mr. Pol—of

114

spreading his perfume on the most disgusting stench! You are my witness!" Boadi behaved as if he had not heard what Sackey said. He took a long draft of his beer, and put it down with a sigh of satisfaction, saying, with what Pol thought was an amazing innocence, "As I was saying, Uncle Professor, there are figures in Ghana politics that you must make compromise with before you can even function. It's a humbling process, and I don't think you could last two days in government! And don't forget, I haven't quite entered yet, I am still learning, in the background. You are the pure people, playing with your theories and your purity; and one day you may give us a little honor by entering the unpainted doors of politics . . ." "Honor?" Sackey asked with a snarl, "My good friend, don't insult me! Have the courage to get your commissioner friend to stop harassing innocent people. Courage in politics here exists only when one politician fights another politician. Can't you understand that courage must relate to Ghanaians as a whole? It's a tragedy that eighteen years after independence, we're still going backward!" There was a pause which the crickets filled with a vengeance. Professor Sackey's intense restlessness magnified the room, pushed the furniture back. And he looked so alone to Pol, as Dr. Boadi spread his ease with triumph . . . as if to say that he was completely relaxed, that he had no impossible goals to carry around on his back. Then on an impulse, Boadi asked Sackey, "Professor, who is more Ghanaian, you or me?" And as Sackey stormed out of the house with his bottle still half-full, Boadi burst into uncontrollable laughter, heaving his fine belly north and south. Okay Pol ran after Professor Sackey, as if he wanted some answer from him, but his mouth remained as silent as Sackey's back. And as he went back stooping into the room, he remembered this green professorial back pushing back the darkness with the tautness of its stoop.

Boadi seemed to be looking with mock surprise at the hole left by Sackey's sudden absence, and was unaware that something had broken inside Pol that evening. Then, almost everything Dr. Boadi did was a discord to Kojo Pol. "Ahhh well," said Boadi with a shrug, "the professor wants to solve Ghana's problems from the sidelines, but I should have told him to solve his good wife first! Can't you see that he treats Ghana the same way they say he treats his wife? Hahahaha! . . . But seriously, Professor Sackey is wasting his voice, wasting his talent. In Ghana you do everything from the

115

inside, and no pressure withstands this inside. Such a man should have built up his connections long ago . . . doesn't he know? Professor Carry Yourself indeed! He won't join any lodge, he won't go anywhere, he won't fraternize with those in power, he won't flatter the chiefs! All he does is talk and think and write. Kojo, answer my question: who is more Ghanaian? I'm asking because we've all got to be realistic about our own environment . . ." "So, Dr.," Pol said, "you are not interested in making any changes at all in this country of ours? Professor Sackey wants to make changes . . . even a small boy like me wants to make changes." "Ei," laughed Dr. Boadi, "are you one of those that must take the revolution so seriously? I am trying hard to make you realistic: you see, with our revolution, you let your talk go far ahead of your action. You leave room for maneuver behind the principles! It's the only way to keep this society together . . . besides I thought you were with me for the money!" Pol looked at Boadi with pain and distaste on his face, and said quietly, "It's partly that, just to live and enjoy life a bit; but it's partly a little search of my own, too, as I've told you!" "Told me?" asked Boadi, absentmindedly, "maybe I was then drunk, eh?" "Yes you were," Pol put in rather too quickly, "but you say you always remember everything, especially when you are drunk." "Young man, young man," laughed Dr. Boadi, "if I get drunk on Star, I remember everything; but you should know that it's Club I have been drinking lately . . ."

There was an insistence in Pol's voice that irritated Boadi, who had at last been able to push thoughts of Sackey out of his head. Pol rose, finished his beer with a sudden burst of energy, saying, "Dr., it doesn't matter if you've forgotten that I believe that something different is something worthwhile—" "You are too young to wax philosophical," Boadi interrupted. "Wax?" asked Pol, confused. "Look it up in the dictionary when you reach home," Boadi said flatly. "I am now extending my training of you to language matters!" Dr. Boadi's laughter went down to Pol's departing feet, dictating the rhythm of the latter's walk down the drive. "Kojo Pol," shouted Boadi as Pol disappeared down the trees, "your airport job could have been far neater! If you are carrying out another job, pay attention to the details of fate, eh!" "If!" shouted Okay Pol back to Boadi defiantly, getting his own rhythm back, and marching out into the jaws of the night. But Beni Baidoo brought the night right back into Dr. Boadi's house. He was so silent that

Boadi was surprised at his tongue. "Ei, old man boogie! What's wrong with you this evening? Have you put your tongue to sleep? Or has some woman left her slap on you . . ." Boadi began.

"Dr., have mercy on me. My problem now is that I have a good cause to beg for: I have been promised three acres of land to found a village on, so I need money to get the other things—" Boadi interrupted: "Three acres to found a village! The smallest village in Ghana! Why don't you just found it on a coin . . . that should be small enough for you. Haha . . ." Boadi's own belly translated his words with its heaving. "Oh, the advantage about the small land is that I will be closer to the girls . . . I love immortality! In the land of sunshine, there's nothing that makes you happier than the touch of eternity. Dr., if my little village fails, then I will enter the church, I will become the most priestly priest you have ever seen! always praying before fornication. But Dr., with you I can go straight to the point: give me money, and I'll tell you how you will fare in politics . . ." Beni looked imploringly at Boadi, who postponed his laughter so that he could smile first, adding, "Boogie Beni, tell me about my politics . . . am I going to be president?" "Nononono, you will always fluctuate in politics, you will betray one man after another," Baidoo said, with a grimace. Down came Dr. Boadi's laughter at last . . . "Old man, what are you saying? I'm planning to have a Benz soon, so don't spoil my plans, Oh." Boadi broke the silence and filled it with gusts of laughter. "Treat Professor Sackey better, and you will progress. I don't like his hot words, but he has his sense of direction, and he goes straight to it! But about my village . . ." Baidoo said raising his voice with the last few words. "But I thought you said Sackey was not speaking to you because you shouted at him in front of his wife . . . We shall see about your village. But about my politics, I'm too smart to reach either too high or too low. I will fluctuate without going up and down at all, koraa!" Boadi said laughing, and added, "Beer for the old man, more beer!" Beni Baidoo smiled, drank, smiled, drank; then sat back in anticipation of the money.

Chapter 10

Her hips gathered the best glances in Accra fast . . . and dropped them off with indifference, stinging the eyes they came from. She had a use for the haughtiness they accused her of: she hitched up her skirt with it, she swayed her life with it. Araba Fynn was the third generation of money, and had the skin of sunlit bokoboko or of groundnuts baking. That look of wild and calculating innocence did not quite fill all of her eyes; for at the edges lay a kind of mercy for the world. And everywhere she went she had to fight against her own beauty. When she spoke English in the airplanes, her Mfantse touched it, and her Ga touched her Mfantse; so that in this world of languages touching, her mouth became complex yet beautiful, even when pressed shut in anger: at those who suggested that her money—not as much as they thought—was inherited. She made her money fresh, her mother made it fresh, and her grandmother made it with fresh fish. The three of them still lived together in the family house at Asylum Down, living like three flowers of different seasons. Their cloths and rare dresses were planned together, sometimes even their smiles and their disagreements; and usually when the sun shone, they took it into their eyes together. But the only one in danger of abandoning herself to beauty was Nana Esi, the grandmother; but then even with her, she was only trying to balance a natural stiffness of character. Besides, a few fineries were a good thing to tame an empire of fish with. She was thus fine, fish and fair, but she had something which went deeper than her extraordinarily deep voice: an obsession with continuity and propriety which she broke, especially in her younger days, with any ruthlessness needed for her money to grow and grow. And she used to measure her daily money by the sound of her own footsteps: the slow heavy steps told of a large amount of fish sold; the light steps, of a restlessness for more money, a restlessness tempered by the style with which she fought and lived.

As more money came, Nana Esi mastered her obsession with it, she refused to cast a shadow of pounds and cedis. Money had to be moved . . . into tomatoes, candles and hats; and each move, chosen carefully, became a symbol for important events: the birth of her child, her grandchild, a deliverance from illness, or a period of great energy and understanding. Now she had an obsession which she could not yet master: the need to stay away from other old people, whom—in her own paradoxical way—she treated as children. Then when she was alone, she would desperately count her face to see whether any wrinkles had been transferred there. But such moments were fleeting. She worried more about whether Araba and her mother, Sister Ewurofua, had the caliber to develop themselves that little bit more, or to hold onto their money. She herself had enough self-possession to fill an egg and break it. She wanted a little more hardness, especially from Ewurofua; the fact that the latter had made any money at all was a surprise, a fine surprise, she would say. Nana Esi complained, "Araba, why have you stopped wearing your beads? You are all changing; even your mother, who now likes to rush to funerals as often she can, with old and new friends that have nothing to offer her. And I'm worried about your Fante, Araba, the Ga is pushing it out of the way . . ." There was a pause, during which Nana Esi adjusted her cloth, meticulously sewn by herself, and caught Araba's eyes seeking help from her mother. This reinforced her stubbornness, and she continued with a glint in her eye, "Yes, and it's the beads that will bring you the right man . . . and stop making more secret signs to your mother! She can't help you, she needs help herself! It's as if this mother of yours does not want to grow up . . . she is in fact enjoying a second youth!" The flowers in the veranda shaded the words of Nana Esi, took the gravity from them, as if enforcing the unspoken agreement among the three women that anger was for those who did not know where their next meal was coming from. An unhurried calm usually filled the house, and it was partly the source of their strength outside. Ewurofua interrupted the severity with the shine of amusement in her face, saying, "Mamaa panyin, it's not the beads that worry Araba; it's that height of yours she took, with that proud turn of the head! And as for myself," she continued with the slow amused flow of her words, moving a cushion onto the carpet and sitting delicately on it, "was it not you, Mamaa, that advised me to go out a bit and stop sitting in the house like a piece of banku satisfied forever with the stew around it! I'm only following the direction you've pointed out to me . . ." "Ah, yes you're right, but it's the way, the way you are actually walking in this direction that I'm frowning at." Araba saw her chance, and she quickly said, "And Mamaa panyin, you really are frowning! You have forgotten your warnings about wrinkles! We're all running away from them, and just now I've caught you running toward them, Ei! caught!"

And when they laughed, every shake of laughter went into the ageless glow of Nana Esi's face, and she said with the play still in the front of her eyes, "All I'm saying is that, though I like change, change must be profitable, and not only in money either but in yourselves . . . your strength, your skin . . . and that's when the money lasts longer. And you, Ewurofua, you think you are still with the younger people . . . be with them in spirit, fine, but the young always leave, always go somewhere. How many years did you leave me for, before finding me in my old age? You must take your step faster toward the right direction! And you are almost fifty!" Araba was now doing her mother's hair, and it was thus convenient to pattern the silence for her, to pattern it with smooth hair. But Ewurofua did not feel this serious consideration of Nana Esi's; she laughed at her old mother, and said, "Mamaa, don't put me between the gray-haired and the young too soon! You should have heard the two proposals I had last week!" "But, Sister," Araba cut in—she called her mother, Sister—"we all know that you get the men's hearts more often than Mamaa panyin or myself . . ." "But I know what you are thinking, you are thinking too many people owe me money; and that it's usually the men that pay slowest . . ." said Sister Ewurofua with some heat. "Yes," pressed Araba, "but if they pay with their hearts only it's useless. You can't put hearts in the bank!" "And the annoying thing is that she says No to every proposal she gets!" teased Nana Esi.

Araba's smile was a market: it brought in everything and gave out everything, the warmth being at the edges and only for the few. And there was a sudden line of three smiles traveling in the pink room. They were together again in their silence. "Work!"

120

Nana Esi shouted, getting up with her straight back, her gray hair plaited back in roads leading up to the junction of the fine sharp eyes. "Task-mistress!" the two younger women shouted at once. But Nana Esi walked out steadily, without looking back. And Ewurofua and Araba looked at each other, as if for sudden confirmation of the old woman's impatience, but knowing very well that they both constantly borrowed her vitality and experience . . . in different proportions.

Sister Ewurofua made her money from cloth, succeeding surprisingly in a rough Mammy and Manager world. Money came without her having to force the angels, without changing her easy-oasy temperament. Like the lizard, even though a beautiful one, she nodded when she wished, climbed the heights when she felt like it, and yet was able to catch all the insects needed. She fought, twenty years ago, to be a UAC distributor, using a cunning brand of innocence that surprised her mother. Whenever she fought with any of the heavier Mammies, she would be the first to cry, trying to reason with them through her tears that they should not take everything and leave the new ones with nothing. One Mammy was so amused with Ewurofua's innocence that she had told her cruelly, "Go and marry and have children. You are too soft for this business . . . we know your mother, and you haven't got her strength at all." But she was already married and had her one child, suffering from a weak and drunken husband who fell for her innocence, and never got up to work again. But she persevered, and earned her quota of cunning and respect, respect even from the old iron queens. She still did everything she should not have done: she gave easy loans, she reduced prices usually out of pity. Her weapon was the charming helpless way she had of asking for her money, so that the customer was caught between guilt and admiration and was forced to pay . . . as she did with Dr. Boadi, a regular customer who was swaying between making a move to woo her, or her daughter.

The older sellers at Makola told Ewurofua as much about her mother as Nana Esi herself did. The old lady was a very shrewd seller of fish, but her gift at the beginning was the buying of it: she would go down to the beach at Anomabu or Winneba, bargaining in a most aggressive yet offhand manner, for the cheapest fish in the greatest quantities. The sand could rise with her bargaining. The fishermen used to say that she was tough enough to go to sea, and that her will alone would attract the fish in their numbers to the boat. And the salt air would polish Nana Esi's skin, so that she looked like the beautiful stone woman facing the sea squarely and without a smile. They called her The Million Pebble Woman!

Araba Fynn was much more like her grandmother than her mother; but she had her own vast store of outward indifference which moved others into thinking her full of calculation and precocious wisdom, and which masked her real qualities of boldness, shrewdness, and a strange touch of mercy . . . what she considered very minor mercy, that is raising the gold in her purse at the church whenever she went, and—when she was not doing business—seeing people as needing either sympathy or indifference. The indifference was safe, and kept her beauty in check, usually from others but sometimes even from herself. At the age of twenty-four years she had just finished building and renting out a new bungalow-type house, to which she went to collect her rent in her VW Golf car— she did not take any advance. Around Asylum Down she was known as Araba Quick, a term she detested, and to which she gave, whenever there was a human being at the end of it, her most withering look of abandoned indifference. She had refused to enter sixth form, and her grandmother always regretted this, saying, "If we couldn't go to university, you at least had the chance to go." Araba never gave a reply to this, knowing that it was a complaint that did not negate her present success. Nana Esi vaguely felt this, and did not press for any word from her granddaughter. It was clothes and African crafts, with occasional yam export, that made Araba her money. When she first saw her own success coming, she was afraid to eat anything she wanted, thinking that she would die of indulgence or happiness. This slight sense of reserve finally steadied her and, with the help of her two supervisory generations, she grew a stability that gave her space and character.

Her first visitor of this very new space was John Quartey who wanted two things in life: to court Araba, and to become an Alhaji, eventually. He postponed the second wish for the first, since he did not know how this haughty girl he wanted would react to his intended religion. He was a cattle dealer of means, and had the solid touch to his life that impressed, especially, Ewurofua. Nana Esi's husband had also been a man of some property, but that did not stop him from leading a wild life and dying early; so she was a little more skeptical about the visitor. Besides she sometimes stubbornly insisted that Quartey looked like the shadow of cows: he talked about cows all the time, and would always bring meat for Araba and Ewurofua. When he started wearing his long flowing robes, hoping to impress, he soon became a complete cow to all but 'Ewurofua. His robes flowed away from Araba, but the more he felt her indifference the more visits he made, and the friendlier Ewurofua became, to compensate for her daughter's lack of interest, hoping the latter's feelings would change toward poor Quartey. And Quartey had completely misread the situation: he honestly thought his masterful relations with cows would naturally extend to his human relationships. He had arrived at the conclusion that Araba Fynn was just shy, and that she had perhaps even confessed her love for him through her mother . . . hence her mother's friendliness.

So he decided to persevere, rushing into this tough but—as he thought in a moment of self-comfort—female household, with tales of great bovine deals; there were horns in his words; hide in his openness of detail, and he positively hinted, even in front of Nana Esi—who had disdain in her eyes—that he had a powerful hoof between his legs. Nana Esi rose in disgust, storming out without any traditional niceties. Even this, Quartey did not absorb. But Araba rose, was following her grandmother, then stopped, looking at her mother with an expression of triumphant mirth, and saying with a slight turn of the hips, "We wish the hoof would gallop away to other pastures, fast!" These words, being said slowly, were allowed to breathe, and thus rushed fresh into Quartey's mind; cows and confidence were pushed aside, so that at last he felt vulnerable. He gathered his robes about him, rocking quickly and uncomfortably in the chair. His wounded mind told him again that this was a household of women, and he therefore had to keep his pride intact, without fail. He continued talking inconsequentially to Ewurofua, from whom he instinctively sought comfort. His thick handsome face looked like the emptying room. But her eyes did not meet his, for she had a great feeling of disappointment: she had hoped that her gentle promptings would put a little sensitivity into this successful man's head, and now she felt ridiculous, knowing she had pushed him too fast toward her daughter . . . and the push had led him right into Araba's thicket of indifference. Quartey was hot, paaa. When he finally rose, carrying on a fantastically fast monologue about his exploits of money, he felt the last dropping

123

of his dignity on the bright carpet. His inner moo was gone. He suddenly decided that he would, without any waste of time or women, be an Alhaji. He announced it with a desperate look in his eyes, to Ewurofua, "You are looking at an Alhaji!" Quartey never forgot that look of surprised pity that Sister Ewurofua gave him, nor her words: "Oh, is that what what I am looking at?"

Just as he got into his Benz, his nobility returned and he said a last good-bye with it, waving with the tail of his hand. When Ewurofua took her slow, almost ashamed steps back into the house, she was met with a hug by Araba, and contributed her part of the shaking to the combined laughter of the three of them. The laughter went round and round, and was only stopped by Nana Esi who said rather sadly, "You know, Ewurofua, I gave you a hundred bits of advice about marriage, and you did not take a single one seriously." There was silence. Then she added, even more sadly, "Of course, I did exactly the same with my mother . . . who was so strict and serious with me that you couldn't push any sympathy between her eyes. Well . . ." Araba knew that some of this was being said for her benefit, and she felt, and resented, the weight of responsibility, so she said these words very lightly on her lips: "It looks as if every woman is condemned to choose her man, or be chosen, no matter how wrong the choice may be." "Araba, is this a warning?" Sister Ewurofua said with a laugh. Araba returned the laugh, with its tail a little longer. But neither of them saw that look of profound regret that filled Nana Esi's eyes, and turned her head toward the bedroom where she gladly went, filling its emptiness with the sorrow of seeing choices made and unmade, things done and undone, in the same, old, blundering, human way.

But the third generation of men of mice had to come to Araba, like a curse as Nana Esi later said; and when it came the gentleness of the household tightened, and turned. Kojo Okay Pol had been sent several times by Dr. Boadi to both Ewurofua and Araba, with whom he was doing business. When Okay Pol first entered the house, he looked so thin and defenseless, so earnest, that they almost laughed him back out of it. He sensed this, and was going to walk back out when Araba grabbed his hand playfully and said, "Little messengers do not leave without unloading their message. Come in . . . sir!" The last word burst with the force of sarcasm in it. Pol's formal defensive manner joined with a directness he could not cage: before long he was giving Araba Fynn ludicrously sincere advice on everything from profits (profits!) to religion. He looked extraordinarily neat for a man so clumsy in temperament. But basically she felt sorry for him, wondering where that tiny touch of adventurousness came from . . . so different from his thin defenseless neck where his height still lay. She also wondered how his little punctuations of pride bore the sentence of being sent so often on business and other errands. But there was a part of him she could not quite fathom: a man trying to be responsible, yet tripping over this trying and finally looking ridiculous, yet constantly freeing himself from this ridicule with a reaffirmed sense of neatness in body, with a wonder in the eyes. What made her finally look at him with a sort of puzzled afterthought was the way he completely absorbed her looks of utter boredom, petulance and indifference, with his own look of wonder; as if waiting for her to finish her look . . . and there would be so much more of his left. At first she thought this staring was merely like two children eating fufu and abenkwan, with both of them eating as slowly as possible, in order not to be the first to finish. But just as she would dismiss him from her head, he would reappear with a new strength, walking like his usual mosquito, and offering—with a strange feeling of regret—his usual advice as if giving alms right and left at Post Office Square . . . with his eleemosynary chatting: she should try to get a balance in life, pursue education seriously, reach out for something new and nonmaterial.

This regret: he always felt it when leaving her, and he pushed it out of his head with words of parting that seemed to define the growing levity of their small-small relationship: "I will come back when my real future begins, when it's two inches from the hold of my fingers. Dr. Boadi likes you with the usual type of like, and he would collapse with laughter if he knew I was advising you. But I want to feel fire before I reach the right age!" Then she would ask, "The right age?" "Yes," he would reply, "I'm growing up at exactly the same rate as this country: slowwww! so when Ghana is the right age, I will also be the right age." She would laugh . . . and then yawn and forget all about him when he left. However, Pol became a thin point of laughter in the house, and sometimes looked like one of the expensive pieces of furniture, thin and stuck in the fat corner yet making a presence that changed its space.

Nana Esi laughed at whatever Pol said, more or less, "because of that stupid look of seriousness in his eyes!" She sometimes even

125

left her mouth on the floor for someone else to pick up. But Pol continued with a stiff deference toward her, not only out of respect but out of a vague fear. To him the old lady's eyes were like catapults that could blast him out of existence. And he insisted to himself that she must be cruel to somebody somewhere sometime . . . Sister Ewurofua, however, kept an uncharacteristic distance, simply because of her experience with Quartey; but her gentle nature sometimes shook her and rolled her down a slope where she could not straighten herself out of the little gradients of laughter. This postponed laughter would burst before the surprised Pol. "Do you really, abrentsie, have to hold your ear with two fingers when you are talking?" Ewurofua would ask reluctantly. "Can't you take the same *length* of steps, Owura Pol? Why the short and long steps at different times?" Ewurofua was, however, sensing some sort of addiction to Pol—not love—from her daughter, some sort of building up of the habit of waiting for his arrival . . . when she had a little time to spare; yet she continued to be half-bored in his presence, Ewurofua saw. Part of Araba's languor—she had a natural physical one which brightened her beauty immeasurably, just like her mother's—came from the shock she had two years ago, when she realized that a rumor had grown around her at Asylum Down: that the reason she had rejected so many men was that she was frigid, barren. She put down the weight of making money, and cried almost for days, begging her mother to "please make a radio announcement if necessary" to reject the rumors. In the end it was the controlled contempt of her grandmother for this rumor that strengthened her. After a while she saw all the tongues of rumor lying cut in the streets yet still desperately mongering, much like worms halved and still writhing. Her strength now raised her level of languor and indifference; and a new ruthlessness made her make more money. She raced past the chatterers with an intense sense of direction, which made Nana Esi glow, so glad that there was still someone with her spirit left.

Okay Pol considered it impossible that his "small businesswoman–danger" as he called Araba Fynn, would be emotionally unencumbered with any man, young as she was. But as time went on, he saw no sign of the prospective alombo. He suddenly wondered whether he was thin enough to squeeze through any small space in her heart . . . or if not her heart, then her cloth. He laughed to himself, thinking her both physically and socially beyond him,

126

though he knew that his head had a few more questions—and fewer answers—than hers did. Thus he hid his largely buried intentions toward Araba from himself, by refusing to recognize them. And paradoxically, it was this way he had of abandoning or forgetting parts of himself—even important parts, such as a basic uncertainty in his aims—that finally led him to be almost as bold about his hidden heart as he was about the horses. When you forgot the limits of your strength, nothing stopped you from trying to lift an elephant . . . so that at each successive visit to Asylum Down he seemed to abandon more of himself, until he had almost emptied himself, and had yet made his heart exceptionally *bold*. So this paradox showed, especially in his walk, with his pelvis half-folding over like a dancer's, and pushing his feet further apart, so that he walked along in an awkward and perpetual certainty . . . at least when he was with her.

She herself felt some of this in him, perceived a change in him that she hoped would only be temporary. It had become harder for her to exercise her mercy on him. She threw the pity to one side; it rose again in another side, more complex with a new feeling of attraction on her part. He was becoming a bright point between business deals, and since she felt nothing threatening about him, she innocently allowed the more complex feelings she was observing in herself to grow . . . if the forest tree was not first cut down, it towered above the village. And even negative feelings of contempt and a patronizing amusement swelled her interest. So that she had reached that dangerous point when an act, a gesture, a look—of this insubstantial man—could fix him firmly in her memory, just at the point where other memories converged and gave out significant reflections of the colors of the kente of the mind's shoulder. Thus they both floated, as if in harmattan dust, trying to create a holding transience for emotions that wanted to settle, even if only like butteflies. For a young woman of such shrewdness, she found it ridiculous in herself, under her kotoko hairstyle, that she wanted to prolong little accidental touches of Pol skin and Fynn skin. He did not know this; rather he thought she was becoming more aloof.

Of course Araba did not want to see that growing look of irony in Nana Esi's face, nor that worried look of foreboding on Ewurofua's. "I will laugh them sane," she thought, "they take things too seriously." Having promised herself not to rush into what her "sisters" would consider an emotional embranglement, a thicket in the bush, she reduced, at least, her hidden intensity. And alarmed, he did the same. Immediately Nana Esi and Sister Ewurofua were friendly again, were prepared for a truce in the silent war of watching Araba's heart. But this was where there was a miscalculation: this mutual reduction merely led to a profound desire to touch, to hold. To wind the heart down was to fire the breast . . . trees left close and deliberately trimmed would thicken and touch. So that when he finally held her late and rashly right in the sitting room —with a trepidation that fluttered like a wild guinea fowl—he felt he was holding all the world, all the corners in Asylum Down. He had not realized that her skin could command with its very smoothness . . . its physical remoteness, and her waist was round twice, thrice as his hand moved there. "They will come in," she whispered loudly in alarm, pushing him away and holding him close at the same time. "I'll die if my sisters see me . . ." "Sister of mercy," Pol said, babbling, "forgive me, but I can't hold myself back from you." He had a wild look of wonder, almost bordering on terror, on his face. It was a long time since she took tenderness from her handkerchief, and she did, wiping his bewildered, excited face with it. She laughed when he called her, without thinking, sister of innocence, and when he said that his heart would break.

She suddenly saw him as if she had soared far above him, somewhere in the Aburi hills looking down on the nature of love, and had seen that he and his love looked so small that she could contain both, and feel safe, and in control. She pulled herself instinctively apart from him, just in time to escape the sudden arrival of Nana Esi who, without a word and looking profoundly withdrawn, came, took a book and stormed out with a noisy silence. "Time to go," Araba said, looking slightly drawn, the brown of her forehead looking a little gray. Then he slowly said to her, "I wish you were not rich . . . I mean in the heart." When she looked at him, she only just managed to lessen the fire in her eyes, to lessen the fight. "Then your heart—is it burst yet?—would have to be stronger than this!" she said, too loudly.

There was a cough from the bedrooms. When she was seeing him off, hastily, he found it physically impossible to let go of her hand; so she pushed him out to the gate, frowning in mock anger. He said, "I think you are trying to push me out of your life." She just laughed, adjusted her duku, and ran in . . . right into the stare of her grandmother. "I think, my little child, that you owe me

128

something, you owe my spirit a little peace. It may not be long before I die. Give me that little bit of peace . . . that mouse can't give you anything at all . . ." Nana Esi said, her eyes deep and almost tearful. "You have inherited my spirit, don't stand and see me suffer." Don't give me the wrong dawn, she seemed to say. It was years since Nana Esi had cried, and she was fighting hard not to do so now. Araba ran and hugged her, and said gently, "Mamaa panyin, I was going to say that you should allow me to make my mistakes, but there's no need to say this: I'm nowhere near being serious with this man. If there's something, I'll tell you, and if I have to comfort you I will . . ." There was a genuine look of calm on Araba's face as she led Nana Esi to bed, holding her and telling her gently that, "Mamaa panyin, trust me, trust our spirit . . . maybe it's this trust that I want from you . . ." Nana Esi suddenly shouted, "Not with him! You can't marry a laugh." "No, not marry, because—" "Because," broke in Sister Ewurofua suddenly from the kitchen, "because you can't make the same mistakes we made." The three women looked at each other with a silence and a sadness that none could articulate. Then Araba said, taking care to be gentle again: "Watch me—not so close!—but I'll not make this life a mess, there's no nkonkonte in me at all." "Hmm," was all her grandmother said; and a quietness came and sat in the house.

Eventually, at Nana Esi's insistence, Ewurofua went to Dr. Boadi, straight, and told him in a direct way unusual for her that his young man had come often enough to the house, and that he, Boadi, should do his own business himself. At first Dr. Boadi had looked at her in that angularly smiling way he had perfected especially for women: his teeth said secretly yet directly, "I know you have come for something important to you, but I must charm you first, I must hold you." Ewurofua looked at him with scorn, pulling his smile out of shape with the draw of her stare. The smile went back into Dr. Boadi's pocket, and he held it there, for later use. Then she asked him, without any warning, "Did I not get the small impression that you had an interest in Araba?" "Madam, madam, madam! You remind me just now of a certain professor I know . . . who usually goes far too fast for me. Now, relax . . . sit down . . . for me to offer you something. Beer, or something hot?" Boadi said in one breath, feeling intensely attracted to his guest yet trying to maneuver his head out of the tight corner. "Now, as you may know, madam, I usually prefer something much more mature . . . like errrr, like yourself . . . you see . . ." Boadi continued. Ewurofua remained at the wrong side of the present silence, putting her beer down with finality.

Then she decided to go back to her softness, for her own skin suddenly felt hard to her. "Sir," she began, "I thank you in the Ghanaian way for your hospitality. Well, my mission is this . . ." Dr. Boadi misread this change, and moved his chair dangerously close to Ewurofua . . . who without the slightest flicker of the eyes, and with an equally dazzling smile, moved with style onto another chair. "Where I'm now sitting is the east, the east is cooler and better, Dr., don't you agree? Well, as I said my mission is this: your abrantsi, the one you send so often, is overreaching himself at the house . . ." Ewurofua said evenly. "Oh Pol! Don't mind him . . . he sometimes loses all innocence and acts as if he's got something earnest to give to everybody! But he's harmless . . ." Boadi said. Ewurofua in turn interrupted: "Harmless! Well, we'll come to that; but you didn't answer my first question." And her face looked like a sweet stew. Boadi was confused, but was too preoccupied to think about his confusion: he wanted a way of facing and holding his guest actually in his arms, yet did not want to give the impression that he was not interested in her daughter, in case she had miraculously come to offer her to him. He therefore preferred to look ridiculous in the middle of this confusion. He tried different tactics: "Madam, excuse my little vagueness. The commissioner really taxed me for information this morning . . . and he had wanted to see Kojo Pol personally, to warn him to be more careful with future assignments . . ." Boadi had added these words to show the power of his connections, and to hint at his utter control over Pol, in case a real complaint was going to be made about him.

But then he suddenly felt that he should not have mentioned Pol at all: this woman seemed to bring out contradictions in him, so he wanted her, though he felt his intentions were, in his desperation, far too clear to her for any sense of mystery to be maintained and any goal achieved. "Of course, you don't expect me to express interest in your daughter while I'm doing business with both of you, do you? . . . Look, let me tell you the truth . . ." Boadi said, holding any possible lie tightly in his folded arms, "it's *you*, I'm interested in, you, madam!" When he moved his chair closer again, Ewurofua rose, as if to see the time on the wall clock, and again moved on to another chair. She pretended that she had not heard Boadi's confession, and said, "You see, Doctor, your boy wants to make Araba his girlfriend, and we feel he has nothing to offer her. He just makes her laugh, she likes the power of control over him; and maybe his long thinness is attractive. But you must stop him. At once!" Her voice rose, not only out of anger, but also to distract him from his advances toward her. He looked at her wistfully, as if he had not heard what she had said either. When he finally understood what was being said, through the mist of his own desire, he gave a great burst of laughter, and leaning against his guest as if he were not aware of her skin, said, "Pol! Madam, you must be mistaken. Your daughter is of too deep a temper for a piece of dry season twig like Kojo Pol to capture . . . Haahahaha. Of course the boy can be funny without even meaning to be so!" Then he looked thoughtful, remembered Pol's rather strange behavior when Professor Sackey was around, remembering his little remarks of independence. Boadi's sudden smile cut these thoughts from his face, as he caught himself thinking again of ways to detain his guest further. He said, "I'll speak to the young man . . . in fact even the commissioner could say something about this if he finally meets Pol."

Then he moved toward Ewurofua, who suddenly shouted, "Hold it, sir! I am five whole years older than you. Respect that!" But Boadi was already maneuvering his belly around the chairs, Ewurofua dodging him with an agility that was easy for her. Then she said with force, "You would have to leave your belly behind before you can catch an old lady like me. And your behavior has ruined your trust." There was a sudden voice from one of the bedrooms, the voice of Yaaba, asking, "Now, Yaw, what's the sound of moving chairs in the sitting room? Has the visitor gone? I've almost finished dressing . . . I'll come down right now . . ." Ewurofua looked in the direction of the sound, with shock. She asked in disbelief, "So your wife is in, and you are trying all these tricks? Shame!" Boadi had become absolutely calm, as was his strength in any such emergency. Ewurofua left. "Oh, my dear Yaaba, I tripped over a chair . . . I think it's the beer . . . yes the visitor is going," he shouted over almost nonchalantly. But Yaaba come down just in time to hear the "Shame!" and wondered what was happening. "Oh, it's only the echo you heard, my dear, and as you know, echoes tend to be the opposite of what we think we hear. You see we were talking business . . . No, she didn't say shame, she said

131

March . . . that is when one contract ends. She suddenly left because she was upset about her daughter . . ." Boadi said slowly, with his iron confidence, knowing he was, at least, telling an angle of the truth, filling in the pauses with long drafts of beer. Yaaba saw the truth in the pauses, sadly, and felt a sudden and extreme aversion for her husband. She said with surprising venom, "You would have killed me long ago, if I still had my innocence . . ."

Boadi's jaws were like two carelessly written "L's" poised for defense, poised to receive any crisis of abuse. "But Yaaba, you know we don't quarrel these days; we live in a spirit of give-and-take . . ." Boadi ventured with a crouched smile, waiting for the hurled hate. Yaaba shouted, "Yes, I give and you take; and as for the spirit it's dead!" When she was angry, she herself knew that she lost half her ultimate weapon against him, which was her demure beauty and her quiet reasonableness. In a burst of corrective self-control, she prepared her new tears in a most elegant manner . . . she made these the kindliest tears, suddenly dried of accusation and free of pointing guilt: she just washed herself in them, as if he did not exist standing there before her, and dried herself with the most immediate self-comfort in the world. He comforted her, for he knew he no longer had any deeper comfort to give; and she took the comfort, for she in turn knew that it was better to take this something now from him, than to fight with the meaningless weapons of her tears. Ewurofua's car drove off with its quiet accusation. Boadi leaped outside to wave.

And there was Okay Pol standing by the drive blocking this belated, supplicatory wave. "You, too, you are hiding my wave . . . I want the woman to see it! It's good for business!" Boadi roared. Pol looked at him with that new puzzled look, and said nothing. He had a slight maturing of the eyes that suddenly amused Boadi . . . until he remembered the complaint against Pol. "Now, my young man, I fear you are hunting in deep forests, in royal compounds!" he said, his voice seeming to double with a new screech of annoyance. Pol looked at him startled, his neck held back like an angled throw, and suddenly pink-brown like a turkey's before the slaughter, in the sunlight. "What worries you this morning, Uncle?" Pol asked with more than a touch of sarcasm in his voice, "What questions are you asking me? I have just seen Sister Ewurofua drive off in an anger I haven't seen her in before . . ." "Ah, it's because of you, young man!" Boadi said triumphantly, "You, you, you are

132

chasing her precious daughter, you are—quick, go and take pen and paper—canoodling with her, your intention is to co-habit! But, my brother, seriously though, watch out. Don't go and annoy these old ladies, don't go and spoil my business, they will eat you alive. After all, with all these pretty girls in Accra, why choose a rich, unattainable one that I myself have thought twice before even thinking about her! Shieeee, Pol! So under your meek exterior lies a sleeping lion!" Dr. Boadi's laugh took the room and shook it, took his own belly and shook it, but left Okay Pol alone. Pol watched him laugh with a sense of distance, but decided to hide, as usual, directly under Boadi's underestimation of him: "But Doctor, how can I hunt such a woman? You know my life is complicated enough already. How can I take the weight of a woman, a woman made heavier with a car and a house! The truth is . . ." and Pol paused, "the truth is she's making use of me! Of course nothing has happened, and she finds it amusing that I can appear so helpless yet so full of advice!"

Okay Pol walked around the room twice, feigning an intense agitation, and sending his own height inches above his neck. That was a sign of danger that he retained for special occasions. Boadi looked impatient, and asked, "What about your own interest? You've talked about Miss Araba Fynn's motives; but what about your own?" Kojo Pol looked sideways and intently at Dr. Boadi and said, without moving his eyes, "That, Doctor, is my own business." Boadi glared at Pol in disbelief, then shrugged. They gauged the silence, with Pol looking inscrutable. At last Dr. Boadi said, "Business is business; don't step in that house again. At least give me the respect of remembering my interests as well as your own . . ." Okay Pol immediately felt that Dr. Boadi was—suspiciously—being far more reasonable than he felt. Boadi must be planning something with his now still belly. But Pol was not finished; he looked at Boadi as if the latter were a child, and said, "Uncle Boadi, you yourself know you can't stop me from visiting any house in this good country, not even traditionally . . . it's like me telling Kofi Loww not to leave the airport. All of us are guilty; we want more power than we have." A feeling of self-revelation told him this: he was no longer afraid of Dr. Boadi, and even found something faintly ridiculous about him. Pol suddenly said on impulse, "I want to resign at the end of the month. I can't go around chasing another young man who after all is innocent! Doctor, you are not brutal, but if little people like me don't let you know how far you can go, if we don't show you our little acts of courage, you may destroy us, even in your forgetfulness!" Pol's body was bent like a victory sign, like a chief's sign of appreciation for a dancer. He spoke as if he were speaking over barriers of war, his voice so low that nothing, not even doubt, could crawl under it. And he added, "It's a pity that you could not get a more heroic person talking to you now . . . you could take the pepper seriously then . . ." He could feel the garden egg and palm oil, gentle at the back of his throat, and his eyes became triumphantly oval with calm.

Dr. Boadi did not rise from his furious chair; he sat and watched the height of Okay Pol simmer with this blatant confidence. When he opened his mouth to speak, to insult, a profound calm, a raging quiet heat, closed it again. His belly filled with contempt, just where the afternoon snails and the constant beer were; he forgot his superior smoothness, and held the arms of his chair with sudden coarseness. When he rose finally, his sharp L-jaws joined furiously in words. He shouted: "Look you look you, you betrayer, you will tell what you are telling me now to the commissioner! I thought I was training you well when you started to understand me after I picked you more or less out of the bush, out of that immature and ridiculous openness that was always getting you into trouble! I cannot give you permission to resign! How can you resign with all these secrets? We shall see! You know my plans, you know my girls, you know my bank, you know my commissioner. What else? Abua now, tomorrow and forever! And look at the money you've had all these months . . . for this operation, for that operation, and for all I know, you've been chopping me small! You will refund every pesewa if you resign. Is it this woman who's making you like this? Is it that mad man Sackey? Do you need any money? Tell me! We shall see!" Dr. Boadi was approaching Pol with slow threatening steps . . . "Hey! Papa Boadi," Yaaba shouted, rushing in, "what are you doing? Leave him alone! Do you want a scandal on your hands . . ." She rushed between the two men and, with surprising strength, pushed her husband violently back by the belly. Boadi fell with a scream of anger onto the couch. "Woman!" he screamed, "Whose side are you on? Has he charmed you too?" Boadi's attempts to rise looked like a cockroach's when it was on its back. Yaaba looked at him with pity, walked over and held his hand with both sympathy and force. "Look at me," she said. "Look at me, and everything will be all right. I've been calming you all these years, and I'm here to do so now. Don't look at the spilled beer, there are other bottles . . . as you know, hundreds." She gave him, almost ironically, a version of his dazzling smile, beckoning Pol, with a secret hand, to leave. Pol left, throwing back the beckon, taking a last look at the unspeakable anger on Dr. Boadi's face as his wife stroked it and perhaps found nothing gentler underneath.

The outside air took him with relief, pushed him along with his odd walk. Okay Pol felt extraordinary release. He put his fez on with a little skip, his bones swung to unseen drums; though never much of a dancer, he now danced in his walk. He borrowed all the smiling in the streets as he left Legon far behind, ending up at the Liberation Circle, where he ate fried yam and pepper with his small jaws in triumphant rhythm. Okay Pol had been changing in the inner, slowly but faster than the driving of outer events allowed: as he took in and digested the remarks of human bushfires like Professor Sackey, he saw the great distance which was growing between his maturing feelings and the ridiculous and odd tasks he carried out, and the strange situations he found himself in. That little revelation of self—which elders nurtured with rites and ceremonies in the past—continued in him, opening his vistas of experience and emboldening them . . . so that in an intense way, he was both more and less himself. And all this ended up in a bright corner called Araba Fynn.

"Indeed!" he suddenly shouted without meaning whatsoever, "indeed the smell of kelewele will continue to dominate Adabraka! Indeed!" "But Kojo, what are you shouting at?" he suddenly heard a voice ask, as a car drew up. "Araba!" he shouted, so loudly, rushing into Araba Fynn's car, holding her hand so strongly that she could not immediately change gear. He looked at her with discovery and longing; his look slowed her down. But she looked preoccupied. When she smiled, it was as if she were smiling over miles of other territory in her mind. He looked at her with his questions showing. She pushed his doubt back with the slant of her own eyes, and said, "I was looking for you, but I don't know your house . . ." Pol stiffened, as if his shoulders could talk. "What is it?" Araba asked, a little absentmindedly. He spoke again with his shoulders as they narrowed in the car; and his neck pressed his shoulders down in silence. "Araba," he began, looking at her full in the face as she quickly took her eyes off the road, "my house,

135

or should I say my room, would have to be improved before you come there." For her, there was no real silence, only the reverberation of his words. She put on speed, trying to race past her own quick anger. "Watch that goat!" Pol shouted suddenly. And when Araba smiled, this time, she pushed a whole world behind her: she thought that it would now be almost impossible to be serious with him . . . whether she really intended to or not. She remembered his wish that she were not so rich in heart. It was, without warning, unfathomably strange to her that the very person that she thought could carry so much of her—even for herself—could not so far stand her weight.

He looked at her with a sudden appearance of his old innocence, struggling with thoughts that he tried to see in her head. "I'm not afraid of your money," he ventured, hoping he was talking in the right direction, "I'm trying to experience every side of you, that's all . . . that's why I mentioned my room in that way." She drove on past the contradictions, hoping he would not become any more complex about his tiny budding heart: she wanted simplicity from him, she was a one plus one woman in his presence. He was waiting for her to react to him, to bring the shitoh to the kyenam; but her face had taken on that impenetrable indifference . . . which he, thankfully, found much more reassuring, much more familiar. They were back to the uncertainties of the beginning; but the touch of her skin, remembered as the inside of boiled okros, pushed his quiet bewilderment aside, re-created a need to redefine their relationship yet again. Then he suddenly said to himself: if he could defy Dr. Boadi, then he could defy his own heart, for after all perhaps the former took more courage than the latter. He said to her: "My small-businesswoman-danger is growing away from me, so soon!" There was a touch of irony and sadness in his voice, but his smile brightened the car. Trees, memories, oranges and hawkers reflected in, and filled, the right side of the polished car; the sky put its birds, flying, on the speeding roof. The city passed, with all its commotion, through them. They could be sitting on the fastest stools, without being chiefs: Accra passing by seemed to pay homage only to the speed of a heart, basically indifferent, like Araba Fynn's. The slow hearts, like Pol's, were blasted back through the exhaust, had to pick themselves slowly out of the waiting gutters.

When the car finally stopped, as if of its own will, they were both surprised to find themselves parked behind the Black Star

Square, far away in Osu. That structure of history sat in judgment over them, barren and gray; there was no message in the roar of the sea, which sent its breeze to the other side of the warmth between them. Nowhere cool, nowhere wide. He was still expecting a re-action from her, so she said, "Oh," and then said nothing at all; the Os of her eyes were empty. He said at last, "Don't think I want you to commit yourself seriously to me, at the expense of your mothers . . . I know I can't marry you, or anyone like you; but maybe I can help you to grow. I can see you want to grow, I want to help you with my own hunger to grow." She looked at him, as if to say that she did not want any more of his surprises. She asked, "But does your head really live in Ghana? How far do you think your good intentions can take you? Do you think I built my house through good intentions?" She had never said this before, so she stopped, and she thought almost with guilt: it seemed so long since she herself saw her own sense of mercy. It was as if mercy and love did not go together at the beginning, but that one saved the other, if at all, for the end of a relationship.

Now her mercy was in her shoulders, and he held them. He just looked with bewilderment into the sea, he just held her shoul-ders. And as the sky darkened altogether, the sea hid in it, then looked out through its shining waves. The rage in the roaring water went into Pol's eyes. He climbed, with his sudden touch, into her mind, where at last her body was at a sharp angle to his. Over where the weeds stood still by the shouting and climbing Black Star steps, Araba's eyes also stood still. She was only the center of his moving, as he traveled quietly and with apology around her curves; and even the sea was not rounder. "I am too big for you, I am a woman of miles and miles that men can't reach," she said, laughing. Their passion was where the sea joined the sky . . . but she suddenly rose, pushing his thinness away, yet held his hand, as if the hand was a mere pen she could write off so easily. His passion grew with regret, but his hands only made intense patterns around her thinking back. He looked thin and mad. He looked at the back of her distant and lonely head. Nowhere cool, and he suddenly thought: he had to give up trying to understand her. And they drove away, fast, finally fast into Okay Pol's tiny room in Kaneshie.

The room was so neat that the chairs sat with crossed legs; and the walls, pink and impatient about space, wanted to make the room look even smaller. The lace curtain over the door was like solid mist, and swept the songs of the radio into the uncomfortable corner of the bed. And the bed shook with songs. "What an old-fashioned bed!" Araba exclaimed involuntarily, "And is this the room you did not want me to see? But it's nice, simple and neat . . . like a city version of a neat little village room." Pol looked for a double edge in her words and finding none, thought: her sweetness must have come from more than an acre of sugarcane. He had recently caught in himself a new trend: trying to look handsome in any sudden glass window, or standing erect by any bamboo trees as the goats climbed each other in lust. When she caught him at this bit of vanity, her cheeks rose like the mounds on her chest, bringing her smile almost to the junction of love, creating an edge and a roundness to his life. Now Pol looked rather tense as he saw his room being scrutinized. He was trying to engineer his body into something calm, out of its part-crouch part-withdrawal. And this body became subtle: in worry, he bunched himself, shrank himself, so that she could touch more of him at once. There was a rush to please on his face . . . and so he folded this rush, put it in his almost-empty album, and gave it to her with the offer of the traditional seat.

Whenever she brought out a smile he polished it with the light of his own. Yet they both felt, in the quiet regret that held them now, that perhaps everything would pass away between them: she showing this by the defensive touch of indifference at the corners of her mouth, he by the rhythmic rolling of his short neck. "You are overfilling my room," he said suddenly with a laugh, "you are too posh for it!" They both laughed into the foam of two glasses of Club beer. The bottles stood at attention, much like his heart, now. "Would you like to do business?" Araba Fynn suddenly asked Okay Pol. He picked up his face from the floor in surprise; and said more by saying nothing than he would have done with words. And his face looked like a closed cine door, with more going on inside than showed outside it. "Yes," he finally said without thinking, "if only it doesn't get in the way of the love I have for you . . ." She looked at him with a severity that seemed to go beyond his experience. "You have too much innocence, you have too much innocence!" she shouted, as if he had touched some deep drums in her, the music of which disturbed her. As if she had made money almost too soon, or even as if his slowness defined her speed, her quick life, doubly. Then she added more quietly, in compensation for the outburst, but with equal force, "Don't speak of love yet, innocent people like you shouldn't speak of it. You have to do something first, you have to find some of that new Ghana you speak of! And don't forget, you are older than me!"

As Pol looked out of the window in confusion, the groups of light around the buildings looked like expensive necklaces around the necks of very plain women. The beer stayed pushed against one cheek in his mouth. His heart beat faster than his watch. She said, rising, "After all, I can hold you instead of judging you . . ." Pol glowed like the match of love he was about to strike, and there was a starfruit tang in his mouth . . . which he wanted to transfer to hers. "What's all this kissing? You see that in films only . . ." He closed her words with his mouth. And found her long dress magically loose and open. And so it was not impossible to hold a whole world in the hands after all. If his thinness could be a benediction, a libation, then she wanted it. "What a canoe I've got!" Pol suddenly shouted, as he pulled her onto the bed. "Row me then Owura!" Araba said with her best Coast school mind. He held the seven o'clock news at her waist as the radio wasted its words over their moving. Her softness was endless, her cheeks were the same shape as her breasts. And when he was on top of her, he wanted to be under her, and when he was under her he wanted to be on top of her. This confusion made their love explode, finally scattering like orange seeds in a head-low sky. Then she lay there, frighteningly clear-eyed; she was something impossible he had managed to get at last, but still not quite attained. Her frown was a gift. Okay Pol felt tremendously mature when he was horizontal. Lazily, he said, "Your grandmother is here watching us!" She jerked up sideways, then lay down again with a soft laugh. He went on, "Your mothers don't like me now. I can see the risk you are taking . . ." She just looked at him, holding him by the long middle of his pole. And his words thinned down in her silence. When she shivered it was from the unease of finding herself in a man's room, and lying down at that. And as she rose her whole past rose with her. It shook in her breasts. Pol suddenly became an afterthought, and she went back a few years when she knew that men were only there to be conquered in business deals . . . Makola style. Her past left her as quickly as it came. And she looked at Pol lying on the bed with her touch still in his eyes. Why was he so *definite* about her, she thought. Then she brightened: how thankful it was after all to be going through the experience she had just gone through with a man whom others thought ridiculous, and who thus did not excite a great feeling of responsibility from her; but who nevertheless, she felt, had to be protected. When she finally left, she certainly wanted to see him again. And perhaps again.

Chapter 11

By the edge of the skyline where the trotros took people to and from poverty, to and from different levels of gari, the cock crowed into the city. And the city held the neck of the crow. The early November mist was stuck to grass and gutter, roof and valley, like endless chewing gum locally made . . . the mist would not be imported. Over where the early risers walked, the quiet street branched into the long thighs of a woman sleeping. Accra was a cola nut in the mouth of a Mallam hurrying to spit it out. And the sun was bad: at last it found the shoulders to push aside the lazy mist . . . mist slept a slow sleep . . . and its rays caressed thousands of legs, brown and unbrown, shapely and unshapely. The cries of goats steadied the concrete in a bank building, and pushed Kofi Loww in no particular direction but certainly toward his own sense of being. The glass of the new office block was trying desperately to throw off its reflection of the horror of gutters . . . and twin buildings near Opera cinema reflected two completely different images of Loww; but for a few seconds these two crushed images, cheap in the glass, defined him completely. He was a sleeping snail, a man of quiet trance, so that both his legs were exactly in the middle of his walking . . . the first two-legged man with one middle leg in Accra. Loww, ayekoooo! he carried his head gently this morning for he had goals in it, he had restlessness in it.

As he walked he seemed to be binding parts of the city together with his clumsy broad feet: the old iron sheets of Nima shouted their rust back to the Ringway, where the cars pulled and stretched the yawn of the old dual roads between two exhausted Circles,

141

Liberation and Redemption . . . the rust was a gift from rain, a gift from the neglect of politics. As he rounded Danquah Circle, he could read the roars of the sea already in the mouth of Osu, parts of which—so near the Castle—looked as if they were stolen from Jamestown, down to the last shallow gap of gutter. The invisible binding string of Loww's feet now tripped into Ridge where the streets lined up against each other like giant squares of a draftsboard, neat, and painted. And on by the sane architecture of the asylum, the tall neems chattered senselessly. From a distance, as Loww squinted his eyes, whole horizons would fit into an orange; all the grandeur in the cathedrals, mansions, trees and even markets would fit into fruit.

Two years at the university as a diploma student had increased his need to graze in the quieter savannas of the mind. Thus he could bite the pasture hard there, without professors returning his bite. He cut up his life into little pieces, and did not quite know which piece to pick up first: if he did not reenter university, the sun would only shine through opaque glass and through his father's tears and worry; if he continued to drift through the streets finding aimless hours so healing, so full of herbs, then they would not understand that even in this city there were quiet men—sometimes even noisy ones—who did not make money or status an obsession; if he thought he would not marry Adwoa then the unborn generations would talk with the most accusing innocence. They were not yet born, these children, yet they were defending, through their kind mother, their right to exist. They shouted to his popylonkwe to legalize itself and work . . . work through Adwoa. For months after he met Adwoa Adde, he had tried to keep his little son, Ahomka, a secret from her: he did not want her to accuse him of being satisfied with his one child—a child with someone else at that. Also, since his own mother, for all these years, had made him wary of women, he was determined to use his little bright son to shock Adwoa away from himself, if this became necessary, by suddenly revealing Ahomka's existence. But Adwoa Adde got to know, very quietly, and neither accused him nor loved him less. He merely became more complex in her eyes, and her love moved like a slow ray to cover his son too.

At first he could not understand the width of this love, and—with a strange suspicion—tried to both avoid her and test her at the same time. But little Ahomka had seen this with all his seven

142

years, holding his father with both hands and saying, "Papa, don't let Auntie Adwoa go, I love her better than my own mama." "So do I," Loww would answer. "Then look after, look after her . . . I want a brother!" Ahomka would shout with a serious kind of merriment. Ahomka's own mother, Akosua Badu, was a big fat woman in her big fat thirties whom Loww met by beer and shared the regret of a pregnancy with, later in sober light. She always cooked slowly, ate slowly, traded slowly, but spent money very fast. When she finally came and left Ahomka with Kofi Loww, and Erzuah, she had shouted, "So you think you are going to study books? What money can you get from books? For me I need money . . . take your son! How can I feed him with books?" And the strangest thing was that Erzuah had immediately decided to look after the little boy himself, no relatives, no maidservants and no word abuse for Akosua Badu. Ahomka had grown strong and lively by his adoring grandfather, bringing light into the house.

But now, Kofi Loww walked on, past all the uncovered food for sale, past the jolly kaklo, the gari, the fish, the tomatoes, the cooked rice and stew, past all the flies that few sellers covered anything from. He stopped, thinking: the flies, the gutters, and the latrines had become a symbol far more powerful than all the excuses, including poverty, made from them. He caught, with impudent ease, a fly on the smoked fish he was about to buy. "Owula," laughed the seller, "I hope you don't want a reduction for catching the fly . . . after all it's extra meat!" Loww frowned, catching a second one and dropping it, with his money, on the woman's lap. "Hey, Owula! Are you trying to charm me with flies or what? Am I the only one with flies? Take that look of disgust off your face, and look around you: there are millions of them! After all, you don't have to buy anything, you can take it or leave it, fly or no fly," shouted the seller with growing anger. Then she shouted, with the extra energy reserved for certain afterthoughts, "And there's a fly on your beard, you chief flycatcher! You can't even control them on your own beard! Goway you!" She had dropped her Ga and picked up English for her last exclamation. She was dying to release her arsenal of insults onto Loww, but she eventually felt the laughter of her fellow sellers against him was enough; besides he looked to her rather mad, and you did not waste anger on mad people.

Loww walked on with complete indifference, their laughter dropping from his shoulders like an old shirt slung forgetfully on the back and fallen. He dragged their sound on with his slow feet: he could never understand a people who bathed so often, yet were so actively indifferent to dust and flies on their market food, so careless about spit and latrines. But of course you did not have your European plagues here! At comparable stages, Ghanaians had been far more fastidious than most people, he thought, with their villages constantly swept with fast brooms but slow history. He shouted suddenly without thinking, "Why don't you all bathe your streets and buildings as often as you bathe your bodies!" Some thought he was one of the usual street-corner preachers, others thought he was drunk; yet most walked on with that passing tolerance reserved for those they thought less fortunate than themselves. Kofi Loww regained his silence, after a penultimate grunt by the open stews and sewers. In that corner the bofrots lightened with sunlight, they brightened their country; the hundreds of sails you could have on the gutters!—for in them was a sort of libation of horror. Rows of smoked tuna fish touched head and tail, head and tail, above two Mammy mouths speaking extremely fast, so fat they drove their words straight out of tune, straight out of Loww's mind . . . which was empty but filling up irresistibly with Makola ginger; five hundred kenkeys rolling up the one-way street faster than Loww, and with their sheer number—without even moving; and the large round spheres, wooden trays for this endless variety of wares, could teach them all how to carry the north, the east, the south and the west of Ghana, for they held whole worlds. Over there where the shea-butter oiled his mind, Loww blocked a world of onions with his back, blocked out the purple mourning of the skins, the tears of the sharp flesh; and as he blocked and unblocked the thousandth world of other things, others did the same, at greater speed; there were sparks as he witnessed the infinite crash of different goals, different flesh, different speeds, different directions. And colors moved and crossed to such an extent, in so many patterns, that they were equal to distance, they solidified distance; somebody's fate hung above the spread of koobi, somebody's love was sealed in banku forever, after one hundred white-ball disappointments. At the four corners of Makola number one, four safety pins failed to hold down the profits, failed to stop the rise of steam from kenkey, boiled rice, Hausa koko and waakyi . . . and slowest of all, the smoke from quietly burning lives.

As Loww went inside the walls of the market, he glimpsed a

familiar face full of foreboding. After trying to place the face, he forgot about it, and walked on into that intense compound of haggling, where the walls shook but still held the chattering and bantering of women, still crawled about in sad rectangles witnessing the secrets of life and selling. Loww isolated all the hands holding and passing money—did Adwoa Adde not accuse him of isolating his heart?—and he saw more sadness there than in the eyes: as if the hands held answers to questions that the eyes would not ask. And he got lost in all this movement broken only by the stillness of stopping to buy. His mind was dazed by this tremendous concentration of energy, as if he had left parts of himself at each tray he passed; so that he felt a curious lightness, so that things invaded him. This table of yoyi was the beginning of one journey, the assorted powder was the end of another. The fresh headkerchiefs wrapped the secret heads of thousands of women, thousands of unseen ancestors.

The fat woman by the thin woman wished to sell only so much of her fat . . . the rest of her fat was part of the foundation of the market, was part of the center of this country. And there was more laughter than smiling, as Loww picked his way through the cynical sounds which ate at his heart with the innocence of things remembered years back yet far beyond nostalgia. Makola was a vast and kaleidoscopic kente, soiled, trodden, torn to bits and whole at the same time. And the color of its dirt should have formed the national flag. But Kofi Loww suddenly wished for the color of gray, felt like a heap of old bola about to burn. If only the flies were a medium of exchange, he would change his soul one time, he would push out that mogya inhabiting him. One charcoal seller's eyes were like his own, but this only increased his sense of isolation. The ground rolled with economics. Would this be solid market flesh he was breathing? When she died—the seller suddenly joked to him—she should be buried in a tin of sardine, so that she could be profitable, even in death. Loww looked at the vast straw hat under which she joked, wondering how much sly searching the sun would have to do to find her hard smiling face forever shaded.

He stood still caught in perfect African time—time that existed in any dimension—and blocking the paths of other sellers with this same time that brought ancestors to the market, that touched the eyes of sellers and buyers now, that moved beyond those yet to be born. "Agooooo!" came the impatient voices, their hands finally pushing him out of the way. He moved yet retained this perfect time stubbornly, dragging it to buy tangerines slowly . . . the stillness was in the buying: he saw all sorts of dead faces moving among the living: she that seller of shea-butter, who finally died of grief because she could not have children; she that ginger seller whose mouth outchattered all others and who died of overeating and secret drinking; look at Ama come back, and wearing the borrowed nose of her long-featured senior sister still living, as if even eternity could be borrowed freeeeee. "These groundnuts are fifty years old!" someone shouted from the disgust of the past. And when Loww looked for the source of the voice he only saw the terror of three indistinct sisters struggling to grow up, to learn the ruthlessness of making money. Poor Abena died in salt, she rolled her death into it, and—how sad how sad—she had wanted to sell sugar all along. They teased her that the husband she had wanted, and never got, would always prefer sugar to her salt . . . and when she laughed it was to stop herself from crying. "Naa Dee-ooooo!" a seller shouted with her historical mouth, as the plantain queen passed, "Naa Dee, things are getting hard-oooo, and very soon it will be the hunger that will hoot at us! Can't you put your boogie, afro-queenie-queenie power under this problem and push it to the top? Oh! Only your 504-oooo! But these days, you people are neglecting the dead, you are forgetting the bones you used to honor. And how can I go home to an unweeded graveyard covered in the insult of cassava . . . the roots of cassava in my bones indeed! Naa Dee-oooooooo, Naa Dee." Loww could wrap the sadness in his head with the driest corn leaves, and people would hear the sorrow as the leaves rustled in the market of his head. Then a shout cut through his mood: "Owula! You are bringing sadness to every seller you go to. We don't want that here! Why don't you just buy what you want and leave us alone! I swear that you look like a harbinger of ghosts . . . after all my five years as a head teacher was only a period of training for Makola!" This speaker was alive, and she sent her laughter to the others as they sent theirs back to her. Kofi Loww turned around, and just as he turned around, there was a tap on his shoulder where his face had been; he turned again, as if the world would not stop going round and round.

Facing him was a policeman whose continentally large mouth was open in advance, and was getting ready to form words and throw them in his direction: "Private Mahamadu here, sah, under orders to beg you to meet officers outside; officers de for car, sah. Your name be Kofi Loww, I lie? No palaver, sah, officer want quiet talk. Your eyes look hot, sah." Loww glimpsed a look of triumph on the face of a seller, as if her suspicions had been vindicated. Her underchin could hold water from a whole cooler, it was so deep, so satisfied. "Go, go, go, go! Go where you belong!" she shouted, "Go with the policeman." The policeman's sudden salute cut Loww's doubt into two: to move away quickly and lose this uniformed mouth, or to say Yes and move along with this whole horse process, with these spying eyes continually following him. Private Mahamadu looked like a smoked mudfish in the skin; but his eyes were so bright above the brown of his cola teeth that they looked completely disembodied and alone, more or less in midair, below the lush gray overgrowth of his hair . . . hair that rebelliously pushed itself back out under the cap, in such a way that the only thing that could temporarily yet constantly hide it was a salute.

Kofi Loww followed him out without a word in this harvest of salutes. Mahamadu repeated confidently, "Your eyes be hot, sah!" "Not as hot as your mouth," Loww replied, as if he had not opened his own mouth at all. "You say what, sah?" Mahamadu asked, amazed that he had at last got a response from Loww. "Where is the officer?" Loww asked. Mahamadu blocked the sun with a sprung salute, and pointed to a fine white Peugeot caravan on its mark, getting set, and not yet going. One man inside was more or less fatter than the car: Dr. Boadi; another man was almost the length of it: Kojo Okay Pol, frowning and looking most uncomfortable; and the last man in the car was Sergeant Kwami, a short man with long steps, and eyes like stagnant ponds full of absolutely sly fish. Okay Pol brightened immediately when he saw Loww, but the latter did not return his smile. Dr. Boadi got out of the car after he had put his dazzling smile, for show, out of the window first; but it merely slid unnoticed to Loww's feet. "So this is the famous Mr. Loww!" Boadi shouted, ostentatiously, rubbing his belly with vigor, and readjusting and reshining his smile for effect. Kofi Loww looked at him with a profound lack of interest. Okay Pol went through his second smile, this time directing it at his own inner sense of satisfaction with Kofi Loww's underawed style before Dr. Boadi. Somebody coughed. And at the end of the cough was a C. K. Mann high life blending with a car's horn. "Ei, that beautiful song can't move for proverbs," Sergeant Kwami said to no one in particular, moving onto his toes to look that little bit taller.

"If you want to talk to me," Loww said at last, "we will have to walk over toward the Anglican cathedral, in High Street. I can't come inside your car." "So you can be definite after all!" Boadi exclaimed with mock surprise. Private Mahamadu had gone across the road to buy Embassy cigarettes, and they could see that his walk was a quick march; and even from the back of Mahamadu's head Loww could sense the mouth preparing itself for a smoke. Sergeant Kwami looked at Kofi Loww with a combination of intimidation and doubt in his eyes, as if asking himself whether this strange man should be bullied or pitied. "Get in," Kwami said to Loww with sudden roughness. Kojo Pol instinctively moved beside Loww, feeling calm, but fighting to keep his heartbeats steady. Loww had immediately noticed a change in Pol: the latter looked far more confident, and was clearly trying to be friendly and even protective. Pol began, "Dr. Boadi, you promised there would be no force, and you know that is why I came . . ." "So that rich young lady has really and truly made you masterful, eh, Kojo?" Dr. Boadi said with a laugh, and with a self-assurance that showed he was in complete command, "and of course as you know, when I promise something I do it. Sergeant! We will walk, as the young man says! Perhaps I can even flatten my belly a bit, eh! I am Dr. Boadi—haven't you seen me on the campus?—and I have one foot in politics, and one in the lecture rooms at Legon."

But Kofi Loww was already walking ahead, his beard pushing Accra aside rhythmically as he walked with Okay Pol behind him. "Look, slow down! Ewurade, I'm getting old! The only time I walk fast now is when I'm after something beautiful—or money!" Boadi shouted from behind with his short breathless strides. Sergeant Kwami gave a nasal chuckle so quiet that you would think it came from his shadow; and even though his short-long steps could easily overtake Boadi, he kept dutifully behind him . . . so that the two middle-aged men behind defined the thin height of the two young men in front. And thus brightly and oddly Accra sloped backward down the heads of the four men. Private Mahamadu had now taken the car ahead, filling it expansively with the smoke he had just bought. Would it were mist from the Aburi hills, Kofi Loww thought as the car whizzed past, off its mark at last. Eventually the walkers came together into an odd group just beyond Glamour Stores. "Look at the people," Sergeant Kwami said, "look at them,

148

they sell everything except God! And if He sleeps just for a minute, He'll find Himself on a tray in Makola, being sold above the controlled price!" Four men laughing was no joke, for it was difficult for the laughter to move at different heights. Kofi Loww closed his mouth abruptly, closed his laugh and around Post Office Square he took his silence. His voice was sometimes so low that you could not hear the Kofi under it. "What did you say?" asked Pol, looking at Loww. "I was saying that years and years ahead the sea will claim this cathedral . . ." Loww replied without looking up. The twelve o'clock post office siren added an urgency, in Pol's ears, to what Loww had just said; as if the years and years had become now and now, and the sea was rising into the pews with its roars louder than the organ's. "So it was you I saw in the market?" Loww asked Pol, this time looking up. "I had insisted, to them, on seeing the expression on your face before we could talk to you," Pol replied, and halted, expecting Loww to ask why. When no question came, he added: "I hear you are a man of expressions, that's why . . . that's why I inspected your face to see if any talking was possible . . ."

When the four men finally reached the cathedral grounds, the old neem trees had already trapped the sea breeze and were sharing it in a miserly way among strangers in the compound; and when they sat down on the benches, the leaves spoke in gusts. The sudden determination that lay on Loww's face did not belong there; the open, wide eyes seemed to hold on to some innocence in spite of the heavy eyebrows. They were all looking at him as he stared out to sea. His nose, gentle at the bridge, took short wing at the crossroads of the nostrils, and carried the innocence further till it stopped at the wide firm mouth; his mouth was the limit of his world, especially when it was shut. He now returned their gaze until Dr. Boadi smiled. It was obvious that Dr. Boadi could afford to pay the tooth allowance that his fine frequent smiles demanded. His cheeks were a fund. And Mahamadu snored in the sleeping car, smiling in his sleep. "Look, we are all Ghanaians," Boadi began, "we all know that the right hand bathes the left hand, the fingers are useless without the thumb. We should help each other. This young man, Kofi Loww, with us here, looks kind enough, but from his eyes I can see that he has a hunger for meaning and principle—which may make things difficult for his wife if he has any! It may even make things difficult for us here . . ." "Oh, no!"

Sergeant Kwami shouted suddenly, "A cathedral is a place of compromise . . . and he asked us to come here!" Boadi's eye closed Kwami's mouth, quickly with a stern look. Worry traveled up and down the angular chin of Sergeant Kwami: one side of his face wanted to take charge of the entire proceedings; the other side did not want to annoy Dr. Boadi at all. And since this confusion prevented him from using his whole face at once, he had to use mainly the latter, the safer half, sometimes filling it with a compressed energy that almost made it swell above the dangerous half.

Before Dr. Boadi could speak, Kofi Loww asked him abruptly, "What is it that you want from me?" "Good, good, we are now getting somewhere; we can at least see that we're dealing with a Ghanaian who wants to know what we want," Dr. Boadi said with exaggerated conviction, avoiding Loww and looking rather at Pol with his eyes though not with his mind. He continued: "Are you a Socialist boy? No? Well, I'm also for the ordinary Ghanaian. Would you accept Krobo Edusei's definition of socialism? Mr. Loww, I'm asking you a question! He says socialism is: you chop some and I also chop some! I know what he means philosophically. Well, I also really want to be where ordinary Ghanians are, all the time; I want to see their messy problems, their little humanities, their lust for money. I don't want to be abstract. I want to see all Ghanaians one by one . . . some in daylight, some in the dark, eh! Hahaha! I want to help them with their marriage problems. Ghanaians should eat more . . . and the more they eat the more I can eat! No, no, I'm not being cynical. I am telling you a fact of Ghanaian life: the principles follow the food! Hahaha! And you, young man—I don't understand why the young are so serious these days—are you with the ordinary Ghanaian or are you not? You asked me what I want from you . . . well, just a little understanding. With your education you could completely misinterpret what you saw at the airport, you could feed our enemies with something dangerous . . ."

Dr. Boadi's stomach was punctual: when he was stressing a point with it, it met his lecturing elbows at exactly the same angle and time as when he was making any other series of movements with it at any time, yesterday or last year. His ears were cocked, listening to his own words to Loww; and the sun made his hair look a wild and deep brown. And the sound of High Street cars pressed his words down intermittently with engine and tire . . .

150

Loww wished the round rubber there would rub out these words altogether. The different types of silence in their heads lined up like soldiers at attention: at ease came only when someone spoke. When Kofi Loww rose he pushed the silence up, and then broke it with his head: "Dr. Boadi, I don't even know who your enemies are. I am thinking of other things . . . and as I said, no one can force me to do something—like leave an airport—that I don't want to do, in my own country. I say in my own country! That's all I said to Kojo Pol here . . . and I think he now sees the sense in it." Pol looked away at the mention of the airport: that incident seemed so far from what he was now trying to grow into. Sergeant Kwami also rose, shouting, "You lie! how can you say that you don't know the enemy? My information is that you have been trying to make contact with counterrevolutionaries! Tell us the truth. Is it money you want? I know your type, you want us to fill your quietness with money! You see, Doctor, I have him trapped! He will soon run away and leave his mysterious sandals behind. And look how old they are! . . ."

He turned with triumph to Dr. Boadi, looking for vindication. This time Boadi's smile was dangerous: Kwami saw a darkness in it, something more than a warning in it: as if the future had gone into Boadi's mouth and was being released in disastrous smiles backward in time toward him, Kwami. But this fear of Boadi only made him talk more: "I have interrogated people like him so often! Now he has the confidence because he thinks his eyes are reflecting the calm of the sea . . . and look at this other young man protecting him. They must be accomplices after all! Bone to bone in crime, yes! Permit me, Doctor, to arrest both of them on suspicions of sabotage! Long live the Supreme Military Council!" Sergeant Kwami's great agitation made his eyes bulge and almost stand out from his face. His own hands grasped the worried world together, and crystals of sweat covered the shame on his forehead. He suddenly stood at attention with his head bowed. But Dr. Boadi, unlistening, had already pulled a reluctant Loww to one side, and was asking him, "How much money will you have to keep quiet? As for the rest at the airport we have traced them all and given them 'drink' already! But you are much more educated, and so we are somewhat afraid of you, you see!" Kofi Loww looked with pity at Dr. Boadi standing there like a squat fufu man, with that conspiratorial air that blew from the nether hip. Loww suddenly said with a smile,

"I want ten thousand . . ." "Eiii!" shouted Boadi with his hands on what was left of his hips, "so this boy likes money after all! Kwami, you were right! But you are asking for too much . . . ten thousand cedis!" Kojo Pol looked puzzled and disappointed, and was trying to avoid Loww's eyes. "Dr. Boadi, I can't reduce it at all; it's all or nothing!" Loww said with an unusual animation. There was a pause, during which Dr. Boadi felt a fine levitation that, after all, Kofi Loww was a good Ghanaian: full of greed and ready to please this greed! Then Loww added slowly, "Of course, Dr. Boadi, you know that it is ten thousand leaves I want! Leaves!"

Boadi could not move. He looked with eyes of thunder at Loww. His body was exactly like banku, taken out still steaming, and profoundly round and still. "Wicked, wicked wicked!" screamed Sergeant Kwami, regaining his courage, "I told you so!" Dr. Boadi was rarely puzzled, but he was today, he was rooted to confusion. The neem trees raged, they kept all the mouths there shut, and all the eyes wide open except for Kofi Loww's: his were half-closed with tiredness after all the walking. He raised his head and called out to Boadi, "Don't forget to count the leaves! You can't trust the banks with cross-checking leaves . . ." As Loww walked away, Dr. Boadi at last found his tongue: "Walk on, walk on! I have come here myself, and this is what you tell me. Yoooo, fine! If I come cantankerous and charging at you the next time, don't blame me . . ." Sergeant Kwami was bursting with impatience, and had walked astride Loww as the latter walked on. "You, you are not too strong for me! I challenge you to anything. If the authorities had listened to me, you would have been a prison graduate long ago! Anyone who is afraid of money is also afraid of me! Why can't you look at me straight in the face?" As he gripped Loww's wrist the latter suddenly flicked the sergeant's arm, pushing him off at the same time. Kwami crashed with a curse to the ground, as Pol ran up beside Loww. Private Mahamadu was getting out of the car, sleepily. "Get back in the car, and let's go," Boadi ordered him, pulling Kwami roughly and with surprising strength into the car.

Barclays Bank stood like a loaf unsliced, calm and freshly whitened; but all their shadows, dancing up the wall as they went to the road, were like ants eating out the loaf . . . the white calm did not stretch to the core. The hatred on Sergeant Kwami's face changed the shape of his own eyes as he stared at the disappearing back of Kofi Loww, a back hidden and then unhidden by Kojo Pol, who was trying to catch up with him. "Go with them. Finish your business with them . . . maybe they owe you some unpaid money . . ." Loww shouted back to Pol, intending no sarcasm. But Pol stood, half-angry, half-guilty, balancing his thinness with a steady stare at Loww. But Loww was already round the corner. And a car passed between this corner and Pol's uncertainties. Then he pushed forward, shouting with a smile to Loww, "My friend, I'll find your house. We'll talk. Boadi is nothing . . ." Kofi Loww waved back without turning around. Kojo Okay Pol stood with his fez in his hand, his head suddenly full of the presence of Araba Fynn; this presence propelled his stillness. Then he walked right past Boadi's car which had drawn up to pick him up. He saw Boadi's strange smile and did not know what to make of it. But he did not really care either . . .

Chapter 12

To the disappointment of her flying crew of black and white sisters, Adwoa Adde did not do much with her grandmother's gift passed on so lovingly to her: she became a benevolent witch flying over Accra like an aerial sister of mercy. Her friend, Sally Soon, was in the distance. She was an English witch sent over on a secret assignment against Ghana, but she had now fallen in love with Ghanaians, and had thus almost neutralized her own powers: the weaker she became the more she became Sally Sooner, the weakest she became the most she became Sally Soonest. She usually traveled the degrees of her surname. But she was now huddling behind the moon, crying over her own contradictions. Adwoa Adde had thrown a handkerchief into the universe for her, and promised to return to comfort her later. Accra was low below Adwoa. She made her prayers shine high, and went up to a particular piece of night sky and enshrined them there. Prayers were lights, with or without answers; they were for her a rest—but always moving—in a limitlessly dizzy sky. So her gift was running out of the original blood given to it; she had to beware of the best blood finishing in the sunset. Thus she had already started the rituals of her own loss of power, and the red powdered pepper on her absent body began them. She refused to talk on top of the silk cotton tree, her sunsum rejected the fiery gift; and her last upside down flight barely cleared the tops of trees and buildings in Accra. She was now nearer the lives she soared above at first, and the people began to talk to the human part of her even as she flew with her own time on her own back again . . .

She saw that Kwaku Dua the fitter's business had almost collapsed over the last few weeks: his apprentice boys stole almost everything in sight, including his daily takings. But he had been too busy drinking to notice anything until it was almost too late. As Adwoa Adde passed he asked her, "Sister, Sister, how can I send my boys away? Now that I've taught them all the repair tricks, they will take the customers away with them. I've taught them everything in sight, from overhauling to bleeding the brakes. And the other day—you would never believe it—my chief apprentice went to the house of the girl I'm about to marry, and asked her to advise me to drink and smoke less. He called me Mr. Jot and Molasses to her face. Sister, can you imagine this! When I got to hear of this I slapped him pasaaaa! He didn't do anything at first; in fact he pretended nothing had happened. A few days later he went off 'sick' just when I had a good contract with a government department to overhaul some cars. Then when he came back he 'accidentally' dropped a crankshaft on my finger and it's still swollen, my swollen finger is the biggest thing in Odorna. But the best time to borrow money for a spare-parts store is when you have a swollen finger: I was successful because I needed double sympathy, and Wofa Kwame understood me . . . he hadn't yet heard of my drinking! Ewiase . . . So my chief apprentice finally left me when he saw the first signs of a new success. He paid his apprentice fees with a flourish and left with one other boy . . . and they set up a workshop right opposite me. But too late, boys! I had already changed. I stopped drinking because of my liver, and also because of my new girl who was strong paaa. I can't resist her koraaa. The old one had left me in disgust, and was now bellyful with someone else's pikin. But, Sister, you wouldn't believe that she tried to come back, even with her belly! I think she had seen the spare-parts shop. So I told her to go and put her belly down now now now . . . if she could do the impossible then I would take her back. She went with her tears flowing behind her. As for me I am justice! I did most of the repairs myself, for I didn't want to lose any more customers to my own boys. Soon I competed my ex-chief apprentice out of business. I was kind to the myselfs, they need sympathy and I need their money; most of them cry in the inside when they come with their car troubles. Things are getting hard, Oh! Mansa my new girl comes to the workshop sometimes to inspect my progress. The girl is tough paaa. Some people think she controls me—they call her sheboss or Mansa controller—but she is helping me t-o-t-a-l-l-y! I've paid Wofa his money now, and I'm now bluffing quietly through life, I'm building a house under Mansa's supervision. Her only complaint is that whenever she's advising me, I always want to go to bed . . . with her. Sister forgive me, but I can't resist kindness when it is put together with flesh! But Sister, I got a bit worried one day when my old friend Alhaji brought in a car very early in the morning for me to dismantle for him. I couldn't say No because Mansa wasn't there to give me strength. I did it for Alhaji. But later on when I told Mansa she told me not to do it again. But when Alhaji came again I couldn't resist the huge money he offered. When I went home Mansa forced me to go to the police, in case the cars were stolen. The police thought I was mad! They said Alhaji was heavy, was untouchable; besides where was the proof? For me, I don't make myself know-know man, so I crawled away like a cockroach you've stepped on but didn't quite get. When the next car came, Mansa was there. She faced Alhaji squarely and demanded the papers on the car. 'Ei, she-boss!' Alhaji laughed. Then with a wicked expression on his face, he produced the papers, and everything was perfect, everything was in order. So we had no choice. I did the car again, but still Mansa was not happy: 'One day, he'll bring your own car for you to take apart!' she said. There she goes advising again! Mansa, you know what happens to me when you advise me! . . . and I was wondering whether my laugh was longer than my hard thing! Sister, Alhaji suddenly broke my thoughts by shouting, 'I respect maself, I respect maself!' His beard was the watchman to his face, I swear. And look at him, his jaws are always maidservant to his cola! But I said nothing and Mansa said nothing. Alhaji and me, we trust each other too too mech for words. Sister, say something! or is your mouth sewn to the sky or what? . . ."

The city seemed to be spinning under Adwoa Adde's low flight, Adabraka ended up at Odokor, Akokofoto had dragged itself to Labadi; and some made love to the wrong wives without even noticing. Adwoa hovered above manager Agyemang's house . . .

"Ei, madam Adwoa, it's my hypertension, my manager's high BP. Agyemang's BP! I can hardly even greet you! Whenever it comes like this I get images of ants; ants under, over and above me. The other day when I mentioned BP to my messenger, he said: 'Sorry sah, there was no gas there when I passed BP this morning!'

I thought at first that he was laughing over my impending fatalities! BP gas by my heart! With pain like this I'm sure I'll die twice at least. It all began when I was building my house: the workers stole me right and left, and it wasn't right that they left me so stolen. I mean, I had already suffered to get my degree and my diploma in marketing, so it wasn't fair to suffer twice. I get terrified to see myself outlined in the faces of some of my colleagues: some had it easy but most of us had it so hard! It's the bitterness that gave me the BP, high variety! All my children went to boarding school, so I didn't even have the pleasure of seeing them grow up. So the house was controlled by squeezed-faced maids and a face-squeezed wife. My wife is killing me with respect, yes *respect*! I can see that she hates me smallllll. Her dreams of wealth when she married me reluctantly years ago have been shattered, now in her middle age. I know she secretly sits and cries over her buried dreams, poor woman. And her hate is so polite! In the house she exercises no initiative. She will ask 'Please what will we eat tomorrow?' 'Please the maidservant has misbehaved so should she go?' I'm expecting her to ask one day soon: 'Please here is a knife, should I stick it into your ailing heart?' So the maids laugh behind our backs. It's possible they spit into our soup before we eat and laugh afterward. Have pity on me, madam! You see, I overheard the older maid-servant tell the younger one that I went out one night, maybe to a girlfriend's house—no comment, madam, no comment—and after almost dying of a heart attack managed to struggle home; and that when I was changing, my wife noticed that I was wearing ladies', excuse-me-to-say, panties, and that my wife looked at them calmly and said to me, 'Please you have brought home the wrong pants.' These maidservants are bad! I admit that I was drunk one night, but I certainly don't think such a wicked story was true. I am a prisoner to such stories in my own house, and what a sad house! And Ama my wife never supplemented the home budget: 'Please I see to the needs of the maidservants.' So I usually took my suffering to my work, where they teased me whisperingly about my colo clothes. For that I care less! If I wear obey-the-wind trousers what business is it of theirs? And as for the parting in my hair, the number of rumors that have traveled its path! On top of all this the chief manager doesn't like me, he doesn't want to promote me. Well, as far as I'm concerned, I'm lucky compared to him: his wife towers above him, obliterating his shadow and making his forehead damp;

and the back of his head comes to the same ridiculous point as his tiny buttocks! They say the woman married him for his tiny buttocks, because they can push paaaaa! Sorry, madam, I shouldn't embarrass you like this. But I must tell the truth: they also say that whenever the male workers want anything from the chief manager, they go to his wife. If they lie down before her—and I mean literally lie down, haha—then the wife will order the husband to grant their requests. Ei, pcople are bad, Oooh! Ghanaians have the busiest tongues in the world! And madam, I have one great fear: I have a feeling, usually after I've eaten okros, that my doctor is not interested in me, and that he is telling me lies about my health just to calm me down. You see, when I see him, he says with a smile that looks like the afterlife, 'You better see me again.' I ask him, 'When do I see you again, Doctor?' He replies triumphantly, 'Certainly before you get better, and certainly not after you've eaten okros.' Confused, I ask, boldly, 'What's wrong with me, Doctor, actually? Should I try traditional medicine? Am I going to live?' He looks gravely at me, his Aberdeen training shining through his Northern eyes, and says, 'Don't get excited, Agyemang. Your skin is looking young again since you came to me. Have faith in me, I will keep you alive if God is willing . . .' 'And if He's not willing?' The doctor then says nothing. He just writes out a prescription and sends his greetings to my wife, adding with a smile, 'Come again, you are improving.' Madam, can't you cure me from where you are? Cure me of my wife, then you can proceed on to my BP gas! Madam . . ."

Adwoa flew on shivering straight above Akosua Mainoo who was slipping out to her boy without her mother's knowledge. She had tied her sleeping cloth loose and dangerous over her breasts. When she saw Adwoa Adde, her fine fresh face froze in its alata samina: she was terrified of Adwoa's light, wondering whether it was her junior mother lately dead and presently rising to frighten her. Akosua rushed back to her room, and was just crawling back onto her mat when, as she slowly looked up with a different kind of terror, she saw the base of the legs of her mother standing like two odum trees in a stormy forest. Akosua gave a short scream, and was again running out of the house when Adwoa Adde barred the way with her light. There was a sudden shift of consciousness in Akosua as she suddenly perceived the world to be a series of backward-running forward-running devils, devils of light, devils of trees. She knelt down in terrified abandonment; but the sound of a car passing and its driver cursing somebody brought the ordinary world back to her. She got her usual courage back, and shouted to Adwoa . . .

"Auntie Adwoa of the lowering sky, my mother hates me; she's kept me out of my last stages at school, and she never gives me praise, not even when I sell all her bofrot for her. I know the secret! She wanted me to be a boy, and yet she's also jealous of my fine skin. I plait her hair, I gossip with her, and she still hates me! She says I talk about her cooking, and that it's me that's turned my father against her food. Well, in a way it's true, because my father prefers my cooking, but whose fault is that? I prefer the sea to the river but I don't gain anything by blaming the river. I am only sixteen, but I have my sense and I have my temper. I used to read a lot at school, even though I didn't understand everything. But for my mother I understand her! If she keeps troubling me, one day I'll tell the whole truth, I'll let the whole cloth fall! And I can talk to a boy under the moon if I want. I like Kwesi, that handsome boy with the funny laughter, yes I'll say it! Look at my mother going away, look at her. Auntie Adwoa, forgive the way I talk, but my mother wants me to die so that she can get all the attention I get. Isn't that sad? My own mother! Let me drop my cloth and you can see how beautiful I am. You see, my brown skin can make a lot of velvet! And as for my shape, it's not only Kwesi that I'll charm with it. Auntie, is it not good to be frank at my age? Here we have never been happy together. Oh, let me cover myself again! It's only my father that makes me happy, it's only him that I stay in this house for. But soon I have to stop being my own mother's servant. Auntie, don't try to bring her back, let her fall, let her collapse! What do I care. Yes, I have tears in my eyes, and I'm trying to hold her hand as she covers her face. But I don't love her and she doesn't love me. It's just pity and it's just habit that make me want to help her, just as you get used to the shape of a gnarled tree wanted and unwanted in a compound. And look at her pushing my hand away. Okay! if she pushes it to the east, this hand of mine, I will find comfort easily in the west. And I have dried my tears now now now! After all, every lake has a dry season. Auntie, as for you, I can't hide anything from you: my mother is sitting here almost fainting because I have an awful secret of hers in my head; and now I'm going to break my head open and let you see it. She

159

will hate me all the more, but I don't care! You see I once saw her with a man, yes with a man! She can go ahead and beat me. My back is stronger than any stick. Here is my skin, mother, beat it beat it! I will talk through the beating. I will shame you even as you strike me! I saw her lying with Kwame Oppong, a young boy only three years older than me! Yes, she can swear any oath! I like to see her lies traveling so fast and shameful from her mouth. When we went to farm that day, she left me as usual to do all the hoeing, all the clearing. But on this day she was so long sleeping under the nearby trees that I went to look. I didn't find her, I hoped that a snake had swallowed her! And if I had to rescue her, I would exact a price before I did so! You see, Auntie, I heard some leaves dropping, then I heard the grass cutters chewing the grass, I heard an akyinkyina at the palm nuts; the forest was moving in my head, I didn't know old trees liked young girls! Trees are bad! I was thinking that the sky was lower than usual, as if it had descended to tell me something. Then I heard some strange noises under another tree; I thought it was the roots shouting with double mouths for water. I felt like shouting for help myself . . . memaameeeeee! mew-uoooooo! and I didn't want to be taken away by any dwarfs. But I had courage, I took up a stick and walked slowly toward the sound. Then I saw a sight that made me shake with shock! What a taboo, what they were doing was forbidden outside. There was my mother lying under this young man, and this man was a young boy! So I stared and cleaned my eyes again and again, then I started to beat them with this stick I had. And they couldn't part for the beating. They clung closer and closer. Then I spat on them and left. I don't know why she always tries to stop me standing out under the moon; she has no right. I swore not to tell my father, for he would break down. I am my father's bodyguard. For you Auntie, I have told you, and I will tell you one hundred times just to watch my mother's shame. Yet I'll tell no one else, unless she really tries to kill me one day. Auntie, help me, I still need a mother. I want to be innocent and good again. Don't you see tears beyond my years coming out of my eyes? . . ."

And the tall tree with the oil of the city on its bark covered the moon with its smoky leaves. The exhaust smoke from the huge car with the sad voice passed into the mouth of Beni Baidoo's dog and his donkey moved about in circles. Adwoa Adde saw Sally Soon crying into the airplanes; there were hailstones in her handkerchief. She couldn't be seen in the sky for her blondness. Sally ate long-distance steak and kidney pudding. There was colonial history in the stars where she sat. But Adwoa went on, a little impatient to do her work, to brush the trees with her belly. Old Beni Baidoo's mouth opened at the same time as his dog's mouth . . .

"Awura Adwoa, you see my own dog barking at me? It saw all the world barking at me, so it's doing the same. I am a funny old man, my knees touch. I couldn't look after my children at school, so they avoid me as much as possible. They feed me all right, but they don't want to see me. They leave me food like they leave a dog food. But my donkey is fooler than I am . . . The lines and wrinkles on my skin are the same as the patterns on my favorite cloths, which I can't buy. I love what I can't buy, because it gives me so much power to see my own powerlessness. At my age I live for opposites. I became a letter writer, when I first retired, but now my language is in the old trunk box. Awura, not that I feel sorry for myself or for anybody. No. I walk with too much of a stoop for that. I smile too quickly and too much for that. And I've done what I wanted to do: I wanted to be a clerk, and I was a clerk. So in that way I was a success. After all, if a fool wants to be a fool, let him! But I wish I knew from the beginning, from the time I served the white officers, that the life of an ordinary clerk was so useless, so empty. At my funeral, I know that my own children will be ashamed of me and my life. They hoped for a successful father, and they didn't get one. Sometimes, with their friends, they see me and pretend they haven't seen me. Their mother was a good head teacher, but she's dead now; I know even now she hates me for surviving her! She cursed me for this, on her deathbed! Sometimes my dog and me we share the same sores, it's amazing, isn't it? You see, it's we Fantes: sometimes we don't look after our old; they are so busy with their kyenam, their concerts, their tea and their professors! Awura, I am desperate for recognition, even though I realize there's nothing to recognize. My shabby clothes cover a shabby heart. You do me a favor by listening to me. Do my words sound like words from the tomb? Awura, I know something of the dead: the dead are full of tricks: a few hours before dawn, they send their eyes up to an inch above the earth, and the graveyards shine with the light of dead eyes, for those who have eyes to see such things. Brown eyes above brown earth, that's also my life! But the great thing is that I represent so many lives like mine: if I had money, and hence a little more education, a little more space above the clerk's breathing world, then I would have more style, I could even be dealing with computers and things or making wells in faraway villages . . . Sad, Awura, sad! But what really worries me at times is that my shabbiness breaks a few cultural taboos: as an old man, with so much experience, so much wandering on the very soils of Ghana, I cannot maintain the neatness that is supposed to stretch to the spirit. I can't afford the expense of keeping a neat and modest spirit. And for this I can't sleep: the bags under my eyes are big enough to carry all the worries in my head. After all when I die, I want to be buried largely traditionally, not in some strange limbo by an empty tin of ideal milk full of my own loneliness. Hey, Awura why don't we have a double tot each! Your waist reminds me of my youth, even when I see it upside down. All that softness in Ghana in my youth has become harder. And let me tell you a secret: when I get money, I intend to sneak toward Libo and pay for a touch of woman's softness. I will pay for softness to exercise my own hardness. I will pay for a resurrection of the past, for a little exercise, for my popylonkwe! I am an old man boogie and after all what's the difference between erection and resurrection? People move away from me because of my displaced energy. But this moving away is sometimes part of my strength! I love their rejection, because I know and love the fact that one day we will all grow old! For sometimes I get so lonely that I can't even remember the smell of my dog's tongue. That Afro girl, with the marks-set go-go backeepers will one day sleep *holding her own wrinkles*! Awura, don't go, hold meeeeeeeee! . . . Even if my village will not work, I will pursue my friends, I will help my Adwoa."

Beni Baidoo vanished and left the saliva at the corners of his mouth dangerously close. His laugh was fresh but his donkey was feverish. Adwoa Adde was beginning to feel the venom of other witches in her bones. Sally Soon was conducting an entirely technological choir in the heavens, she was losing herself in the minor scales of a fish without a key to the sea. She was the sole singer above waves she could not turn. The witches were tying their knots and throwing their black powder. They pressurized Adwoa's blood, they wanted to pump her blood out high in the secret blue sky; and make a meal with her pretty bones. Abena saw the besieged Adwoa Adde and shouted to her . . .

"My mother, my flying mother has come! Mother, come and

162

save me from Kwabena Kusi, his jealousy is ruining my business. You know me, Abena Donkor. We have been married eight years now, with two children; but because of my bread baking I had to be unfaithful once. It's bad, but I had to do it to get the flour. And when I eventually got this flour my own flower of innocence was dead. I don't know whether Kusi sensed this guilt, for it seemed that in any matter that came up, I was wrong. And he won't let me talk to any men at all. I have already been to the fetish priest, and slaughtered a sheep, with other rituals, to make up for my sin. But I sometimes feel the strain of trying to be extra-nice for so long, in compensation. My own guilty kindness is, Is, IS a big load on my head, but I prefer this to Kusi's hearing the secret. One day when I was out with him to buy sandals for the children, a wholesale officer dealing with flour rushed across the street to me, hugged me, greeting me like an ancestor come back again, and asked me to come the next day for my yeast. Kusi almost disgraced me by the way he began to walk with fight in his eyes, toward the man; but something made him stop, and instead he stared in a very strange way at me, as if he were seeing me for the first time. Fine! So I also started seeing him for the first time. Four eyes with a new look! The children were caught in the strange silence later in the house. In spite of this Kusi insisted on going with me to collect the yeast. When I refused, he in turn refused to eat my food. I began to wonder where he was eating, because he was beginning to put on weight. Sadly, both of us became especially attentive to the children; but this did not help them, for I could see bewilderment grow on their faces. And they became more difficult to control. They would not listen to Mama, they would not listen to Papa. In spite of the money I was making, I could feel my little world swaying dangerously to the left. So far, my money couldn't protect my heart. So I made more in desperation, and lavished everything on the children, as if I was forcing them to take sides. Kusi was getting more and more impossible: when it rained, he was dry with his words, and when it was dry his words rained down, usually in abuse. Then I secretly built a house over the weeks. I built a house over his silence. I hoped that a shock or a surprise would change him. One day, after I had told the children of my plan, we waited, and waited, and waited. He did not come for three days and three nights; and it was the nights I was worried about, frankly. Then we were told he was in hospital: he had had an accident with a

163

young woman in a hired car. Ewurade! Since he only broke one arm—the woman broke her nose, hmmm!—I seized my chance: his Ghana-gallivanting, his away games finally got rid of my guilt; and I looked after him so well. How he loves the new house! Mother, a miracle has happened, Kusi and I are one again! . . ."

Kofi Kobi threw his moonlit shadow around the corner in exasperation: he had lost yet another wife: she had left him for the man with the long longer longest legs. These leg reasons were getting too much. Neither of the families was in favor of the marriage in the first place, so each accepted any reason as grounds for divorce. The only advantage Kobi had—apart from the payment of drink money—was that he was looking impenetrably handsome that day, so that his wife, already on the divorce bus, was torn with doubt, was dying to jump off; if only to hold his ridiculously smooth neck. To protect her emotions she at last managed to slap a piece of imagined ugliness on his jutting chin, in the form of its exaggerated length, and then that was that. They jumped out of each other's lives simultaneously. And Kofi Kobi landed almost straightaway into the waiting lap of Akua Nyamekye. Immediately, she looked at his doubtfully long legs, with her desire hidden expertly in the look. Kofi Kobi cast his eyes up long-sufferingly to Adwoa Adde, who was suddenly replaced by Sally Soon with two breasts against two planets and holding a pen and a notebook.

"Ei, Maame Broni, the love in this universe is a matter of inspecting legs. I lie?" Kobi asked. "Can you speak a little more loudly please, the universe is very noisy tonight," Sally Sooner said, wearily. Kofi Kobi picked up his education, wrapped it around his waist, and said as if in a dream, "Maame, I think we have a brik notebook witch, I lie?" "Oh, this is very significant. You have used 'I lie' twice. When you do that all the one-way streets in the sky go double. And your skin, all that palm oil has made it a bridge to other skins," Sally Soonest answered, her smile broadest and stretching between two moons. Akua Nyamekye saw nothing, and thought her newfound love was going mad. "Are you trying to tell me that your legs can talk?" Akua asked. "Besides," she added quickly, "how can a man with such long legs make money?" There was a pause during which Adwoa Adde rolled and blotted out Sally Soon, who did not mind, for her name was a bird that flew three times, each with a different call, a different degree. "Oh, Ohemaa, you have come just when I was finding your friend interesting. But you know all my secrets," Kobi said with a smile. Adwoa Adde smiled back with difficulty, for she was still losing height. Akua Nyamekye persisted: "Look at your legs, one is browner than the other. Which one is meant for me? If you give me the right answer, then I'll know we will last together." Kofi Kobi looked at Adwoa Adde again, his exasperation back on his face: "Ohemaa, one woman said my legs were too short, another said they were too long; now, this one is saying that one outbrowns the other. Where do I go from here? Should I walk on my hands to confuse them? Once I swore that the next woman I got, I would quickly talk about *her* legs before she got around to talking about mine. But her eyes when she came were so beautiful that my own couldn't leave hers, couldn't lower themselves down to her legs. So she started the leg inspection first. But, for this one, this Akua, I want to give her a try." "Look at my legs," Akua said without warning, "one of them is quite different. The one you prefer will love you, and the other one will look after our love." "Our love?" Kofi Kobi asked suspiciously, "I haven't committed myself yet." "That doesn't matter," she said with a laugh, "I like all that brown all over you. It's the African style." Kobi was confused but threw off his confusion immediately with this: "When your longer leg is long I like it, when your shorter one is short I like it." Akua Nyamekye rushed to Kofi Kobi, hugged him and shouted, "You've passed your middle school leaving leg test! You've passed the love! You've passed the Ghana love logologo! you are more than a standard seven scholar!"

Kofi Kobi stood there proudly while he was being hugged, as if he were renting his skin to Akua. Thank God I have someone worthy to worship me at last, he thought. "C'mon, stop standing there as if you are being worshiped or something! Return my love, you long-long man!" Akua broke in, pushing him into the room, "And leave your mosquitoes outside, we can't have a beautiful man like you and a beautiful woman like me suffering bites! Kofi Kobi, let's gooooooo!" Akua Nyamekye wrapped herself around Kofi Kobi, like some ruler that constantly measured the inches of his love. "You can go ahead and measure me. I am every tailor's delight! And it may be that I may have to immediately marry you," was all Kofi Kobi could say. And he had completely forgotten all about Adwoa Adde. So when he did remember her, he ran out half-naked and waved twice into the universe: one for Adwoa, one for Sally. He did not hear Sally Soon say to Adwoa Adde: "Adwoa, can you

165

transfer the copyright of your aerial history of Ghana to me? I would love, just *love* to be famous through the people of Ghana!"

They both laughed the laughter of tipper trucks: it carried all the worry behind them and dumped it in some bola far away. The planets were the dancing hearts of vulnerable witches. Accra could harm the hearts of beings hundreds of feet up in the sky. Accra be sweet-ooooo; only, avoid the history, avoid the gutters. When Adwoa Adde ended up finally at her house, she saw Amina standing at her door, waiting to enter with 1976. Her father had thrown her out. Adwoa took her in with her own tall puzzled look, Adwoa was completely exhausted and she had left Sally Soon asleep suspended in the sky.

Chapter 13

The tail of the church rat bisecting the middle of the pews made the biggest cross; the same tail gathered shadows, sudden shafts of light, and all other linear things, and dragged them in rodent holiness toward the circular altar. God's Word crawled. The rat was now at the center of the empty SS church, and was shifting this center as if the church were movable, as if other walls, other beams, other windows could instantly appear and retain the rat at the center wherever it went. Silence bred a new architecture. The church was dizzy with this movement. When Osofo rose early that cool January morning, God rose with him and put some fire in his hands. As he prayed by the outside walls his words scattered into the church, moving the rat out with their force. Words prowled around the running rat. Osofo took the worries and troubles of the absent flock and pressed them against the morning walls; and the walls touched them as they raced toward the ear of the sky, toward the ear of God. Last night's drum, dance and song still lay inside the church, calm, as Osofo entered it with broom and reverence. Then as the morning wore on, the sufferers came; suffering broken marriages, poverty, disease, witchery, shame and hopelessness. He laid his hands on them with such zeal, such intensity, that some of them were frightened by him. Different shrubs took in and gave out different prayers to Osofo as he sometimes pulled at their leaves in semitrance. While Bishop Budu calmed and cajoled the sick, Osofo overwhelmed them. The bishop's clothes, his lavender, and his utter satisfaction with his relationship with his flock drew out a different world of healing. But the flock would wonder: how many times had

Osofo burned his own head? With his changing moods, his un-
predictable preaching, his trances and his passion for selling Bibles?
He roamed over airports, markets and football parks with God by
his cassock, and he was filled with a burning desire to keep the
faithful uncomfortable, to make the comfortable faith shiver for a
new beginning. Somebody thought: Osofo's passion was just like
roast plantain kept on the ashes too long.

Osofo ended his healing with the announcement that the extension to the church should move more quickly than it was moving. It was now time for the Weekly Exchanges between priest and
congregation, which formed part of the church's ritual. "The building should not move too quickly at all," someone shouted with
annoyance. Osofo retorted, grimacing with impatience, "If God is
saving you, would you say he should not save you too quickly?"
A member replied, his high voice moving fast: "But before we give
ourselves totally to the water in God's moving hands, we ourselves
must have some surviving to do, even before God's hands move
again; besides the water we choose may be too deep to begin with.
After all we've got to make things a little easier for God. If we
move too fast we may rush past Him as He takes his afternoon
sleep, even if He sleeps with one eye open; and after all His work
is hard enough already." Osofo rose and put his enormous hands
together in exasperation, saying: "My Brother, do you understand
what you are saying? You should know that God's speed is lim-
itless!" "Look," the old man cut in cruelly, "some of us have families to feed, we can't preach at concerts and parks all day . . ."

Bishop Budu, sensing tempers rising beyond bounds, raised his
hands with a smile and said, "God is a man of many cars. Some
are big and fast, and others like myself are slow and deliberate.
Give according to the size of your pocket or according to the end
of your tied cloth. If Osofo will use your offerings like a fast trotro
toward completing our extension, then God and all of us will be
happy." First of all there was laughter, then there were murmurs
of approval. Osofo, trying to calm down, took his peace under the
papaw trees. But other deeper questions were not solved for him.
So he climbed a high neem tree in the church grounds—four acres
of fruit, crosses, trees, goats and vegetables—and started to preach
loudly and without care for any ears that may be listening: "And
so if you think the church is facing west, I think on the contrary,
that it is facing east. Have you ever seen the importance of okros

to Jesus? When you catch a herb young and find its uses, then you have put your heart as close to this earth here and now as you should. Away with your daily plans for food. You are all lost in food! How many fat fetish priests have you seen? Is God fat? You are here to improve your spirit. Look at this branch shaking, shaking in the direction of Christ! Which way do you shake? You love rumors, you love funerals, you love ludo, you love drafts! What's all this? If you really want me to pray before you, then give me the spiritual speed I want! Where is our African Bible? There is too much lavender and beauty here! Go to the concerts, go to the parks; then you see the sort of lives we are witnessing! We are looking in while thousands of eyes are looking out! We will miss our own eyes! Where is the search that began this church? Go on, say it: I am in the wrong place! I am a desert in your fine gardens. But I know those of you who suffer with me. And I love you all, I love the fufu you eat! If you think you can't tolerate me, then bum me. After all, your law fills this big compound. Burn me!"

When Osofo finally looked down, his eyes met the calm face of Bishop Budu. The ground widened with Budu's smile. No one else was there. "Brother," Budu said, "let me go and call the delegation that the members left behind, to ask you a few questions." Before Osofo could speak, the bishop had left, and he returned almost immediately with a group of five members. "Why up a tree?" one brother asked abruptly, getting strength from the strange smile that he thought he saw on Bishop Budu's face. "There are some people whose eyes cannot see through trees." Osofo stood stiff and silent halfway down the tree. "I'm an old woman," a sister began, "will you put me on your back and take me up the tree to listen to you? You have shown me something I have not seen before, Osofo! You see you are making my voice shake, an old woman like me. I need peace!" And a young brother asked almost before the old sister had finished, "And isn't God everywhere? You are always talking about libation. Can you pour libation from a tree? Won't the wind carry away the drink from the mouths of ancestors? Osofo, we don't want the young ones to see you disgrace yourself like this. Sorry I've used 'disgrace,' but I think this is the truth. Wake up, brother!" "Osofo, you need a wife!" another brother declared flatly. Bishop Budu's eyes twinkled at this, and he held his hands together in prayer. "Osofo," yet another voice said, "you sometimes remind me of palm-nut soup, the real abenkwan. But

169

it's your fufu I'm doubtful about: it rises up too high and too bold, and I think it's too hard. I prefer a softer fufu, if you ask me!" Osofo had been climbing down slowly through the thicket of words and leaves. He was shaking with anger, but all their hands remained in prayer, in defensive prayer. They knelt and continued to talk to Osofo in the same way: "People climbed trees to see Jesus; Jesus didn't climb trees to see people. Ah! Osofo paa! He needs both hands of God to direct him. Sometimes I think your water boils too fast for us; your coal pot can boil a whole river!" "Is this an attack? Is this an attack?" Osofo asked with the quietness of the deepest anger.

Before he could say more, Budu rose and demanded silence with the slant of his eyes. His silks were hard with concentration. He began: "The tree is a good thing. Osofo may be trying to say that to be nearer God we must be on a higher plane, and this height I see as a height of the heart, a height of the soul. There are neither trees nor even enough crosses for all of us to climb here. Some of us can lie down, some of us can sit. We shall some day meet some of the high demands of Osofo, for I know there are enough hearts striving toward the height of purity! From this day we shall take a branch into a corner of the church as a symbol of the upliftment that we need. And we will wave our love to God with the leaves. We will have a new item of worship with this branch. I am thinking this is what Osofo wants: instant ritual." There was not a single trace of irony on the bishop's face as he said this last phrase. He in fact now looked slightly absentminded. Then he added emphatically, "And God oversee Osofo for he is still our engine of the church." Osofo had held his anger down by the soles of his sandals. He prayed for the patience that let gari rise with the temptation of water, yet stop rising just at the right level. The bishop burst into song, and the whole compound was in song. Some threw flowers at Osofo while he prayed, still with an air of defiance. The drums came, the dancing came, the handkerchiefs waved, all below the rustling of leaves. Osofo suddenly rose and hugged Budu. The latter asked him with a smile that told more than the lips it came from, "How many more tests do you want to pass? Be patient with them. When I go they are yours in Christ." Osofo went with his sharp strides to his house wringing his enormous hands.

But in the times ahead, what eventually calmed the complaints of the flock was Osofo's growing gift for laying on hands and healing.

Old Man Quartey, who had made a strong stand against Osofo's eccentricities, was put in a deeply ambivalent position when he brought a sick nephew to the church. He had tried to bring the boy in when Osofo was out, but Osofo was in: he had returned unexpectedly from Labadi. Osofo saw the weak, wasted boy, and also saw the uneasy look on the old man's face. He went over to them near the first cross, and said, "Old man, why didn't you tell me this before? I was with you yesterday and you did not say anything. Does your boy get fits? Yes, I can tell. He needs God's attention right now." Old Man Quartey waited a few seconds, as if in deep thought, as if full of hate for Osofo yet unable to show this openly. "Well, well," Osofo said almost playfully, "you were not trying to avoid me were you? Forget that you hate me, and leave your boy to the hand of God." Quartey opened his mouth to speak, but just shook his head and looked away. Osofo knelt before the sick boy, and said brusquely to Quartey, "Leave us now but get water for bathing him." The boy's mother, standing close to the old man, started to cry, "I have brought him into this world for nothing! He is going to die." Osofo looked at her with pity and concentration, saying, "Never anticipate God. Now move away with your crying!" Osofo went behind three crosses, and called God; Osofo went behind four crosses and called Jesus. Then he rushed back from the fifth cross, lifted the boy gently, and asked him, "Which side of Jesus is hot, which side of Jesus is cold? I can tell by looking at your hands that you are very good at alokoto. You won't die, I can see God's light in your eyes." Little Quaye wished that his body belonged to another boy, so that the pain in his head could, at least, be shared. But he felt at home with this quick, squat, friendly man. Quaye said weakly, "I'm sick now, I can't play alokoto, and my mother says I will die." "You won't die, you won't die," Osofo almost shouted, holding his own chin in chinned prayer. He took Quaye's hands and brought them together gently. "There," Osofo said, "there's no space between your hands for any sickness to pass through."

Suddenly Osofo's eyes opened wide, and his mouth moved at great speed, praying in a mixture of Twi and English: "God is coming, God is sending his angels to you, little Quaye. God, owner of this earth, this is my child, I look at you with the middle of my soul for the beginning and the end are already finished with worry. Take my life instead, I give you my crying in the wilderness, I give you my useless bones. God, you have seen this child of yours run and play, cry and work. Give him back his movement. I give these herbs to you for blessing, so that when I use them they know which wound to heal, which blood to rush through. I give you for a second blessing this new incense mixed with herbs. God, God, three times God!" As Osofo prayed, Quaye opened his eyes with a feeling of utter weakness, his hands shivering under Osofo's. He saw that a few fire ants had gathered on the sandals of Osofo. He tried to tell him, but he couldn't move his mouth. When Osofo finally saw what he was trying to say, he just smiled at the ants on his sandals, though he felt the pain of their bites.

Osofo finally rose, in great sweat, and Quaye noticed the tiny drops of blood where the ants had been, with a few claws still embedded there. Osofo looked at Quaye and smiled again, but Quaye could not return the smile, no movement could stretch the corners of his mouth; though he had absolute confidence in the white cassock standing before him with this Osofo in it. "You will stay with us for a few days, my son. I can see that you and I are not afraid at all. I will play with you soon. After all, we've beaten the ants, so what else is left!" Osofo said, then turned with a look of utter impatience to Quartey and the boy's mother. Osofo did not speak; he just stared straight at Quartey. When Quartey finally moved his eyes away, Osofo said severely, "Leave him with me for two days; if he doesn't get better then you can try elsewhere." He had said this quietly enough for Quaye not to hear, though the boy was now fast asleep. Quartey suddenly bowed and left. Quaye's mother, who did not belong to the church, fell at Osofo's feet, crying and imploring that he should heal her son. "Get up woman! It's not me that heals, it's the heavens! Go and eat, go and dry your tears," Osofo shouted, without taking his eyes from Quaye's face. Old Man Quartey came back glowering, wanting to say something to Osofo, but Osofo spoke first: "The bishop's trances would not be useful here, in this case. Did Bishop Budu not tell you this? I'm sure he did!" Quaye's mother now pulled the old man away, asking him, "Don't you want my boy to live? Give the man peace to cure him, Ah!" Osofo did not wait. He had already lifted Quaye gently, and was walking with him to his little house.

Osofo prayed and administered herbs the whole night, sweating and muttering, sometimes rushing into the second room to fill it with desperation and supplication. He thought: if the weight of this prayer and these herbs cannot hold God's mercy for this boy then we have to try something lesser than God Himself . . . the doctor, yet again. The next day Quaye slept, waking up only to ask for oranges and milk, which Osofo mixed with herbs shown him by his own father. Quaye had only one fit that night, shaking desperately under the small bright eyes of Osofo. On the third day, Quaye could talk a little, and smiled widely, his face weary but rested. He asked for guavas. Osofo thanked God that whole morning, ringing his bell in praise every hour, and then repainting the nearest Cross so much whiter. The Smiling Saint had given his love to Quaye, to the church. Under the palm branches suddenly cut, the songs spread in praise. Old Man Quartey lost his ambivalent feelings toward Osofo for a while, controlling the cold cut of his lip, and blessing Osofo whenever he saw him. Bishop Budu, who had not been well himself for a few days, came up to Osofo and held him without speaking. Osofo saw, also without words, that the only way to make his little innovations possible was to have this easy almost totally worldly man anchored there beside him, yes even ahead of him, giving him, Osofo, a weight to pull against, a light against which he tested his dark and inexplicable moods. The two men made a bond, there and then, to push God's work on and on and on, together, but alone if necessary. They were still huddled in God when Quaye walked up with a small bag, and announced that they should tell him what they were talking about, for he also wanted to be an Osofo, and that he was now going to stay on the compound. Then Quaye added as an afterthought, with his face so serious: "I think healing is easy enough for me to learn."

Chapter 14

The snail of the small rain took the path of September past itself
and on to other months, past the speed with which ½-Allotey was
trying to make a living and a life. The moisture then was the
understanding in his life: it took the dryness out of his lack of
answers to the questions of change that he sought. The grasshoppers
jumped over the world, leaping onto the bush to bite his farms in
small fast concentrations of teeth. And the sudden gusts of harmattan told a different story, pushing his feet harder against the
shrugging shoulders of the hills. When he toiled, part of his head,
part of his heart raged over questions of fetish, farm, fate and man.
He was feeling himself odd and ridiculous this morning, like so
many other mornings. Why did he uproot himself from his own
haunted lands?—full of spirits, yes, but familiar too. Why did he
end up sloping his back constantly against the sky as he cleared
land, same slope of hill, same slope of back? And when he was
confused he would hoe this sky for answers—the skyline could be
the earthline. A row of boundary shrubbery behind his hut stopped
at a flattened mound on which the guinea grass had thinned out,
rushing into the muffled frogs singing a song in quick moss. The
akyinkyina's cry joined together the sad horizons, heavy with long-
spaced trees, trees waving him on past his own perdition. And yet
this bird's wings, desperately like his own sunsum, made its flying
like a series of short embraces of a willing sky. Everything was
brown and gray with dust, but the vast greens could shake this off
in any burst of sunlight, in any burst of mood. Everything was
short wings, short rise. When ½-Allotey screamed and complained

to fate, the hills shared the useless sound among their mounds and merely restored the silence which he now carried on his back, almost tripping over the giant grip of the roots of trees. Over to Allotey's left the cassava stalks hid each other, sometimes creating amazingly long unbroken lines on the horizon. The clump of wild banana remained wilder, scattering the suffering in its inedible fingers and swinging its aloof silent, purple horn.

Yet Allotey's fish and beans grew, which he sometimes regretted since the little success made his roots go slowly deeper into this desolate place. The more fish and beans he supplied to Legon, in small amounts, the more he believed that Professor Sackey carried a mad restlessness that could eventually lead to disaster. He found himself consciously separating his fate from Sackey's, sometimes changing the time of meetings, or even avoiding them altogether by taking the produce to Legon in Sackey's absence. It brought a smile to ½-Allotey's face again to think that at Legon they thought he was leading an interesting life, a life of "traditional" searching. Trees enjoyed him, made fun of him then protected him, but to say that his life was interesting would have to mean something far easier and far more answerable than he could see. Allotey sneezed into the hard earth, putting on his old batakari with a grunt, his enormous shoulders working solidly, like rocks holding and guarding the whole plain. He looked like the son of trees, bending and weeding among the vast trunks.

As he looked to the east across the small ridge on the senior hill he saw the certainty of dislodged stones rushing down in full stops punctuating his life, scattering the birds in an uprush of wings. The birds, soft against these stones and countering their downward drop with the sharp height that their wings gave, restored his sense of doubt. This was nothing like the doubt of stars—it was less cosmic—but much more like the doubt in the belly: he lived with it when the harvest failed, he lived with it when he decided to throw away his sense of stagnation. All that stagnation around him bogged him down, Ah. And for ½-Allotey the more doubt he stored, the more compelling became his need to make a decision of deep ripples, even pulling up more implications than he needed to, a decision that by the nature of its depth, contained its own doubt even at the point of being made. He planted his beans, his corn, his cassava, leaving the usual regular spaces like deliberate lengths of uncertainty, sometimes rushing about the trees, seeing which ones could

175

truly absorb the wide spaces in his heart. "It is the insects, it is the insects," he shouted to the hills. "They want to take my manhood! My ex-wife is an insect! They don't want me to make a comfortable life in the bush, where my spirit is!"

½-Allotey looked calmly at his friend, the hut, whose thatched hat could not hold back all the rain, when it came, at its heaviest. Sometimes he would hold the shoulders of this hut that he himself built, hoping that the little history he was going through—no matter how ridiculous it looked to another part of his brain—was being witnessed by the eyes of the small windows. The different browns and greens came at him with different whispers, each a diversity that did not make a whole with the other; and when he was really tired he almost closed his eyes away from the desolation of God's plenty country. He was waiting for the coming dusk to give a democracy of color to the shouting infinity around him. As the wild hens cried, he took their cries and shaped them, so that they could enter the quiet of his mind; the beaks, thus changed, becoming themselves the symbol for the utter quiet and cunning of this bird. "Let them hear your wild cry!" Allotey shouted, wiping dust the color of dusk from his big forehead, where one frown led to another and another. Then as he suddenly smiled the frowns were driven away fast, by the stretching skin. His calm body seemed to take in, and not reflect, more of the lessening light. The crickets sang with their legs, and as he slept under the power of the trees, in his watching hut stuck in the stony wound of the side of the crouching hill, he asked himself in a dream: did he have the courage to keep house and to keep farm in these strange and lonely places? The darkness was heavy, almost too heavy for dreams, except when dreams were full of questions. And the only light that challenged it when the moon was asleep was the kerosene lamp with its one dull eye shining one way . . .

In the morning there was no trace of questions. Early birds cleared the ears. The sun's legs crawled over the earth, and the barks shone. ½-Allotey threw handfuls of small stones at the small birds eating his beans, and the morning was in his throw. And at this time, everything seemed smaller: during the night, the hills had sprung down to the valleys to press and press down the low grass, the low height; and when they rose almost too late and staggered up again they seemed smaller, they had lost some bush, they had left below a valley of free bush. After sweeping, he fetched water

from the stream below; and he was startled by how big and searching he saw his own eyes in the clear water, even with the traces of
mosquito bites under them. In his surprise he decided to leave his
eyes in the stream, for they were safer there; and it was only when
he rereached the top of the hill, after the stream's glare disappeared
behind the trees, that he saw his eyes back in his face. Then he saw
that these eyes had become more complex than they were: each leaf
beyond had a story, each stalk had a jutting presence, and they all
spoke to him, and to him only. He suddenly shouted without thinking, "Who borrowed my eyes?" The tops of the giant trees were
not telling the truth: the rustling was too quiet for the time of
morning. The truth behind the borrowing of his eyes lay higher
now than necessary; for no tree kept a man's eyes long, especially
when snatched in secret.

½-Allotey stood by his hut, staring with a squint at the narrow
road climbing its own space so slowly. He saw a smaller car behind
the climbing, and the car looked angrier than the slopes pulling it:
it stopped its winding, and almost overtook the road it was traveling
on, the exhaust pipe snarled in reply to the silence. Now who would
be passing this way at this time? Allotey thought. Oh, was this not
Agya Sackey in his blue Datsun? What was he doing here! Was he
taking a shortcut to Nsawam? The car had now stopped, surren-
dering itself at last to the road. Its driver, looking like a pinpoint
of agitation, got out, and looked up and around at the hills as if
lost. Then he left his car and started to walk up. It was Sackey,
Allotey thought, waving down rather unwillingly. Sackey instinctively waved back, his midhead shining like a new pesewa, even
from that distance. Sackey's impatient climb looked extraordinarily
thin, even impertinent, among the soft edges of the mounds and
leaves. He did not belong to the growth around him at all! The
leaves hid and unhid him as he pushed his way up, looking even
less natural than his benevolent little car . . . which had tolerated
its master for several years, years of carburetor kindness.

Professor Sackey was already regretting setting out into "this
wild nonsense of trees." He carried all his energy in the chew of
words in his cheeks, words scattering like doves surprised by other
doves of the same feather. "I am in an inappropriate place! I am
being swallowed by these valleys!" Sackey shouted from below,
his forehead like a colonial cannon with some extenuating burr on
it. "Besides, aren't you going to welcome me?" "But you haven't

177

reached me yet!" ½-Allotey shouted back irritably, then waited until Sackey was almost face to face with him before he said, with mock ceremony, "Akwaaba, yewura Professor, we are glad to see you in the bush!" "We?" asked Sackey. "Yes, my hut and myself!" Allotey said with finality, his eyes holding the irony they contained, so easily. Sackey kept his face absolutely straight, and then stumbled with a curse over an old dusty stool, ending up holding Allotey's batakari for balance. "I hold the world!" Sackey shouted, sarcastically. He continued: "What's all this! I feel absolutely crowded out, with all these leaves and branches marching up and down. And there's something stupid and selfish about the roundness and the foliage of the hills . . ." "Selfish?" asked Allotey, getting ready to defend the plains below, the hills above. "Yes, selfish!" roared Professor Sackey. "Look at the space they take up, prodding the skyline like that. I hate their motionlessness! I don't want any of this nature worship on the soil of Ghana. I am amazed you've been able to stay up here so long! But change this place, change it! Develop the leaves into something else!" ½-Allotey took up his hoe and starting clearing, to stop himself from saying something angry to the bronze man standing before him. He laughed, and put the hoe down again, saying, "So you have been here only a few minutes, and you are already telling me how to deal with my life . . . it is business you and I are doing, not life! Everything you see around you is my life. And I'm changing it in my own way, small-small. But I want *more* leaves, more and more, not less!" A few gray clouds wrapped up the sun but could not take it away, and left wandering for other rays; the sun reappeared naked beyond Professor Sackey, whose silence at last rested his overspeeding mouth. There seemed to be a rebuke from ½-Allotey in the way he turned his back and started hoeing again. Allotey wondered how long Sackey could absorb the silence around. "I'm worried," Sackey broke the silence at last, "it's worry that has brought me up here so early." Allotey looked extremely surprised, yet still felt himself on guard somewhat, wondering what scheme the professor was going to spring on him; or what price he would have to pay later for the confession he was about to hear. In Sackey's presence, ½-Allotey's restlessness seemed to lessen considerably: otherwise, one wind would blow away another.

There was silence again and the slopes held it still, and the professor now seemed to be counting his fingers over and over again. Sackey's fortyish face took on some gray in that light, his eyes glaring sideways at a single crow opening and closing its wings, opening and closing the sky. His expression then took on a most brilliant black, moving beyond the crow a few feet to where it had left the last cry from its sly beak, and then, allowing his eyes to dim, he formed, beyond, bright memories of regret that pushed with sorrow against the leaves that pushed them back at him, again and again. And the way his orange shirt held him with no flesh to spare, as he himself held, still, his own moving fingers, gave Sackey a vulnerability that Allotey had not seen before. So even Sackey would die one day, he thought, and those that he spent his time blasting when he was alive, would wail and shed tears, some smeared with pepper and charcoal, others eating furiously in the funeral rooms.

"You see," Sackey continued, "we are all human, aren't we? We can't be hard all the time . . . not when the consequences of our actions affect others. You have never heard me speak like this before? All the better, for Ghana is changing . . . for the worse! I am the barometer for Ghana! When they start making things unhappy for me, then things are getting serious! Well, what happened was I took my little ball of temper to the ministries and exploded it right in their faces. I blasted their privileged teeth! The thing is, there was some political pressure to have two students admitted to the faculty. They were not qualified, and in any case there was no room; so I said No . . . you should have seen my mouth shaping itself into battle! All manner of officials tried to calm me down, but I was busy in my little palanquin of the mind, in my own head I detonated their appeals away. You see I had taken my car and roared through the streets of Accra, ending up at the wrong commissioner's office. I blasted him anyway! And when I finally ended up at Education I gave the culprit commissioner a real blast. I fumed. They would never get Sackey to bow down before them! After all, what is a uniform? I threatened to expose the underhand tactics, and stormed out rejecting the apologies that the whole lot of them were trying to make. I was an African bull! But what is worrying me now is this: in a sly way they have reduced the vote to my department i.e. the foreign exchange component; they have even stooped so low as to cut some development votes due my wife's school, just at a time when we are quarreling in the house! And again, when I wanted to travel out for a conference, I found it impossible to get a visa . . ." Professor Sackey paused, staring with indignation at ½-Allotey, as if it were the latter that was doing all this evil.

Allotey, totally absorbed in what Sackey was saying, returned Sackey's gaze rather impatiently, waiting for him to continue with his story. "I can always fight them on my own behalf but they are punishing a whole range of innocent people because of me. Look at the double trouble they have created in my house. Just when I was beginning to get comfortable with the balance of power, or balance of complaints, in the house, they come with this! Now Sofi is like a martyr, she feels right on top now. She thinks she has the chance to defeat me in the house. Ha! We shall see! And you see, she talks to the children in that overconcerned way that is meant to give them all the attention, and punish me on top! Isn't it sad that I have children who never understand my view? I do have a heart you know, I do have a heart! But I hate this female right-eousness in the face of these political and other pressures. Also, outside in the senior common rooms I hear very few have a good word to say about me. To them, this is all a kind of rumor's revenge. Revenge. You hear! You see it's this: Sackey takes the risks, and he must by all means suffer the consequences. I wish I could suffer it alone! And when they meet you face to face, the sympathy they give to your face they'll never give to your back. If I had a beard I would scratch it on one of your trees in exasperation, or give it to that impudent crow over there to pull at! . . . Look at your fish! How skillful of you to build a pond on the side of a steep hill! And your beans, they dominate this hill . . . I've been advised by many to go and apologize to the military politicians. Never! You see how ridiculous we are in this country? I'm right, yet I should apologize! You see how we turn things upside down in this country! They are now even beginning to trouble a young niece of mine: Efua Atta is shrewd about bofrots, and she has been making money from them since the age of twelve, that's about five years ago. And you wouldn't believe, Allotey, that she actually left secondary school to make and sell more bofrots, against everybody's wishes . . . except mine: I knew that she had my spirit, and that she would be truly successful in selling them. I'm sure I would have been a bofrot seller if I hadn't wasted my time trying to be a good academic! Don't smile, I'm serious! Her bofrots have made a name for her already, and people come from as far as Winneba to buy them in bulk. She knows how the sun shines on her bofrots, she knows what weight, as opposed to size, will attract people. Sometimes she bakes for money, other times she bakes to impress: something for the future, as she says; she knows how to make bofrots one of the most important things in the belly world. She is so clever that she sometimes bakes *ideas* and not just things: symbolic bofrots! Hahaha. What I mean is sometimes her shapes go beyond the round bofrot: they either relate to her own mood or they relate to something traditional. And you know, she's very outspoken! She came to my house for a visit one day, and she told Sofi quite frankly that she thought I, yes I!, wasn't looking very happy, and that if she didn't look after me properly, I would waste away. I loved it of course! Sofi was livid and had been made basaaaa. Then to top it all, Efua Atta took out a whole range of bofrots saying that each had a meaning, and that the most important meaning she wanted to convey was that I looked very worried and needed attention! I basked in her attention, I soaked in her truth! And oddly enough I spent most of the time looking at Sofi's face trying to see what effect Efua Atta's show—what a show!—was really having on her. I wanted to see beyond the anger. Eventually all I saw there was a deep sadness in her eyes. It looked as if she really and truly wanted to have a better life elsewhere, away from me. Then Sofi did something which broke my concentration: she got up and pushed Efua Atta out of the house, without a word. And Efua went so willingly that I became suspicious: ten minutes after she left the house, she stuck her face through the open window, and threw in the last bofrot, saying to me with a huge smile: "Uncle, she may be a good woman, but she's squeezing your spirit dry! Stay with her for some time, and if she doesn't give you more peace, then come to me for advice, *free*!" Then she ran off laughing and laughing. She has not stepped in the house since then, but I see her when I can. All this was about six months ago. And now that Sofi has almost succeeded in rinsing me out of her head, I must admit that I sometimes rely on my own niece for emotional support. But, what's happening now is that she once spoke her mind freely about soldiers troubling her uncle small; she also said that if they really had the courage, they would leave me alone and try her for size! She boasted so much that her enemies—and because of her success she has made many —made use of this: she started having problems getting flour, and even oil. But she's fighting this beautifully . . . through her customers: when she tells them openly what's happening, those that can help, help her. And she now has enough stock to keep her going for weeks! But it troubles me that people in this basically peaceful country can stoop so low. Bofrot politics, hmmmmm! Because of all this, I have come here to warn you that don't be surprised if they turn on you next . . . and I don't want that to happen. How can you suffer politics in addition to your farming and searching? You are at liberty to break your little contract with me . . ."

½-Allotey stood still for a long time looking down at the valley. "And look at me thinking that you were rather going to involve me in something else . . ." Allotey murmured to himself quietly. "I didn't hear what you said," Sackey said. ½-Allotey remained silent. He looked so self-contained that it worried Sackey, who wanted to break into his strange world. "But you know I was fighting with my own people at Kuse . . . How can I run away from a friend when others are attacking him? We'll go on as we are!" Allotey said slowly, but brightening up considerably. He knew and loved this type of fight. "Agreed, then, agreed!" shouted Sackey, with joy. They could farm in their mutual glow. "Can't you feel the beans growing, Professor?" Allotey asked Sackey suddenly, the usual irony back at the edges of his eyes. "Look, young man," Sackey said with a severity that he soon put in his pocket in mid-sentence, "I know I don't agree with leaves, but have pity on me. I have a secret desire to farm, I want the earth to yield to me, before I finally yield to it in my death. That's all!" Their laughter drifted down, though some stayed in their faces, brightening more than eye and cheek. Sackey could feel ½-Allotey's thoughts beating against each other like afternoon pounder and mortar. He interrupted these thoughts: "Allotey, your thoughts won't get me beans and fish! And your hut won't help you either. Finish your thoughts now now, now! And you know another thing? Your batakari is political cotton: it says something against all the fine cloths, smocks and suits; it's a condemnation of most of the types of people that wear them. Had you ever thought about this?" "What do I know about politics?" Allotey asked in mock surprise adding, "In this country do you have to be a rebel before you set out to find your own way?" Sackey looked a little absentminded, as if he had thrown his attention elsewhere, then he said, "You have ventured a new soil for your roots, and I have ventured my anger!" He was speaking slowly in his deep voice, his body bent before the onslaught of morning shadows. He picked grass and chewed the stalks between the flesh of words, adding, "And this anger covers all six feet of me. In fact there is not enough of me to be covered with!"

"And what are you angry about, sir?" ½-Allotey asked suddenly and heatedly, pushing the horizon back with the irony of his gaze. "Are you angry about garden egg stew? Are you angry about the tang of atua? Do you think that the way Ghanaians make history is too slow? Tell me! Are you afraid of the spirits in the bush? Do you hate the lack of consistency in the people's ways? Tell me! are you angry that most of us are political, moral, philosophical and economic cowards? Uncle Professor, do you think our leaders reflect the lowest common denominator—I did this arithmetic, sir, in class five—instead of reflecting real leadership? How many witches' heels touch each other in Ghana, especially in the sun? I'm serious! Do you think my wife had the right to show her friends how my okros grew? And okros of flesh are the most dangerous! Are you angry about the Akans' philosophy of the human being as made up of the Okra, Sunsum, Ntoro and Mogya? With all respect, sir, how much sense have you got in your shining motoway? I say with all respect, for you are now in my territory! Uncle Sackey, do you know that I have been suffering at the hands of trees? Are you angry that I come from a long line of fetish priests, and that I want to make alive my own type of farmer-priest? Sir, how many herbs have you analyzed in your long sociological life? Do you know that we are a free-floating people: when we float we sink, when we are free we get caught? I mean that we have kept most of our roots in terms of certain obvious addictions—drums, funerals, greetings, body movement, language (half, ha!)—but that we are not self-conscious enough! And yet you would be surprised, sir, our culture is too heavy, too slow! And we are experts in undermining each other! Have you ever poured libation and noticed that the gin has remained in midair, has refused to descend until the whole oman changed? Uncle, I am getting breathless, you have never seen me breathless before, but I mustn't stop! Are you angry that sometimes the river does not flow backward? You know, I dreamed that God has two eyes, one is the sun, the other is the moon; and did you know that every evening He polishes His moonshine eye? God is His own shoeshine boy! Are you angry that principal secretaries exist? How principled are they, and do they love the secretary bird, as it flies over the ministries? Can they kill snakes like this bird? Professor, help me! I can't understand this country! And that's why I'm in the leaves here! But it's your anger that I am worried about, your six-foot anger! Only don't let it bury you the same six feet under, hahahahaha! Uncle, would you be angry if I asked you to fetch me water from that difficult drunk, wet, stony stream? Can you imagine a professor fetching water on his head for a half-educated madman like me? Are you angry about the harmattan? Have you ever written a love letter on kenkey skin? Do you hate rain? Which part of the sun would you find hotter than a woman's heart? Do you remember that my woman and child are waiting for me? Are you angry that I am talking to you like this? You see, up here, there's no one to talk to, so occasionally the words come out of my wet mouth like a true African storm! I must get some kind of new information of the soul to take back to Kuse with me. Do you know something, Professor? I suspect that all my women are witches! As soon as they leave me, I start loving the memory of their absence; and whenever they reappear I hate them again! If you had a camera that could take a picture of the whole of Ghana in an instant, how many people would you see making love? How do Ghanaians make love? You are the sociologist, you should know the answer to that one! The professor has ventured his anger, and he's suffering for it. Uncle Sackey, do not worry, I'll suffer with you from a distance. Look at my broad hands, they can take all the suffering in this country now! Any surplus sorrow will be planted in my farms. I know the plant, I know the flower of sorrow. I can treat them all. When my mother died, she died of a broken heart . . ." ½-Allotey was absolutely breathless; the horizon now contracted again. His huge chest heaved as he changed his hoe constantly from his right to his left. You would think the earth grew on his back, you would think the earth was trying to bury him.

Professor Sackey was sitting on the bare ground with the biggest frown in the world on his face. The world was an impertinent place, it scattered the best people into the wilderness. Professor Sackey could never sing the humility in his heart, not even when it came to him once or twice a year. He looked at ½-Allotey with contempt, spreading his gaze over the continuing brightness of the former's eyes. "I'm going, you hear!" Sackey shouted. "I'm going! Come to *my* territory, and I will give you some of the answers! And I certainly won't wave to your hut. I'm glad I came to talk to you. I say I'm glad, you hear!" And this was the closest Sackey came to touching Allotey's soul. Sackey went down the hill abruptly, he never waved and he never looked back. He slapped at the usual morning flies as he entered his car. And the exhaust smoke couldn't climb the hill not even up to ½-Allotey's feverish gaze, his great gaze at the cantering car.

But Professor Sackey had an unpleasant surprise when as he drove he felt a bony finger tapping his shoulder. "Professor, surprise! I am here with my bones! I know you told me not to talk to you again but you can't push me out of your life like that. I am sorry if I took Sofi's side in the argument about who is a fool and who is not a fool. I sneaked into your car right from Legon. I heard everything you said to yourself, I noted all the curses you threw out to the world . . ." Beni Baidoo was smiling, giving his lips such a stretch that they almost snapped.

The livid Sackey looked on, speechless. He stopped the car abruptly, shouting, "I have no room in my car for mathematics: one man plus another man will not be in my car! Out! I have already forgiven you about Sofi, but I don't want you unauthorized in my car . . ." "Professor, I have known you since you were a student, and you haven't changed much at all. You know, Dr. Boadi's fate depends on how he treats you, And try as I can, I can't change him . . . He will arrest you one day . . . Professor, I would like you to bring some sociology into my village when it's completed! I mean, I want a learned village where in between fornication four times before a rich breakfast I learn hard things harder than, excuse me to say, my popylonkwe about how the world should be! Professor, I think it was your thoughts that burned the hair off your crown . . . but never mind, you have such beauty in your skin and your eyes, especially when your eyes are not on fire as they are now!"

Sackey put his hands together in exasperation, and gazed back up at ½-Allotey's hut. Beni Baidoo never failed to excite his feelings of pity and anger. He said surprisingly quietly to the old man, "Why don't you go and visit Allotey up there? He could do with a bit of wisdom . . ." "Certainly, sir! Just wait for me for five minutes and I'll be back down . . ." Baidoo began. "I don't wait for anybody, old man. You either come now, or you make your own way . . ." Sackey said, opening his door. "But you said I could visit Allotey . . ." Beni implored, then started to run up the hill painfully, casting his arthritis left and right into the wild flowers.

185

As ½-Allotey squinted down the valley, he saw Baidoo Beni at the end of the squint. Allotey had a wry smile on his face as the old man struggled up. But Sackey had not yet moved, he seemed to be searching for something. "Owura-½, I give you my half-good afternoon. I sneaked a lift to be up here with you, and I have played a trick on your friend the professor: I have his key in my pocket, so he can't return without me! Haha . . ." Baidoo said with a beaming face to ½-Allotey. "But . . ." began Allotey. "Oh I know he will beat me or something. But I wanted to tell you how my village was going. Now the only land I could get was farming land for one season, so I'm going to have a one-season village! I have to plant the village just as I would plant cassava . . . if only the girls I haven't got would come to fruit just in time before I give the land back . . . Can't you get me more permanent land, sir?" Baidoo said, keeping the same beam on his face and fingering Sackey's car key, "And while you and the professor were talking up there I had already fallen asleep . . . then my own snores woke me up." "Elders don't usually give land for founding one-season villages . . . But why don't you return the key? Can't you see Professor Sackey's in great agitation down there? Give it to me to return," ½-Allotey said, taking the key and making his way down.

Sackey fumed but the valleys did not catch fire. And after snatching the key from Allotey with a curse at the old man, drove in a fury back to Legon.

There, sneaking miraculously out of Sackey's car again, was Beni Baidoo, who had crawled down Allotey's valleys with rolling speed and slipped into the car before the agitated Sackey snarled off. He was satisfied that he was again witness to the swearing and snarling of the professor as he talked to himself in the belief that he was alone in the car, all the way to Legon . . .

Chapter 15

When Kofi Loww finally went to the house of Adwoa Adde, with a dead butterfly unknowingly in his pocket, he found a hostile Amina, whom he had never met, barring the door and demanding to know his identity. So Amina had at last found her spiritual mother Adwoa, whom she had been serving with a fierce loyalty; for in Adwoa's house she had found a peace that her uncle's prayers—said through the roof of a fez—could not give. So now her uncle had disowned her, just as her father had done in the North. For Amina, everything was fresh: Kofi Loww was a fresh intrusion; he looked so empty that he reminded her of a huge pile of fresh cola chewed and spat out. "Papa, so you are that sleepy man who doesn't come here very often, and who sometimes wants to marry my sister Adwoa!" Amina shouted out, laughing and running away with a lazy akimbo run, and leaving one of her eighteen years unclaimed and ungathered at the feet of Loww: as if she had become one year younger by her running which was both bold and shy. Kofi Loww smiled in that detached way of his, as if his teeth did not exist. Coming, he had bought bright fresh bananas from that woman glad for a buyer in the deepening dusk where her three small children cried. The woman was agitated, and had said in her high, loud voice, "Why should all three of you have colds in your noses all at once? Have you no pity for your mother? I have only one bit of cloth. Hold your noses and stand in line to be wiped! Look how I suffer and your father doesn't even look after you. Hmmmm." As he stepped into Adwoa Adde's room with three bananas, he knew that she would complain above the confused blink of his eyelids. All the stones of a guava

187

pointed in different directions, and each stone could be subversive of love and action. And any love or power that did not have this infinite direction of seeds, this patterned way of variety, could neither fit into his heart, nor his head. Yet what did he in his withdrawn openness, in his slow explorations, have to give toward this very same variousness that he wished for?

He smiled a smile of small shame at his own contradictions, and slowed his steps in the room, expecting a fire of words from Adwoa. He met no fire: he just saw her sleeping, her long body curved like a question mark, and asleep so early. He touched her leg protectively, and pulled the cloth up to cover her left breast. Over the wall he saw the dog whose barking was out of rhythm with its own jaws. A dog of four legs and four doubts, and very much like himself: in this country of sun, juju and wisdom, where did he get his bouts of absence from? The richness of his own country was a fine pattern outside, but not inside, him. The problem was how to faithfully wear the kente inside his inner shoulders, or how to eat akrantsi with his inner mouth. Then he threw Ghana out of his head, and looked down again at Adwoa Adde. She stretched slow and rich in her sleep, opening and shutting her long fingers, pulling the world in, pushing the world out. In the corner he saw her lamp on low, and wondered whether his heart was still on, whether it could still give her light. He suddenly thought: any woman who could sleep so innocently in front of him, must have his love. Poor Adwoa, it was not that he had no love, but that the only way to make sure of it was to make sure of himself. After all what was wrong with a crisis of identity, for himself and for his country, even under the brightness of the sunflower? It was precisely the yellow pull of sunflowers and mangoes, dances and wisdom, that hid so many problems and crises underneath. This quiet man thus wanted to kill beauty and energy, so easily available; or at least to postpone them until the way was clearer. And would it be possible to postpone love too? It would be ridiculous. Old Erzuah had told him that he Kofi Loww always saw the edge and not the center of life, and that even at the edge he would drift in circles; then Erzuah would stretch his moustache over his mouth, keeping the agitated silence there, and staring into the confused future of his son. "It was your mother that broke you!" the old man would suddenly say, then would lock up his moustache again and free his beard. All this further quietened him, but he was still determined to drift through the type of world that would, perhaps, finally become defined and important enough for him.

His eyes had traveled miles when Adwoa at last woke with a start, feeling a presence in the room. "Ho, Kofi, how long have you . . . you should have wakened me . . . I don't like being watched when I'm asleep . . ." Adwoa said all this very quickly. Then she looked at him severely, as if she had remembered something. She said, "Sit down, sit down, there's more love in sitting down than in standing up! You know you have been neglecting me . . . let me go and tidy myself up a bit." As she was going, he caught hold of her wrist timidly and squeezed it lightly, looking into her eyes as if he rather and not she wanted an answer from them. His expression changed to something quizzical as he saw behind her eyes a fund of sorrow he had not seen before. He wondered what she had seen these past few weeks that had given her this new dimension. She seemed to stand there indifferent, but he did not know that she was trying to adjust to his presence, to see whether love itself, now present, was stronger than its own memory. She was now demanding both more and less from him: more in that if he wanted to make a serious relationship, he had a much more considerable person to love, he would have to deepen the space of his soul; and less in that if he did not so want, then she could support her own emotional self-sufficiency, push his lack of seriousness away, and walk on as if she had only broken off a piece of sugarcane and thrown it over a wall that she would not look over again. Though he wanted to hold her there and then, he let her go, turning around to watch her lithe long walk as she went. He was wondering whether he was doomed to love things that always went away . . . Then, as if in desperation to stop himself from falling into deeper levels of interaction with Adwoa, or even with any other available human being, he started to dust and tidy the main room, shifting little stools and photographs into positions he had known them some weeks before. Perhaps it was his own heart he was tidying and rearranging, since the room did not need it. The curtains did not blind him, he thought, they blinded the world.

By the time Adwoa returned he had almost completely changed the room, and his heart had moved to other parts of his chest, with a different beat. She gasped in surprise, for him and for herself, holding a finger to her bright chewing stick teeth. He touched her hand with both of his. And his trembling would not exist if he did

189

not acknowledge it in the sudden breeze. It was as if some buried love was suddenly rising again and that he, taken by surprise by himself no less, was desperately trying to throw off the shroud around this love before anyone else saw it. He would be lost in fufu and abenkwan if that was where his soul belonged that minute. Then, in his moment of inner surrender, she suddenly withdrew her hand from his. He shook. Her look said: if he wanted her they would have to start off on a different footing, a different bedding. He was lost in her subtleties of feeling. But when she put her hand back in his, his surrender returned; returned through the way he filled the long slope of her thigh with his own, the way his chin parted her breasts and moved them into his hands. Odorkor was breasts of East and West desire. She was as strong as he was, and when they rolled he could not understand the fullness of her cushioning. They held each other's necks exactly where he felt her extraordinary patience was. "Time is a neck!" Kofi Loww shouted, his face on fire with its own feeling. She pushed this shout under her and lay on it, so that it rocked and moved them both, lengthening every moment yet breaking this same lengthening into bits of healing and peace. When she smiled it was a complete definition of the geography of the heart and the moving stillness of the moment. He suddenly looked at her and thought: it was the magic of the beads, it was the magic of the waist rainbow. The dead butterfly in his pocket would flutter now, without even knowing how it got there. And as they formed together two flats, one above the other on the bed, they made around each other's hearts buildings of the future. But Kofi Loww's future was a thirty-minute one: not his commitment to the woman now under his body and over his soul at the same time, not that. But he was often afraid that his sunsum came only in thirty-minute bursts, and that nothing was certain again after each burst. He dreamed of a hundred sugarcanes being trained on him, with each a burst of sweetness and a type of death for him. "How to keep the sweetness," he said aloud without thinking. She looked at him, she was half-asleep; but awake enough to feel so much of her past come to the shine in her long eyes: at moments of intensity, love never failed to push Adwoa's own history forward into her pools of eye. This was how she washed this history. It was the smell of new kelewele that finally brought tears down from her eyes, and she wondered how many events she was losing through tears. The new year was mixed up with the kelewele.

190

Loww studied her face which the lamp's glow had taken over. He took the tears from her eyes with one finger and put them on his own eyes. As he grimaced, she laughed at last. Over the outside mango trees now flowering in January his gaze went. What was flowering outside had already flowered inside, inside the room and inside the body.

Then he suddenly asked her, "Adwoa, what is it that has changed you? You look as if you can leave me any minute . . ." "They've given me some work to do. I fly when you are asleep," she interrupted, with no sense of hesitation at all. Her eyes mirrored the universe. He laughed, but the puzzle in his mouth did not come out with the laugh. "I like mystery, but I still don't know what you mean," he said. "I think my grandmother has made me a witch, a witch for Christ, a witch for Ghana . . . Will you stop loving me?" she ventured boldly yet defensively. He was lost in the weight of this information, he was silent. Then he looked at her with a new wonder, as if admiring her for her sense of invention; or as if about to meet a big, new mystery which would finally stop his own searching: that big space of questions he had would be filled with something concrete at last, something so strange in someone he loved so much. She looked at him with apprehension, worried about his silence. "But I'm losing my powers!" she added hastily. He said, "I love you and it's enough. And I love mystery too. Only, don't leave me . . . not even when you are flying." Then he fell asleep.

They woke up to a long column of black ants in the room. "Oh, quick, Kofi, I'll get the broom, you get the kerosene!" Adwoa shouted, rising quickly above the dawn. He looked at her for a moment, wondering what dream he had wakened up to. Then he rushed for the kerosene which he had seen when tidying up the room. "Kofi, stop it! How can you hold me when we're getting the ants out, Oooooooh!" Adwoa laughed as she swept.

Loww had sprinkled the kerosene on the retreating ants, and was now sitting watching Adwoa sweep. He felt a quiet exhilaration and the smell of ants and kerosene took him far back to when he was a child making cars with old sardine tins, sea-acorn wheels, and broomsticks: he often drove the meaning of his mother in little roads all over the compound dust. These convoluted lines complicated his love for her. He drove her memory mad, with the speed of sea gas. And every corner was a father, where he had to slow

191

down in case this father, this corner, would not understand the reason for the speed. Even then, his father, Erzuah, had become responsible. So responsible that sometimes little Kofi felt guilty that he thought about his mother at all. Then he would fix a neem stick onto the little car's steering wheel, and drive faster than the contradictions in his head. Bare-footed three-dimensional speed. And he would crash heads so often with the big sunflowers, chase so many bees away. Sometimes his friends were witnesses to the circles in his head, for they would look at his sudden bursts of speed and wonder where his sardine gas was taking him. They noticed his intense concentration on the little holes in the sardine tin, as if the stares in his eyes would, or should fill them. Then he would build long graveyards by the road, killing the bees, often after suffering stings—and burying them with ceremony. Sometimes the tiniest unsolicited tear could fit on the tiniest petal. "Kofi, are you playing with us or by yourself?" his friends would ask with irritation. "And how can we make more roads for the cars when you've filled up all the space with dead bees . . . your graveyards are in the way . . ." "They are not dead bees!" Kofi would shout indignantly. "They are dead friends." "Are any of us among the dead?" someone would ask. "Oh, I know, he wants to use the bees' wings for angels' wings! You see, let's dig up the dead and take off the wings . . ." another would add. "Ancestors don't have wings. And no one is going to dig up my dead friends!" Kofi would scream, standing guard over his graveyards. Then they would all start driving again, and Kofi would not notice as his friends surreptitiously dug up some bees and used the wings in their own way. Kofi's friends used sly wings beyond his head. Someone would ask him suddenly, "Has your father got no sisters or mother to look after you?" Kofi would ignore that, and try to hold his heart down, for this question led him back to his mother. And where his mother was, the heart could rain. Then he would eventually reply, "None of your business, eat your alasa in peace." The small rivers of time under the tin bridges flowed into urine and bees. Paani was the policeman when anyone crashed into another's crash. And the more collisions Kofi had the more wholes he made, there and then, out of his little life. The penny in his pocket had a hole of sympathy which bought another hole: a circular bofrot, that he shared by his double-crashed heart among them all. "You see this bofrot?" he would ask his friends, "It's my father that made it possible, so don't ask me again about sisters and mothers looking after me! You hear!" Kofi would add in triumph, feeling that he had now settled that question.

"I've finished the ants, Kofi," Adwoa said, bringing Loww back into the present. "It's not ants, it's bees!" he shouted without thinking. She looked at him, noticing the preoccupation on his face. "It's all right, you can go back to the past!" she said with a smile. "For me, I'm going to bathe. There's some sawi on the table for you . . ." Loww finally stretched himself back into the present with the longest yawn. "I didn't know there was this type of peace at Odorkor, in your room . . ." he said.

She had already gone, with her long strides which walked inside his head. Then he decided to talk to her, as if she were still in the room: "Adwoa, you make me think more clearly, or at least you can send me back anywhere in time. But I'm used to being alone, so where do I fit you in? I said where do I fit you in? *Where in my heart do I fit you in?*" "Right in the middle," Adwoa Adde whispered from the doorway. He turned around startled, his beard crowding out the morning. "Am I so much of a problem?" she asked, sadly. "Oh, no," he said gravely, "not you, as you know. It's myself." He looked at her with an intense stare, which she returned. When they lay down again, it was to continue the silence: when she thought he was about to speak, she kept her own words back; when he did not speak and she was about to, then he moved . . . the words could have been in his shoulder; she would restrain herself again; the silence was building up in different dams; two mouths were vacant but filled with love . . . with that large tail of doubt behind his. "Do you sell nice biscuits," he suddenly asked her, "and would you sell me some?" She laughed from a distance. "Keep some of your biscuits, you may need some for when I marry you . . ." he continued. She laughed again, but now from the closest distance of the heart. "Don't tease me," she said. "I'm serious," he added. "One of these days, you'll go to sleep single and wake up married!" They shared a long ironic smile.

Then there was a sudden knock at the door. Kofi Loww was startled with a start higher than Adwoa's. Amina was behind the knock, and behind Amina was Jato, and behind Jato were Adwoa's people of the night world crowding the compound. "Oh," Adwoa shouted, "Kofi, they have come to me when I have no powers left at all! How can I help them?" Kofi Loww rose in bewilderment, he took deliberate steps to a deliberate seat; and rose again like a released spring. He looked at Adwoa with all the angles in his eyes. "Help them, help them, whoever they are. I'll help you. Maybe this is my only chance to be together with you, somebody or something . . . and look, how sad, we are in a country of togetherness . . . do you really see the togetherness?" Adwoa Adde looked at Loww's mouth to see whether it was the same, and to see whether any more new words would come out.

Outside, Jato stood stiff with the same overbroad chin; you could never have seen a wronger chin on a more reluctant jaw. And now, there were a few surprised hairs on it. They blew into his left nostril as he spoke: "Sister, my eyes are browner than when we last met. I eat too much nkonkonte. And my brother Kwao is so rich now that when he goes to the toilet, money comes out. I don't know what to do: I've tried stealing, but whatever I steal is always stolen again the next day. I once stole a child to smuggle to Ivory Coast, but halfway there the child turned into a beast and severely bit my, excuse-me-to-say, my popylonkwe. And Sister, when I look at any woman now, my thing rises the wrong way . . . so now I have come to you to help me find a woman who is also made the wrong way. We have to make love with our skins inside out, we have to pump backward. Sister, how is it? Could your Amina here help me? She has a face pretty like a fresh okro . . . and when she walks I have trouble tracing which direction her buttocks want to go."

Adwoa Adde looked bewildered and full of pity. She looked at Kofi Loww, whose eyes were shining with an intensity she had not seen before. "Let them talk, let them come. We will know where to send them," Loww shouted. He saw some sort of direction for himself in Jato's outbursts. In the corner of the compound stood Kwaku Duah the fitter; and his eyes were like headlights in daylight: they shone, but they were wasting the light. His ears were shaped even more like Peugeot 404's. And when he spat he was terrified because the spit never reached the ground. Kwaku Duah was crying, his tears reflected his wrought hands, his big shoulders were soft and he shivered. The whole of Odorna far away was a puncture. He said, "Sister, do you know that Mansa died? Sister, I'm broken. They say that Alhaji killed her. Yes, I have money now. But she toughened me, she made my money for me, and now she's not around to share it with me . . . I now want the spirit to kill this Devil-of-an-Alhaji! I have filled my buildings with silence. I only hear Mansa's voice in them. This morning, Sister, you must give me the power, the power to kill. The other day, I was looking at my workshop: every oil stain was a bit of memory. I thought I saw hundreds of Mansa's footprints; and each one was jumping up and down, each one was jumping out of my life, out of my life. I repaired all twenty cars in the yard in two days, and had the compound swept. I sprinkled schnapps all over it, and prayed in the tire marks. I prayed through gaskets, I prayed through repair kits, I cried into gas, I called God through an overhauling gasket, I begged the ancestors through dirty carburetors. Then I saw Mansa's vision in a cracked windshield. As she smiled at me, the broken glass joined. Yes, Sister, joined! I tried to hold her face, but she just smiled again. Sometimes you have no shock absorbers for the bumps of life. And do you know what, Sister? I set one of my own cars on fire, I was going mad! And as the smoke filled my mouth I blew out cigarette smoke, as if I was going to start smoking again. The shape of every smoke in every city is Mansa. I have tried several other girls, but I always end up loving the same coffin. But, Sister, I'm trying to be whole again. When the glass joined, Mansa was trying to tell me to join myself together. Together and together! Mansa has promised to get me a new girl! See! But I must have the heart of Alhaji. Sissssssster!" Kofi Loww was holding Kwaku Duah, and wondering when last it was that he really comforted someone. Adwoa Adde saw the dawn rise three feet, as high as the nearest sorrow, as high as the nearest knees. And all the shadows seemed to join in a strange way. Bits of Odorkor became bits of Labadi became bits of Kwabenya, became bits of Odorkor again, just as when she was flying.

There by the gate was Manager Agyemang, and his eyes were full of laughter, and the laughter followed him around like a frisky dog. His head was like a wizened mango being examined under a 25-watt bulb; but there was happiness in it, the stone of inner mango was happy! Agyemang shouted, "Sister, I'm freeeeeee! All these years I didn't know that my wife had a lover. All that politeness was a way of telling me that her thighs were transferable. When I saw that she had a lover—through the same troublesome maidservants—I made some investigation and discovered that he was a civil servant who was even more polite than she was! I understand they say *please* to each other several times before going to bed and business! So, Sister, you know what I did? I let my BP go right down by force, and then wrote a letter to her and placed it on the pillow. She was very very late from the market that evening: imagine walking in at 10 P.M. from the market with the words, 'Please, I had to wait for them to catch the fish before they could sell it to me.' Well, Sister! I was wondering whether the heavy market mammies went out in their own canoes . . . and can you see a canoe carrying a supertobolo market mammy? It would sink before the fish could even scale the nets! Ewurade, my polite wife, went marketing on the high seas! Can you see her buy tomatoes among the tossing waves? Anyway, it took a long time before she saw the letter on her pillow. She glared at it, then smiled . . . I had not seen her smile in the house for several years . . . Sister, my letter said: 'My dear wife, with effect from today, your thighs, and whatever cargo they contain, have been transferred to Owura Puplampu. I understand that his ruler measures your thing much more straight than mine. Yours delightedly, *please*, your dear husband.' Then without any other comment she told me that she was pregnant. Pregnant! 'Pregnant by whom?' I asked, knowing that there was a trick somewhere. 'By you, of course, please, my dear husband.' 'Nonsense!' I shouted. 'But we haven't had any fikifiki exercise for over two years. It must be Puplampu that pumped! Don't go hunting and come and put the harvest at my door! I tell you again, it was Puplampu that pumped!' I was beginning to get angry at her lies. This woman had no shame. She stood there silent, then said quietly, her head down, 'My boyfriend is impotent!' I shook with laughter, I surrounded her with the roaring of my teeth! Then she added, with her head still down, 'One evening, my dear husband, when you were asleep, I forced you to do the thing. I did some kalabule with your thing! You never woke up at all!' Sister, the woman is mad! I was rolling on the floor with laughter, and then the maidservants came in. I had a sudden idea: 'Now, you girls, you always used to hide behind the door when madame and I were busy doing it . . . you think I didn't know? I could always hear you laughing. You are bad girls. Now, my point is this: have you within the last two years found it necessary to hide behind the bedroom door? Tell the truth!' At first they were terrified, but Kokor, the bold one, suddenly shouted, 'Uncle, you are right! We have tried and tried to hear some entertainment from your room . . . but we hear nothing! Madame has been having her entertainment elsewhere!' My wife looked with evil eyes at Kokor. So I protected

Kokor with my own staring and she was looking good, too. Sister, have you ever heard of bedroom kalabule? She's a great liar! So I eventually divorced her. And all she could say to me and my family was, 'Please, thank you!' But Sister, my only problem now is that I have conceived with Kokor. But I completely forgot that she was not educated! Darkness plus skin equals forgetfulness. I can't take her to important parties, which I now attend very often with my oiled arms, You see, I'm free, yet unfree. Please terminate Kokor's pregnancy for me. Sister, I beg you! I can't risk a clinic. Then my laughter would come from even deeper in my mouth! Besides I've caught her looking at my office driver . . ."

Adwoa Adde rushed into the room, shouting, "Kofi, I can't cope! Help me. I have no power." Kofi Loww took a chair and stood on it, shouting out, "Bring your lives, bring your lives here! We are all suffering together!" When Adwoa came out again, there was a new determination in her eye. "I've prayed," was all she said. Over there sitting on top of the shrinking wall was Akosua Mainoo. The wall loved Akosua's knees. She was waiting for her smile to reach the end of this wall before talking. Her skin had taken on even more velvet, and there was a triumphant swing in her breasts, which she had wanted to place in her own hands for inspection. Her words finally pulled the smile out of her own face: "Sister, is that your husband? I like his beard . . . it reminds me of the forest I caught my mother in! After all, Sister, my mother has run away. Shame! She kept troubling me, so one day I told the truth. I told of her lover in the forest. My father nearly killed her, so she ran away. Now, I look after my father. I sell the whole world if you like! I'm far too busy selling to chase the boys—and they are now men. What I am doing is to save all the looks I get, save all the proposals until I meet the one that will make my heart beat. Then I will empty all my knowledge onto his lap. If he wants me, then he must also want the information in my head. Isn't that smart, Sister! After all what I want to avoid is the same shame that my mother had. Sister, I sell soap. Because my mind is now clean. Before I sell soap to my customers I wash them all, especially the men, in my head! My problem is that I want to know whether my life will always be successful. I want you to see around the corners of my life for me. I don't want my father to die and leave me, when I haven't yet given him a child or a house, or both. Sister, I want to know the future. I want to know how many times I will chop fufu and abenkwan in my life. Will I marry a copper-colored man? And I would prefer somebody with hair on his legs! Sister, I ask you about the man standing beside you. I want you to be happy. Tell me! Is he nice?" Akosua ran to the gate laughing. She came back carrying different types of soap, from Lux to alata samina. "Sister, use these when you marry. But I want my answers!" She went and sat smiling on a stool.

But that stool was Beni Baidoo's knees, from which she shot when he tried desperately to caress her. He laughed bitterly, and shouted, "Ewuraba, you are not afraid of my skin, are you? It's like the most expensive corrugated iron sheets!" Then he turned to Adwoa Adde, looked at her for a long time, and said, "Sister, you remind me of the life I missed. I wish I had the dignity you have when I was your age. My dog has finally deserted me, it left only its fleas behind. But I don't really care: it used to go into my small food cupboard and bark as if it was chasing away a thief, then steal everything itself. And my dog is a sergeant, my dog is the police force of Ghana . . . which is just full of fine men with rotten bellies! And laws so wide that they swallow the good with the bad. For me it's only been God's laws I have suffered under. Fate has been my counterback. I am yet again an old man boogie, with two eyes and one vision: to see and feel with one heart all that I missed, and to have this heart sometimes wild. I am too old for dignity now! But I do want one thing, Sister; I want to learn how to fly an airplane." There was laughter from most of those present. But Beni Baidoo just remembered portello; he mourned the deep purple now, but rejoiced over the memory of the fresh taste. "You can all laugh. And that young Kofi with the beard can want to laugh. But if sister Adwoa is not laughing, then I'm happy. I know I look dis-dis-what? ah—disreputable! I smell of stale bread. My culture is still in the Mfantse wastes! But I still want to live, I want to live now more than ever. You young ones, listen! I can live more life than you! I can boogie and dance rough, pasaaaa! my donkey, my donkey, my village, my village! The years wear on me wearing them." Then he rushed with lust toward the scattering girls. Akosua Mainoo's smile finally fell off the wall.

Over in the eastern compound, Adwoa Adde rubbed her hands together, as if she were rubbing the world down or away. "So you've borne all this yourself, all these months," Kofi Loww said, the intensity gone from his eyes, his face full of pity and admiration for Adwoa. She said quietly, "We are supposed to be together as a people, we go to each other's funerals, we laugh at a lot of things together. But we don't really care for each other at all. This made me so sad when I was flying, it makes me so sad now . . ."

There was a whisper: "Sister it's me, Abena Donkor, Kusi's wife. Sister you gave me blessing just by looking at me, just by listening to me. But I am worried about one thing: I am worried about being so happy. Kusi loves me more and more . . . Oh, sometimes I turn my face away from his girlfriends, because they come quick and they go quick . . . but I get up and look at my happy face and then I spend a few minutes worrying about why I should be so happy. Kusi has put on weight for the two of us, for I am still the same. We have one heart, one fat, one bed. I think we should be a good example for all Ghanaians! I wouldn't have come here at all, I would have found a better time to thank you; but something just pulled me here, as if all of us here move with one body when we are coming to you, no matter which part of Accra we find ourselves in. Just before I came here I felt a sudden breeze inside the house—no one else felt this, not even the children. Then it was as if someone had switched off the lights of the whole city. Then I felt that the soul of Accra was a smoked fish finally going bad, with worms in it and no head. But then all this passed, and I felt happy again. But Sister, you yourself you look different. There's something more human about you. As if you are now sharing the light in your eyes with someone else. Leave us with our troubles, go and live your own life. Sister, greetings from Kusi, I told him about you. He doesn't believe you exist, but he still sends his greetings. He loves planning our life from our own house, and the children now obey him beautifully . . . sometimes they even obey him before he gives the order! Sister I want you to laugh small."

Then there was Kofi Kobi standing in the yellow light beside his new wife of old, Akua Nyamekye. Their love was more than legs now, but it had not produced any children. It remained only a four-legged love, the sixth leg was missing. He was about to fall out of love with Akua when she pushed the love back, with force, into his surprised heart. She did this with a meal. Then he fell in love with this pushing. "Sister," Kofi Kobi lamented, "tell Akua Nyamekye to give me children instead of so much love. I don't want to have to throw her away. She must Must MUST give me sons!" Then Akua would cry small, in the distance . . . she had moved away. "Do you think your tears will give you children?" Kofi Kobi asked her impatiently. Akua stood on one foot, Akua stood on another foot. Then she rushed to Adwoa Adde, and whispered something. Adwoa smiled with relief. Then she in turn whispered something to Kofi Kobi of the long legs. He held his hands up to the sky with joy, shouting, "Two months? But why didn't she tell me? But why then was she crying?" "She thought you didn't have faith in her," Adwoa said simply. "You Kofi Kobi, you are too known!" Akua Nyamekye suddenly shouted, "Let's go home. I was trying to tell you I was pregnant, and you wouldn't listen! Let's go home. From now on till I deliver, we sleep on different beds. I don't want your long legs spoiling things before they are due! Sister, thank you, God give you blessings. Move, Kofi Kobi, let's go, move!"

True nobody saw Aboagye Hi-speed as he stood there between the moon and Accra. True he was close to death, with all his drinking; he was so thin that when he stood sideways, he disappeared . . . so that he had to face anyone he was talking to, or he would talk out of nothing. His tongue was fat with death, was like the oldest bit of pink chale-wate; and his teeth angled back toward the cave of his throat. Adwoa Adde had to touch him, hold his shoulders, to keep up her resolve, to show some sign from deep within herself that she could help the unhelpable. His shadow was full of akpeteshie, and his voice was hoarser than sandpaper: "Sister, I'm going. I've bought my own coffin, in preparation for my automatic funeral. Life has been hard . . . lazy but hard . . . but I don't want them to fool me in my death with this communal living nonsense. When I was alive—I think I'm dead already—they couldn't help me. Why should they come around wailing and performing rituals that betray my life? Sister, I tell you, I am a fool, I lived a fool's life, and I should be buried like a fool: I care less for some of these Akan and other taboos, like the fact that even strangers must be buried . . . with their feet facing their hometowns. And what do I need the ancestors for? Why should I forge a link between the living and the dead? They thought that because I was a drunk, I knew nothing; that because I lived in a dirty room with a stupid wife and mocking children, that I had no head. Well! I've taught myself to read, I've stood and preached whole sermons to myself about life. I dragged myself out of akpeteshie once a day to study.

Before they sleep, I will be on my deathbed. When they wake up, they will find me already buried. They will find me an abomination! They will think I am the devil! Sister, let me tell you a secret: I have tipped a Dagarti man to watch out for my death: as soon as I stagger onto the steps in the midnight compound, then he will carry me to the coffin I have hidden in the cemetery, he will reveal the grave that I myself dug secretly over the weeks and hid with wood and leaves; then after throwing the Big Box in, he will look away while I crawl like a rat down into the five feet of grave . . . I was too tired or too drunk to dig six feet! Hahaha. Then he, my cola-chewing gravedigger who never dug my grave, will hand me down twenty bits of rope tied on to boards that contain all the earth needed to bury me. When I pull it, the lid will crash on with its glue, then all the red earth will follow. He will only need to smooth things over. Sister, you don't know how rotten the underbelly of this city is! Or you do? If you do, it doesn't show in your face. I've already prepared a letter to the *Graphic* about my automatic feat, so that they will, for once, laugh and marvel when I am gone . . . At least strangers will; the family will have to purge my memory, they would not want my bad spirit to return, if it could at all . . ."

Kofi Loww stood there as if in a trance. He could not push the darkness out of his head. He moved forward to touch Aboagye too, but he was gone, gone even from Adwoa's touch. His absence tied everybody's mouth. The others had a feeling of revulsion. "I wish I could write to Aboagye," someone said, imitating Aboagye's hoarse voice, "but the devil has no P.O. Box number. Sister, we need to see the Osofo in Madina to do something about this. Aboagye is too strong for any of us here . . . and you should not go after him with your sympathy. Leave him alone to the Osofo, that is if he survives at all . . ."

Then it was suddenly morning, the compound was deserted and Kofi Loww had already led Adwoa Adde by the future of her elbow into the quiet, quiet walls, where marriage could start filling the rooms.

201

Chapter 16

Okay Pol would sometimes forget the Kojo in his name because he was confused but Beni Baidoo would shout it back against his surname, with the Kojo shaking. Ever since the horses at the airport, Beni had warned Pol that if he Pol were not careful, he would turn into an old man like Baidoo himself . . . except perhaps with his habits a little neater than the old man's. Baidoo made Okay Pol both slightly odder and more aggressive: he would abuse Baidoo for bathing infrequently, and drag the old man in an absentminded way to the nearest tap and soak him . . . and then he would regret it as the Beni shivered as hard as the abuse leaving his old mouth. Then after he was satisfied that enough abuse had weakened Pol, Baidoo would boast about his village: "I have now got a woman to inhabit my village even before the buildings are up! Hey Kojo, listen, and stop dreaming about your Araba. She will never marry you . . . you are so light that she can carry you on her financial back! My woman has agreed to live under a big tree until I build my first atakpame hut. She says she would love walls being built around her . . ." Baidoo stared hard at Pol, watching to see how much mock the latter's eyes contained. Pol said, "But Ama Payday is mad! Have you no pity, forcing a mad beggar to stand under a tree for hours every day? Her bones will weaken her head more . . ."

"Oh, no!" Baidoo bellowed, "I feed her . . . food and ideas. I have her saying the alphabet, I have retrieved part of her brain from madness. I am talkative and she will be fuckative! Soon I will retrieve her beauty . . . and consider some romance . . ."

"Beauty and romance!" Pol shouted with a scowl. "The madness you retrieved has gone to your own head . . ." Pol would suddenly leave Baidoo, reluctant to share what he saw as their mutual ridicule.

Okay Pol's fez sat on his head like a child sat on a block of wood, and became liable to fall off when he was eating: his upper jaw chewed far faster than his lower jaw, so that this counterpoint of chewing shook his head, shook his fez. He had taken to trying to play the thumb piano with a wise beggar in the streets, but gave up in disgust when Araba Fynn passed one evening and pretended she had not seen him there. Pol was confused because even though he felt extra confidence with the coming into his humble bed of the proud Araba Fynn, he could not shift some of this confidence to tone down his odd ways, to destroy the inevitable pull that little oddities had for him. Araba Fynn had continued to treat these ways as entertainment, and as flavor to her attraction. After all, his long fastidious body was handsome, and he was also partly a source of rebellion against her mothers . . . admittedly a source that she would not be willing to push to the ultimate. But strangely, as she saw him more often and became more attracted, she began to feel an alarm: how many places could she take him to? The odd-colored joromies he chose to wear, the overthin trousers that gave his legs the look of propelled pins, all changed her little passion for him. Changed it, but did not completely destroy it . . . as if when it rained, only half the rain wet half her face, so that the dry half was still presentable to the mirror. And to top all this, Okay Pol had taken to loud whistling in the most unbecoming places. She would at first close his mouth with a kiss, where possible, but then it became necessary to pull his hand, and look away.

"What is happening to you, Kojo?" she would ask, out of an exasperation that had not yet gone deep enough to lose the touches of irony at her mouth. She had been glad to get rid of her sense of mercy toward him as she had become more involved, but this mercy was now coming back . . . and back right through the back door of their love: she did not like this unsuspected breeze at her back, but neither did she move away from it. So she nipped him in exactly the same place, whenever she felt this doubt, though he mistook this for a strengthening of love, at first. When she asked Pol this question, he would turn on her his look of inspired buffoonery, blasting her eyes with the concentration of stored laughter in his own. He would ask her as the store burst: "Do you want me to laugh above the control price, or what? This is what happens when you hoard your tongue . . ." All this won Araba over for a bit, all this made her sleep in his pocket for some time.

Part of the problem, also, was that Okay Pol had crossed the path of Dr. Boadi, and Boadi was on the warpath: Pol had been taken several times to Boadi's house, partly for questioning, partly for persuasion. Dr. Boadi had come to the conclusion that Pol was far more dangerous than Kofi Loww. He knew far more, and he, Pol, was—in his mad moments, as Boadi would say—much more ready to make something political out of this knowledge. Perhaps not against Boadi or anyone else, but as a means of clearing his own path toward a very vague clarity of life. "Kojo," Boadi would say harmlessly, "I have had you brought here of your own free will, I'm sure, to discuss our small problems again. Don't let the distant influence of people like Sackey or Loww—look at the name even—guide you. For you, you can never make politics: you are not devious enough! If you want to study, then study. But help us part-time . . ." Dr. Boadi had lost weight slightly over the months, and was feeling that he was surrounded by fools who were incapable of carrying out his orders. No small matter to serve a commissioner, especially against the inclination of one's own wife, who was at last beginning to neglect his physical needs more and more. It was not only teeth now; it was shoes and hair. But this only meant that Yaaba pushed more and more on to the maidservants: Boadi still had this whaaaaat smile, and his whaaaaat jacket. He liked Pol, in spite of himself, because he felt a touch of honesty in him, felt a certain awareness that Pol, coming from a Northern father and an Akan mother—both dead—had no great loyalties, no sharp axes to grind. So that he both overestimated and underestimated him. Pol would say with his tight face full of indignation at Boadi's house: "Look, Dr. Boadi, it is immoral of you to keep picking me up, as if I was a prisoner. I owe you thanks for giving me a job. But now, I am no longer interested in that job. It's a wicked job, trailing people for information . . . and you know you are wasting time with the wrong people. The Sackeys, the Pinns and the Lowws just don't want to be pushed around, just don't want their intelligence underrated. That's all, Mr. Doctor! You could, excuse-me-to-say, spend more time in solving real problems, rather than in flexing political muscles at the wrong audience!"

"Ei," Boadi laughed, "have you really grown up or what? Or are you getting some more money elsewhere? Now we see this before us: Kojo the Master!" Sarcasm always raised the pitch of Dr. Boadi's already high voice; his cheeks would look even more like ripening tomatoes unhandled. Dr. Boadi had seen the other dimension of change in Pol that Araba Fynn had seen, and this was another reason that he did not want to arrest him outright: Pol was drifting into a ludicrous existence, and ultimately, no one would probably take him too seriously if he chose to betray him, Boadi, or his commissioner.

Another reason that Dr. Boadi held himself in check—as far as all political irritants were concerned—was that he thought his commissioner was falling slightly out of favor with the Castle. His highly sensitive political skin forewarned him, so that he had decided to move more slowly, to tread on fewer toes. This had been in his head when he decided to visit Professor Sackey in the company of a reluctant Pol. He had told Pol that he was now trying to make amends with the professor, and that it was not he, Boadi, who had arranged for the rough interrogation of Sackey some weeks back in April of the new year. When they arrived at Sackey's house they found a great deal of surprising silence in the mango tree which refused to rustle its leaves in spite of a strong breeze. And the red ants ate the sky. "Agooooo." There was no reply. "Agoooo." Then, without warning, Sackey in an angry vest, flew at the soft flesh of Boadi from a door which suddenly opened, and he was squeezing the arms of Boadi's rich body of beer and chicken.

"This could have been your neck, Boadi," the professor screamed. "You are a scoundrel! How dare you hound and bully me like a small child? What did you pick me up for?" The two men shared one sweat as Pol tried to separate them. "You see, Kojo, I told you that the man was mad, mad! I come to be friendly, and he attacks me! Is this how a professor behaves?" Boadi was panting hard, as he stood there separated from Sackey by Pol's big push. Sackey had stormed into the house. "I hope he has enough sense not to be going in to get some weapon or other," Boadi panted, wiping his sweat with a curse. He still wanted to cultivate patience, for after all he had come here for a purpose. Professor Sackey rushed out holding a glass of water. His eyes, on fire, threw light on the snarl over his teeth: "Boadi. you are lucky you are with this young man . . . if you were alone there would have been no witness to your destruction! However, I must remember the civilities . . . you can report me to the police or anywhere you like. Today I have squeezed you back. Now, sit down. What do you want?" "Now, Uncle," Dr. Boadi began slowly, "I would advise you not to do things like this. Some crazy people carry pistols on them for emergencies like this. And I wouldn't like a brave Ghanaian like you shot." There was a shade of intimidation in Boadi's eyes as he spoke. The shade suddenly vanished under the sun of his smile: he had put his ruffled body together again. He said: "I must thank Uncle Sackey for providing me with some gratuitous exercise this morning! And is today not April Fool's Day?" Okay Pol had put his sense of shock aside, and was busy adjusting his fez to the same mad angle as Sackey's eyes. He felt a touch of release in his hands. Mrs. Sofi Sackey had walked through the room, with a perfunctory nod, and was determined not to partake of her husband's excesses any longer. She was now a complete expert in instant neutrality: Sofi, only your haughty look, was what the walls said. Professor Sackey never seemed to want to take his eyes from Dr. Boadi's smooth face, as if his wild anger had now turned into a quiet venom. Boadi preferred this look, for he parried it better than that anger of the arms. Okay Pol suddenly whistled into the silence. "Aha," broke in Boadi, "this is the signal for me to explain my mission: Uncle Professor, I have come to explain to you that I have not been behind your recent troubles . . ." "You could have stopped it," Sackey interrupted brusquely, and with utter finality in his mouth: "Yes, you are right, you are right, you are right in a way, but I wanted to wait to rescue you from more serious trouble!" Boadi said with his dazzling smile now firmly stuck at the right place in his face, much like a badge of resewn honor, of chewing gum. "And as I talk, you will be able to see the wisdom in my restraint. You see, in Ghana politics, we don't usually try to be vicious. Bombs and killings are rare. We value consensus, provided we are holding the reins! You can choose either the 'con' or the 'sense,' and if you really want to count on us, choose the census! Hahahaha. But seriously, I have come to offer you the chairmanship of an important economic committee . . ." "I am not an economist . . ." Sackey interjected. "Precisely!" Boadi continued unperturbed, "it's so important that we cannot leave it to the economists alone! We want to use your outstanding energies toward improving the life of the people. And of course we are prepared to listen to any reasonable conditions you

206

may set . . ." Boadi's smile stretched to an amazing length, the symbolic chewing gum gained inches.

There was a silence as Sackey smiled into the past, as he moved a sudden feeling of disgust from the back of his head to the tip of his impeccable lower lip. "I thought I had told you before that I was not interested in politics . . ." Sackey shouted. "Politics is life!" Boadi shouted back, "and you can't escape that!" "Politics is life, but life is not politics," Sackey replied with surprising calm. Then he called through to his son, "Kwame, come, come, I want you to tell this doctor something for me . . ." Kwame came rather reluctantly, for he had just been listening to his mother's complaints about his father. So he had suddenly decided to cut his resentment into two, and he was carrying the bigger half in his face straight to his father; the smaller half was left with his mother, until it was necessary to bring that, too, to his father. "Yes, father?" Kwame's eyes asked. Sackey did not even notice the resentment on his son's face. Father put his hand on son's shoulder; and the hand felt so heavy on this shoulder. "Kwame, tell this rich-skin gentleman sitting here that if I don't do politics, even with civilians, then I would never dream of doing it with soldiers!" Kwame repeated this to Boadi, with the resentment still on his face. Sackey at last noticed his son's frown, but thought that the boy was trying to intimidate Boadi on behalf of his father. Sackey's proud smile only made Kwame more angry inside himself, and he felt as if he were being torn in two. The boy suddenly shouted, in tears, "Dada, can I go and call somebody else to do your talking for you? My throat is sore. I am going to my poor mother, I am going to my poor mother!"

There was a silence, with no tail whatsoever on it. Sackey rose slowly, walked through to where Sofi and the two children were, in the kitchen, held Kwame's hand so hard that there was almost a squeal of pain, then said, "If you do that to your father again, he will beat you for the first time!" Sackey was about to throw some words at Sofi, but quickly changed his mind. When he stormed back defensively to the sitting room, he found it empty. The two men were walking down the drive, at the insistence of Pol. "Keep your committee," Sackey shouted. "Can't you see that even my house committee can't meet!" Pol waved back sadly, as Boadi smiled with great satisfaction: "I have done my job. After all, he can't even control his house." Pol finally went his way, after ignoring Boadi's triumphant chatter. But he did manage to ask Boadi this: "You won't arrest him again . . ." "Of course not!" Dr. Boadi replied in triumph and triumph again. "If I arrest him I will be doing his poor family a big favor! Hahahaha!"

Okay Pol left on his own way. Over by the Tetteh Quarshie Circle, the motorway rolled its breathless carpet toward Tema. No taxi stopped for Pol as he walked his uneven walk. "Massa," one driver shouted out of his taxi, "ibi your hat, I no fit have room for it in this my posh car . . ." Pol made a decision: he would visit Araba Fynn, whether she liked it or not. It seemed she preferred to meet him outside her house . . . or wherever Nana Esi was not. As Okay Pol reached the airport, he avoided looking at it: the radar looked like an obscene wave. Then down dipped the road, rushing on in a shrug of badly patched potholes, and keeping its cars in check with a combination of advertisements and an absence of pavements. The two gas stations by the Continental Hotel were like displaced elbows permanently stuck as the body of this hotel crawled squarely out with its gray beyond its own rectangular world. Pol met another two elbows, Mobil elbow and Texaco elbow, and then slid to the adinkra symbol of the 37 roundabout. Then under the huge neems the squat military hospital pressed its walls further down, under the cries of the disturbed bats, stretching Pol's thoughts and feelings into arabesques and adinkrahene, Nyame Dua and Sankofa. A nurse passed, defining the suffering in the walls with her uniform, and with the vacant look in her pretty eyes. And her neck reminded Pol of Araba, but then the nurse would not smile, at aaaaaall. Redemption Circle pointed its long tarred finger back toward Flagstaff House; and standing behind this was the Broadcasting Corporation with its wired world and the sound of its government grunts scattering over an apathetic nation. Pol smelled bacon by the embassy residences, and wondered whether Nana Esi still liked her sausages Mfantse style in jollof. Pol's neck disappeared further as he approached Asylum Down, through the square but affluent Lebanese houses, up to the last jump of street with more embassy buildings, toward the Catholic cathedral junction. And if a life had no real clutch, it would slip back down the steep roads, and throughout his walk, it was the people that made the buildings move, that gave them history. Pol suddenly wished for the world of the thumb pianist as he approached the house of Araba Fynn. He wondered what he was doing out of his depth and forcing himself under the roof of the Mfantse matriarchs who were still suspicious of him, of his advances toward their daughter.

He reached the gate, and stood there scrutinizing the beat of his own heart. He sent his height over the gate. There was complete silence. The heart of the house seemed to be slower than he knew it some weeks before. Then suddenly up above the bedroom window he saw the form of Araba Fynn. He waved frantically, but she had moved back into the room, deeply away from him, he thought. He knocked at the gate at last. No one heard. Araba appeared at the window again, this time holding a handkerchief to her eyes. She looked so overwrought, he wondered what was happening. His old tenderness came back as he saw her. This time she saw him, and gave a start. And then abruptly waved him away, while her eyes looked as if they were asking for help. The afternoon sun rose into a shroud of clouds, so that the cathedral tower could not reach it. The organ music could stretch this tower with its thin concrete. Pol refused to go away, and was beginning to climb the gate when Araba came down, crying.

She spoke first, and quickly: "Is this the time for you to be here, Kojo Pol?" She had not called him Kojo Pol, just like that before. He wanted to be gentle with her, to get her to tell him what was wrong. "You are not one for tragedy, are you? I can't even speak Fante with you, can I?" "Just tell me," Pol said simply, and the look in his eyes drew on any deep experience, any at all, that they had ever had. "Don't underestimate me," Pol said, to his own surprise, standing there looking immensely odd in his clothes, in his ways. "My grandmother is dying, and she won't let us call any doctor. She has hidden the key of my car . . ." she blurted out at last. "But where's sister Ewurofua?" Pol asked with a strange excitement, a strange foreboding. "She's gone to try to get the abusuapanyin to try to persuade Nana Esi . . ." "But is he in Accra?" Pol interrupted. "But what about the neighbors . . . or what about getting a doctor here?" He added without waiting for an answer, "I'll get a doctor. She shouldn't have a choice . . ." and with that Pol ran off, jumping with a hop over the gate.

Araba rushed back into the house, confused. As soon as she reached Nana Esi's bedside, the old woman, looking gaunt and gray, but with especially brilliant eyes, asked, "What was that tall groundnut doing here? Is he still clearing the bush . . . around your heart? What does he hope to plant and reap there? He just can't afford the harvest . . ." There was laughter in her eyes. "And don't cry!" Nana Esi added with a startlingly loud voice. "You are the one that is to carry on the spirit, my spirit. Don't disgrace me . . . I don't want any doctors or any of the family. I only want the two of you, especially you, even though you are younger, to be with me." There was a calm in her eyes which was a calm of stone, a stone just out of the bottom of the sea. There was a packet of cream crackers by the bedside table, and some raw ginger. "I like the smell of unripe mangoes . . . but maybe God doesn't want me to have that . . . Have I been a little too unbending in my life? No, don't answer me, I don't want too many answers at my age. Do you know that I never took the bandages off my heart for anybody? . . . at least not for long! I even went to church less often at one point because I thought it was opening my heart too wide. Perhaps after all, I am only a fisherwoman with a few words tied around my head for show. That's all . . ." "Mamaa panyin, won't you rest?" Araba asked, keeping the tears back, with the strongest of efforts. "Rest? Araba, you can't be serious! Help me to turn over to my side. I want to face you completely. Rest! That's the last thing I want to do. With these quick few moments left, I want to take the bandages off . . . or at least take some off, because I don't want to die from a broken heart." "But Mamaa, who can break your heart here?" Araba asked, her eyes wide. "You won't know yet, child. But the telling of all your life sometimes breaks you. For the last thirty years I have lived my life through you and Ewurofua. And you wouldn't know, perhaps, that Ewurofua too in her soft womanly way—I am not that type of woman, I certainly am not!—is beginning to live her life through you. Oh, it's no responsibility to you. Just ignore what I've just said now, I don't want to give you the weight that could age you quicker than you deserve . . . At least I can say that thank God I don't dip my bread in my milk! And my skin still bears the sea, or at least the scales of fish!" Nana Esi's right hand was shaking slightly, there was a weight on her chest. "I don't know who is trying to make it difficult for me to breathe . . . Do you know that if someone else were to be here, I would be robbed of the peace of my own death. I would be stiff, and I would take my stiffness to the grave. Stiff body, stiff spirit!" The old lady laughed, looking, from close up, like a child about to receive a last and important gift. Her white sheets had never looked whiter; and she had ironed them herself. She had in fact almost finished ironing them when she collapsed. She had been imperious even in her fainting, for though her eyes had been closed, she had not lost control. There was a silence, during which Nana Esi stared intensely at Araba, and Araba never lowered her eyes, not even when a tear dropped out onto her purple blouse. "That's it! You have truly inherited my spirit! And I have just transferred more to you! I hope, God forgive me, that Ewurofua does not return until I've gone. You see, her softness may force a few tears out of me. And I don't want that at all. I have been planning that things happen just like this for the last few weeks. She will never be able to take a hard, dignified death. She would think everything would be too cold. So you can tell her everything . . . she can survive a second-hand tale! Araba, I want to ask you something: am I dying as a typical Mfantse woman? When I'm ready for water I will tell you, I have sometimes preferred to think of dying in a shrine, rather than a church. There's real dust in a shrine, the type that would have received my own dust without any contradiction. Even now, all my old classmates—or at least those who have survived, and whom I tease so much—think I have always moved in high circles, that I was born with a natural coast elegance, and that I advanced and hardened with a few European touches. They make me laugh! I hate little circles! especially the high ones . . . I would be too blunt. The only friends I have are the same classmates that think so definitely that I have a better circle of friends . . . Isn't that stupid! Araba, make more money, and more—I am now being the devil's advocate, I'm speaking with a hardness of truth—because there's nothing else to do for the likes of us. And making money makes it possible for you to combine so many other things. I am not saying that you will be completely happy making it . . ." Nana Esi hesitated, she let out a sudden gasp, and then smiled. Araba shot up, then sat down again, " . . . but in this country now, there are too many other frustrations if you forget about money . . ."

Araba suddenly hoped that Nana Esi would not touch on her relations with Kojo Pol, for the finality of any judgment on it would probably break it altogether . . . "But I mustn't forget one thing: that Kojo, that Kojo, that funny man. You can't have him. He will turn into a rather vague man and he will be full of impulses, little ideas, and he will be far too open for you. He has no guile, he can't bring up our type of children with his odd ways. Oh, I admit, he's fine and fresh with his laugh. But Araba, you must not betray me.

I'm telling you again not to make the same mistakes we made."

The room was stiflingly still as Araba digested these words. And then she became too busy with the watching of the beautiful old face before her to think more. "I wish I could share your death, Mamaa Panyin . . ." she said more to herself than to Nana Esi. "Nonsense! that's what you're doing! And I mean the best nonsense . . . all your sharing is ahead of you. You know, I have never taken to this city . . . all these years I have been here, I have learned only the smallest Ga." Nana Esi's voice was lower, she moved her feet under the sheets as the afternoon wore on. She asked for her water, and she was holding her ginger; the cream crackers slipped further down the table as her left hand moved up and down the sides. "Is it the Bible you want, Mamaa Panyin?" Araba asked, shaking. "Oh, no. I've already finished with it. I want my ring, I want my finger to be surrounded," Nana Esi whispered, her eyes closing.

Then there was the desperate sound of a horn outside the gate. Both women stiffened for different reasons. Pol vaulted over the gate again, and let in a harassed-looking doctor, who was complaining right at the gate, "Look, young man, I do not like the trick you used to get me here. You said there was an accident . . ." Pol was knocking at the front door unceasingly. "Sorry, Doctor, I thought a life was a life . . . Araba, the doctor has come!" Pol shouted, his fez falling off. Upstairs there was triumph in Nana Esi's fading eyes. "I've beaten them to it!" she whispered to Araba, with a smile. Araba stood there torn between staying at the bedside and opening the door. At last she rushed to the door, and let the doctor and Pol in. Pol stayed downstairs. "Young lady," the doctor growled, "next time use your car to come to me . . . there are other patients waiting for me. Where is the old lady? I remember her, and that's really why I came . . ." When they reached the room, the ginger had fallen out of Nana Esi's hands. Her ring had surrounded her whole life, for there was no breath left, no room between skin and gold. On a piece of paper on the side table was scrawled "Thank God they came too late." Nana Esi had begun to write Araba's name but could not finish it. The ferns at the window waved to the cars outside, in the sudden restrained breeze. The doctor checked Nana Esi's pulse, listened to her chest. "She's gone. Control yourself, and be thankful she lived so long," he said flatly. Sister Ewurofua was already crying at the gate, where some members of the family were slowly getting out of the taxi. They followed her. She knew instinctively that her mother was dead. The house had the silence of a shell with no sea in it. Okay Pol took his leave of Araba with three pats on her shoulder. He did not want to get in the way. His fez was wet with sweat. All he heard Araba say in the distance to Sister Ewurofua was this, this delivered in a harsh voice with only a touch of pity: "Sister Ewurofua, my mother, hold your softness, hold your tears . . . you have come just at the right time . . . but take proper control of yourself . . ."

Chapter 17

The two hot voices, Celsius and Fahrenheit, blended from two different dwarf walls of the bar, in argument. The one blowing double fuse went lower, suddenly: Ebo the Food's voice always lowered after four bottles of Club beer drunk quickly by his resting limp. His barrel chest echoed with the speed of words scattering like gravel, as the kerosene lamp took over after the power went off. Shadows lengthened, climbing over the bent backs, over the low words. And several faces looked smoother, as the kerosene glow hid spots, scratches and frowns. The lights came on, then off; the darkness bit the bar, it was so sudden . . . by the Food, in the ugliness of Madina, could lurk supernatural, electric teeth. Cut, cut. And there were two levels of darkness: the external one, above his limp, which enabled him to steal from someone else's beer; and the one in his heart, far below his limp, which grew out of him with an intensity of worry over his wasted life. Beer was useful, but it could not wash down all the pain that Madina could hold. So Ebo was here, doing all the washing he could.

"Hey, contrey!" Ebo shouted hard, "that was the wrong leg you scratched! It could have been my wife's leg if she was here . . ." "But you, you Kanda mosquito, have you a wife?" jeered Kwame Ti, drinking from two old glasses he himself had brought along. "Hey Kwame Ti, you don't know I am a carpenter? I will lock your mouth just now! You have two other mouths inside this mouth of yours, you have three truths! All lies! Watch your scratching . . . as for me I worry about what people will do to the wife that I haven't got yet. You Kwame Ti, you are trying to commit something stupid this evening. If I hadn't given my belly the donkey work of holding my beer, I would put down my limp and fight you, jot to jot!" Kwame Ti blew the contempt through his smoke, but no one saw the abuse in his cigarette, perhaps only the surly kerosene lamp. The Food said: "Look at Kwaku ne Attah, dancing bone to bone. It's a mad Madina, this place! Churches, corn mills, latrines, bars and potholes! CM,L,B & PH! I can't bring up a child here . . . I can only bring up wild girlfriends: we will leap from bars straight to the churches! And after making love in the potholes, we'll troop to the latrines. Hey, Kwame! you brokeman, you. You see all these beauty-beauty ladies with guarantee shoes bought from the sweat of some sugardada, with his sugar finishing fast . . . you see them? They need help! Beauty needs help. Hey, quiet, don't say what you don't know! Kwame Ti . . . where did you get that name? You are a bush balanga! I will tell you one thing: I am good for other people's goodness: when they practice it on me, then they get blessing. And the more blessings they get, the more goodness I also get . . ." "Yes, and that is why you have become bad yourself," Kwame Ti said without hesitation, his contempt lighting up as the lights came back, right onto his cigarette. "For me I work. I type. I know paper. I understand the thoughts of professors. As for me, I'm me, paaaaa. You, you just hold on to other people's broken bread. The man of crumbs! Rural! Rural! And you can't even run straight . . ." "Except after women, except after women," Ebo corrected, half-listening to Kwame Ti, "and Kwame, I want my mouth to be bishop-and-beautiful for one night in this Madina Bar . . . after all, bishops too drink smallllll."

Bar breezes were different: they followed the beer and cooled it. Foreheads did not matter. Ebo's finger arched a story and bent it: "And you know the story about the man with the giant balls which he always quarreled with? He was in Korle Bu suffering from tennis balls which had grown into footballs. And when he put the pearls, God forgive me but I have love for people, at one end of the bed, he himself would crawl away secretly to the other end. And if they dragged along behind him, as they must, then he would shout: go away, everyone has his sleeping place. Go away and leave me in peace, in the name of—" "—of the almighty balls!" Kwame Ti interjected without a blink. "And poor man," the Food continued regardless, "poor man. His wife has left him. She is looking for smaller things! Kwame-ooooh, Kwame, I have to dance.

It is therapeutic!" "Ei, Ebo. What's wrong with the food in your head? You said it's thera-what?" asked Isa, sauntering up to the table. Ebo replied: "I said thera-beauty. I mean your wife, her beauty is in her tribal marks! And Isa, I have been telling you for the last one hundred bottles of beer that you should commot me your daughter. She is so tall that a strong man has to shorten her! And I've been seeing her eyeing fitters' trousers. Isa, sit down, if you haven't come empty-handed; as for your empty head, don't worry, don't worry, we shall fill it soon, soon!"

Isa was a clinic watchman, and he usually watched his own sleep, hoarding his snores openly. With the rushing bar girls all buttocks were beautiful and democratic: you just transferred the vision of beauty from the bigger ones onto the lesser ones. This was part of Ebo the Food's view, part of the success of his failure. "Yes I have to dance," continued the Food, "my head wants to see more of the sky as I rise, up, Up UP to dance!" The Food considered his dance a way of stretching his body in wide possibilities, a way of remolding his experience. He made allowance for the slight short-ness of his left leg, so that he seemed to be in a perpetual crouch, with his deep belly rounding in impudence, almost hanging on to his knees; then without warning he would send the bar into an uproar by executing intricate, supertobolo steps, while bringing in a few hand movements symbolizing a challenge for any woman present to come and test the size of his thing. "Bring me food, clapping is not enough, bring me food, bring me eat," Ebo would shout. "I am the Food, and I know the way of life in Ghana!" Ebo the Food was the man with his left space bigger than his right space for life could be a higher limp than you thought. If any mother were alive, she would put sweets and money on him, and then retrieve them later in disgust, as the Food continued with his in-decent gestures. He suddenly stopped dancing and looked at Kwame Ti with sorrow, saying, "Kwame, I wish my mother was were was were was were was here . . . to see the dancing I've done with my life, to see the smiles I can dig up freeeeee. Give me more beer to enable me to cry better. I troubled my mother, paaa." "Yes, and you killed her with all your troubles. I hear you shouted at her funeral: 'You have the wrong corpse! I'm the one that is dead!' What did that mean, at alllll? You killed your mother, and you're killing yourself. What do you want her to see you now for? She, she would be ashamed!" Kwame Ti's mouth was set with authority.

The snarl there traveled around Ebo's head. The music huddled in one corner, and waited for the Food to pull it back. Ebooooh stared in bewilderment at his friend. Then he said, "Never be serious when the country is dry and one man will never save another, except when others are looking. Killing is a serious matter. Mothers are even more serious . . ." The small tension was broken, and people returned to their breeze. Kwame Ti got up and suddenly talked to the khebab, he meant his meat at last. By the chipped glass, the tide of swaying flies looked for a share of the beer. All flies in bars were commas, for they never fully stopped on one glass.

Kwame Ti was now lecturing the adjacent empty table, which should have been full of beautiful women and jewels of beer about to melt. He was a thin, short man, with a detached intensity, and his coughs gave rhythm to his talk. He had known, loved and despised his friend Ebo for the last five years. His loyalty was at the tip of a cigarette. And, apart from other things, their bond was a jug of beer, or the share of jot. Ebo sat and stared at the concrete. He could sometimes see death there. He saw marks on the walls, the insults of other people's carelessness . . . There was always one thing he felt he could do when he was dead: eat, Eat, EAT. Then there would be a resurrection of the bottles, the *drinking*.

Ebo rose, then Kwame sat down and beckoned him over the few feet. Kwame needed Ebo's ear. He whispered something into it. The Food rose with dignity and walked toward that fat woman whose surplus skin was still fresh on her tray: "My friend says he wants to marry you immediately, now now now. Never mind any huge boyfriend you may commot. But I must try you first, I must see what the taste is like before I permit my friend to eat. Madam, no woman ever refuses us. Besides, we have beer and money; one never finishes and one never ends. We are the men!" The Food stood at attention, a salute plastered on his forehead. The languid owner of human fat looked at the Food with the utmost contempt. All the cheeky thrust of Accra was in her eyes. She took a long draft of beer, and made the slowest swallow in Madina. She sent her eyes back to the high and low of Ebo, and said, "I hear foko. Tell your friend if he's soldier boy, then he should come and do the fight himself, Or, is his thing too small, or what. Go, and don't waste my time!" Ebo about-turned, with the same dignity, and marched slowly to Kwame Ti. "She said you are handsome, and come over straightaway, because marriage is hot and shouldn't be allowed to cool at aaalll. My brother, go and attack her fat!" Ebo said in one breath. Kwami Ti rose, with extreme pride at the tip of his nose. When he walked, the breeze held his untidy waist like a chief was held when dancing. And he had arranged with God to give him an extra five inches in instant height, whether he walked on tiptoe or not. He rushed like a bullet, suddenly, toward his prey, and sat down with a familiarity that had become absolute. "Awura," Ti began with regal disdain, "I hear I am just too mech for you. Don't fear, koraaa, okay? I am only human. I type. I would very much like to type you . . . and Yes mama, I always do my typing, my best work, lying down." Ti's smile remained in midair, pulled out of his face and held high for effect. His assured elbows propped up the whole bar, even in spite of the heavy music, which shook the fat mama's arms as she raised her glass without even looking in his direction. "Madam, your head is facing the wrong way. And won't you let me fill your glass or attack your fat? . . ." Then, without thinking, Kwame Ti turned to Ebo's table down the bar, and shouted, "Is she deaf or what, it seems she finds it impossible to look at my sssweet face. She hears foko. Ah." Above, in the open roof, the neck of the universe could not wear all the necklaces of stars nor could it fit the neck of Club beer. Kwame Ti's hat hid the moon, hid this woman's heart . . . if she had any. She suddenly rose, and shouted over to a small fat man drinking by himself in a corner where the music would not reach: "Hey, Kemevor! I told you you were too short. I can't understand why I married you. All these years I've been telling you that you are too short, and too-too fat. And still you follow me everywhere . . . even when I want to drink beer. At least try to leave your height and shadow behind! And look, you are now attracting other short men toward me. It's a short life! Look at this mad runt before me here proposing love. Are you jealous? And you haven't even got the strength to beat anybody. You can't even beat your own fear. Imagine that I have to lean down six inches to give you your yearly kiss, or something. And that is even when I want something from you . . . Yieeeee. I'm suffering-oooh. I want to look up Up UP to a man, not down, koraaa!" Kwame Ti rose, pushing his chest out with a crushed look, with a twisted smile, as his indignation lay on the floor. He shouted to Ebo, "You, Ebo, you are libilibi. Your brains are like guavas, stuffed with a thousand stones signifying nothing! You are nkon-konsa-ni. You should know that I didn't mean *this* woman. Come and let me show you a really beautiful one . . . After all, have you ever seen a lion chasing a mouse's fat wife?" Kwame Ti walked back to his table with his own dignity tucked desperately between his tightened legs, his sideways cigarette making up for the lack of thrust on the other side of his life, the other side of his smoke. But he soon forgot himself again as he took another beer. Meanwhile, the Food's own crooked cigarette was bending furiously by the absence of straightness in the opposite side of his life, the darker side of his regret.

The Food chattered among the drinkers, supplying wisdom, in groundnut paper, on politics, love and money, that trinity of bar language. The watch in the moon was fast, faster than Kwame Ti's drinking: he talked so slowly now: "Ebo, when my wife left me, she finally came back to pick up all the abuse she had left behind. At that time I had just collected some heavy advance. So she stayed to help me carry the money; and we have been quarreling ever since it got finished. She likes waakyi too much. In fact she would rather go to bed with waakyi than with me. She would abuse me by asking me how I managed to have such tall children with such a short, short . . . thing! Ebooooo! We are a faulty people-ooooh! Half your fault is mine, and half my fault is yours, one moral ball each, and so if you multiply us by ten million, you'll go mad! Ghanaians are all waiting to squeeze the money out of 1977! Very soon, we'll start taking the years in advance . . . we will eat in advance, love in advance and die in advance. This should make it possible for me to attend my own funeral. Time will become so mixed that it will become one abenkwan. But all the fufu will be dead. Ebooooooo! Sea, never dry, at least not in the glass, not in the pocket. You see, it was these professors that spoiled me. You should see the type of nonsense I type! They think I'm stupid, but I notice everything that I type! Even that mad professor, Professor Sackey can't fool me. For him, he lectures his wife . . . I hear even in bed! He lives on beans and is always blowing his air out backward. That Legon place is another-Oh!"

The Food was dozing with his jot unlit, so Kwame Ti saw his chance to steal some beer, just as he had seen Ebo do. But he chose the latter's beer. "God forgive you!" Ebo shouted as he saw his jug at his friend's mouth. "For me, I can hear my drink move even in my sleep! You foolish man with banku in your bashi. Even if your build was kosrokobo, Lebanese style, I would bash you. You think coming from Kodie gives you the right to vamoose my drinkable! I love my blue beer made blue by the light . . . and you too! You are not sweet koraa, you are not sugarcane! You would steal the golden ring around my popylonkwe when I'm dead! Useless jot, man of nothing." "Ei, Ebo. What's all this?" Ti asked with justice in his eyes. "When you were stealing beer in the darkness I said nothing. Now, listen to you! You call me ewi. Beer kidnapper!" Kwame Ti stared at Ebo, but that justice in his eyes had already rusted there; and he blinked into another subject: "These days you can't get guavas to buy; and papaws are not sold much, they are only eaten or stolen. And the annoying thing is that when they steal the papaws on your farm you can hear the chewing yards and yards away . . ." "How? Are you going mad, beer kidnapper? And when did you last see the inside of a farm? It looks as if the beer you stole has gone to the wrong part of your head," the Food said with a grimace. "Oh no," Kwame Ti insisted, "you see I have the same problem: as soon as my life comes to fruit, someone else picks it. The other day I lost my nose in a spiritual church. I couldn't smell my own kwee! True, true, don't push me away, my gas won't go: . . . it was in Madina here, at the church of the Smiling Saint, where that crazy Osofo is, the famous Madina Osofo who talks about God to goats . . . I swear! I talk true! Now, about my nose: I went to the church to reclaim all that fruit I have been losing spiritually, to see who has been commoting my sunsum. And you see, I went with my sense of smell, my nose was working when I arrived—the gutters are the best test for that—but as soon as Osofo heard my story, and told me to close my eyes and pray for my wife, I couldn't smell anything . . . not even the incense. I couldn't locate my nose—and you already know how big it is . . . Then I had been confused: why had he asked me to pray for my wife? My wife did not need prayers, I told him. She needed waakyi. Osofo flew into a rage, and I thought I could see the gods scattering with the abuse from his mouth. Then I smiled, to try to calm him down; but I was warned that no one was allowed to smile on Thursdays. So I frowned, in compensation. The Osofo is now treating my wife. She said his sometimes holy anger is now beginning to heal her small, small . . ." "But what about your nose?" Ebo asked scornfully. "As soon as my wife is cured of trying to destroy me spiritually, it will come back. It will be the wisest smell, and Al-leluya for the spiritual nose," Kwame Ti replied with a look that showed how hungry he was, all of a sudden. He added: "And there's one thing all my years at Legon have taught me: a typewriter is only a porcupine with the alphabet on its back because what these lecturers write is wild!"

The space between Ti's eyes usually narrowed when he was getting drunk. And in the absence of his nose, his ears held all the smells and sounds around. His mouth had become the bar, and all words there seemed to be spoken through his amplifiers of beer and cigarettes. Some twenty legs, crossed, bent and mixed in the bar, formed his name, and that was as far the alphabet would go, as far as porcupines and names; as far as the world moved further and further away from him.

And then in the middle of the silence between the Food and Ti stood Dr. Pinn. "Welllll, Doctor! So you have chased me to this place again," beamed Ebo. "I know Madam EsiMay has been worrying about me again. Please tell her that I am sober in one lip, the upper lip; the lower lippp is really low and hanging, is secretly kissed pink by witches that fly on and around it at night . . . the low lip flight! Apart from that I am fine. But my ear is sore from listening to all the wisdom—of the left hand—from my grrrreat frrrriend here, Kwame Ti. Have a beer, Doctor, there's one whole jug in one whole world waiting for you! And as you know, Uncle Pinn, when I drink I lose half my limp. Kanda and Madina don't usually go together, but I know that your blue eyes are as wide as the whole of Accra, that is if you leave the sea out . . ." "Ei, Ewurade! The more I see of this white man the more I admire his teeth. Chief, were they shined by your wife? They look like the keys on our church organ! Let me press them to see whether any music comes out. Excuse me . . ." Kwame Ti said, staggering forward to try to open Pinn's mouth. In the middle of the bar, even teeth had music. Pinn took Ti's hand down with raised eyebrows, and said, "Good evening, gentlemen. Very kind of you this Madina evening. It has to be the quickest beer, since there's someone in my car. Kofi Loww's father Erzuah is sitting there in great confusion . . ." "Oh, Kofi's old rascal of a father! He should join us. The old goat used to drink far more than me; and now he's been so busy looking after his grandson that you would sometimes think he was a saint . . ." Ebo shouted with a laugh, as his belly blocked his empty glass. Dr. Pinn said simply, "I don't think he will drink anything this evening . . . his ex-wife Maame has taken away little Ahomka without

221

telling anyone. Erzuah says she's trying to steal him . . . and he can't find Kofi Loww, so he has come to us for help . . . I've finished my beer now." "Did I not tell Kofi that this woman was a witch?" Ebo shouted, clasping his hands as if in prayer, "I swear we will look everywhere for this woman! But where is Kofi? So he is not even at Odorkor? He can't be wandering about now, these days he doesn't wander so much."

When they went out old Erzuah looked so grave and so big in the car that the car seemed to be sitting in him instead of the other way round. His grief swallowed the Fiat. "Old man, don't vex, we'll find the witch. How did she manage to take Ahomka?" Ebo asked with his hand on Erzuah's shoulder. The old man took his pipe out of his mouth reluctantly. All he said was, "She managed to take him through chewing gum. Why doesn't she leave us alone? As soon as her lover dies, then she starts trying to break the little life we have built up in this city . . ." He closed the words again with his pipe. The Fiat filled with silence, but would not burst. They went and left Erzuah to the comfort of EsiMay and then sat down to ponder what to do.

Chapter 18

Clothes-lines of Accra unite, for all your washing ropes were higher than Maame's great head of duku. This April morning, with the clouds still undecided, she took her certainty along by stooping under everything: stooping under her own history of the head and the heart, stooping under the stares in Mamprobi, and stooping under her own lowering world. Her face had changed shape slightly, with the lower jaw setting—there was no sun on her face—and pushing up her lips so that you would think they were together in prayer. A desperate prayer which rose up to her eyes with two types of doom: doom for her decision to take her grandson whatever the consequence; and doom for her fear of Erzuah, mixed with the pity she felt for her son who had suddenly been arrested by the Special Branch for a reason she did not know. Her sandals pointed in two different directions, pulling the contradictions along, tightening her hips which had fallen several divisions in flesh over the last year. But curiously, her loss of weight also led to a loss of height. Under the whirr of passing trucks, she suddenly stood sideways: the profile of her waist was the same width as the plantain tree leaning over the wrong wall. She could not think properly for two days, and she had eaten only once, not counting the ghost of one sugarcane she had half-chewed, half-thrown away. In her bag were four packets of PK chewing gum, with which she would take away Ahomka. One Peugeot horn made her stop, one Datsun horn made her walk on. When she looked right, she expected a visitation, any sort of blessing for her impending abduction; when she looked left, she knew a curse would descend through the glare of a traffic

223

light. The time she was a little girl, she was fat and fearless; when she was a young woman she defended herself with her fat; but now she was running, so vulnerable, in and out of her own thinness. Her plan was to reach little Ahomka when there was no one there, when Erzuah had sent him to the next house while he went to the market. Another old woman stopped her just before she turned to the junction to Erzuah's house, and asked her with concern, "Now, my dear sister, my stranger-sister, where are you going in such a rush? You know, at our age we don't hurry; we don't know which bone or which memory will break. Walk slowly . . . already they think the thin ones among us are witches. They will burn you alive. Walk! Walk!" Maame pulled herself away with a quick shout, thinking the curse had come, even without the deed being committed.

But she was free still, and walked on, slowing down as she neared the house. Erzuah's house snarled at her, stared at her through its evil windows. She had no eye to stare back. When the sky breathed in, it choked her; when it breathed out, she would burst. That cashew-nut tree with the flies under its leaves was draining her heart with its blowing. Maame almost crept, crept through the dangers of her own life. Then she called a little girl she vaguely recognized: "Hey you, my daughter, go and call Ahomka for me; tell him his father has come," she ordered, trying to hold her shaking hands together. The little girl looked at her for a long time, then turned and ran toward an unfinished wall, with a thrown-back "Yooo." Maame went under the nut tree as if to hide. After what seemed such a long time, Ahomka skipped along, his smile as unfinished as the wall. Then he saw Maame and stopped, a look of deep concentration on his face. And he said, "Stand back, Nana Maame, stand back. Don't embrace me. Why did you trick me? Why did you trick me that my father had come? We are looking for him, and we can't find him. So it's not a trick that an old woman like you should play on her own grandson. Now, there's one thing I have to do: I have to hoot at you twice: one for annoying Papa Erzuah when you came last time, and two for not coming when it was my birthday." Ahomka stood back and started to clap and shout at Maame. Maame rushed forward, holding two chewing gums, and begging him to stop. The little girl who went to call Ahomka was standing near them, laughing. "Now, Maame, I have finished my business, am I not such an understanding hooter? What do you want with me? I am now a big man of eight years, and

Papa Erzuah has taught me not to be afraid of anything. I can scare dogs, I can scare people," Ahomka said, looking straight at his grandmother. "My little husband, come with me. We will go and look for your father. Only I know where he is. He's in some trouble. Take the chewing gum, and let's go; give one to your little friend," Maame said smiling, but with her eyes full of desperation. Ahomka looked at her with a combination of pity and alarm. He asked, "Nana Maame, why are you looking so strange? What's wrong with your eyes? There's fire in them. Now, if you want me to go with you you must go and tell Auntie Lili; she's looking after me till Papa Erzuah comes back. Or, let's wait for him then . . . Oh, Maame! Why are you crying? Can you hear me through my chewing gum? All right, we can go . . . but if we take too long, Papa Erzuah will hate you again . . ." Ahomka removed his hand from Maame's grip and strode ahead, asking, "Where are we going? Tell me, and I will lead the way. Don't I walk like a soldier? Come on, Nana! You are too slow . . . no, don't run, old women don't run . . ." Maame's eyes were burning, but behind the hidden eye-flames was a look of triumph, which moved her thoughts, her rights and lefts, into one life again. Then she panicked: she had seen Erzuah coming far off in the distance. "Let's go round this corner quickly, to see whether we can get something to eat . . ." she said, pulling her grandson along. "But there's no food there," Ahomka insisted stubbornly. She pulled him along all the same, smiling her desperate smile, so that he shook his head at her like a wise schoolmaster. Erzuah passed innocent and invisible, moving behind his beard with his confident walk; but his eyes seemed to look through and beyond everything he saw. "I told you we will get no food here," Ahomka said to Maame, with a frown, "I am the man, listen to what I say!" Then they passed the roast plantain and groundnuts, which Maame did not buy. Ahomka brought out his second frown, keeping it firmly on his forehead like a wound. "I hope you are not going to kill me . . ." Ahomka said suddenly to Maame. She stopped, and almost cried out. Then Ahomka continued: "What I mean is, I hope you are not going to kill me with hunger. After all, I can't live on chewing gum, can I? And there's only one plaster for the wound in my stomach . . . Food!" "Yes, my little husband, I will make you happy . . ." Maame said, without looking his way. "When?" Ahomka shot back impatiently, "Don't forget Nana Maame, I can always hoot at you again!" Ahomka laughed at himself. The laughter cleared the stare in Maame's eyes. Then as they got into the taxi for Labadi, Ahomka asked Maame, "Why do you still want to mix your life with ours? Papa Erzuah wants to know. Tell me secretly, I won't tell anyone. If you knew the number of secrets I had in my head, you would promote me to twenty-one years old!" Maame smiled, aiming her teeth over all the sadness she had accumulated. "I don't want you to smile like that, Nana Maame," Ahomka complained. "When you do that you look like a witch!" "But what secrets do you have, my little husband?" Maame asked quickly, adjusting her cloth. "Well," began Ahomka reluctantly, "but anyway, this one is not a secret . . . at least they didn't tell me not to tell anybody . . ." "Yes, and what is it?" Maame persisted. "Give me a chewing gum, please," Ahomka demanded, "and don't cry when I tell you." Maame brought her eyes back into the taxi, back from a long look at the palm trees by the sea. For a moment she thought Ahomka was Kofi Loww, and she was almost broken with this deep feeling of guilt. Her past was sitting right beside her, judging her. "Nana Maame, get yourself ready, and I hope the driver is not listening," Ahomka said, lowering his voice. "You see, Papa Erzuah says he has at last stopped loving you! He says you broke his heart, and broke my father's heart too. And he loved you, still, for many years . . . but one morning, he woke up, and he knew that he had stopped loving you! Maame, you must be a very bad woman, are you?" The tears in Maame's eyes stayed there defiantly, and did not know, this time, the touch of her slightly feverish skin. "Maame, look," Ahomka shouted from another world altogether, "the sea is in your eyes!" "Ahomka, you have the feelings of your father, and the spirit of your grandfather. I didn't want to be a bad woman, but your old Erzuah drove me away with his own bad ways . . ." Maame began. "No!" Ahomka shouted, "don't say anything bad about Papa Erzuah, his name is *Papa* Erzuah. Let's stop talking now. Let's accept that you were a bad woman, then I will have the chance to forgive you!" He looked with a long suspicion at his grandmother, then asked her, "Did you love Yaw Brago?" "Ei, my little husband, how many extra years have been added to your old head!" Maame exclaimed, as if looking at Ahomka for the first time. "Well, I'll tell you. Since you told me one secret, I'll tell you another. And you are the only one I can talk to now. That's why I have taken you! I've taken you for a long time . . ." "I knew that was your plan, I knew it! But Nana Maame, it can't work. I'm too strong for you, and also, these days I often cook for the house. If you take me like this without telling anyone, who will do the cooking, and who will listen to all the nonsense of Papa Erzuah? Besides, I want to help find my father." "We shall find him!" Maame said, with force, her face shining through skin folding over one by one with the years. Then she added, out of the darkest corner of her world, "Ahomka, wouldn't you like us all to die together . . . one day? I mean if we all start loving each other again, then we all decide to die, before we lose that love again . . ." "Ooooh!" Ahomka howled incredulously, "I think, in fact I know, that I am older than you! With all respect, Maame, I am far older than you! If we die like that, some of you will cheat some of us! I want to be somebody big and rich, and with more books than my father has! But I don't think I will have a beard, because Papa Erzuah says that sometimes hc hides his sadness in his beard. He said the whole of Accra goes to sleep in it! But one night when he was asleep, I searched, and searched, and I couldn't even find Mamprobi in his beard! I will never die . . . the best I can do for you is to spare you two years from my own long total . . . I hope you're not going to try any harm against me . . . remember I'm so, so, so strong!"

Maame just held Ahomka's hand as they got out from the taxi. Ahomka said, rather irritably, "This time I will let you hold my hand, but strong men don't want too much of this holding! I'm here to protect you, not to feel the sweat on your hand! And do you think I have forgotten that you still haven't answered my question about Yaw Brago? Did you or did you not love him? Don't fear, don't fear, if you don't tell me, who can you tell? After all, he's dead! . . ." Ahomka saw with surprise, as they entered the compound of a newly painted, starkly rectangular house of five bedrooms, that Maame was shaking violently. "What is wrong? Do you need nivaquine?" he asked with agitation. "No," Maame sobbed, "I am only giving you the answer to your question . . ." "So you did love him!" Ahomka exclaimed with disgust. "Then you better stop crying. I can't comfort you, I can't wipe any tears that are not being shed for any of my family!" "I only started to love him a few months before he died," Maame said, wiping her tears, "and I don't even know whether it was pity . . . but he has left me this house . . ." "And I will not enter it!" Ahomka shouted. "What Papa Erzuah said was true! You are a bad woman, bringing me into someone else's house . . . I will not enter." And true Ahomka stood at the gate so much stiffer than the metal there, for two hours, while Maame cooked sadly inside, after finally giving up trying to persuade him to enter. "As for the food, I'll eat. Yaw Brago didn't build it!" Ahomka finally said as he walked into the compound. "Come, my young man," Maame said with relief, "soon we will go and find your father . . ." Ahomka did not speak at all as he ate his ampesi. He sat with his back doubled to the house.

And so it turned out eventually that Erzuah, Ebo the Food and Dr. Pinn were looking for both Kofi Loww and little Ahomka. After one whole day of searching, even the Fiat became bigger than any hopes they had of finding them quickly. Erzuah's eyes kept shifting into angles of desperation away from the hopeless thrust of his beard. Pinn lost his little ironies, with the fatigue, and Ebo just ate into the future, beginning with groundnuts and ending with mature coconuts. They combed and unwrapped Accra, and found nothing in the waakyi of the unwrapped leaves. The police went around with them for two hours, then gave up, fixing a new date for more searching. It seemed as if, when the sergeant was around during the search, that Pinn could hear the entire police force eating in his car . . . the sergeant's chewing, the Food's chewing were amazing for their noise. Erzuah had never been so withdrawn, for after all he usually reacted to misfortune with bursts of energy, bursts of agitation. But for the first time, there was no gesture or commit- ment he could send out to the world: Accra, rather, started to move into him, as it had never done before: he saw something which he insisted to himself he would tell Kofi Loww when he saw him; that is, the buildings, the architecture, which Loww so often disparaged, had a long history and an amazing variety, which he was seeing for the first time, after all these years. He was seeing this because his emotions had wrung out of him different pressures of looking. His enormous energy had turned inward, and was pushing him into new areas from the back; he led himself from the back of the head, with his pipe showing the wrong way and smoking inter- mittently like a train. Most houses had taken on a loneliness—quite different from his mood—through being so utilitarian, so useward. The first use was that people did not much identify themselves with buildings, they did not see much of their history in mud or in cement. So that the space between body and house was constantly growing, just as Kofi Loww said . . . with the result that the body took all the inner and outer presences it could from the house, and the body became stronger, more vital, at the same time as the building became isolated from meaning, getting caught only in the confines of its own use. The second use came out through the hot smoke in Erzuah's pipe, which was not used to having too many thoughts passed through it with the tobacco and which was feverishly remembering his son's words . . . but if you had energy, and your sons were lost, you could shake with your own recollections. As the second use repassed through the pipe, it proved that the body of the Ghanaian was too heavy, too crowded, and too comfortable: it carried all the symbols, it carried the universe so easily; and in this way, it felt so much less reponsibility, so much less adventure, for all the external world beyond itself. The body, in a completely nonsensual way, was the First House; all other houses were at a distance, were for rent in a part-neat part-squalid way. Kofi Loww had once told him that everything would change for Ghana's good, if the body could be made lighter in the load of the head, in the load of the heart, but Erzuah had dismissed it as more, mere, book talk. Now he himself saw some of this in the buildings. Erzuah suddenly shouted, "Eboooo! You know what Kofi says our secret should be? Our secret should be to keep our link with life, with existence, while keeping clean and light that passageway that joins us with the world outside us, and which others have cut, and which we can keep with only a little hard work . . . a little of the midnight thinking, a little of the humility that Kofi Loww makes use of! Ebo, Accra is giving me a headache . . ."

"Things will be all right, Uncle," the Food said with sympathy, thinking that the worry was getting too much for the old man. Pinn listened with interest. Erzuah continued as if possessed by his son's presence, his son's words, "After all, do you think that after all these years of bringing up my own son, then my grandson, I would not have the time to think small-small or to listen? Dr. Whiteman, you are kind, as if the world has not yet touched you . . . you are wasting your gas. But don't you think that we in Ghana can keep life itself human! Let's have a little machine life, yes; but I hate the type that we see in other lands as I used to see in your films! Perhaps I'm getting old . . . at least I know that today I haven't had anything to drink . . . or maybe it's *because* I haven't had anything to drink! I have the answer, and it's all these buildings that have given me the answer. First of all, let's talk about what we can get rid of: as Kofi says, you lighten the body by throwing off some rubbish, without—he says *without*—losing sight of the ancient way of bringing the world to the body, rather than the body to the world. This means getting rid of, excuse-me-to-say, poor latrines, spitting, the amazing comfort of the body, or at least the part that is almost the same as being lazy or inactive . . ." Ebo laid his hand on the old man's shoulder, feeling generous with more of his easy sympathy. "Take your hand away," Erzuah shouted to him, with something like a little more of his old voice, "I'm not mad, nor is my worry making me talk rubbish! As for finding my boys, we'll find them! Only let me make some use out of all this searching in the street." Then Pinn asked, with more eagerness in his voice than he wished to convey, "You've talked about what to get rid of; what about what to keep?" "Oh," exclaimed Erzuah, looking with pity at Pinn, "it really does look to me now that the world not only hasn't touched you at all, but it shouldn't! After all, from what I have seen of your strong wife, she can always touch the world back for you without you moving your hand, at all! You are right . . . Kofi says this is what we must keep; the body itself hasn't become a mere shell—is it a mere shell in your part of the world, Doctor?—and we must continue to oil it with palm oil, we must keep its balance, rhythm and natural beauty . . . none of your physical obsessions! You see, even an old man like me can talk with you booklong people! After all, where do you think Kofi gets his brains from? We must keep that wide wide experience that finds almost nothing odd, now . . . we accept the old, we move with cripples, we rub shoulders with the mad. Even some taboos must stay, or at least their spirit must stay, not necessarily each real one. Then we must continue to modernize faster . . . look at an old man like me talking about something like modernizing. But there's been so much change already in my life that I want more and more! Change everything except the roots that do the changing! And in change we must look both backward and forward . . . what are you people forcing me to say? It's my son that should be talking to you, not me! It's his head I'm speaking out! And as for Ahomka, you'll see the type of body and head he'll have when he grows up! We are letting our great chance slip in this country. Our war cry should be, to be histo-, historical and to be smart! Hahahaha!" The old man looked almost hysterical, and then added, "I'm sure our doctor understood some of the Mfantse that I used to express my-self . . ." Ebo patted Pinn on the shoulder and said with a smile, "Madam and I are trying to teach him. I am the standing-up teacher, and madam is the lying-down teacher!" The Food had been trying to get a word in, and now that he had got it in, it wouldn't go back out: "Old man, I didn't know that Kofi had filled your head with so much . . . nons—— . . . errr, I mean so many words. And he doesn't like talking either. It's amazing! So after all Kofi is not the first generation of brains. Hmmm! For me, the minute I think too much I start to get hungry. The only thing I see wrong with this country, at least according to my mood now, is poverty: there should be more food, more women, more cars, and more more . . ."

The car moved on. "Look, look!" shouted Dr. Pinn, with great excitement, "I have just seen your little grandson in that red Toyota taxi coming from the direction of Labone. Quick let's turn around. Chase!" Erzuah shot up to look, banging his head on the roof of the car, and shouting, "Yes, you're the one driving your kind car, onward, please! chase him! He must be with that witch!" The Fiat moved like a drunk dancer, abruptly changing lanes in the Ringway, by Danquah Circle as its color fell off unwhite with the speed. True, ahead was the Toyota taxi, with five cars, five angers between it and the Fiat. Erzuah's agitation added nothing to the accelerator. The Food started to wave madly out of the car. The world would tear. Then the first car ahead of them stopped, thinking they were signaling it. "Not you!" Ebo screamed out at the driver as they passed him. "Hmmm," said Pinn philosophically, "this car was not built for grand prix racing!" "On, on!" screamed old Erzuah, riding the car like a horse. As they whizzed past an unsuspecting policeman, he jumped back, almost out of his uniform, pointing at them with a thumb of curse. The Fiat moved like a lion's haunches, bursting with sprung muscles, with absorbers of the sky, the tail of smoke snarling back onto the mane of white roof . . . where Erzuah's hand lay drumming, as if the fontomfrom fingers could raise the car and let it fly. Accra narrowed, the whole world got in the way, the distance became solid with other cars, other obstacles. And through it all Erzuah's heart was on fire, with his pipe dangling uselessly from his mouth. "Old man, control your heartbeats, Oooh!" Ebo shouted to him. He did not hear. The key to his locked ears was in the staring of his eyes, which framed the Toyota in a circle of intensity, pulling it out of its field of vision altogether and flat-

231

tening any other background around it. The crippled boy begging at the Liberation Circle did not exist at all, nor did the sky on his head. There was now only one car between the Fiat and the taxi, one whole world; then the Toyota suddenly stopped, at the same rate that Erzuah's heart sped. But this heart would have pumped gas if it could, for coming out of the car were Kofi Loww, Ahomka and Maame. With the speed and the sudden short distance Pinn stopped only with difficulty.

Old Erzuah was almost out before he stopped. "You, woman here," screamed Erzuah, ready to make a wild scene, "what devil has sent you here? What are you doing stealing my boys? I will pull you to the ground in the street here. Then you will be taken to the police to explain your abduction!" He lunged forward, his beard tossing on his flailing arms. "Papa, take it easy!" Ebo shouted, holding the old man. Like ants around a piece of dropped meat, the crowd started to gather. "Ei," someone shouted, "are you people trying to disgrace us before that white stranger? Go and solve your matter at home, this is not a compound!" There was some murmuring. Pinn quickly took the old man and Ahomka to the Fiat, and drove to the opposite side of the Circle, stopping in front of the Lido nightclub. "Papa, papa," Ahomka said at last, "I've hooted at Maame already. She's done some bad things, but she's also done some good things, she took Dada Kofi out of the police station. We found him there, and then she used her money to take him out . . ." "She's a witch!" Erzuah shouted, holding on to his grandson. He looked across as Kofi Loww, Maame and Ebo crossed the Circle. The taxi had driven away, and the crowd had scattered. The heat was returning, but with a breeze, and the water in the fountain at the Circle suddenly dried up. Erzuah broke away from the watchful eye of Dr. Pinn, and raced toward his son. He hugged Kofi Loww, who looked tired and absent-eyed. Ebo walked behind Maame, looking at her back with suspicion; and she turned around as if she knew what he was about to think, then walked on again with an even steadier gait, with her expensive lavender following her. The Food said to himself: imagine a woman trying to catch the men of her past with all this lavender, trying to trap them in perfume and iron sheets and a dead man's iron sheets at that! And after all if she had a song to sing, she had to sing it from a distance . . . otherwise she would drive the old man to his grave. Kofi Loww then said to Ebo and Pinn, "I thank you so much my friends . . . it looks as if you've been looking for us. Thanks. I know Ebo will pay for the gas bill . . . And I hope you can see the gratitude in my eyes. You see I was arrested—they thought I was Kojo Pol; but then later on they discovered I had a link with him anyway, and they kept me for a few days . . . I almost starved until Maame here, and Ahomka, found me, and somehow managed to get me out. They were still, unbelievably, talking about secrets I knew from the horses at the airport. The two of you can go and have some rest . . . we will make our own way. Thanks." "Now we have a prison graduate!" Ebo said laughing, as they shook hands and left. "We'll see you soon." Kofi Loww became absolutely clear-eyed, knowing that if he did not remain aware, old Erzuah would pounce on Maame in his rage at her presence, no matter how helpful she had been.

Father and son seemed to raise each other's beards, one powdered, one unpowdered. Accra was under hair again. Erzuah was completely unaware of Maame, even though he still held tightly on to the hand of Ahomka. He said to Loww as they walked along to find a taxi, "Kofi, I was talking to them about your body and building ideas when we were looking for you!" There was a shine in the old man's eyes. Kofi Loww laughed, wondering what odd variations Papa Erzuah had given his small thoughts. "I'm hungry!" Ahomka said suddenly, bringing them down to earth. Maame crossed the road to buy something, as Erzuah looked over his shoulder at her, with contempt. He said to his son, "We must talk about this mother of yours. She can't keep on crossing our fate with hers like this. We must find a way of letting her lead her own life. She may even be trying to get you to choose between me and herself!" Erzuah looked at his son full in the face as he said this. Kofi Loww playfully picked up his own son, and said to him with a laugh, "The old man thinks we are going to forget all the years he has spent looking after us! He doesn't know that it's now our turn to look after him!" "But sometimes we may allow Nana Maame to visit us. Papa Erzuah can be out whenever she comes . . ." Ahomka said, returning his father's laugh, but keeping a guardedness in his face, through which the laughter showed his double meaning. Maame had been looking at them from a distance as she bought the bananas and groundnuts. They seemed so set and happy. She could wrap her past in the groundnuts, throw it away, and look for fresh land to farm her meaning on, to plant her expectations on. She had been surprisingly patient these past few months. She now went over with defiance in her eyes, and shouted to Erzuah, "All right! If you don't want to see me, I'm going! My sons still love me, and that's all I wanted to know!" Old Erzuah did not say a word. He turned his back on her, and sent the triumph in his eyes to the short horizon beyond Kaneshie. Maame came closer and hugged her son and grandson, saying, "You now know my house, you can come to me any time you need me." Then she left, without glancing back once. Her back was infinite, but so was Erzuah's.

Then she saw Beni Baidoo in the distance, but she could not replace the sadness with new anger. She let him walk beside her chattering about his village; and thanking her ironically for the bread she threw at him when they last met . . . Then she turned into a different road abruptly, handing him two cedis with distaste, and going on alone. Baidoo had already laughed into 1976, with the same grade of laughter as the previous year, but was apprehensive about whether 1977 would come at all . . . the number of coughs he made in a day was beyond one hundred lungs . . .

Kojo Pol was looking for a new fez. Either the old one had shrunk, or his head had grown . . . the brains may have at last wanted to come out properly. Shrunk hat, shrunk life, the same thing; but he still knew how to send enough kelewele to his mouth and enjoy it. His room was even neater, and so was his heart, for there was less of the extravagance of Araba Fynn in it. Her powder had gone out of his window with a swirl, especially since Nana Esi died. Like a child, Araba Fynn would insist that Nana Esi had just gone, and not died. She was the stern watchwoman at the old lady's gate of memory. She had to hold Ewurofua's grief in addition to her own, for Ewurofua had completely gone to pieces. She cried all the time, did not eat unless forced, and talked about nothing but Nana Esi's life. Pol had been moving in and out of Araba's house, doing little errands, feeling much more of a ghost than the living that had just died. He was being used and was being useful, mainly because Araba was determined, abusuapanyin or no abusuapanyin, to keep the family as much out of things as possible. Nana Esi had given her more than a hint of this when she said, "I have made some sort of provision for them, even though they don't visit us, but I don't want them running around planning my funeral, as if they loved us. No one will be allowed to love me new when I die!" But his errands were now becoming complicated: Private Mahamadu had rushed to his house one morning as he lay flat on the doubt in his bed, and warned him . . . it was a kindness without reason or reward . . . that Sergeant Kwami was now an inspector, and was planning to arrest both him and Kofi Loww, but that he, Pol, was to be the first. Okay Pol had thanked him with a hug as he rushed back out into the jeep. But, at this time of grief, it was impossible to tell Araba Fynn about this. Neither did he want to go to Boadi's, in case Boadi was really behind it all. So he did the errands the best way he could, though sometimes he would stay away for days at a time . . . and come back to meet the cold stare of Araba who could not understand his absences, just when he knew she needed him so much. But she did not seem to need his heart, he thought to himself with a laugh.

Pol got a black fez for the burial, wanting, just at this perverse moment, to wear a batakari to emphasize his Northern links; and even perhaps to throw Araba Fynn into confusion, so that she either finally rejected all of him, or took only those parts of him that he himself found acceptable. People came like ants, cockroaches and mosquitoes, as Nana Esi would have said. Some of them could feel the old lady's contempt swell in the coffin; and there was at first an unusual amount of silence. Then the fishermen and all the other people she dealt with in fish, took the courage to whisper, then talk openly: "How can Nana be dead at this time? Did she not boast to us that the sea would have come to Asylum Down to get her before she would join the ancestors? . . . No, she wasn't a hard woman, she just wanted standards, she just wanted others to drive them-selves as hard as she drove herself . . . Isn't she so beautiful? Did you see her skin, even as she lay there dead? I wonder where she got this secret of her stone skin from? And look at her daughter and granddaughter, they have the same skin, but the granddaughter has taken the hardness. Do you see how she talks to us, like some queen mother in some town somewhere? . . . They say she almost didn't get her water to drink, the doctor was saying she refused to see him, and that she turned off her own heartbeats just before he came. Ei! Nana Esi! Where is she taking all that mystery that she built up around herself? Some of us simple fisher-dealers believed when we were children that she could sometimes walk on the sea! And you wouldn't believe the number of people she has sent to debtor's prison! It's not only her skin which is like stone, it's also her heart! Oh, but that is not fair: she would always give plenty of time before acting. She didn't want anyone to take her for a fool. And as for her late husband, he used to say: what sort of woman is this, with this massive dignity? I must pull it down with all her clothes! Poor man, they say he never saw her naked, excuse me to say this. Ah! . . . Our Nana Esi is so rich that they say she has more money than one hundred thousand customers put together! The day she would withdraw all her money, she would need five articulators, plus one tractor for all the gold! Oh, don't say that: she was a very spiritual woman. She went to church. She in fact built most of the churches that she went to, by Adabraka side there. It was a pity she couldn't build her own Jesus! . . . I think the bishop himself is going to bury her, both in the cathedral and at the graveside. I don't know myself whether I would like this type of funeral. I would prefer to drown at sea! Ei, Nana Esi! Dammirifa Due! Sleep, Amen!"

The words formed a gray light around the hearse, above, below, across, but not in. Every ditch in Accra had a lie to tell: the lie of going down when it should be going up, the lie of space when it should be earth. The deepest ditch was the grave, deepened by a whole life, and defined here by the impudence of Pol's height, with its upper afterthought of fez. No one knew that the head could define death with the roll of such irony, such felt. Pol looked ludicrous with his sudden sunglasses, as if the deep gray sky had descended onto his eyelids, and had refused to move from there.

He looked left, and then had to look sharply again: there, unmistakably there, was Dr. Boadi, also in sunglasses, carrying his belly along like a second coffin. Only his dark secrets were buried there. Pol had a momentary feeling of fear and contempt, as Boadi flashed his whaaat smile in the absence of the silver jacket. Boadi mourned by producing this flash as regularly as a firefly's. Pol tried to mix more deeply, more inconspicuously, with the crowd; but to be successful, he would have to take his own neck and fold it under his arm, so that his head could get the chance to be short and unnoticed. His irregular walk, which used to make Sister Ewurofua laugh so much, irregularized itself even more; and after tripping over two mourners, stood still altogether, as the black and red waves of people flowed past and even through him.

There were three quick taps on Pol's shoulder, and he turned too quickly, crashing into Boadi. Boadi managed to drag his smile out of the heap, and showed it dazzling, but reluctant, to Pol. Pol stared with unusual severity at him, and remained silent. "My friend, don't vex," Boadi laughed, "why have you been avoiding me these days? . . . Oh, incidentally, may she rest in peace, the old lady! Are you still hunting on dangerous territory? Or you now think that the lioness of the savanna has been removed, so the plains are safe! Be careful, the prey itself will turn on you and devour you! Hahahaha . . ." "Aren't you laughing rather too loud?" Pol asked, looking around. The two of them walked on in silence, and by the time they reached the Catholic cathedral, they could not move forward for the crowd. Pol asked Boadi abruptly, "Why are you trying to cause my arrest, and Kofi Loww's too? I thought we had solved all this already; and I also thought that in the old days I saw a little decency under your fine skin . . ." "Stop, stop! What are you saying?" Boadi asked, with a dark frown which made his cheeks, especially the left one, stick out even more, "I am not on that level anymore . . ." "You are doing it through your inspector . . . Inspector Kwami!" Pol finally revealed, tilting his fez away from Boadi. "And I wish your security dogs would not continue to waste time with the harassment of innocent people that are not the slightest dot interested in your affairs . . . Do they feel they have to earn a living or what! barking into people's lives like that!" Pol's voice had risen, but he remembered where he was, and let it fall back gently into the funeral. His voice darkened and quietened.

"Listen to me young man . . . Inspector Kwami indeed! Is that stupid man still on this dead schedule? Then he's doing it purely from personal hate . . . Now, listen: haven't you noticed that after losing a few pounds I'm beginning to put on some weight again? Well, my commissioner is no longer a commissioner, and I'm far too busy trying to maneuver my way elsewhere to be bothered about chasing young and idealistic . . . mosquitoes! You see, confidentially, I'm getting quite close to some SMC members. They like my confidence, confidentially! And you know all about my way of life! I'm sure you know me well enough to write me a testimonial. Of course I certainly wouldn't like my wife to write me one under any circumstances at allllll! Hahaha . . . I sometimes think poor Yaaba is preparing to leave me. True this would be regrettable, since she would be taking away a third of my past, and even I have some interest in the past . . . if it profits the present. But if she takes this courageous step, I would have to respond with equal courage . . . by racing immediately into the small beds of other girls! And, Pol, Kojo the Pol, these are confusing times, both for the heart, and for politics. But don't worry, once I regroup my forces, I will destroy Kwami! I will soon get my inner Asafo Company moving! In the meantime, be cunning with him, you and your friend Loww. You see, Loww should not get too high, and Pol should not be on fire!" With that, Dr. Boadi moved off abruptly without another word. Pol stood there stiffly, wondering whether to chase Boadi and beat him with an upright stick, or to let him take his matter and go. He chose the latter, and pushed his way around to the back of the cathedral, hoping to get the smallest glimpse of Araba Fynn; or even to see Ewurofua's tears once more . . . anything to take his mind off Dr. Boadi, and to get back into the mainstream of mourning with the eyes or with the heart. All sorts of societies that Nana Esi had been patron of were fully in evidence. For such a private woman to have such a public farewell . . . As the bell tolled and the drums boomed subtly, Pol felt like sleeping.

Then an old man with small sharp eyes shuffled up to him, and said, "Young man, I've been watching you. You look confused. Did that fat rascal trouble you? I am the brother-in-law, the akonta, of the deceased. Let me tell you something: I was the one who was really in love with Nana Esi. I tried everything, but she could not or would not look at me. She took that hopeless brother of mine, may he also rest in peace, and she was never happy! That was my triumph! That is what has comforted me over the years. Last year I came to see her, with my Mercedes, yes I am not ashamed to admit to any young man that I have a good car, for which I worked like a demon. And I must confess that I worked so hard just to prove a point to this woman lying flat in this church. Yes I came to see her last year, I came all the way from Winneba, from my poultry farm, brought her some eggs, even bought a good akrantsi on the way. I came in my immaculate political suit. When Esi saw me, she gave a short laugh, as if she were laughing all the way to the past. I looked at her quizzically, wondering, rather wickedly, whether she was overawed by my university education . . . She invited me to sit down, with mock ceremony. I kept my back absolutely straight. I must admit, young man, I had really gone to see her out of revenge. I wanted her to see what she had missed . . . of course with a woman like Esi, you don't talk about missing anything in life. She had that stylish Mfantse shrewdness! She offered me her famous cream crackers, and a little wine. She sat down and stared defiantly at me. Then she suddenly said, 'Acquah! I'm not going to ask you your mission, because I know what you have come for. You are wicked! Do you think you are coming here to make me regret part of my life? Don't try at all! I don't care for your car, nor your suits!' I returned her gaze, eye for eye, for after all these years, I was no longer weak! Then you know what happened?" . . . Pol stood there, almost hypnotized, and shook his head. "Well," continued Mr. Acquah, "Esi came and sat beside me, and started to cry! I almost died! I held her, our two old skins together: leather to velvet, for hers was smoother than mine. Then she quickly wiped her eyes dry, and said, still holding me, 'It's true, I don't care much for your attempts to impress me . . . but I did love you, I did. I only thought you were not strong enough. And yet things turned out the opposite way! This is the secret I give you, after all these years . . .' She spoke as if from some blue light beyond her cloth. Then she put her face against mine, my poor, wasted, Mercedes Benz face, bare and brown, and she said, finally, 'Don't come here again, I am not going to change my heart or my life now! I can't put fresh palm oil in an old cracked dusty bottle, can I?' She never listened to my protests . . . and here we are after these burning months! I am here, she is there . . . I'm vertical, she's horizontal . . . Young man, I must leave you. Here's my card. You look like a sincere person, and your eyes are ready for education. There is something generous and odd about you. For me, I'm the typical educated Fanteman, with the words always ready in my pocket to either bolster or destroy the heart! Visit me when you can, but never on Fridays. I always pray in a shrine on Fridays for I belong to several worlds. I'll see you . . . even your wave is generous . . ."

Kojo Pol started to walk away from the cathedral, thinking to himself: Araba Fynn would do the same to him, she would come for him when he was old. She would remember the innocence, or something. He remembered his meeting at the other cathedral, the Anglican cathedral, with Boadi, Loww and the rest; he remembered the first provost of the cathedral whose voice used to fill the walls for the Bishop's Boys' School children. Churches. Priests. Death. His fez led him gently back to his Kaneshie room, where his sadness filled the wireless that filled the corners. And Okay Pol, the man with the crowded neck and the multimetered walk lay there asleep, and he did not dream.

239

At first when they all returned from the cemetery, Araba did not notice the absence of Kojo Pol. She was exhausted, but was overseeing what she thought was the shocking habit of feeding many of the guests after a funeral. She could not bear the noise of their jaws, and thus she went up to Nana Esi's room, where she saw Ewurofua sitting, reading and crying at the same time. Mother and daughter did not say a word, for a while . . . Ewurofua spoke through her sobbing, and Araba through her frown of exhaustion. In spite of her grief, Ewurofua felt very guilty at her incapacity, at the pushing of all the responsibility onto her own daughter. But there was nothing she could do. She was sliding down emotional plains, emotional savannas that she could not control. And it was exactly as Nana Esi had predicted . . . which made her even more helpless.

She rose, her beads rounding her vulnerability, and went to sit beside Araba, and hugged her. "Forgive me," Ewurofua said, still crying, "I should be helping you more than this . . ." No more words came. Araba wiped her own eyes, but she refused to sob; sobbing was for soft mothers, or for clean horizons without duties given with the last breath at the deathbed. Araba's old look of indifference had now become a look of beautiful dignity, a look heavy with the quickening future. And oddly enough, she sometimes stopped herself from crying by remembering Pol's funny antics.

This was when she suddenly realized his absence. "Sister Ewurofua, where is Kojo Pol? You know, he has been so helpful . . . he had a certain type of strength that I did not realize, and which I found I was sometimes leaning on . . ." Ewurofua just shook her head. Araba was suddenly filled with deep foreboding as she remembered Nana Esi's words on Pol. She thought, with a boldness that she could not hold back: after all, Nana Esi herself made a mistake in her marriage. How can she advise me on my affairs? When I have finally put my grief down, I will talk to Nana Esi in spirit, and then make my own choice. She will not grudge me that! Araba went downstairs again. She could not see Pol. She only saw the jaws still eating.

Chapter 19

At last the gods and trees were refusing to protect ½-Allotey any longer . . . he was becoming too successful, and too inventive about the ancient ways of his life. They thought ancient ways should remain ancient. Five years ago, Allotey had been sent to a shrine, in the true line of his ancestry—and after serving his father's shrine for years—to serve the god there through his new master, the priest. But before the first year was over, he had been sent away, because of his impudence, his constant questions, and his own ideas about the rituals and the divinations. The priest did not have the patience of his father: "You, young man, you cannot tell me to try a different mixture of herbs . . . are you mad? You will bring the wrath of our ancestors upon you! I suspect it is already an angry spirit speaking through you. Do you not remember the night you were bathed in the cemetery? Or, you've forgotten the knowledge of the leaf that you can eat, and not be hungry for days? Be careful!" The thunder of his priest at the shrine merely doubled the questions in his head, and enlarged the rebellion in his heart. But it made the love he had for his father grow. "I was born this way!" he would say with indignation. "Can't you speak to the god, and ask him to help me to push my own meanings in among the thousands that have existed for thousands of years? My father did just that!" Even then, ½-Allotey's stupendous shoulders carried the beginnings of authority.

So he was sent away, with this warning: "Young man, your father tried much the same way of demanding answers . . . if he had not reported back to another shrine for treatment years later, he would have gone mad!" But ½-Allotey rejected this. He would still smile into the past, in spite of his experience in the forests and Kuse, and in spite of the growing loneliness of these hills, where the language of silence was pursuing him threateningly, and where he could feel drums and war in the air. This dusk, he stood with a large stare on the hill line. He was stroking his hut. The darkness was coming out slowly from somebody's left heel, coming out almost with the richness of smoke. It could be that his own heel was the dispenser of this darkness. He could feel the evil, the shadows of his own Kuse people crawling up the hills. He pushed his shoulders against the darkness pushing back, and he thought he heard a song from deep under the hill he was making his life on. Perhaps the rocks were built on songs, on warnings. Allotey pressed a herb used for boils, in his hands, and said to himself, "When the forest made me ½, I survived. If I can't fight this war, then I will betray my father and my own self." His words rolled tightly down the plains, pushing the first fireflies out of the way. The trees chattered at him, they would push the angular movement of their long branches into his history. By the different grades of leaves, dark and light, there were different grades of fear. And the biggest roots would seem to uproot the moon, would seem to push the light underground, to brighten the secret deeds there . . . and to darken ½-Allotey's eyes. Over where his fish talked purely with their movement, he heard two stones falling into the pond. When the water jumped up, it took so long for it to join its own ripples again. The crickets were silent every five minutes, betraying that there was something or someone among them. Far, far off in Pokuase, the last light went off so early . . . the last wink was gone. That stalk of guinea grass that Allotey thought he saw moving, was another stalk of grass altogether, and that too was another one, and yet another. When all the grass, this central grass, came together and touched, they touched the bunched fingers of his courage.

Suddenly, someone was climbing steps into his mind, and warning him to leave the hills immediately. Allotey broke the steps with his swinging fist, but he turned around and saw nothing. He smiled because he felt his own eyes so intense, so much clearer than the black sky. The owl had the eyes of the entire hill, and was defining his rebellion with the relentless circles of its stare. Then without warning, he heard his own name screamed out three times. He refused to look in the direction of the sound, and asked himself,

242

"Is this a war of the head, or a war of the plains?" He walked around his hut with careless stealth. He saw his entire young corn farm walking stiff and in accusation toward him. He blinked the vision away, but heard footsteps rushing away, rushing away into the future . . . where every answer was itself a question, darker than each last one. The future would move back into the past, and deepen and darken as it moved; then it would move sideways into the present, standing in its own deep rind before the raised hands of Allotey.

The hills were revolving, for he saw that his back had become his front, and his front had almost vanished . . . with all the memories of survival that he had. Into the beans strode ½-Allotey, frontless and headless, carrying his own head in his hands as he should in any war. He laughed as the beans tightened in their pods . . . they were growing away from him, they were rounding away from the square prison of his own head. "Allotey!" he heard a voice shout. "Allotey, come back to us at Kuse, come back to the earth in the way of your ancestors. Bury your questions! There is a hole behind you ready for their burial!" The wind would blow in the opposite direction, taking the words away, and bringing them back again in a game of coercing echoes. The words were whips, and they kept missing him by inches only. Shame! But why had the sky raised itself and gone? The sky was streaking away! He thought: would that his father were up there pushing the heavens back down. The rain was beginning to fill the darkness with the worst type of May . . . under the circumstances any screams would be wet, any blood would be diluted. By the bamboo coop, Allotey's cock crowed to have its throat cut. The rain came down in slants of "We said so, we said so!" He lay down in the rain, and the earth lay down with him but he had to leave fast this eternal twin lying there; so that he got up. His neck found his head, at last . . . as he touched his father's old talisman. But his body stiffened, for when he wanted to smile, he had to tear his lips apart. And he did smile on and off, for that was the best way to keep his head on. He suddenly stamped the ground to stop his shadow moving of its own accord. And the light that came from the west and died, was met by the darkness from the east of his head.

"Let not the darkness come from my eyes!" he shouted. At the end of the echo of these words was a laughter that his mouth had not made. In the plains, the strange mouths were busy: the contemptuous chatter came in shifts of different tone, and each sound was passed up the hill stalk by stalk, leaf by leaf. Allotey remembered how his mother would quiver at all his blasphemies. She quivered no more, for she was dead, leaving behind her vast memories of the most beautiful nkontommire oiled in the village . . . green spoonful settled by the plate, beside the fresh authority of new yam; and under jaws already chewing before the food even entered. He remembered his father saying with a smile, "You young boys still don't know how to park food properly in your big mouths! Yet you are so keen to learn how to drive! Be careful you don't end up driving bones down your stomach!" His house was full of echoes, strange, but happy . . . and other boys thought twice about visiting him. But even then, he enjoyed playing against his own strength . . . ½-Allotey had this strength long before his manhood followed.

The darkness now formed hundreds of half-symbols, with its loops, lines, squares, circles and hearts; the meanings and insinuations were suffocating him. "Allotey!" came the voice again . . . and this time it sounded like old Kwame Mensah's voice . . . "Allotey, we are giving you the meaning of surrender! The easiest thing is to surrender to your own forefathers, when they are advancing toward you in the darkness!" There was a thin man—his legs stuck in the middle of the world—with a terrible face sitting on the tallest tree, driving the whole horizon, with the plains and trees following in zigzag, like poorly joined timber trailers. To cut all the timber in the head would leave a clear mind. ½-Allotey frowned at the thought, the frown climbed the lines of his forehead, and stared down at his bitten lower lip.

Slowly by the northern side of the hill climbed the black goat with the perfumed beard. Its droppings were of thunder, and spread down the plains in words of damnation: "Allotey-ooo! We are now a goat, we are coming to get you-ooo! Do not resist, you can neither resist the past nor the future! We own the midnight, and the hours of midnight are the sharpest weapons! We are the goat, we are coming to *get* you!" ½-Allotey shifted so that his dagger met the shadow of the goat at its own angle. The drum music that rose from the tail of the goat seemed to drain away his strength. His own dagger would suddenly turn toward him, toward his heart; and he could only control it with the greatest effort. The hide of the goat hid nothing, not even its own bones underneath. It sent

244

its eyes ahead to survey him. Allotey missed with his thrust at the eyes. And the hooves danced to the music of the tail. He rushed behind his hut in desperation, gathering wet twigs and kerosene for the fire that would burn time and fear. The rain had stopped, and had sent an interval of wind, so that the fire roared and roared. The goat was bleating by the fire. "Kwame Mensah!" shouted ½-Allotey. "Don't come any nearer! I have overpowered my own knife. If you come any closer, I will kill you and roast you in this fire! I am not alone here! My father stands beside me. I have his strength!" Sweat could make a small well, when it was intense enough. Allotey jumped and shook, as if in a trance. The goat laughed and spoke at the same time, "And your father is still mad. We have standing before us, beside us, and behind us, the strong hands of history. Can you defeat them? Can you defeat the hands that never end?" More laughter bound both man and goat together. Allotey laughed back, so that there were two concentric heaps of laughter.

A sudden understanding rose in ½-Allotey's head; his head rolled back with the heat of the last answer: with a scream, he stuck the dagger lightly into his own left arm. He watched the goat intently. And from it came an enormous bleat: "Leave me alone, leave me alone. We are Kuse. You can't destroy a whole village. Who told you the secret, the great secret?" Allotey raised the knife and plunged it into his arm again. The goat fell down, and was rolling downhill. He chased it, stabbing it several times in the beard . . . where the blood and the perfume met . . . and in the left side. He dragged it back up the hill, throwing it with a curse into the fire. The words burned: "Allotey, you have killed us, you have won your peace. Come back to Kuse!" Then the words died.

And the suddenness with which the dawn came shattered ½-Allotey. He lay by the ashes, which had the shape of his wound, the shape of his words, the shape of his spirit, the shape of his own stubborn path. Apatupre, the first bird of the morning, pushed the baton of the dawn along, above ½-Allotey's wound, which he was staring at with surprise, and which was gray with ash. His own goat lay half-roasted, with its teeth fresh and shining in a gruesome grin. The black carcass was the world: you ate the cooked half, and tried to store the raw. Allotey rose with an extraordinary number of mosquito bites . . . as if his skin had a small range of absent teeth. Both his hut and his hoe were still asleep. And if he wanted to eat, he would have to chew through the morning, for it followed him everywhere . . . African gum morning, to which his thoughts were stuck. The rain had poured all its words on him, for the back of his batakari was wet and the front dry. Everything was ½. The corn farm seemed exhausted with walking. What had he won? After all, was he not just after a little revelation, a little irreverence in all these rituals?

He tore a piece of roast meat, before the poor morning could move . . . and you should never chew looking at the teeth of a dead goat: the doubt would stare at you from the mouth. The charred tail was a one-finger blessing: Allotey had found part of his freedom attacking the mad music around it. The hut opened its mouth and let him in. He had never looked at his small belongings so sadly, except for the leaves and herbs, which reached a different part of his mind. He saw how to burst through the propriety of ancient ways, then boldly sew the bits together again in different patterns . . . yet within the womb of the earth, Assase Yaa. The earth was the basis, the earth was still the boss . . . even when you flew, you left your footmarks on it first, even if you would land on a different slope. He felt complete peace standing beside his herbs, and thinking: you would invent the impossible, you would make your life move fast; but you would always come back to the earth. Then he had a sudden vision of telling this to Professor Sackey, in spite of any scorn that his friend would pour on it. He went back out and had a long look down the hills: the eye was speed, it moved around trees . . . different traveling for different trunks . . . it parted the bush for the sudden path of an akrantsi; then as it moved over the roots and leaves, it came to rest with surprise on the dots of two heads walking up the hill.

½-Allotey wiped his face and looked again. It was two people, dragging the flatness below them up the slopes, very slowly. There was a man in Northern robes, and a woman who, even from this distance, looked familiar. He started to move down for he did not want them to put their strangers' feet in his little world, so disorganized at that moment. His visitors started to move up a little faster when they saw that he was coming down. "My dear husband!" were the words the woman sent up to him from below, "My dear husband, please wait up there for us . . . it is me, Mayo. No, don't get angry . . . I have come all this way in peace . . . receive me well, for I am not alone." Allotey stopped with a sudden anger, his shoulders broadening with suspicion. He continued to go down, knowing then that meeting them halfway down the hill would make Mayo uncomfortable. And what did this silly woman want here? he asked himself. Mayo continued to wave to him to move back up, but he ignored this, remembering the impertinence with which she had always interrupted his searches. When they met, Mustapha smiled for all three of them, for the other two mouths were shut. Mayo had been thinking: was he still so stubborn that he would not even stay where he was to welcome them? She had changed over the months, she had become much fatter. But this had no particular interest for Allotey.

"My dear husband, are we going to stand upside down here and talk, or will you kindly lead us to your house as custom demands?" He was about to say: we should stay halfway, so that I hear only half of what you are going to say, for I am not interested in the other half. But he took them near the top, suddenly sitting down, and saying, "Here I have no chairs, only one old stool; and I haven't fetched my water yet. Welcome. What's your mission?" Mustapha continued to smile, for after all, this was the man that Kofi Loww had said he should see about his . . . illness. And Kofi Loww had said it because he had heard it from Kojo Pol who had in turn heard a chance remark from Professor Sackey. Mustapha had been trying desperately to trace ½-Allotey for the past four months; and he finally traced him to his ex-wife, Mayo . . . who made Mustapha understand that she was still married to him.

The truth was that, for some strange reason, Allotey's reputation as a healer had soared at Kuse, in his absence. Stories reached the village about him . . . perhaps from some of the scattered hamlets around in the hills, for they found his ways, his farming, his aloneness strange. Who had grown such beans on these hills before? Who had made a fish pond here? And they saw him with herbs. And he would eventually heal one or two isolated cases, more out of exasperation than anything else. Mayo loved gossip and fame, and she had wanted to see this famous man whom she had wronged last year. So she had braved it with Mustapha all the way here. Mayo thrived on Mustapha's embarrassment when he was telling his story, for the simple reason that she had no great feeling of responsibility toward anything, except where her curiosity was alive. If she were to see an ancestor, she would immediately want to be entertained by him, with her mouth constantly shaping different circles of curiosity. This sense of energy and laughter had drawn Allotey to her, but he discovered that there was nothing behind it: it was this sole quality that filled the confines of her being. She was a child and she had joked about the middle of his legs, had put okros where real flesh was. Now she had struggled up here because she was intrigued by his reputation. She did not feel guilt over her past relationship with him, since so many others had praised her for bearing so courageously the ways of such a strange man. Her lightness of being fouled the plains for him, the leaves grew thick beside her.

When Mustapha talked, he had a habit of putting his face very close to his listener. But as soon as he started this with ½-Allotey, his face was pushed back hard but politely by the latter. So Mustapha, without a protest, found his face a different geography, his words came from a different map. Then they flowed again, like his robes, some dark, some light: "Okomfo Allotey, me I de call you that, you be heavy pass all small-small shokolokos . . . me I call the other fetish boys that. Your shoulder ibi strong paa, strong pass hill self. Your madam here, e try for me proper, e fit come with me all the way here. I see she be good woman paa, she love you teeee . . . Now my matter, ibi man-to-man matter, ibi two-man talk. Now I come here, I feel better small, my leg too fit make strong small. You see, massa . . ." Mustapha turned to look at Mayo, who was listening intently. The two men pushed her back with their eyes; but she parried the push with a dazzlingly innocent smile, allowing only the hills to move her away a few yards, and leaving her perfume exactly where she had been sitting. Allotey turned his neutral eyes back to Mustapha, who continued: "Massa, me too my wife be beautiful paa. I take her when she go for school. She fit do one plus one, and as for two plus two she fit do it in bed! Massa, I lie? I tell your woman here that something de tack me paa. I no fit take my wife, I no fit do the fikifiki. She go shake her buttocks aaaaa, but the thing no rise. Ibi serious-ooo. So, I de for your hand . . ." When Mustapha talked, it was as if it were cola talking in embodied form. The world became brown, in brilliant contrast to his cream robes. His body had an extraordinary dignity, an upward thrust with a wise stoop at the top of it; the thin wings of his moustache moved with style around the edges of his face. His respect took root, but sometimes became withered by the arrogance of his gestures. He controlled the air boldly, with his cuts of hand and with his height: but then all of a sudden he would be begging the world with the humble bowl of his mouth.

There was a silence which redefined ½-Allotey: he looked like a rock crouching, his skin had taken on the entire plain, and the world moved in and out of him easily . . . for spirit was now holding his bones together. And Mayo stared at him, she was shivering with love or admiration . . . as if she knew that his realization of this would form barriers beween herself and him. The hut looked at Mayo, Mayo looked at the hut. She said from her distance, "As for your house here, it's higher than everything at Kuse! But if you won't ask me to go and see it, I won't go . . ." Hawks held the sky above them, moved the thoughts of the three heads below," much more smoothly than the heads themselves would. When Allotey suddenly stood up, the high claws had pulled out his last thought: to sweep Mayo's eyes from around his hut. As he went up to sweep they looked at him in silence. Each step of his had a meaning for them, a destiny. By the time he had finished, noon was already burning. He came down. Mustapha rose and asked him, "My thing, make a bring it? Make a take it out for you to see? Boss, I beg you, talk to my thing, make am rise!" Mayo moved her face and laughed together with the breeze of this noon.

Allotey put his hand on Mustapha's shoulder, and took him up to the hut, ignoring the questions of Mayo's eyes . . . she should sit a little longer in her laughter. And she yawned after them, her interest was dying. There was so much that Allotey remembered from his father's cures. But like his father, who was far more temperamentally agitated a man than this son, he was at the beginning reluctant to heal: he wanted to build up a ritual related to each case, he wanted to have his herbs and potions analyzed, he wanted to add his own dimension . . . but often the anguish of the sick, the worried, would not wait. He could sulk as he administered his medicines. Sometimes only a touch would heal, sometimes a long crush of herbs and roots. So he began with Mustapha; one hour of grinding and tying, of staring and laying on of hands, led to another hour, then went into three hours of complete concentration. Allotey suddenly rushed out and looked at the nearest trees . . . he did not even notice the absence of Mayo. He then called Mustapha outside: "Come to Kuse, next week, you hear? I have not finished. I will go to Kuse for some business, or to stay small . . ." Mustapha nodded with satisfaction. He had complete confidence in Allotey.

He said, "For me, I no go go for any Mallam, at all . . ." Then they noticed Mayo's absence, saw her far off. "Ei, as for woman, no patience, koraa! I go catch madam!"

If there were golden stairs leading out of the valleys, then Mayo and Mustapha had already climbed down them, right out of ½-Allotey's mind. The spaces around leaves were questions . . . leading space by space unbroken all the way down to Kuse, where his absence was now sharper than his presence, and where his okro farm had become famous far beyond Mayo's trick. This same Mayo was now taking his name there to polish and polish it, to let his new powers, his new goodness show. Name shoeshine woman. Allotey knelt down, eating more of the goat, direct with his teeth and indirect with his hands. He went and cleared up the used herbs, the ritual shellless egg skins, the peeled twig strands; he swept out traces of his deep powder, by the grinding stone where the old feathers lay; he had tied and untied the old man's penis, the po-pylonkwe of the hour; and he had read the signs of the old palm, the right hand, until all the sorrow there was finished, until the interpretations prepared the legs for the initial healing. The seat of Mustapha's soul, usually either in his mouth, his heart or his pocket, was now in his legs: the confidence already had an invisible pipe there . . . and the hope was that something would flow through soon. With a look of scorn that could be determination on other days, Allotey started to gather a few of his things into an old gray bag; knives, stones, shorts, batakaris, underwear and cloths. Before he fully realized it, as if something were pushing him to the north toward Kuse, he had decided to pay a visit there now rather than later . . . to stay for a few days, if he could get someone to come and stay in this hut for the time he was away: for the fish, or for the spirits. He spent an hour looking at the hut and cleaning it. No one could stay in his absence, he saw. Before he left, he put the sky on the hut, with the angle of his eye; he pulled the thatch further down, nearer the windows; he put his tongue three times against three walls, each third pressure longer; then after spreading good-bye leaves at the back and the front, he descended the hills. After a score of steps, his brother hut started to pull him back, by the back of the head: he forced his legs to move on, but his head turned back at quick intervals. He turned around fully at last, using the paths of his descent to push the sky back off the hut. The palm thatch moved in salute. His early corn complained in its rustling, from west of the hut. Then there was a complete cut in upward vision, for he did not look back or up again . . .

The mouth of the bus on the Nsawam road was full of the teeth of other people, but he took it all the same, he bit his thoughts through to his seat, and finally reached Kuse far from where he got on from Achimota village . . . and right there at the entrance of the old path to Kuse stood his brother Kwaku, with his teaspoon mouth holding out little measurements of his smile, part-welcoming part-resenting him. Kwaku's smile had not changed, it had only come lower, stretching halfway down the semibridge of his nose, up the street of this Akan village with its Ga relatives. But as he embraced Allotey, the impudence was asleep in his nostrils. "Ei, brother to brother! Welcome, akwaaba! Do you now have all the spirits you want in your bag! Let me lead you to the house. Don't ask me about the forest till you've eaten and you are in a good mood. But watch all the stares. They now say you are a magician!" Kwaku was truly glad to see his brother, but he sensed a new silence around him; as if the traveling had killed a few words in his head. ½-Allotey saw several people waving at him, as if they knew he was coming. But out of charity, he kept his irony only in one eye.

The land of Kuse had shrunk by taking on two new houses, one of laterite and the other of sandcrete blocks. As they passed, Kwaku casually pointed to the latter house, saying, "They say your Mayo wants to marry Paa Ababio, because he has come back from his travels with a little money; but that she wanted to have a last look at you first, to see whether there was something she could yet make of you! . . ." "I saw her today," Allotey said, with little interest. "Oh, so only today! So that's why she was trying to rewrite your whole history with the stories on her tongue! She was saying that if she hadn't lost her sense, she would have had a child with you by now . . . And your old friend or enemy Kwame Mensah, died last month. He spent all his time talking about you, good one day, bad the next . . ." "He sent his voice to me last night," Allotey said flatly, as if nothing was a surprise anymore. "He was challenging me to live properly or perish." Kwaku looked at his brother as they entered the family house.

In the compound stood Fofo, the woman who bore him a daughter almost a year ago. She had almost grown to love his absence too, but was now standing rather stiff, her daughter in her arms, and an element of reproach in her eyes. Allotey held her shoulders,

251

as if he were holding her life; then he took his little daughter, but she struggled back to her mother. "I've come. When did you return from your mother's? I've come, and I'll always go and come. Coming is the important thing . . ." Fofo was already surer of his traveling than his staying, so she just smiled, welcoming him, wondering whether he would finally marry her or not. She ignored stories that he had taken her and had a child with her just to spite Mayo . . . but she had already decided to ask him when he finally came. She would wait until he had settled down. Then she would ask.

By the morning some excitement had come to the village, and ½-Allotey watched their views and beliefs about him stand on the opposite side of the path that they had first stood on. Pillars of houses marched to meet and welcome him: there were smiles of baked mud, there were smiles of cement plaster, there were thatched teeth smiling from above, for others came with curiosity from their buildings . . . they had smiled into the roof, and brought the thatch along. There was incense in the morning which had become only as cool as the feet that went up and down carrying it. When Allotey rose, some anger rose with him: he knew that all this celebration was from exaggerated tales told by Mayo, with dubious motives. Either she wanted to raise him so that if he fell, it would be a hard fall; or she wanted to bribe him back with goodwill. Both reasons brought scorn to his face, so that Fofo thought it better not to ask him anything yet. By the time he went to greet the elders, his anger had gone down with his food, and there was an odd sparkle to his eyes. His shoulders were as wide as the red streets, yet no one bumped into them, in spite of the crowd that gathered at the odikro's house.

After the exchange of greetings, Allotey was given a seat opposite the semicircle of elders, and he sat beside Kwaku, and Wofa Anim, his uncle, who, for some reason, looked so nervous. Allotey had always considered Wofa Anim weak, and open to swaying by almost anybody holding a gift. Wofa Anim crossed and uncrossed his arms, with one eye looking east and the other looking west. Allotey told them his mission, as a son of Kuse: "Nothing strange, nothing bad, nananom; I went and I've come. When I was leaving I told you all, especially Kwame Mensah, that I would be back. Some of you thought that this was a threat. Well, you can look at it the way you want. I went to see what I could make of my life, to talk to the ancestors and gods a little; perhaps even to make some money. Now, I've come for a few days. I will go and come again, doing any healing that I can . . ." There was a murmur among the crowd, and Wofa Anim looked away from Allotey with a contemptuous shake of the head. Allotey continued after an almost imperceptible stop: " . . . any healing that I feel is within my power, or the powers of the shrine of my father. I see many people here. Did they come to see me I wonder? I take the chance to thank them all for their welcome." Then he sat down abruptly, feeling that there was a mood among the elders and the crowd that he could not gauge properly. After the okyeame retold Allotey's answer to the odikro, the latter called for silence and then spoke to Allotey through the okyeame: "Well, our son, we welcome you. It looks as if you've given us good heart, for look at all of us that have come out to see and embrace you. You left in anger, and you have returned in love. That's what we want. But there is something troubling us. As far as we know, your father left the shrine in the hands of your uncle Wofa Anim. He is the one we know; he has been healing us and advising us . . . okyeame, tell Allotey not to talk when I'm talking . . . as I was saying, we know that Wofa Anim has the shrine. If you want to be at peace with us, then you leave him to do his work in peace." There was silence as the okyeame did his word work.

½-Allotey rose with a sideways glance at Wofa Anim, who still looked away. Beyond the wall, wild flowers absorbed the commotion as Allotey said in a rising voice, "Wofa sitting here is old enough to tell the truth without fearing anything! Where was he when my father was dying? I have all the objects of the shrine, and my father told me to carry on his work, if I was satisfied with the changes I wanted to make. Wofa Anim can't build his house on someone else's back . . . if he does, his house will come crashing down!" Wafa Anim rose with the confidence of what he thought was general support showing in his voice: "I don't usually argue with young men in public. True, his father may have left him some things, but the old man was going mad! . . ." There was a look of fire from Allotey which pierced the side of Wofa Anim's temple. Wofa continued to talk with one side of his face: "All the elders understand my view. A young man like you has much to learn . . ." "Wofa Anim, what you are doing will only bring you trouble!" Allotey interrupted. "You were never the old man's pupil, and so by what rules are you claiming to carry on his work? I was with him for twelve years! So, I now understand why you are all here. You want to see me driven away in disgrace! Well, let me tell you: I will soon start a drug store here. No one is going to drive me away anywhere again! If you think this man sitting here is going to spoil my plans, then we have a big palaver on our hands! Look at him, he can't even look at me in the face! Has he really been healing you? We shall see! . . . Nananom, I beg to leave . . . I live in different centuries at once, so I'm busy, and I know when to be humble. I'll give you respect. When you decide what to do, do it. But you know my mind already!" There was an uproar as Allotey pushed his way fiercely through the crowd. Some patted his shoulder, others stared at him. Someone shouted, "Allotey, you want to move them forward, and they don't want to go!"

Kwaku followed him with a smile and whispered, "One day you'll have to show a little fear! That's all they want, a little fear. Then you can get your way." Kwaku looked as if he wanted to say something more to his brother, but the words did not come out. Not before Mayo accosted them at the entrance to the house. "Mayo!" shouted Allotey. "What were you doing inside the house? Why this interest in me now? . . ." "Oh," Mayo said in the quietest of voices, "so you still have that temper. I thought you would have reached here before me from odikro Kyei's place . . . I only greeted Fofo, and held your child. She looks so much like you! You have to cure me, so that I can marry . . ." "Yes, so that you can marry someone else," Kwaku put in impatiently, throwing his look beyond Mayo's open mouth. "I know, I know," Mayo said more loudly this time, "but don't be sure that this young girl in the house will marry your brother!" She straightened her cloth and her body in defiance, facing Kwaku with contempt in her eyes. She continued in the same voice, "Besides, you are not the one to marry for your brother! Anyway, all I came here to do was to tell Allotey that Mustapha says he's now cured, and he will come with his thanks very soon. I don't know what's wrong with this brother Kwaku of yours. So many people want to marry me. Yet I'm taking my time . . . the very day Allotey marries, yes, you Allotey, then I marry too . . ." Then she ran off laughing, trailing her legs after her like two brown bits of firewood not yet ready for the fire.

When they went into the house, they saw Fofo in a corner crying, with her child on her back. "From one woman to another! You women make one trouble and share one trouble!" was all

Allotey said, in anger, as he passed her into the room. Kwaku went over smiling to talk to her, but Allotey called her in. "Are you trying to tell me that you are too young in the head for me? This is what your tears are saying! Don't listen to the things that Mayo says. She is a little confused just now. She wants to live in the past and live in the present, in a way she can't do. She doesn't have the heart. She'll soon marry and settle down. Only don't listen to her! As for you and I, I won't cheat you. If you can grow along with me, then I'll make you a life that others will respect. Mayo drove herself away from me. For you, I know you will grow to understand me but I am a difficult man. Wipe those tears, and go and make my food. Afterward I'll start to teach you how to read! . . ."

Fofo went out with a smile, and Kwaku brought almost the same smile back into the room. "To business!" shouted ½-Allotey as soon as Kwaku sat down. Allotey continued: "How were the farms?" Kwaku hesitated, his frown of old coming back. "The dwarfs of the forest were too much for me. For me I haven't got the patience you have. They drove me out! It was only after I pacified the river god, that I was able to have one harvest. Then I had to do many things with the money . . . repairing the house, looking after Fofo and the child. I know you left some money, but it wasn't enough . . . No, I'm telling the truth, don't look at me like that. After all I have two hundred cedis for you now, now, now!" Allotey looked at his brother hard and long, and added, almost as an afterthought to the look, "You Kwaku, you'll never change. I am changing, but you will never change! . . . Don't let Wofa Anim step in this house until everything is settled . . . you will never change . . ." ½-Allotey kept repeating this in a distant way, almost as if now that the lines of his own life were clearer, he could savor the disgraceful luxury of his brother's disorganized life; and also, as if this disorganization would serve as a warning against failure, against which he would measure his own growing success.

Chapter 20

Bishop Budu finally married Ama Serwaa. The tree had at last broken into flower, and was shaking with the breeze of its own surprise. For the brothers and sisters of the congregation it was as if ordinary things, ordinary worlds had at last come to the church: plantain was plantain, the new mushrooms of April-ending were as fresh as the wedding . . . which had no ceremony, for when the heart burst out, as the bishop said, it had to be put back in the breast with the quietest dignity. But the brothers and sisters were singing, filling every corner, every bush with song. They had to have their own ceremony, and they had it, with Old Man Mensah leading them, in vindication of his years and years of persuasion. "God has brought the heart out! You cannot hide the heart forever!" he would say in greeting to those he met. The home was in the church, the church was in the home, and the center of the dancing was the sweetness of the compound. Today the compound was married. The bishop had naturally told Old Man Mensah first of his decision . . . for the old man had outcalmed and outreasoned him. "You almost made it too late, father!" Mensah had said. "But Ama can still have your child . . ." The brothers and sisters were rejoicing for an additional reason: it seemed to them that the traditional forces of warmth, light and dancing had defeated the hard spiritual ways of Osofo. Some of them wore white for this reason as well.

When Bishop Budu first broke the news to Osofo, Osofo had said, "I know, I know. I've had hints of it, I've felt it! That's what they all want . . . only as I once told you, don't leave! If you leave, you'll one day find a whole congregation outside your house, on strike! They will pray you out of retirement! They will wail for you. Brother, I have to tell you this, so that you make the right decision. After all, you will see how much they will celebrate your decision. They will celebrate for you, and against me. You wait and see . . ." The bishop had looked at Osofo for a long time, without a word, with no movement left in his eyes. Then he patted Osofo on the shoulder, and left, gathering his deliberate walk about him as he went . . . as if there was a rebuke blasting out from the engine of his back, the back looking especially heavy then. Osofo suddenly thought: there were two pesewas in different parts of the sky, and when the sun shone, only one reflected its light; the other one hoarded the heat, and . . . burst! scattering onto his heavenward eyes, eyes that closed and ran in defense. They would hoard their sense of surprise, they would use the heat against him! He looked up and saw that little red-breast bird, God's African robin, singing a new tune somewhat shorter than of old . . . in God's country, even songs were getting shorter; songs and spirits. There seemed to be no power, no trace of trance left in Brother Budu's eye. The bishop was preoccupied, and Osofo wondered—with an instantly withdrawn scowl of remorse—whether God had now been pushed sideways . . . to make a little more room for Ama. That thought had violence in it, and Osofo knelt exactly where he was, for forgiveness. When he rose again, he had a smile of inspired herbs, he had his new herbal smile; which appeared a little dissociated from his mind, and which stood out like a flower would too long from a girl's hair. His own hair had not been combed for days and days; time had passed through it with its holy dust.

This was when he locked himself up for two days to contemplate the bishop's decision to get married. The others, of course, misinterpreted this, storing it away for future use as yet another charge against the tides of his moods. Bishop Budu himself, as usual, wanted Osofo to live out his tensions; and he was ready to help if necessary . . . but he passingly wondered whether, sometimes, Osofo should not make more often the distinction between spiritual pain and emotional pain. For Osofo, the latter was always the ready pipe for the former, and when it flowed through it, pipe and flow became one, If it were possible at all for the bishop to feel demented, he made sure he chose cheap silk, against which he would flagellate his mind, with sharp bits of palm frond in suffering for Osofo. He chose Ama's arms now partly because he had finally seen the true path that he thought the church would take. His spiritual clarity had at last landed fully in the ordinary plains, because he was overwhelmed with the humanity of his congregation, their vulnerability and their short spiritual lease . . . for them the church was a way of life, not an adventure before the presence of God. He had also seen, with great foreboding, that the brothers and sisters had taken as much change as Osofo would give; they had struggled through one man's vast spiritual thicket, and now they were ready for the home bush, for the home thorns, for the grass that could receive some dancing easy, easy; for the incense that stretched far back into memories and not into spirit. After all, many of them had almost as many years as the pillars of the Lord's Smiling Saint church; or if not, then as many as the few years of the carefully planted shrubs. Osofo had often warned, in a different way, of this before. But now, Bishop Budu had finally let the reluctant realization come home, and he grieved for the uncertainty of his brother priest's future. With his marriage, he felt one huge weight cast down . . . only to be replaced with the weight of Osofo's precarious balance. Had there been a tall tower to the church he would no doubt have seen Osofo standing balanced on one foot at the top, swaying uncomfortably, mixing and pushing the thoughts of all the lesser beings below. And what about Osofo's healing? What about that wild energy he had that often attracted the young to the church? What about the excitement of the herbs, which Osofo refused to see as mere gifts to be cast down? Bishop Budu stood with his solid hand holding up his solid head, a head needing that little bit more support, for it was heavy with doubt, yet solid with the certainty of his own chosen paths.

Osofo had a shock: when he looked at the compound this gray June morning, he saw the earth divided into hundreds and thousands of little squares; each square had an eye, his own left eye, from which there was an impossible glare. The squares were drawn with a matchstick still lit and lonely in the distance, and some had even spread up the barks of trees. God's fragments, or the breaking up of his mind? he thought. Then his eye disappeared, and the spaces were filled with the visions of the brothers and sisters of the church. Each face had a warning, an accusation. Each face looked at the past, but glared at the future. It looked as if they had screened the future away from him. But to him, the future was not dark, it was only different. Then they all vanished. The goats guarded his usual corners of prayer. The breeze could hold his throat. "Brother," he shouted to the absent bishop, "what are your children trying to do to me? After all these years I've served and healed them with you, why are they trying to drive me away? . . ." Then he caught his voice sharply and put it back into his mouth with his enormous hands. His hands could obscure the entire world, if he held them close enough, and if they would not shake as they were shaking now. His mind was now creeping strangely through his body and it crept slowly into his house, followed by his reluctant limbs. "To heal myself, to heal myself!" he shouted to the returning walls. The walls took his strength, returned his strength, took his strength yet again. The nkontommire in his stomach was expanding, his bowels shortened. Over there where the bed slept on its springs, he sprung, with his unbuttoned cassock flying and catching a stray chair, turning it crashing, just as his worlds turned. The prayers gathered on the left side of his forehead. God shrank, crowded in half a head. The light which he had put on so early shone through the corners of the room only; and when his eyes shone back, his eyelids pressed themselves down in anger. Light yet no light. "You are not an Osofo! You are not a man of prayers and herbs! You have failed your people, they don't want you!" he heard himself say. The goats he gave leaves to were now at the window. There was a mixture of bleat and prayer. And the young pear tree shook, shrinking the vision of windows as the goats raised their front legs in agitations of climbing. Osofo cut the world in half with his praying hands, which moved together and separated constantly, patterning exactly the movements of his inner head. The stale bread was either bread or manna, so that he opened the window and threw it to the goats; and the prayers in his mouth were moving far faster than his feet did one after the other, nowhere. His whole house, like his body, must have become compressed, for he could hardly breathe. God's air was thick, the air of his ancestors was thick. He took his cross and hugged it so hard that it broke. As the walls changed places, like broad mountain dancers, he rushed to the corner of his mightiest prayer, the prayer that had not yet cooled, and screamed, "God, destroy me! This is Madina! This is the lost place!" Then he drank his old brew of herbs, blessing himself with a wide sweep of the hand. When he suddenly rushed out, the goats pressed against him, crying against his own crying. Bits of the cross scattered. "Over to the Lord! I am going! I am leaving my compound! If I have to go with some dancing, if I have to drag my heart out of here I will go, Over to the Lord!"

Osofo sat on his small outside stool, feeling the drips of his own sweat. His cassock's open buttonholes let the world pass through at last, at last. His skin began expanding, with the tightest joy in the world . . . okros were good, he could make a life out of pepper, round and round the orange, not yet in season, could go a whole life, and that odd shape of ginger: it had all the shapes of this world! Let the mango move, for there were still a few left in the markets with which he could gladden his mouth, who would not consider the priest fit for fufu during the service, for after all did Jesus not eat plantain? And bless the red beans, bless the white beans, bless the bananas asleep against the hundreds of groundnuts, bless the pito, bless the palm wine for they deepened the gathering of the calabash. His heart now was so slow that one beat had to chase another. The quietness was a drum unbeaten.

But Osofo looked through the trees, and there was noise coming, there was a crowd coming. Some were calling his name. Ahead of them was a tall young woman, her head bent to one side with listening. Her brightened eyes carried questions, carried the pull of worry. But she had absolute dignity. Not far behind her was an absent-looking young man, who looked as if nothing could perturb him at all. And around them were a few people of all ages, of all men and women. Osofo remained sitting as Adwoa Adde came slowly over with her long, sad strides. They all stopped some yards away, at the absolute stillness. "Yes, that's him. There's Osofo, he's in his silent communion . . ." Then the same person whispered, "He can be wild with God, so don't be deceived!" It was Beni Baidoo speaking, his face twisted into both a knowing smile, and a frown, as he stood by the shoulder of Kofi Loww. Kwaku Duah stood his engineer's stand, stood in the broken bolts of his heart, his cheeks shone a little less with the absence of his Mansa. Behind him stood an ironic smile, and behind that smile stood manager Agyemang adjusting his mouth every few seconds, and still trying to recover from Kokos's pregnancy. Jato was there without his unfinished chin, which had finally sailed at an angle out of his face. And he kept whispering, "Kwao is constipated, his money still won't come out!" Kofi Kobi had at last managed to shorten his legs, out of love for Akua, so he had decided to come along, leaving his vanity safely by the mirror. Akosua Mainoo and Abena Donkor were too happy to come; Aboagye Hi-speed was dead, but he only managed to half-bury himself: they buried the other half immediately, and, as he predicted they held no funeral for him . . . his children all changed their names, and his wife sold all her worries and her shame away on a different tray in a different town. They all stood before Osofo. One group and one Osofo studied each other's silence.

Adwoa Adde greeted Osofo quietly. Osofo returned the greeting with a penetrating look saying: "My only seat is my grass; and sometimes people who are really desperate can sit on a goat . . . Strangers, let that young girl go behind my house and fetch water for you. She may even see a bench." Osofo nodded at Amina, who cast a glance at Adwoa before going. Quietly behind the group, by a tree, stood Bishop Budu. He had wanted to see Osofo, but he stood and watched, his face calm. Osofo put his head on his lap; his lap was like the sound of the sea in a shell. And he spoke from that position: "Sister, what is your trouble? We are all roaming about confused. God is sense. I have my own troubles, but I have no sense. The more sense I don't have, the more sense there is for God. And that's why I'm humble . . ." Adwoa Adde felt a compassion for this man, and said, "Osofo Ocran . . ." Then she paused, to see whether his head would rise from his knees. It did not. "Osofo Ocran, after a little searching, we have found you here. These are my spiritual children, and that man over there is my heart, yes if I can say so. We chose each other, all of us. I was called to listen and they were called to tell me their suffering. Some of them are with us now, others are not. I think their absence is your presence, and your own presence is the absence of their sorrows . . ." "Hey, sister, stop!" Osofo interrupted, "Are you sure you are talking to the right man? I don't calm people . . . not now, especially. I blow up their worlds! I hound them with my restlessness. They say I'm dangerous . . . and in the end they begin to hate me . . ." There was a sudden silence. Adwoa Adde stood there erect, her hair plaited back severely under her duku, so that her large, round eyes stood out almost in daguerreotype . . . stood out, vulnerable and firm. The blacks and greens of her cloth—the printing and styling of which she had designed herself—emphasized her height, throwing a vision of cropped pines in her direction, with she herself straightening the vision with her straight spine. She went over to Osofo

261

and touched his hand, with her eyes closed in silent prayer. All the heads bowed down in sympathy, even Jato's; all except Kofi Loww, who could not keep his eyes off Adwoa, for he did not yet know . . . and perhaps would not know for years . . . how to make use of the active depth that she had given him. He had his own passive type of depth, which he had used to survive this limping life, and which would, now, probably surge forward, if the years nurtured it. He had now a strangeness of manner and temperament, rather than a strangeness of heart and spirit. Ahomka had put it like this, "Dada, you see me better now, don't you; now that Auntie Adwoa has changed you!" Osofo glared hard at Adwoa after the prayer, but she only smiled without wilting. She moved back.

Then without warning, Beni Baidoo took six, hard, long steps toward Osofo. He saluted so quickly that his wrinkles almost fell down, right by the imprint of Osofo's knees where he had knelt down to pray for forgiveness. "Osofo, sir! Our young lady here is an angel, she has stopped some of us from dying or going to pieces altogether. She has cured most of us, just by listening, she has saved us expense at the shrine or in the mental hospital! But some of us feel that there is a last devil left, which we would beg her not to try to fight with. We beg beg beg beg! There is evil in Ghana! certainly in my old bones . . . And look at that young rascal, is it Jato he's called?, over there; is he not evil? We don't want to take over her life. We Ghanaians are freeeeeee! We are not obsessive . . . this is a word I didn't use once in my letter-writing days, at aaaallll! And you see this fine young man here? Odd as he looks—his eyes contain more dream than his beard can hold!—we want to leave sister Adwoa alone to build the foundation of her heart into his lonely wall. We are now getting in her way, leading her into areas of experience that may even pull her away from him. You, see, if you save us, then you save them! We have heard of you, we have been respecting you from a distance . . . And you see, some of us are managers! And I once wanted to study Law . . . if only they could give me the degree for my good intentions! Hahahahaha! Osofo, if you were laughing, then we would have a case of holy laughter! I hear you love ancestors. Well, help me to change and be good, so that when I die I may be good enough to be made an ancestor! You see . . ."

"Ahhh! but you too, old man, you are something, paa. You talk too-too mEch, too mEch, true." It was Jato speaking, with an exasperation that filled his absent chin. He was an angular young man, stooping in two directions at once, at the waist and from the shoulders. His hair had been allowed to grow so thick that if you were not careful, you would think he had a two-story head. Manager Agyemang put in quickly between the space where the last two speakers were regrouping their forces, "Hey young man, respect age. Hey old man, respect your mouth; and be careful not to mind your wife chop bar! I am the manager of managers. This Osofo obviously looks strong enough to grapple with the devil. At first I thought I was coming for the curiosity, but now I see that it's a matter of life and devil! This Osofo is a one-man army!" Then Agyemang turned around with his thin squint, and boomed with a sort of sad authority, "Who is laughing in the bushes? Come out! Come and laugh in this clear corner!" No one else had heard any such laughter.

Kofi Kobi thought things had gone far enough. After all, it was not easy to tame his legs for once, before coming this long way. He said, "Nana Osofo, the ant and the anthill give each other no thanks. But my world is crowded with legs, as if my fate is wrapped around with them. What we want to know is this: will you or will you not accept a spiritual contract to cure us of bad luck and the devil?" Adwoa Adde held Kofi Loww back when he moved forward to speak. "Let him hear them as they are," she said in a whisper, as if whispering a whole life from her mouth. Kofi Loww steadied his eyes to let her truth pass. "Thank you, Kofi Kobi," grinned Beni Baidoo, "your legs always do go straight to the point. I lie? Osofo, sir, Sir, SIR! We can't bear your silence . . . there are other things I would like to bare now . . . hahaha!" and he looked salaciously at Amina, who did not take the slightest notice, for she just lived for Adwoa and often noticed little else. But there was a roar of protest from the rest at what they considered profanity and playfulness in a place of God, before a man of God. They thought old Beni Baidoo was either drunk or mad. "Sister, it's the cross bringing all the badness out of him," Amina shouted, to everybody's surprise. She became shy and overawed again, looking away with a grin of regret that she had spoken at all. It was the old man on his sleeping donkey, who laughed loudest, suddenly saying, "Let me ask you this, Osofo: if I say herbs herbs herbs herbs herbs herbs herbs herbs herbs herbs; then I say Lord lord lord lord lord lord lord lord lord lord; then divide this ten-ten draw with very fresh palm wine, equally, what chance would I have of being thought a holy Ghanaian? . . ." Manager Agyemang and Kofi Kobi immediately pounced on Beni Baidoo and his donkey, pulling him along the ground so quickly that no one had the chance to stop them before the old man's shirt became half-torn and so muddy; and there was donkey-body mixed in a sprawl with Baidoo-body. "STOP, Stop, stop!" screamed Osofo, his voice trailing off, its power going into the wild stare of his eyes. He quickly buttoned his cassock, put on his sandals, raised his hands high to the skies, and shouted, "Otumfo Nyankopon! God of all foolish and all wise people! You have at last shown me the way! They must see us in procession through the streets of Accra. It has to be a procession of truth! Praise God! Praise the Lord!" "Alleluya!" Beni Baidoo shouted in reply, as he rose from the dust. "And more Alleluya! Alleluyas are plenty everywhere like kaklos! I will find my ancestors soon; but I'm hungry, so I'll eat first, then I will praise the Lord, then, and only then, will I become spiritual . . . after I've washed my long, dirty hands . . ."

Slowly, Bishop Budu at last came out of the trees. He went straight to Osofo, and held him, saying, "Brother your place is here! Heal these people right here!" The others looked at the bishop in surprise. Adwoa Adde took hold of Kofi Loww's hand, and went toward the bishop. Budu saw her out of the corner of his eye, and he immediately turned to her and said, "God bless you, you are a gifted and blessed young woman. Go now, go now. Your place is not here. Go and make your life. We will see to your children, your spiritual children. You go and start your earthly children. They are God's real children too!" Adwoa Adde's face took on an intensity that Kofi Loww had not seen before, as he led her away, instinctively. She kept looking back, but he took her forward, forward into their life, with his long grave steps, with his new eyes and his new commitment . . . Amina had already gone ahead, home. "Joy to the young woman!" Baidoo shouted, but Adwoa did not hear. She had gone, she had gone, she had given her handkerchief to poor, rich Kwaku Duah who had stood praying all the time. He waved so hard, for he was left standing, tottering at the edge of his world, with a car's horn blowing a benediction. "Brother!" Osofo at last answered Bishop Budu, "the Lord has spoken! Today we break barriers, we go to war, with our Asafo company right here! We shall heal them through the streets—with the marching and the dancing! Bishop! Look at your congregation coming, *your* congregation! They are calling you, they want you!" Bishop Budu looked left, and true, some of the flock needed him for something, and desperately so: "Yaa Badu is dying, Bishop, and she has asked just for you. Please come, she's desperate!" an old man shouted. Bishop Budu's eye's looked, for the first time, totally agitated, trapped. He kept his physical calm, except for the violent shaking of the hands that still held Osofo. The eyes of the two priests met, Osofo's a strange mixture of irony and farewell, farewell in the spiritual sense . . . after all he could not leave his humble compound house, he would wall it, pull his heart away from his first church, and form his new one if God so wished. Bishop Budu's eyes remained agitated for a second more, then they took on the usual firm, fatherly look, with a great glow of sadness at the edges. Osofo was already moving ahead with his little band, as the bishop hurried through another path, holding his strong back, in a run to save poor Yaa Badu, who would have chosen another time to die, if only she knew.

"Tsoooooooboi!" came the cry from Jato. "Yei!" replied Beni Baidoo and Agyemang. "The war is on! We will march against Acheampong!" Kwaku Dua had already left in his Peugeot 504, and Kofi Kobi was moving off in that smile that carried so much confusion: he felt too long in body to march and dance; but he felt the excitement, the excitement he could not join. So he smiled his way out, missing Akuah piercingly, though he knew she would be angry with his lateness. A cloud and a hope had covered the sun and then released it again. Beni Baidoo had got a drum from somewhere, and manager Agyemang a whistle. With their souls in drum and whistle, and the donkey majestic in its dung at the rear, the four stalwarts moved down the street of Madina as if they were twenty, Osofo's eyes kept shutting and opening, and as they went along some joined them, some laughed at them. The gutters of Madina had closed, for Osofo would not fall. The afternoon had rushed into the dust, as the crowd grew, so that they had to breathe outside the day . . . breathing from yesterday's deposits of darkness. One gift of whistling from Agyemang's mouth brought tens of additional dancers, and new hands waving. They could wave in, wave out whole worlds. But don't forget the faces covered by the waving hands! These faces would push through the flesh in the African void . . . they too wanted to see the history that ran past them. And the air was swollen, for not all the people could fit into it. One leg of the crowd was Osofo, the other leg was Ocran: surname and first name both stamped the entire street so that bits of groundnut paper rose; heads, hearts, and heels rose; sugarcane rose, agidi rose; waakyi would rise if there were any left outside all these bellies. Beni Baidoo shouted, "It would be dangerous to let Madina pass its own post office." "Why, why, old man?" someone asked. "Because it's moving so fast that it would be posted with force, air mail all the way to Accra!" "But how can you post a town?" the stranger asked in annoyance. "Wait and see, wait and see!" Baidoo sang back. "He's mad, that's all! . . ." was the cry. After the air finally burst, there were arguments about who should breathe what was left: "I've rented this bit! So take your head go! . . ." "The air is the same as the earth: there are plots in it; I have six plots. You can't bring that big nose of yours into my air!" . . . "As for me I have already put up a Don't Breathe sign. In Ghana, the air must always have something in it. We fill any type of absence with any type of presence. So I intend to fill my air with hundreds of kaklo for sale. Even dancers must buy!"

Now the universe lowered; the sky had joined them, the clouds bursting in among them with the broad promise of rain. The key to the crowd lay asleep in Osofo's cassock pocket, and no one wanted to be opened, nor to be shut. When they reached the airport junction, the police thought it was a grand picnic; so they fanned the crowd on, either with their own dancing, or with their indifference. Osofo dragged the junction along for a few yards of prayer. And in front of Flagstaff House, he tore a quarter of his cassock off, sticking a sudden stick through it and screaming, "The flag! we have our flag! Our Asafo banner with Jesus behind it!" There was a roar as the crowd saw him and moved on, surging like a dry sea roaring in human form. More drums had joined, so that the different centers of sound deepened around the spreading movement . . . and all around the electric passion of one man: Osofo Ocran, whose huge hands tied the crowd . . . the people could not burst through his hands at all, and the donkey splayed and tripped four dancers. Manager Agyemang had long ago given up trying to create little squares of order and elegance among the acres of fury. With whistling, his lips were exhausted by his chattering jaws: "You people are cutting off the sound at my mouth, as soon as it comes out! What sort of self-reliance is this? I can't hear anything," he shouted hopelessly. "Masa, ibi mouth reliance, I swear!" someone shouted behind him barely audibly. Agyemang was glad that someone at least had heard him; not every soul was deaf to his goodness. Then his new friend added, "Masa, I no sleep with woman for long time, so you fit help me find some sweet balanga . . ." Manager Agyemang moved on as if he had not heard koraa. Then he had a vision that all the dancers and marchers were tied with one sharp, thin rope, with an infinity of allowance for individual movement, yet holding, invisibly, the entire number together. Agyemang stopped, petrified . . . until he was pushed along, and told in a shout to blow his whistle and dance his dance. And only his bones danced, under the laughter of the inexhaustible Jato Dakota. Jato was so happy, for he was being swept along, and he was part of the broom doing the sweeping. And he had made a friend: Jojo Toogood the frightened dancer who smiled only after you left, only after all smiles were exhausted. Beni Baidoo, for some reason—"repentance," he said, "repentance"—was eating a lime, his eyes full of lechery as his hand found some unobtrusive buttocks to put itself against, slyly. There was a "Hey!" as he was pushed strongly forward, carrying the ridicule of his own momentum, bumping into scores of equally pushing dancers. Behold, the donkey attempting to nuzzle a perfumed thigh . . . Someone beside the woman snarled, "And he swore he was a priest!" The rain was dragged out of the sky, as if by music. And while this light rain was falling down, the heavy tears of this city were falling up. UP . . . as if the drums alone were cleaning the sewers of the heart. After all, if you cut Accra into two, you would find that one half was the proverbial kenkey, and the other half would be thousands of fish dying out of the cynicism of the seawater . . .

Suddenly at the Redemption Circle, Osofo stopped, and demanded silence except for the braying at the back. Miraculously, they gave him this silence. He looked around as if he had traveled around and touched all the eyes. Then he asked with a roar through his taut body, "What are you all dancing for? What is all this beauty and fury doing in your bodies? I know why I am walking, dancing and marching here! What about you? I am dancing against the slow speed of the spirit, I am dancing against the churches, against the latrines, the asylums, the hospitals, the politics, the societies, against the terrible waste of beauty! I am marching by the cathedrals to the Castle! Be brave, brothers and sisters! Come with me! Walk to your salvation! Praise the Lord! the Lorrrrrrrrrd!" There was a huge "Alleluya" as Osofo fell down in prayer. Then an old catechist, who was so thin that his cassock was more or less his skin, screamed out in the fattest of voices, "One whole country cannot fit under a soldier's hat! ONE WHOLE COUNTRY CANNOT FIT UNDER A SOLDIER'S CAP! I say God help us, God help us to push them all out!" "Ampara!" was the refrain. The old man's cry became a song; then it became a burden as they carried its meaning uncertainly along; then at last it became a weapon . . . they would attack the center of Accra with the power of prayer and the song! Osofo knew how to put a smile above the higher reaches of tension. The smile climbed the stiffness of his face, and burst . . . into the roars and the cheers, into the power around him. The suspicious sky was beautiful now with the beads of a double rainbow . . . thousands of women's waists in the sky. Then there was the chanting: "By the peppers . . . there is power!; by the key-soap . . . there is power! by the cutlass . . . there is power!; by the chale-wate . . . there is power!; by the sardine . . . there is power!; by the Akurugu . . . there is power!; by the Kojo . . . there is power!; by the tama . . . there is, there is what? . . . there is *bottom power*! Forward! Forward! . . ." Somebody shouted that the whole of Accra was in a sack, and that they would pound it to death, just as they used to pound cats to eat. Ghana was a photocopy country, and they wanted the original truth! Cars and trucks, which had been impatient all along, partly joined them with their different types of horn making one tune of solidarity. You could hold the hope in the air and powder it; all the salt could leave the sea and flavor this stew still on fire by the roadsides. The tied rope dragged their sunsum along, the rope with the thousand directions all going to the same place. "Forward to the plasterists, Dooo, do for me, me for do!" shouted Beni Baidoo, when he had regained his confidence.

"Old man, what are you talking about? Plaster-whats?" Jato asked, slightly irritated at the interruption of his drumming. He had taken the drum from Baidoo already and then had given Jojo a try. "Oh, are you the one I should explain myself to? Which one of your ears is literate so that I talk to it? Well, the plasterists are the politicians and the soldiers: they can put plaster around the mouth of a whole country. And this is what we are tearing off . . . but as for you, your mouth is too big. You can chop Madina one time. You have to tear off a whole roll of plaster! Okay, I've finished

explaining. You can open your illiterate ear to the others now."
Beni Baidoo had a different smile at each side of the face, and
cigarette smoke came from the middle. He found it impossible to
dance for long, for others laughed so much that the laughter locked
his legs. And at other times he had to dance regardless, like now:
his tiny bottom stuck out like a halved kenkey with half its leaves
off; and his legs became alphabetical: the knees were bent into *V*'s
and *W*'s and then crossed into *X*'s, while his mouth formed the
vowels. He could get stuck in this oven of words, this bellows of
the bottom. So that by the time his hands started forming their
delicate shapes, their subtle meanings, the small uproar had already
begun: "Hahaha! Old man boogie! We are the men! Bokoorrr,
careful! Don't form any more wrinkles than there are already! Old
man, that coconut head of yours will fall-oooh! Hey, look, look,
look, look at the buttocks, he's dancing so rough! Beni Bai-
dooooooo, Yeahhhhhhh. Yeah! And your donkey is sexyyyy!"

Then he suddenly stopped, for now that he had an audience, he
wanted to say something quickly before they were all swallowed
up in the dance and drum: "This road has done well, paa . . ."
There was an ironic silence which he loved, for the power of his
own knowledge overpowered him: "Okay okay, I'll tell you: this
road has done well—better than any woman . . ." Then he savored
his silence again. "Hey contrey-old-man! Hurry up or you may die
before you finish! . . ." someone shouted. "Okay okay," repeated
Beni Baidoo, "this road is better than any woman because it lies
down soooooo long. You see, humility! But I warn you, very soon
the road will rise and dump you all!" "Including your jokes, old
man! They will be dumped first, I lie?" someone shouted from the
back. "Yoooh, you think I'm joking? Wait and see! . . . You all
say follow the leader, follow the leader. I say we can't, why? Because
the leader has gone to the toilet, that's why!" "Ei, as for the First
Class Boogie-Woogie, the only name we can give him is Mr. Wait-
and-See! Baidoo Buttocks and toilet leader!" Then all the laughter
scattered, but none touched the real Osofo: Ocran, at the head of
the crowd was in his most controlled trance. In charge, soul and
all; with his three-quarter cassock bitten by the jaws of God, they
thought. The Smiling Saint was grim in his head.

They were now approaching Makola . . . some of the heads
were already reflecting in the large oils of sweet stews, for Makola
could reflect anything. Beni Baidoo said: "Osofo, forgive me, for

my head is lost in all the cooked rice, all the shining stew . . . I'm hungry . . . Oh, you MAMMIES!" he shouted to the laughing, dancing women. "Give us food, give us water, we want to free you! Show your love, your luuuvvvv!" And the women obliged, entertaining with a generosity that was not usually in their trays. There was pandemonium as they rushed to devour what was offered . . . and what was not offered. Food flew. Mouths had not chewed so fast before. Beni Baidoo had sat himself on a fat mammy's lap and was eating and laughing. He roared, "Mammy, I will marry you after we finish our sacred march, I will, of course, have to feel how soft you are first, then eat more food; then if you pass, we have the wedding straightaway!" The fat mammy's laugh completely swallowed Baidoo's, even though hers was so gentle and relaxed. She could not have children, so she had impregnated herself with a massive dignity, with massive smiles. As they moved on, Baidoo rose and left his promise where he had been sitting. The mammy shook it out of her cloth with a laugh.

"One whole country cannot fit under a soldier's cap!" came the old war cry as the crowd surged toward the Anglican cathedral. Someone shouted, "We forgot the Catholic cathedral! Let's go back!" Osofo held up his hand, and said through the screen of his sweat, "We will pass these churches with our silence . . . the silence will tell more." Feet shuffled feet just like cards, the silence was in the leather, or in the skin of the sole of the feet. There was disappointment, for some had wanted to howl in cathedrals, to take their sufferings there; to protest without undue reverence . . . or perhaps at last to do something totally unGhanaian, whether in church or shrine.

"We can march the guns down!" was the cry, as they wound their way toward Osu, with the sea roaring on the right, and Parliament House dead on the left with the donkey grazing impatiently on its lawn. The neem trees passed them along as if they were batons. Tsoooboi, Yei! There was a change in the air, as they passed the Riviera Hotel traffic lights, under the stare of the Public Services Commission building, that baneful stare of concrete . . . by the Passport Office in the distance, crouched there like a painted elephant. And ahead was the Freedom Arch, free only to the Black Star Square and the sea . . . not free to this country, Osofo had thought. "We have arrived! Now on to the Castle!" Beni Baidoo shouted. But there was no enthusiasm. Manager Agyemang was

270

leaving already, "to find out whether Kokor had got rid of her pregnancy yet or not, God forbid." The waves of the sea were now quiet behind the Square . . . the sea could be in the Square, the Square could be in the sea . . . but the shells under the waves were busy underneath, hitting each other hard and making a tremendous amount of noise that the water pressed down out of earshot. Like the crowd, like Accra, the shells were at war, but you had to get at the movement through deep contact . . . even the poor sea lived on contact. Part of the silence was due to Osofo's meditation, his sense of hopelessness that he had arrived here with his new flock, and he had one reason for coming, and they had another . . . if any at all . . . for being where they were. It looked as if the Freedom Arch had spread its stone and was blocking their way like the hardest love with thighs closed. Osofo strode up to it and prayed in slabs of supplication. There was some aimless chattering behind him.

Then from behind the Square itself came a group of policemen, some in uniform, some in plainclothes. No one took much notice of them until they were very close, with their gray shirts under the gray skies. "They've come to take us!" the old catechist said, with a gleam in his eye. "Not at all, old man," one plainclothesman beamed, "we have a message from the Head of State for you . . ." "But we want to see him personally," came the cry, for they felt rejuvenated even in their tiredness. "Serious matters of state forbid him. He heard that . . ." the officer was continuing. "So do you mean that there were some security men dancing among us? Shame!" someone shouted again and again. The plainclothes officer had more than enough patience for he continued again: "He heard that you wanted to discover spiritual truth in Ghana, or something like that. First of all, he wants you to be entertained here at the Black Star Square. You must be tired! We have ricewater, bread, corned beef, sardine . . ." There was silence. "Corned beef politics!" Osofo shouted, rising from his prayers, "We want some sanity in our lives . . ." "Yes, spiritual sanity, isn't it? Any other sanity is playing politics!" the officer said laughing, as if he had no objection to his own sanity being stretched in an unwilling dialogue. He added: "Reverend, your followers are hungry. Let them eat, then you can decide whether you can solve all of Ghana's problems in one march, in one dance . . . or even in one prayer!" Another officer, in uniform, shouted, "This way to the food, brothers and sisters. Dancing from Madina to Osu is something big! Fat . . . or you want to leave it all to us?" Then all the policemen laughed. Jato winked at Beni Baidoo, then shouted over to Osofo, "Uncle Osofo, Yeah, why don't we go chop, so that we are all freeeee?" "Why not?" smiled Beni Baidoo. "We can say a heavy prayer before we start eating . . . I've lost half my skin dancing here. God is always willing to wait for the hungry. Officer, we have solved the country's transportation problem: tell the Head of State, Kutu, that there should be a decree ordering everybody to dance everywhere! It's cheaper!" Then there was a roar of "Food!" as the crowd, considerably thinned, made its way away from Osofo's open mouth to the Black Star Square, under the watchful gaze of the law. Baidoo dragged his donkey along.

"Where's the message from the Head of State?" Osofo asked defiantly. "The message is food for the hungry!" shouted the plainclothes officer, turning to the crowd. "Don't worry, you'll see your reverend later, if he doesn't eat now." Osofo's mouth could be God's open mouth . . . and the sea could not shut its waves. The flock flocked to food . . . that was all. Osofo suddenly turned around, and was walking away in fury. Two of the officers followed him immediately; the plainclothes leader tapped him on the back, and whispered: "Reverend, the Head of State's brother is a good friend of your bishop, and that's why we have treated you so nicely. But be careful, keep to the prayers. The enemies of the Revolution can misuse you!" Osofo pulled the policeman's hand away, and walked on with a "Praise the Lord!" as they laughed. The flock, the flock ate itself out of his life . . . even the old catechist himself, taking his badly-fitting false teeth out of his cassock, wearing them over satisfied gums, and attacking the food like the rest. "I'm flea, I'm flea!" shouted Jojo by the Freedom Arch. "But don't scratch your fleadom so much!" Baidoo shouted back at him. Then there was a cruel remark from a mouth furiously full of corned beef, a remark that Osofo could not hear: "So after all this, he didn't really waste our time and you know, I think he has cured me of my devils, but he's one of those zagazogos who can't discuss God without going off into a spiritual fury, He can't last in Ghana! He's God's man, but he's mad!" Laughter and food now mixed with policemen and the waves of the sea, nicely. Something went through Osofo's head as he retraced, deliberately, the same route they had taken, and this time it was so quiet that the road would have to rise: "C'mon, you

272

can't sneak a look at the heavens like this! You are a Ghanaian . . .
all you have to do is to throw a symbol, play a drum, burn the
incense . . . then you can touch the infinite!" He shook this thought
out of his head and put another there: "Start again, start again, start
again for they will always betray you . . . !" The eating Black Star
Square vanished behind him, but he would not let Baidoo's donkey
follow him away.

Chapter 21

This mid-June morning with the corn in full flower, the sun was all-correct sir. The flowers snarled in Professor Sackey's grass. They grew in war. He usually looked at green when he was brooding, so that the immediate vegetation grew as much out of fright as out of anything else. Oranges would fall from Sackey's height into August. His head and heart were reflexively blasting, and his shirt drew the entire blue of the sky to him. His strong mouth was walled, full of the teeth of silence . . . and the same teeth had traces of zomi, beans and gari, vanishing under his chewing stick. This chewing stick was as horizontal as his back and beliefs were upright. Straight was the strike at life, and straight would the strike ever be! The shadows of his life had deepened: some of the elements that formed his general background had suddenly moved to the fore: Sofi had finally left him, and was crying in Saltpond; and the politicians in uniform had picked him up yet again for some ludicrous questioning. He now had one hundred qualifications after his name: all degrees of interrogation from the university of the Special Branch. Under his anger, he was truly amazed that they still thought him somehow dangerous, in spite of his basic lack of political interest. Ah! Perhaps it *was because* of this disinterest, Sackey surmised, pushing his subtlety beyond the security perspective. Some sort of stature grew from this apathy, or something. And in this country, you had to beware of stature, especially moral stature. The politicians did not want to breathe the air with anybody, Sackey thought, his motoway rising over his eyes like a fist. And if they were more efficient, they would be much more troublesome and dangerous.

These elements all came to the same root: Sofi and the special branch amazed him. He admitted his impatience with Sofi, but her drastic decision, he thought, was rather senseless; he wondered whether she would even survive emotionally without him . . . for after all, the hand that bullied was the same hand that also protected. He was constantly prodding and pushing at her centers of peace. But, granted his own impatience, he really thought this was a sort of complement to her easy, almost lethargic nature. She was leaving, she was leaving, she was leaving . . . and now she had finally left; part of his bank had ripped off into the river. Thus he had less earth to stand on, just at the time when he had so much walking, so much inner moving to do.

But a little child became one of his little, surprising areas of stillness: his own son Kwame had refused to go with his mother. He had told her: "Mother, I want to go with you, but it is my duty to stay with my father to make sure that he is looked after properly." Kwame had said this with his usual solemn face, his eyes as bright as his father's. Sofi had tried everything, in the absence of Sackey from the house at that time, to persuade Kwame not to stay. But Kwame stayed, much against his own wish; and he did not cry. He just waited patiently for his father to come in, then handed his mother's note over to him. Sackey stood there struck for a full two minutes. Then he went and put his hand on his son, asking, "And you, Uncle Kwame, are you following later? Do you want to collect your ten cedis from me before you go? . . ." Kwame looked hard at his father with a mixture of pity and alarm: he was used to tenderness only from his mother, and he did not know what to do with it from his father. At last he composed himself, and told his father, stiffly: "No, Father, not the money. I am staying to look after you. Excuse-me-to-say, you quarrel so much that I must make sure that you do not get into any serious trouble . . ." Sackey had begun to open his mouth, but he closed the new Yale lock instantly in-stalled there . . . as if he were discovering the value of silence, the value of premeditation. "But Father," Kwame continued, "we must make our decisions together, and I insist on doing the cooking." "Insist? . . ." began Sackey, then stopped again. Over by the win-dow, the sound of distant, passing cars punctuated his thoughts: this little boy standing before him must be just like he himself was, only a little more sombrous, perhaps a little deeper! The tall trees outside brushed the light in, brushed the dark out. "Democracy,

275

Kwame, eh? We shall see, we shall see . . ." Sackey said, still somewhat confused, "But do you think your mother will come back? I shouldn't ask you such questions!" Professor Sackey laughed out of context, and his hands held his head. "Father, sit down. I think you feel a bit shocked. I have already arranged for your palm wine. You know, I'm not like mother. You can't boss me about. But, excuse-me-to-say, I think I can make something out of you yet," Kwame said with the same detached solemnity, and with the complete confidence of his father. "After all, I'm now eleven!"

Sackey sat down. The discarded wings of flying ants made a silver mound in the corner. And when Sackey sighed, they scattered hard, back against his own legs, silvering them too. "If only the professor had a silver heart!" Sackey laughed, whispering back into the corner at himself, driving his heart over into the ordinary streets of his descending mood. "Kwame my beloved son . . . and it's not as suddenly beloved as you think! . . ." Sackey said, rising with his thin body arched for laughter, "You have one uncle, and he's a very funny man: you know, when his trousers fell down—and they often did when he was drunk!—when his trousers fell down, his buttocks usually fell down with them!" "Hahaha!" Kwame laughed loudly, in spite of himself, and he asked, sitting beside his father, "Father, what if he visits us and this happens? Who will sweep away the buttocks?" Sackey's roar of laughter was faster than Kwame's, but they reached the same line of friendship, at the same time. The walls flew apart and came together again, the house touched their hands.

But at Saltpond Sofi was wrapping the cloth of her past round and round and round the speeding circles of her waist. For three hours she even dropped the name "Sackey" from the end of the cloth, and from her head. Then she started unwrapping again. Her mother watched this unraveling of the past with alarm, for she saw that Sofi was in danger of unwinding everything, including herself, from her life's reel. Sofi finally stopped spinning, when she saw her mother's face: "All right, maa, I know I have the children and I know I built up a life; but I couldn't find my own direction under Kwesi's roof. He was shattering my life. And he won't keep his mouth shut. The police have started picking him up, and that was just too much for me: just when I was feeling so far away from him, so aware of his little cruelties, that was the very time he would have needed my sympathy. Now, this is one thing people would not understand: how can I give sympathy to a man who has given me so many headaches, and who is giving himself this same pain? This would be too much for me. Besides, he didn't want my sympathy! I can't understand the man, there's nothing in his heart but pepper . . . he doesn't even want to lead a normal life on the campus with his colleagues. Maa, what do you want me to do? . . ."

"Bear it! How do you think I managed to stay with your father, that cantankerous contractor—may he rest in peace—without any trouble? Don't forget, you have to complete your life, you have to give it shape and pattern . . . if you break it off now, who is going to form the missing spaces for you? Anyway . . . you rest; don't let your head and heart go round and round like this. I thought you had inherited my patience . . . I didn't know you could explode like your father used to!" Sofi's mother went over and hugged her, with a smile, and added, "Go and rest. A few days' rest will clear your head . . . and perhaps Kwesi will have come by then."

Sofi laughed and looked incredulous at the last remark, but she went and rested all the same; though the sheet covered only a quarter of her head.

Back at Legon, the house bowed to the sun, as Sackey took off his shirt and watched Kwame cook the evening meal. "You know, I have never really seen anyone cook before . . . does food exist? You look as if you are cooking the whole of Legon!" Sackey said, absentmindedly looking at the onions. Kwame looked back at his father, with a little irritation, and said, "I don't think too much talking is good for a cook . . ." "Yes, yes, I think the words slow down the fire, eh!" Sackey interrupted, and moved to the sitting room. Was that a knock at his door? Be careful! If you knocked at Sackey's door, it could easily knock you back. Sackey jumped to the door, preparing the ice in his mind, in case it was Sofi coming back already, ready for the coolest reception. He would wear the deep freezer just for her . . . But at the door stood the very blond Sally Soon. England was all finished in her blue eyes . . . the Channel did not toss or cross there . . . for she had been eating enough kenkey. She had lost her powers of witchery, at the same time as Adwoa Adde had lost hers. She felt so vulnerable without Adwoa, but she had to continue her interviews, now that she was normal again. Professor Sackey looked at her as if he were waiting for her flesh to ride through its embarrassment, before he would say anything.

"Yes, young woman, what is it? You look like a sabbatical I did years ago . . . are you sure you haven't got the wrong house? I may not be Sackey standing here you know!" "Oh, sorry," Sally Soon said with a confused smile. Her teeth showed themselves one by one through her fine mouth, "then where can I get Professor Sackey?" "You have him!" Sackey laughed, "You have him! Come in, if you can leave your hair behind, because I don't think its length would fit into the room . . ." Sally Sooner laughed, collected her laugh, and carried it, so light, into the sitting room. Her legs were not quite as long as the light from the James Town lighthouse, but they tried . . . Sackey reluctantly got her some water, African style, and asked her mission. Kwame looked in and looked back out with his kitchen eyes. "What a lovely boy!" Soonest said. "But Professor, I have really come along to book a date for an interview on aspects of the Ghanaian intelligentsia. I'm trying to do my doctorate on 'Development and the Informed Ghanaian Psyche' . . ." Sooner quiet than say too much to this restless man. But Sackey had already laughed, and was asking Sally, "You have, I presume, decided that the Ghanaian psyche exists? As for the 'Informed' I wouldn't bet on it! 'Out of form' more like it, 'outformed!' Now, young woman, I must warn you now that I don't give interviews! Certainly not to fresh, young London rabbits . . . ingenious ingenues who are experts at instantly reducing their intelligence, just to get what they want! How much of London are you prepared to throw out of your head?" "But Professor, you are being unfair!" Sally Soon said, stealing a bit of justice over the expanse of her reserved manner. She had wanted, Soonest, to stretch toward the use of superlatives, and perhaps say "most unfair," but she suddenly thought that with this man, you kept your superlatives in reserve for future use. "This is my third time in the country. My first time here was when I was in secondary school. I was here with my parents. And I was taught by a Mrs. Sackey, who may be related to you, In fact . . ." "Which school?" Sackey interrupted. "Achimota Secondary school . . ." Sally replied, sensing a shift of interest in Sackey. His eyes looked like shining water in two potholes. "Well, I won't tell you that the lady had the misfortune of being my wife!" "Well!" Soon interjected, ignoring the tense Sackey used in describing Sofi Sackey, "this is providence! She was such a patient and systematic teacher . . ." "Sometimes patience is left under desks after lessons," Sackey said brusquely. "I don't quite get you," Sackey's young visitor said,

278

feeling that it was time to risk the personal angle. "Young woman, you are angling for information already!" he boomed as the wall boomed back. "You are trying to sneak in your questions . . . Now tell me, how much nkontommire have you eaten since you first came to Ghana? Seriously!" "I eat all types of Ghanaian food," she said guardedly. What was he driving at? "I asked because I think you deserve to retain your complexion! Eat our fine foods while you are here. And let me tell you: fufu is a light food . . . don't fall for the nonsense about its weight! Now, we have found ourselves in a strange position . . ."

Kwame suddenly brought in his father's palm wine, gave a quick stare at Sally Soon, went and touched her hair, left his "good evening" hovering in the room, and went back to the kitchen. "I find your little boy's self-assurance fascinating! What is he doing in the kitchen?" Sally asked with her eyes wide, waiting for any possible rejection. "Cooking!" Sackey replied, and said nothing more. Sally Sooner was confused, and wanted to ask why Kwame was cooking, but then decided to take a bold course: "Can I go and help him? I can see through the crack in the door that he is reading a book. I can take over and let him finish his book . . ." Kwame heard her and rushed in with his lips more solemn than his eyes: "Lady, I do my best cooking when I'm reading. Nothing gets burned.., and if you stay long enough you can taste my wonderful work. I don't want any help!" "What a way to invite me!" Sally said, laughing. "But I'm afraid your father must decide that . . ." "We are democratic in this house! So I know Father will not mind if you stay," Kwame said with finality. "Don't believe my son," Sackey said with a little exasperation, "this is a democratic dictatorship . . . he wants to be the boss! For he knows the political history of Ghana! I was saying we were in a strange position: look at all the talking we've done about not doing any talking! What's your name, if there's anything in a name at all?" "Sally Soon." "Of course I'm not surprised! A name with not a moment to lose . . . and how did you find me?" Sackey asked. "It was Dr. Boadi of . . ." "Boadi!" roared Professor Sackey with distaste. "Then the interview is closed!" "Oh!" was all Sally Soonest said.

But then Kwame suddenly brought in the yam and bean stew the excellence of which he threw as a challenge, and shouted with satisfaction, "Food ready! The little woman will get her palm wine now. You see, I kept some for you!" Sackey now turned sharply to his son, and said, "Uncle Kwame, what are you doing? Why are you inviting her without asking? Do you want to outdo your father? You know that when I say something, I say it! . . ." "But, Papa, you promised!" Kwame said with determination. Sackey looked puzzled: "Promised what?" Kwame looked at the ceiling for a few moments before answering, "I've forgotten what you promised, but you did promise!" They had no room to put their laughter down when they reached Kwame's little table, so they swallowed some with the food . . . and Sackey's face was left with a preoccupation on it. He was thinking that food spoke through the language of oil in Ghana, oil the okyeame! "This is delicious!" Sally said, looking at Kwame with genuine admiration. She did not ask him who taught him to cook, but he himself said hastily, "And no one taught me how to cook! Does this beat British cooking?" "Of course!" she answered, spontaneously. Then the silence was in the chewing. "Immediately after this meal, I will give you half an interview . . . yes, half! You can see Boadi for the other half. After all, he should find more time for his academic duties," Sackey said rather sourly. Kwame was looking with great interest at Sooner, wondering how she would take the half-world she was being offered. He was delighted when she answered, "But Professor, half a contribution from you will be worth so much more than anything else!" Her smile came again, starting straight from second or so gear, and rushing with satisfaction into the full fourth . . . it was the type of skin engineering that she sometimes did so well. Sackey got up from the table, shook his son's hand and laughed, saying, "We will manage perfectly well without So—" He stopped when he saw the frown on Kwame's face. Kwame chewed his own annoyance away, and was already absorbed in watching Soonest drink her palm wine with such extraordinary daintiness. "Poor palm wine," he said with a smile, "it's never been drunk with such care before!"

Sally smiled and finally got up from the table when Kwame went back to his book. She sighed and felt oddly at home, in spite of her feeling of intrusion, of sitting at the edge of a chair. She tried to take the comfort of the dining chair to the sitting chair, but this comfort only trailed in her hair. She looked at Sackey sideways— with her angled world—and suddenly saw that his head looked like a huge cake, with all its icing in his cold eyes. She wondered where Mrs. Sackey was, at seven o'clock in the evening, but lost that thought when she saw Sackey looking at her rather impatiently.

The world being a mad watch, had to be watched carefully.

"Professor, if you would prefer a different date . . ." she began. His proud, shining, silent forehead pushed her on; as if her questions had to test this rare silence. Sackey was thinking of all the research work he had not quite done over the last year, of all his new ideas that remained just that. Harassment, paa, he thought, rationalizing this failure. "I hope you are not thinking that I was lost in some telling profundities . . . It's the lack of them that was bothering me just now . . . as if I haven't yet reached the bottom of my gourd of water, as if my cooler was still shallow and quite without recent research. Now, about your topic: I hope you have been advised on its focus . . . has no one told you from the Britannic plains that it is rather vague? Or is this the latest style in the usual series of ludicrous academic fads! Seriously, though, it depends how you want to modify it. But I'll leave that to you . . . I am not your supervisor. Kwame has taken to you, in his hour of need, in his mother's absence. So let's rush on, it's getting to seven." "Professor, can I ask you a rather embarrassing question? There are whole stretches of social and psychological background that I'm not sure of. I am not 'in' on Legon Society at all . . . But why do they call you Professor Carry Yourself?" Soon would swoon if she had to, to defeat that glare in Sackey's face . . . which suddenly turned to laughter. Sackey beamed: "Now, what sort of a question is that? It shows the perversity of the Ghanaian academic community, and your own naïveté! I generally carry my own friendship, that's all —at one point I even encouraged this nickname—and the professorial clubs find that both proud and odd. I do have friends, but there's a limit. Now, how do you expect to trap the Ghanaian psyche—whatever that is—when even Ghanaians struggle with its very genesis! And when you eventually finish, you will take your information home, and become an instant expert on Ghana. True?"

Sally put in quickly, "I intend to settle in Ghana for years, if Adwoa would agree. You see, we flew together . . .Oh!" "You what?" asked Sackey with interest. "We studied together," Soon corrected herself, blushing. "Adwoa is my closest friend in this or any other country. I trust so much in her that I would let her choose a whole life for me without prior consultation!" Sooner's eyes had lit up, and then dimmed again back into Sackey's orbit. "Fine! I'm interested in anyone who is emotionally involved with this country whether through flying or whatever! Now, talking about the psyche, the "informed" psyche: first of all, onions have an interesting place in its interstices. No, I'm not making fun of you! nor pulling your leg! I'm trying to say that there is a sort of kitchen materialism in this psyche. You see, the mind that finds itself among concepts and the like—and quite at home with them in a polemic, examish sort of way—does not yet want to lose touch with commonsense reality. That togetherness (a mere concept in many ways, for Ghanaians can be so untogether!), that so-called communality is really an inverted intellectual democracy, as well as an obstinate sort of preference for the earth, the rural earth . . . Don't take notes, young woman, not yet! What I mean is this: in the psyche may lie the concept of, say, Marxism; this concept would fill its own space in the mind, but then would turn around, invert itself, and stretch toward the onion, because the onion pushes his pretensions down, reminds him of the vast rural stretches that have nothing to do with such alien concepts. But Marxism itself would rarely take transformed or original forms in his mind, unfortunately. Then a little guilt comes in: is he going too far from his roots? Should he, ultimately, be in any sort of ivory tower at all? (Ivory is the right word: we are in elephant country!) Then this psyche gets rid of its guilt easily because, one: he can still fairly easily communicate with the ordinary Ghanaian—he may rush to Madina to have a beer among our symbolic roots—and two: he sees the structure of his life as a broad continuum, stretching from the village, the uneducated or the onion, to the high-flying jets of the mind! You see! You see, you must understand this! Never underrate the complexities of the Ghanaian intellectual's psychic territory!"

Sally Soonest was mesmerized, but feared that Sackey's eyes would burst; she wanted to rush and get a glass to catch them in if they did . . . "Of course you have the different elements, actors, forming this inner structure, with their different levels of space and importance, and with their own histories in relation to the head they are in: wives, children, relatives; colleagues, friends, chiefs, clientele such as students—some of this is a little arbitrary, but I want you to see a point; then you have the attitudes relating to these elements, and the general world view, if any (you have professors that think about nothing but money!): funerals, ancestors, spiritry, tribe, politics, lavender, business, goats, religion—with a fine amount of sublimated and raw ritual and participation—common rooms, football, envy, symbol, status and intrigue. At any one given time any of these combinations may come together through agents like shock, sex, need and action . . . Are you with me? Good! And of course binding much of this together is the belief about what is proper, what is Ghanaian, and what the individual mind itself has made of its experience. Is my mind cycling at the right speed for you? Hahaha. So that you have a fairly easy flow between abstract, symbol, action and thing . . . usually too easy here, in fact! If you have a well-oiled Ghanaian psyche at full speed, it is a sight of beauty: it has a breadth, an expanse of experience beyond the narrow Eurocentrism I've so often met in the cold lands where your hair grew! Otherwise, this same kenkey mind I'm talking about, can be crowded with snails (plenty of calcium in them, but how much can such a mind use of it!), pettiness, rote learning, an unending positivistic gathering of data, data, data, with very little structuralizing, very little shaping! The pedestrian laborers of the mind! When will we ever get "all the facts" about this country? Let's use and manipulate what we have . . . Well, I'm glad the interview hasn't started, because I haven't begun to warm up yet! Now, young woman, it's late. Come tomorrow afternoon . . ."

"I was especially interested in the ethic-forming structure of . . ." began Sally Soon, as if stirring herself out of sudden dreams. "Hahaha!" replied Sackey. "You can bring that mouthful with you tomorrow! We are too tired to prod such lively corpses tonight; besides this is not a night for resurrection!" Sackey stood up abruptly. "Thank you, Professor Sackey . . . Goodnight, Kwame!" she shouted with more feeling, suddenly looking through to the kitchen. And there was Kwame asleep by his book. "Oh, poor child!" she said, and went out into the night, one girl in one taxi, in one Legon, in one Accra. As Sackey walked back from the door with a slight sway of fatigue, Kwame met him in the hallway. The professor's tongue was bluish, as if the words had singed it. "Papa, I wish you had wakened me to see that woman off. Don't forget to bathe; and your clean socks are hanging at the bottom of your bed. Be careful how you dream!"

When the morning came, it had to push the professor out of bed, for he was very tired. "Sofi!" he shouted down the hall. "Is breakfast ready?" He realized what he had done, with a loud ironic snort. Kwame came into the bedroom also half-asleep, rubbing his eyes. Breakfast was a fundamental decision needing strategy . . . so Sackey went and made it; and the poor ideal milk, eggs angrily boiled, and the bread barely survived the onslaught . . . He may have been gentler with his kenkey and kyenam, with shitoh, for no cooking would have been done. As father and son sat down to eat, there was a knock at the door. "Ignore it," Sackey said instinctively, as Kwame rose to go. Son sat reluctantly. Father looked with disdain toward the door. "So now, we have breakfast calls! Who can it be?" "We will only find out when we open it!" Kwame said, with a solemn mourning, morning face. "All right, all right, open it! And tell whoever it is that I am bathing or I'm not in." "Then I'm sure they'll hear your voice under the water!" Kwame laughed as he went to the door. "Oh!" said Kwame sooner than Sally, "you are back already . . ."

"Yes, I'm sorry. When I got up at dawn, everything else seemed to have its own morning different from mine . . ." Sally said apologetically. "But I've brought breakfast. I saw you asleep yesterday, and I thought I would let you have a rest." Kwame just stared at her, quite happy against his own inclination. "But we've eaten already!" Sackey shouted from inside. "Well, I'm . . ." began Sally, but Kwame had taken her hand and led her into the sitting room. He had put on a cunning, pleading voice as he asked his father, "Papa, I am still a little hungry . . . I can eat more while you talk." Sackey calmed himself down, rising with a reluctance that rose with him right up to his head. He had powdered half his face only—the professorial half—so that Sally Soon could not but laugh from a respectful distance. And her laugh was like carefully planned bubbles. "Have you ever heard of interviews being held so early in one's house?" asked Sackey. "Professor, I just came to give Kwame a little breakfast. I didn't come to interview you . . ." "Kind, kind. And cunning too? I hope not, I hope not. At least your style is a little unorthodox . . . something strange at the back of your eyes. Well, I'm free until eleven this morning . . . thank Kwame again! To work straightaway then. Get yourself a chair, Miss Soon, and leave your Sally standing! Hahaha! . . . You were waffling last night about some ethic-forming whatever . . . is it an ethic-forming grass cutter or what?"

Kwame was eating his oats and cake noisily in the corner, and watching the leaves rustle against his father's words; his little jaw broke up Legon with its chewing, eating departments, halls and offices . . . and his mind was far from school . . . "But for what it's worth, your question may carry something: without prejudice to defining any moral action, I may say that the moral psyche of our Ghanaian in question—even in general?—is frozen! It is fish in the freezer. Why? The psyche becomes perverse because it has internalized a contradiction between the traditional and the contemporary—I wouldn't say 'modern'—and this contradiction reflects, in terms of development, and in terms of its own processes, the deepening dichotomy between action and thought. This is doubly painful because, traditionally, very little clogs the channel between the inner and the outer . . . in fact in many cases the distinction may not exist at all. The psyche sees this distinction as unnatural, and therefore feels little responsibility toward its own processes, nor much toward the external world either. Now you see the problem with development! And therefore, any action that, however temporarily, transcends this psychological cleftstick is either taken completely out of its real scale (someone may 'invent' an idea or something which may turn out to be a known process in another country), or viewed as a great sacrifice . . . and of course sacrifice is interpreted both in religious and social—traditionally speaking —terms. Now this poor psyche is really stuck in a bush trap, big enough to catch the rat-spirit! It can't make any fundamental move, and sometimes it can't move at all. So this immobility tries to create meaning for itself by assuming a trinity of roles: the role of paradox, the role of sacrifice and the role of rest . . . that eternal rest of the head that treats new *facts* in themselves—and not even necessarily their interpretation—as forms of originality. Now when you come to action, young woman, when you come to moral action, then all is lost! . . ." There was a heat and a tightness to Sackey's skin which held Sally's face prisoner . . . she did not know where the intensity would end. " . . . all is lost," continued Sackey, "for the basis of righteousness or goodness for each specific moral action would be so twisted from its psychic root that the consequence may not be related to ethics at all even if the original motive could have been! . . . Have you ever seen a confused koobi? You will get justifications, denials, helplessness, shrugging of shoulders, an intonated aaah-ah, the projection of responsibility on to others; and then very conveniently this: a sly taking advantage of the availability of different cultures, different ways to justify one action based on one culture whereas it should properly be based on another. There is a relaxation and a festival spirit just when there should be a work-ethic spirit, and the ease and stupor is wrongly justified as 'true' to one's own

285

culture, and left at that ridiculous junction of authenticity! I say shame to them! They have betrayed everything! We should be thinking of atua squared times guava cubed! I put it to you, if you have any lawyerly leanings, that your European intelligentsia share the same type of moral horror, only with a different etiology . . . I am thinking of the race thing for a start! Fools, fools! . . ."

Kwame came over to his father with concern, saying, "Papa, calm down; remember mother used to give you the same advice . . ." Sally Soonest was going fastest with her pen, but stopped abruptly when Sackey said with irony, "Don't forget to write down all the exclamation marks, insults, pauses and even silences!" "Professor, no! I'm trying to write down my disagreements . . . on some of the details, but you are going so far so fast! Am I not right, Kwame?" she replied with some spirit, looking imploringly at the boy. "Yes, I agree. But Papa," Kwame said quickly, "today, no school. I'm trying to recover from the shock of mother's . . . move!" Sackey hardly heard at all, but nodded vigorously in his son's direction. Kwame had asked Sally hair permission, and was now measuring this hair, as she continued to write. "Hey!" Kwame shouted as the others turned in his direction. "It is nearly three feet! your hair is nearly thirty of my toes placed one after the other!"

Sackey looked across to Okponglo where the new houses crawled over the mud, multiplying and twisting in their new cement; and every car that passed wiped out the crawling, only to have it begin again. And when a leaf dropped down so far, so brown, and so late in season, it lowered the breeze; it took Sackey down the steps of so many years . . . all the years were corrugated, with memories that would not lie flat . . . to when he was dancing in an Anglican church picnic, sweating beside the tall, little girl whose Asante lips were taller than her head. They were surprised to see him dance, for he was a difficult child; and one old lady, who was a miser with her perfume, let only one drop fall on him . . . and that drop could have been a whole acre of rain brought together especially for him, for after all, the old lady was also a difficult child . . . Then the cycle of his head stopped moving backward, and rushed forward in time, again:

". . . and at the same time, as I was saying before all this hair measuring started! re Kwame, my son of sons . . ., the work ethic itself is used very badly at a communal level—isn't it odd that a communalistic society should be so poor at coordinating itself, i.e. working together and through each other, these years of all years!—or it is used only on an individual level. Now, in moral terms, how this individual psyche fits itself into a society of psyches . . . can we use the word 'mind'? psyche is getting on my nerves! . . . is another devastating problem: one, there is a feeling of responsibility for the so-called masses; two, there is the recognition that the masses expect a certain moral and nonmoral standard of one, considering one's position; three, there is a wild race to keep one's status and position intact, with all the accoutrements involved since standards are material as well as moral; four, one must never forget the sideways glances, the moral sidesteps, of one's colleagues as they notice, with a nod or with envy, how one may be piling up the material things, say, a new car or a new freezer; five, one remembers all the relatively new research about the riches and propriety and smooth interpersonal relations of one's almost idyllic ancestors . . . I will never forget this cacophony of screeching, screaming wind-ed anthropologists creating their noisy music over such a quiet past! Can we not at last internalize all our spirits, totems, ancestors, ghosts, okra, sunsum, ntoro, mogya, our Nyame, our God, our *values*! We do it on the quiet, we fall back on them at our leisure and pleasure. But seriously, how many would choose a soul rather than a Benz, if given the choice? The god of your shrine asks you: would you, Owura so-and-so, like a perfect soul or a brand new super-dupe Mercedes Benz 450 automatic? No doubt, all Ghanaians . . . almost all . . . would prefer to postpone their souls, and rush after the Benzes! Six, we sometimes think we are the only nation with paradoxes, moral or otherwise, and this leads us to almost complete inaction . . . we jump, at the opportune times, into the hundreds of little pigeonholes available in the transcultural carpenter's shop! So consistency dies, we can't sustain anything except our careers, or little segments in little systems. Oh, we have *style* all right! But there's no breath to blow a trumpet clean! We can't go back, we can't go forward, the content is dying and the fine form will shrivel. I believe your Ghanaian intelligentsia, including myself, should be morally condemned; politicians, laborers, clerks, soldiers, teachers, businessmen, farmers, everybody, should also stand trial for the way the country has been, and is, going: we should not delude ourselves into thinking that a multiculture is the basis of our problems. Some use their multicultures as a great advantage in the corridors, in the paths of history . . . So should we."

"But Professor," protested Sally Sooner than you thought, "we can't take Ghana's problems in isolation: as recently as the 1930s, in Britain—and that is only a little over forty years ago—there were marches, 'hunger marching,' against the food problem, against poverty, and in 1936, half the population in Britain was too poor to afford an adequate all-round diet, with nearly one third suffering from serious dietetic deficiencies. And this is not even the moral problem. Think of the way factory and mine owners treated their workers, think of child labor, think of the treatment of women economically and politically! Right in the midst of this twentieth century, there were still de facto slaves, in Britain: long hours, seven-day weeks, terrible conditions, the horrors of certain areas of housing, and so on and on and on. And it wasn't so long ago since leprosy and plagues, and other dreaded diseases, left British shores. You would also be surprised to have it confirmed that there are over a million illiterates in the Kingdom! . . ." There was a smile of determination on Sally's face, there was history in her eyes.

"Again we find ourselves in a strange position . . . there you are lecturing me on the imperfections of British society, and here I am doing the same service for Ghana . . . and I wish I could put bougainvillaea on your words . . . but you would agree that by 1929, poverty in the actual sense of malnutrition had really diminished . . . but the real point I'm making is that you made use of your advantages rather more seriously than we are doing now. Of course, as you know, there's nothing genetic about it; and that is what makes me so angry. I carry this anger, because I think of this criminal waste all the time . . ." Sackey said, looking far away again. "And so you must go deeper and see these paradoxes: You see—and forgive me this insufferable parlance, it has a dead gray kente on it—it is this same moral positive that lets the Ghanaian intellectual identify with the ordinary person that also leads the former astray . . . paradox of the opposite side of the coin: he can't fly the kite of his ideas too high, in case those with their two feet firmly on the ground cannot stretch high enough to see it flapping beyond the Kwahu scarp, among the clouds. The ordinary is the traditional is the ordinary . . . and be careful about originality, since you may be going against your culture! So that just when banku is cooking, the poor fire is out! And the more the fire is perceived as being out—reluctantly, reluctantly—the more cold, uncooked banku is made. Then this: the survivability of the Ghanaian—the ancestors would condemn me for this abstract convolution of language! this pontifical paraphernalia of the mind!—can be simply explained: his body-mind has been stretched through suffering, and the successful sublimation, in symbolic terms, of suffering; and through the depradation of politicians which has been partly possible through the slipperies of different cultures, different tribes . . . the Ghanaian is indestructible because he has got formed in his head, deep ravines of opposites; if he feels too hot with one being or with one presence, he just hops onto another, thousands of miles away if necessary. And there's something I find very odd: there is no territory between the supernatural, and the purely factual . . . you get the factual explanations that do not fit superfactual situations, and you get supernatural answers that fly off at a tangent to the merely factual; and all in the usual polemical stew, with no insight at all for any salt of any worth! The Ghanaian likes argumentation! And of course, having an inkling of all this, your Ghanaian intellectual is a proper posturist! Forgive my little local philosophy of the black pose: all the little hesitations of morality—usually only for those sensitive enough for such things, for the rest are all so *certain* of their day-to-day living!—are not moral hesitations at all . . . they are immediately, or to be a little more charitable, ultimately, the status posturings of social- and self-oriented men, rather than moral men. And you know, there are a whole lot of interconnected contradictions. The feeling of historical, political and plenty other helplessnesses is, ironically, considered positive by the intellectual . . . Don't get tired, Miss Soon, I'll soon finish this Ghanaian lobotomy . . . for he has an ample psychological fund of *power:* power over himself for passing exams, and meeting some of life's obstacles with style, with style; and power over his people above whom he has risen without cutting all cords. Now, at the crucial moments when there should be a moral assertion—for example, in political terms—you rather get your head-head man choosing to feel positive by *subtracting* moral value from his fund of power *by not acting at all* i.e. inaction is moral abstinence is a good in itself, thankfully, since the psychological humility it may have led to reduces the fund of personal pride and power; don't we have our convoluted mea culpas! This act of dodging wastes a whole country, we have our dodgers of the mind! You see our problems! And of course we must be confident enough to discuss our faults, even in front of comely strangers like yourself . . . And I laughed when Acheampong named a roundabout 'Redemption Circle.' The poor circle is still going around in circles trying to find out how and what it is supposed to redeem! We really must learn that ideas do not exist merely in relation to the past or to exams, to books, articles or to other countries. Our soil can grow completely new things here too. The contours of the mind's geography are rather tired here . . . the weight of our past seems to be crushing the present . . . and the future will not be born! Listen to my talking! There are very few ways in which I myself am different: like Ghana, I feed off my own sins only, I'm complex enough to choose these sins! And I have to commit them to feel whole enough to exist. And I love the liberation of feeling no original guilt to struggle with! Your intellectual here does not quite know the freedoms available to him to create new worlds, new wholes! The poor tatale intelligentsia! They believe in very few single-minded cogitations, they think obsessions are alien—except as forms of defense or attack—they don't want their relaxed minds to do a little crazy thinking, certainly not for its own sake! . . . forgetting that nature's little obsessions are what have created the whole universe! The choice: you either find your own way, and develop it—you can't escape that either—and link it with other ways, or you are doomed to a series of well-rehearsed shrugs . . . and these are shrugs from shoulders the size of a whole country! But of course, this doesn't excuse the metal homes of countries where astronauts and cosmonauts come from: all their glory is an interim glory, a narrow glory. Let them sail to other planets: they will take their cigarettes there, they will fail there, just as they have failed this world too! Young lady, don't speak, don't speak, my mouth hasn't found a parking space yet! Over at Ghana House, sometimes the only space for parking the soul is right on top of the wide, wide sea . . . See? . . . And I feel that it is the symbolic meanings themselves that must change, must be dynamic. You keep the form of symbol and you change the symbol in action. You keep the drum, you keep the paraphernalia, but all relationships with them must change, must move . . . so, so, so . . . "

Sackey was the biggest kayakaya for this country; Ghana was a troublesome baby on his back, and it was the crying of this baby

290

that he himself cried out against. "But you know I've written a book on all this, don't you?" Sackey asked Sally casually. There was a quick pause, as Sally's eyes rose and flew, the tiny muscles behind them revolving. "Well, I didn't know at all!" Sally Soon said, in agitation. "But how will this affect my project? I, I'm a little confused . . ." "What are you confused about? All you have to do is to read this book, make the usual use of references, and go ahead with your own thesis . . ." Sackey interrupted rather irritably, "Besides, it's a recent book. It could be useful for a new thesis to make use of new books!" There was another pause, then Soon said, "What if you've covered all the points I want to chart? I have to start again, and tell them back home . . ." "Wait, wait, wait! Don't be emotional about purely academic things! You haven't read my book yet. There's of course a sociological bias. but I do touch on some of the moral points. Yours is a whole new thrust," Sackey reassured her.

Sally Soon usually felt that her name was too glib to stand still by itself, so she would have loved a "Dr.'" guarding it, after receiving her doctorate. She was adventurous, but sensitive, about obstacles in the way of this goal. "No more interviews until you have read my book," Sackey declared, as Kwame came in, wondering what was wrong, since his friend Sally had a worried look on her face. "It will soon be lunchtime!" he declared, and went back out. Sally asked Sackey, "Professor, could I please take Kwame to the Hall for lunch? I know I'm being a bit forward . . ." "Why not! He has so taken to you that there's nothing else I can say! And if you were my student I would of course have to be a little more circumspect. And how's your Adwoa?" Sackey added as an afterthought. "Oh, I'll see her tomorrow. And she's going to be a student! Isn't that wonderful? . . ."

When they left, Sackey decided, on an impulse, to write to Sofi that he had decided to go on his long overdue sabbatical, and that she should send little Katie over within the next few weeks. As soon as he stepped out of the door, there was Sofi coming up the drive. He froze for a second. "Kwesi, hello," she said quietly. Sackey looked at her sideways, then handed her the letter, ordering, "Read it! And where's Katie?" Sofi did not reply, but read the letter. She felt oddly thrilled, with the thought of reassessing her life alone for one year. "Are we not going into the house, Kwesi?" Sofi Sackey asked. Sackey's eyes looked suspiciously down at her sudden happiness. "I have an appointment. You can go in. You have read the letter? Good, now we know our plans. Kwame is out with an ex-pupil of yours. A whole year should crystallize your thoughts. You can go back for Katie and we'll all plan this. A whole year here should be good for you . . ."

Chapter 22

Kojo Okay Pol had just come away from Araba Fynn with her laughter tight in his pocket . . . he could be bitter in the groin. She had called for him, but she laughed her new disinterested, mature laugh when he suggested marriage. So Araba was now missing from his life. She was the big, rich boss, almost the mother of her own mother, Sister Ewurofua. And Okay Pol had eyes all over his head now, looking for the cruelty and unfinished ends that he thought trailed him. But he retained the strength that came from this same association with Araba Fynn. Cinders of charcoal used in roasting plantain were an affinity to Pol's head . . . there was a glow coming from the center somewhere . . . and this head and hands had now taken to photography.

He took the most amazing photographs of people, of goats if required, and of buildings; and the people had no stilted reserve at all when they were being taken, for Pol still looked like something slightly out of this world. And perhaps it was this quality in him that Dr. Boadi really sought, something to balance the g-o-o-d doctor's cynicism . . . otherwise he would have chosen more efficient people for his intrigues. Pol had also acquired a motorbike, with the sad arrears Boadi had paid him; and as he went around Accra, he was said to look like a cross between a policeman and a scampering squirrel, all fezzed, FEZZED. As he flew through Accra now he would remember his dream of the magic bottle of Star beer with its neck growing high and sharp into the ceiling, with a thirsty man standing forlornly by the bottle, with an empty glass . . . it was getting more and more difficult to offer drink to himself, to the gods, and to the ancestors.

Over by the tiny bit of pasture, the goat was in arrears with its own dung, it would not fertilize its own grass. It was as if the constipation had spread to the small nearby houses built through years of strain and sweat, with hopes often caked like cement; and the eyes that built them had become off-brown, almost gray with reduced feeling, for all the world had been seen before, and there was no innocence left. Pol remembered passing a house where he knew the children were so spoiled that when they blew off it was immediately framed . . . and hung up against their future. And out of that other crowded house in Accra New Town, a cough and a laugh alternated: one hundred coughs, ninety-nine laughs . . . all tiered one above the other, so that if you were not careful, you would heal the wrong one. But the way some people laughed at everything, from war to accidents, it could have been the laughter that had to have the treatment; for after all, the goodness and the innocence—that were turning into apathy and cynicism—were now placed far above the controlled prices. Hens were the cheapest, best coordinators in the country . . . they went and touched everywhere, clucked their messages, carried news of lotto wins, death, promotions, marriages, and orders from above. And the only real togetherness that Pol found, fitfully, was this: if one man urinated, he did it for the whole city. Through to Dansoman, where a few of his customers were, Okay Pol saw the morality of the underbelly: whatever was not outright bad, was toooo gooood . . . anything, from the water and the electricity to the open gutters that mirrored this morality: you never showed your underbelly in a hard pioneering place like Dansoman, for someone, somewhere, would put a dagger in it, or steal it, steal your underbelly just like that . . .

He went westward toward Odorkor, where he had been visiting the happy household of Kofi Loww, Adwoa Adde, Erzuah and Ahomka, with the everpresent Amina. Kofi and Adwoa had decided to pursue or even run after their studies. Loww had a new brightness about him, he no longer looked gray under the tropical sun, for Adwoa was carrying half his weight; and Erzuah was delighted with the marriage; he even shaved off his beard—much to the annoyance of Ahomka—in thanksgiving; and when he grew it again in August, he and his son called each other "beard, beard," with the old man teasing Loww that he was brought up on bofrots and nkontommire and that was why he had made it to university. Maame never came again, she was growing old against Brago's walls, and only slithered down when her grandson visited her.

Here in this polite and conservative country, they killed their thieves. You could predict the hawkers selling their own sweat; and you could see the sidestreet palm nuts, and see why they were red . . . their thorns were useless against the civilization started thousands of years ago. Mallams looked for the skins of Accra lizards, looked for big birds' beaks, and Olla Balm. All the ordinary people were the real people: they lived beyond the slogans, they outlasted the politicians, even those that wanted to label and measure their very blood . . . there was the ruled blood, and there was the unruled blood that did the ruling. By the Chorkor beach Acheampong's Revolution lay exhausted in the sands, being pushed up and down by the damnation of the tides.

Then, tearing across the plaster of wounded roads, by the sea route, Pol eased through Bukom around that corner which the September kelewele defined, in smell and color; and where that passing buyer was desperate to drop her buttocks, for they were all looking at her when she walked. And most people were busy with their rumors: one mouth could house ten other mouths in the same face. Pol was now looking for a contract with a dog, to bark the thieves and witches of his soul away. Or perhaps he could ride his bike into the sky, for he had earned a little goodness there: as a matter of principle, he had not spat for two years now on God's Ghana earth. Shifting direction back to Abodwe, Okay Pol's mind climbed with the sponge plant climbing the fence of somebody's life with its yellow flowers. There he took the picture of an old lady so wizened and so rough that his camera shook involuntarily: it was as if Accra, dead long ago, was now reincarnated in one human being sitting throwing out her obscenities, as the ready gutters received them. You would not want to divide this morally sakola city into tribal groups, SIR, for it had devoured all the different tribes long ago . . . and the Gas, the land being theirs, were spat back out, only to be reswallowed the more. The mosques were built on swallowed mouths, for when Allah was called, there was a double resonance, there were several stories of lips; the robes expanded with praying. Then on to Ridge Park where the gamblers slept by the chacha flowers, and there could be ghosts on the swings and roundabouts, for very few children used them, for most of the time the mouth of the watchman was shut. The park belonged to the western crows with their dog collars, and when they talked with their raucous cries, it was through the language of the backside shifted without feathers to the mouth to blast through. BLAST! said the crows, so that the sounds crept into the Ridge bungalows like aural thieves. And the gamblers were asleep with early mosquitoes suspended on their backs. Over again to Adabraka, by the few Lebanese and Indian houses that were as potbellied as some of their masters. Pol ate a little Lebanese bread before he took twenty pictures, some smelling of curry from the next house. But he loved most of all the smell of thick abenkwan down the old, narrow Adabraka alleyways, perhaps useful as conduits for hasty souls running away at night to count their money . . . or at the very least to dream of it. He had forgotten himself and he was dragging behind him the cathedral roundabout, still at Adabraka, just because this roundabout was dangerously the waist of Araba Fynn. He avoided Asylum Down, for all the kerosene there would ignite the small wick of his heart. You could not, *any nana*, have fire on a moving motorbike.

Behold! he sighed as he remembered: Adwoa Adde had been crying over the death of this Beni Baidoo, and she was telling them all on Pol's last visit about him: he had died with a last twisted smile on his face, with a lit cigarette still fuming away and almost setting fire to his tiny room; for it was crowded with the dried elephant grass of his jokes and his escapades; but oddly, she said he never recovered from the betrayal of Osofo at the Freedom Arch; he pined away while scattering sparks of jokes that the fire brigade could not put out . . . for you could not hose hearts, especially broken hearts. And his old, old dog reappeared and licked his dead face. And before his illness, Baidoo Beni had received a letter from Professor Sackey imploring him, Baidoo, to keep alive, and that there could be a little survey on his attempts to found a village. The old man had thought that Sackey was getting desperate for research material, though he didn't realize that Sackey had at last seen that Beni's ridiculous standards helped some of the rest of them to define their own, even far away on his sabbatical. Sofi Sackey was prospering on her own . . . Dr. Boadi had at last got his Benz from the proceeds of a special assignment of confidence for the Supreme Military Council; but he had smashed it into a cow, with his latest girlfriend thrown out and lying over the dead animal screaming over her cuts from the broken windshield. And Beni Baidoo had rushed to Dr. Boadi to implore him to buy him another donkey, since the first one was dead . . . dead from the weight of two buttocks that Beni used on it when he forgot that it was definitely a one-buttock donkey. Boadi did buy the donkey, but Beni Baidoo was already dead himself when the stubborn animal was led into the sad old room with the shilpit dog on guard . . . Old Baidoo had created a great scandal by trying to make love to the mad woman Ama Payday, who was peopling his village for him with her alphabetical presence. He had furiously denied this, but he used to secretly boast that she had good skin, and that besides she had stolen all his money when he was trying to embrace her . . . Kofi Loww had decided to give Beni Baidoo a little monthly dash, which Erzuah reluctantly agreed to, seeing how shriveled Baidoo had become with his unorthodox village failing. It was as if Baidoo had cared enough to die over it . . . Okay Pol used to go for medicine for Beni, and discovered the old man's body . . . ½-Allotey had agreed to bury Baidoo, since his relatives had miraculously disappeared . . . and Adwoa Adde had talked to the body for hours, not knowing why, but wishing Baidoo a safe journey to make up for a dangerous life . . .

Pol was tall and open, and he saw all this, but his heart was yet narrow, it needed space for some of his own suffering. So when he really wanted to show his sympathy for an uncaring city, he just put his fez on the highest towers, and watched the emanation of long-distance mutual suffering, he watched his fez on Legon tower. One city, one fez, one eye, would cry together. By fezless Labone, where the two circular houses with their single tower sitting rooms lay, Okay Pol stopped to buy groundnuts. There was the usual extraordinary neatness here which could not quite be called beauty, for it was too pretty, too regular, and there were too many watchmen guarding it. He imagined smooth orange juice being passed around from house to house, and then being consumed at exactly the same time with exactly the same types of glass . . . but sometimes the boys' quarters screamed, scattering the suppressed envy like harmattan dust. And there were only two photographs he took in Labone: somebody's breasts with wine poured over them, and one old watchman with fine cola teeth. The evening came in a flash, and that was what he had to use for more pictures from his camera. Osu mixed its old and new parts as if they were sisters that would speak to each other only once a year . . . and the Castle was now the master of different slaves, the controller of graded blood. Then Pol became so tired that his motorbike was already driving in its sleep, as he thundered back toward his room in Kaneshie. He carried an unusual rain on his back, straight from the horizon, as he went. And all the lights showed the different angles at which the rain cut this city into bits; into jigsaw puzzles, in restrained African razzle-dazzle; and through the beams, there was yellow rain and white rain, but most of the vast stretches of wall where the concentrated light could not reach were shadows, were black rain. There was a lot of running for shelter, from the gods of sudden puddles. But those that decided to be leisurely and get wet, were speaking in flooded words . . . they talked about the wet country that was yet thirsty. At last Okay Pol reached his long, neat room, which always stood at an ironic attention to welcome him in . . . and he never failed to bump his head at the threshold, for that was also another type of welcome.

And he had heard that after all the galloping at the back door airport, all the horses were dead. Diverted horse-O, undiverted horse-O, they were dead! Boadi would have another chance to do his shoogmadoodle, to fry his own onions; and perhaps Kofi Loww, Professor Sackey, and himself would be left in peace, if the good professor could control the gun of his mouth. There was too much politics, as Sackey said, and most of the wrong kind, too. Photographers could make money, but he had to move a woman out of his head first, and not come across her decades later, as poor Mr. Acquah did with Nana Esi . . . just like flesh turning into ghost turning into semiflesh, again and again.

Thus Pol lay shivering in his old-Ghana room, whether with the rain, or with malaria. Wooden low-beam ceiling, old calendars, old moods for a city crawling toward its own suburbs. Old cards, shriveled palm fronds from an old Palm Sunday service that a girl-friend had forced him to go to. The newly dusted, empty penicillin packet lay exhausted with healing other people's children in the neighborhood; he tried and tried, but he could not heal the whole of Kaneshie. There were minialleyways beyond, just like in Se-kondi, leading up to raised inner and outer chambers . . . and sometimes the steps would be missing, lost to the soul that wanted to climb . . . where the sitting room was so low that good people were better sitting. Two pale sticks held up a window, directing

298

the traffic of mosquitoes toward the light toward the flesh; Pol drank beer through the mercy of mosquito bites: take in beer, take out blood, the *rhythm* of *the city*! And the doormats were on strike because they did not like the extra pressure of guarantee shoes. One pink wall held another pink wall in granite embrace, Pol's home cliffs, Pol's old cry that Ghana was beyond its own history. Look: bags, wires, buckets, and a sieve lined up, and ascending the walls. A second, hung door curtain shaking in the different breezes that were powerless against the heat that they were supposed to trap. Homowo in the distance. Oh, to be more Northern in the next few years, he thought to himself . . . this secret had to be kept away from the wise bed, that knew so much. Memories of hundreds of fishing generations in one single, simple, calendar. The grandfather clock sought a grandson in Accra, a true grandson of sound. Look: and Pol was half-asleep.

When he met Professor Sackey last week, the professor had told him of his friend ½-Allotey who was becoming rich, and who was putting more flesh on his already huge shoulders. There was a wicked little moss under the Kaneshie steps, against which the percussion of the crickets was slipping with speed into the ear . . . the people had been assured that the rain would be banned by decree if it came to a matter of floods; and the sun was suddenly under the authority of the Supreme Military Council if it came to drought. Pol loved kelewele, so he jumped up dreaming, and bought five cedis, even ate it in his sleep, with the laughter of the women, mocking his sleeping cloth, still in his ears . . . if only the crickets would allow, allow. The story was that Kwaku Tia had resigned from his airport job, and that his legs were now so short that they had to apply for extra inches before they could touch the ground. If Tia had his way, all airplanes would be in the asylum: for they rose while this country was falling, and this was mad! Some children thought Pol was so tall that he would be privileged to know some of God's answers to Accra's questions, such as this: if all the safety pins being sold in Makola market got finished, what would happen to all the stars hung up and pinned so precariously over the villages? And Osofo's new church was growing and growing as he mellowed. There was a whole papaw tree growing across his life, thickening Pol's horizons, and he was waiting, a little more mature, yet still desperate to pick the fruit *when it finally became ripe*.

He remembered: he and Araba had been whispering very close

in this same room, sharing the different teeth of one same-same smile, and she had looked with a glance beyond surprise as he scratched her head by mistake . . . he felt they were so close . . . that he could even put food in her mouth by mistake . . . but now he was putting into the neglected corners of the relationship the hidden sorrow that none of these proverbial unfinished young men wanted to reveal, not even in this careless city. Pol would never forget Araba's smile breaking out in her recent grief, like a Bedford entering a sunlit corner with polished mudguards gleaming into somebody else's eyes at the wrong time. That smile now was jailed, shut. The secret for both of them now was to burst through someone else's life, but gently enough to catch the old memories when they fell.

If Pol had a yet unfinished sunsum, a yet unfinished soul, it was because Accra was the same: that was partly his self-appointed excuse; after all, if an "i" was searching for its dot, and had not yet found it . . . When the great owl hooted, there was no answer beyond its still wings. Pol's landlady would come in the morning for the rent. What a woman, with a body from the forest: a few inches after she had passed a corner, her buttocks stayed behind, almost at an acute angle with the field of vision, protesting against the shaking of its own flesh before finally following her around out of sight. And she could never quite trust the look of innocence in Pol's eyes. A few months ago, it was the harmattan—with its strange and suspended dusts and lights—that he shivered and stared meanings through, with ancestors breathing their ancestry all over the islands of city grass; and that was when the black skin took on an astonishing number of colors. After all, there was some hope under this haha sky . . . where people usually laughed their troubles away though the fund of laughter was finishing. But Pol knew they could not take the future away from him, for the innocence that lay beside him in the bed could either be picked up and carried around in the morning, as usual; or be put safely in the trunk to mature, then used, Used, USED at the best time . . . for, if he were not careful, the rainbow would continue to dress him up again and again, to give his skin beauty, only while the colors were there, only while they lasted so sad . . . For after all, if you placed a thousand pairs of trousers empty and upright in ascending angles as blue as the sky, all through the city up to the Freedom Arch, random legs, with their kenkey perfume, would eventually force

300

their flesh into the thousand pairs—hanging like angels or witches —and then swagger in their easy symbols, as if something had at last been achieved. And what was that something? After all, the purveyors of the Arch were typical and waakyiful, had betrayed all time before and after it, were worth just one tutu-ni . . ., tomorrow was Okay Pol snoring through his own ideas, chacha by national chacha . . .

Glossary of Ghanaian Words and Author's Neologisms

a	I
abenkwan	palm-nut soup
abrantsi	young man
abua	fool
abusuapanyin	head of family
Adabraka	area in Accra
adaka	box
adinkra, adinkrahene	symbolic patterns on funeral cloths
agidi	a soft white staple
agoo	give way
akimbo	hands on hips, elbows turned outward (*usual meaning but applied unusually here*)
akonta	brother-in-law
akpeteshie	locally distilled gin
akrantsi	a type of bush animal used for meat
Akurugu	*a name*
akwaaba	welcome
akyinkyina	hornbill
alasa	a bitter-sweet fruit
Alhaji	a Muslim who has made the pilgrimage to Mecca
alata samina	soft black soap
alokoto	small snail shells (*played with by children*)

alombo	girlfriend or lover
am	her, him, it
ampa, ampara	true
ampe	a girls' game
ampesi	a staple and stew
Ananse	mythical spider of oral tradition
apatupre	a bird
aplankey	a driver's mate
Asaase Yaa	Mother Earth
Asafo Company	a youth clan originating in the Central Region
atakpame	made of mud
atua	a fruit
awoof	suspiciously easy
awu	it's dead
awura	young woman
ayekoo	*a complimentary greeting*
babooning	giving up one's room for a time for a friend and his lover
baked-block	swish
bambala	large
bankoshie	*part of a ditty but used here to mean* nonsense
banku	staple corn food
basaa	confused
basabasa	confusion
bashi	thick growth of hair above nape of neck
batakari	a smock
bebree	a lot
blow fuse	to smell of alcohol
bofrot	a doughnut
bokoboko	a smooth spinach pureé
bokorr (bokor)	softly
bola	rubbish heap
boogie	to spoil
book-book	intellectual
booklong	intellectual
brik	clever
brodo	bread
brofo nut	Indian almond

brokeman	man without money
bush balanga	*an expletive*
calabash	traditional bowl for drinking palm wine
cassava	staple root
cedi	Ghana currency
chacha	gambling
chale-wate	slippers
cheche-kule	*part of a ditty but used here to mean* foolishness
cine	cinema
C. K. Mann high life	a popular musician's high life music
cocoyam	staple root
colo	outdated
commot	*a general doing word, which can mean* eat, take, have, loosen, etc.
contrey	comrade
Dammirifa Due	condolences
duku	headscarf
durbar	gathering of chiefs and people
easyoasy	relaxed (*Scottish word*)
ewi	thief
ewiase	the way of the world
Ewurade!	good God!
fikifiki	sexual intercourse (*coined by author*)
flamboyant	large tree with brilliant flowers
foko	*an expletive*
fontomfrom	talking drum
fufu	food made from pounded staple roots
Ga (adj.)	of the Ga people of Accra
gari	a ground cassava staple
GBC	Ghana Broadcasting Corporation
gidigidi	boisterous
GNTC	Ghana National Trading Company (*general merchants*)
goway you!	go away you

304

green–green	a type of stew
harmattan	dust-laden wind from Sahara, in dry season
Homowo	a Ga festival
i	it
ibi	it is
jolof	a rice dish
joromi	brightly colored smock
jot	cigarette
juju	magic, witchcraft
kaklo	plantain and flour fry
kalabule	sharp trading practices
kayakaya	porter
kelewele	ripe plantain, chopped small and fried
kenkey	staple corn food
kente	colorful traditional cloth
Keta-school boys	small fish, widely eaten
key-soap	brand of washing soap
kofi-salanga	*part of a ditty but used here to mean* nonsense
koko	porridge
koobi	dried fish
koraa	at all
kosrokobo	thin-legged but heavy-chested
kotoko	a porcupine (*emblem of Asante nation; but in this case the word refers to a hairstyle*)
kpa	*onomatopoeic word suggesting a crash*
kpakpo shitoh	a round pepper
krontihene	a subchief
kube	coconut
kyenam	fried fish
kyinkyinga	khebab
libilibi	litigious
logologo	genital (*coined by author*)
lotto	number staking

Makola	largest market in Accra
Mallam	healer
masa	master
mogya	blood
motoway	receding forehead
myselfs	private car owners (*usually from professional classes, and so called by taxi drivers*)
nananom	elders
nkonkonsa-ni	troublemaker
nkonkonte	type of cassava dough
nkontommire	stew made with green leaves
ntoro	character inherited from father
nyamanyama	foolish
Nyame	God
Nyamebekyere	God will show the way
Nyame Dua	designs on funeral cloths
odikro	village chief
odum	large forest tree
ohemaa	queen mother
one time	immediately
okra	soul
okro	sticky, slippery pods of the okro plant
oman	the state
oware	a game
Owula, Owura	Mr., Sir
panyin	elder
pasaa	completely
pesewa	Ghana coin, equivalent to penny
pikin	child, children
pioto	pants
pito	a beer traditionally brewed in the North
popylonkwe	male organ
portello	mineral drink
PWD	name for a type of grass (Public Works Department)
sabe	know

sakola	bald
Sankofa	a bird which symbolizes how the future makes use of the past
sapo	sponge
sawi	chewing sponge
shea-butter	moisturizing cream
shilpit	mangy
shitoh	pepper, ground and fried
sika na ya	money is scarce
Shokoloko Bankoshie	title of a ditty
shokolokos	*a term used by one character to mean* healers
shoogmadoodle	nonsense (*coined by author*)
showboy	showman
SMC	Supreme Military Council, government of Ghana 1975-9
sunsum	soul, spirit
supertobolo	big and fat (*coined by author*)
tama	waist beads for women
tatale	plantain and ginger mashed and fried
tee	too much
thumb-pianist	player of the small African piano
t'in	thing
tongg	so far
trotro	private van/truck transport
Tsooboi, Yei	a war cry
tutu-ni	prostitute
UAC	United African Company (*a store*)
UNDP	United Nations Development Programme
waakyi	popular meal of rice and beans
whaaaat	stylish
Wofa	Uncle
wawa	a forest tree
Yewura	term of respect for a distinguished man
yoyi	small, black-skinned fruit

yoo ke gari	grated cassava with beans and palm oil
zagazogo	wild man (*coined by author*)
zomi	a type of palm oil

93
1